Susan Meier is the author of over fifty book~~~ Mills & Boon. *The Tycoon's Secret Daugh~~~* ~~~nce Writers of America RITA® ~~~ ~~~ny *for the Millionaire'~~~* ~~~st award and was a fin~~~ ~~~e awards. She is marr~~~ ~~~ eleven children hers~~~ ~~~out the complexity of familie~~~ ~~~ves in the power of love.

USA TODAY bestselling and RITA® Award-winning author **Marie Ferrarella** has written more than 250 books for Mills & Boon, some under the name Marie Nicole. Her romances are beloved by fans worldwide. Visit her website, marieferrarella.com

Also by Susan Meier

The Spanish Millionaire's Runaway Bride

Manhattan Babies
Carrying the Billionaire's Baby
A Diamond for the Single Mum
Falling for the Pregnant Heiress

The Missing Manhattan Heirs
Cinderella's Billion-Dollar Christmas

Also by Marie Ferrarella

The Cowboy's Lesson in Love
The Lawman's Romance Lesson
Coming Home for Christmas
Dr. Forget-Me-Not
Twice a Hero, Always Her Man
Meant to Be Mine
A Second Chance for the Single Dad
Christmastime Courtship
Texan Seeks Fortune
The Maverick's Return

Discover more at millsandboon.co.uk

THE BODYGUARD AND THE HEIRESS

SUSAN MEIER

FORTUNE'S GREATEST RISK

MARIE FERRARELLA

MILLS & BOON

First Published in Great Britain 2020
by Mills & Boon, an imprint of HarperCollinsPublishers,
1 London Bridge Street, London, SE1 9GF

The Bodyguard and the Heiress © 2020 Linda Susan Meier
Fortune's Greatest Risk © 2020 Harlequin Books S.A.

Special thanks and acknowledgement are given to Marie Ferrarella for her contribution to the *Fortunes of Texas: Rambling Rose* continuity.

ISBN: 978-0-263-27874-3

0420

MIX
Paper from
responsible sources
FSC™ C007454

This book is produced from independently certified FSC™ paper to ensure responsible forest management.

For more information visit: www.harpercollins.co.uk/green

Printed and bound in Spain
by CPI, Barcelona

THE BODYGUARD AND THE HEIRESS

SUSAN MEIER

For Selena Blake… Brainstormer, blurb-writer,
marketer extraordinaire…friend.

CHAPTER ONE

"GO TO PENNSYLVANIA, they said..."

Jace MacDonald mumbled to himself as he walked through three inches of mud coating the little hills and valleys created by a dozen pieces of heavy equipment digging what looked to be a foundation for an enormous building.

"All you have to do is tell her she's one of the heirs to Mark Hinton's estate, get her on a plane to New York and keep her out of the public eye until her vetting process is complete."

His fancy Italian loafer sank into the unstable dirt as he took another step, and he groaned. Charlotte Fillion was a bigwig in some highbrow construction company. Yet when he'd called them for her location, they'd sent him here... to a jobsite.

Luckily, he was almost at the worn and rusty trailer housing the office where she was supposedly working that day. He took the last three steps, scraped the inch of mud off his ruined shoes and opened the trailer door. Wood paneling and the scent of three-day-old coffee greeted him. And silence.

The two desks in the main room were empty. No one stood in the cramped space. No sound came from the offices on each side of the trailer.

"Hello? Anybody here?"

The squeak of a desk chair moving across an uneven

floor came from the room on the right. Then suddenly *she* stood in the doorway. He barely recognized her as the pulled-together executive from her headshot in the company's annual statement. This woman wore jeans, a plaid work shirt and a hard hat. But this was her. Charlotte Fillion.

"What do you want?"

She was one long, tall drink of water. Slender, with jeans that slid along her body like a second skin and blue eyes boring into him, she stood like a goddess.

His heart stopped, then bumped to life again. It had been so long since he'd been unexpectedly attracted to a woman that he'd almost forgotten what it felt like. Still, he dismissed the sensations oozing through him. He'd had the love of his life. Or so he'd thought. While he'd believed Mary Beth was supporting him through two tours in Afghanistan, she'd been cheating with his friend.

"I'm Jace MacDonald. I own Around the World Security. I've been sent here by the estate of Mark Hinton."

Charlotte Fillion actually laughed. "Huh. So, you finally found me."

She turned and walked back into her office.

Confused, Jace scrambled after her. "You know about the estate? You know Mark Hinton is your dad?"

"Of course, I do. My mother might have had to raise me alone, but she didn't make a secret of who my father was." She fell to the noisy desk chair, one that obviously needed a visit from an oil can. "We didn't go around announcing it to the world because the man was trouble. We didn't want any of that showing up at our door." She picked up a clipboard and began reading.

He inched his way to her desk. "The man wasn't trouble. He was rich."

She didn't lift her gaze from whatever she was reading on the clipboard. "You call it rich. I call it trouble. Bodyguards. Kidnapping attempts. Death threats. We wanted no part of that. Still don't."

"Well, brace yourself but you're in line to get a big chunk of his money."

"What would you say if I told you I don't give a damn?"

He gaped at her. Were all Mark Hinton's heirs going to be pains in the butt? Seriously. The first one they'd found, Leni Long, hadn't wanted her share of the money and now Charlotte Fillion was acting as if she wanted to bow out, too?

"I'd say you're crazy. But it's not my job to talk to you about this. It's Danny Manelli's. He's the attorney for the estate. Whether you take the money or walk away, you have to sign papers."

"Fine." She held out her hand. "Give 'em to me."

"You can't sign them as an heir until you prove you are an heir."

"I'll tell my mom to send over my birth certificate."

In a lady's presence or not, he cursed, then told himself she was probably accustomed to it because she wasn't merely prickly; she also worked in construction where a man who hit his thumb with a hammer didn't say, "Oh, gracious me."

"We have your birth certificate. We need irrefutable proof. DNA."

"Want to swab my cheek?"

He shook his head. "Are you being rude deliberately?"

She set the clipboard on her desk with a thump. "I have eight weeks to get this building under roof. Eight weeks. Do you know what the weather is like in Western Pennsylvania in April? I'll tell you. It's unpredictable. So, I don't want to spend even ten minutes arguing with some fancy pants from the big city. I have work to do."

Jace couldn't help it. He laughed. When she got all fired up, she was like poetry in motion. Her forehead wrinkled, causing blue eyes flashing fire to narrow. The image implanted itself in his brain and he knew all he'd have to do would be think about it and he'd laugh again. And get that weird shot of attraction again, because the woman was like nobody he'd ever met.

But she was about to find out he wasn't like anybody she'd ever met, either.

"You're going to have to call in a replacement. Because come hell or high water I'm getting you to New York."

"Guess again, Ringo."

He frowned. "Ringo?"

"Ringo, Gringo, take your pick."

"You think I'm a greenhorn?" He chuckled and plopped down on the seat in front of her shabby desk. "Lady, I wrote the book on stubbornness, intimidation and getting my own way. You wanna have a contest? Give it your best shot."

"I can call the police, and have you arrested for trespassing."

"I invite you to do that, except then you'll have to explain to the police why you don't want to go to New York and accept billions of dollars from *your father's* estate."

She scowled.

"You think I didn't catch the fact that you've kept your biological dad's identity a secret?" He stood and leaned across the desk. "You think I didn't catch the fact that you know three million reporters will descend on this jobsite once I make it known that you're a Hinton heir?"

She glared at him.

"Oh, honey, that glare might intimidate guys who push dirt and hang drywall. But I did two tours in Afghanistan. I started my security firm right after I got home." His chest tightened when he remembered arriving home, remembered finding Mary Beth kissing Dave, remembered the two weeks of drinking himself into oblivion and then the day he picked himself up and started the company he'd always planned. "I've dealt with rock stars so high they didn't know their own names. Socialites who threw temper tantrums and billionaires' spoiled kids." He leaned in so close he could smell her scent. Not soft or floral, but pure female.

It jolted him that he noticed, but he had a purpose here. He refused to be distracted. "Give it your best shot."

Charlotte held the gaze of the absolutely gorgeous guy, and—damn it—the fierce expression on his handsome face made her swallow. His eyes were as dark as a moonless night. His black hair and the angles and planes of his face gave him a severe look, a countenance that probably scared lesser people. With a name like MacDonald, his ancestors undoubtedly wore that same expression when they fought with William Wallace for Scottish independence.

He meant what he'd said. But then again so had she. She didn't get to this point in her career by backing down from what she wanted.

"Okay. So, you have ammo. You could out me to the press." Her instinct was to move in closer to show him she wasn't afraid of him. But she stifled that urge and leaned back. Casual. Composed. "But I have a job to do. I don't disappoint. I perform. Since we're at an impasse, let me suggest a compromise."

He retreated to his seat.

She smiled. Some days the way she could get people to do her bidding made her giddy. "Give me the time I need to get another foreman here."

"You don't have one on standby?"

She laughed, easing up, making him think they were friends. "There is no such thing as standby when a company is trying to make money. Some of our foremen get tapped for double duty."

"So, you gonna call one of them?"

"I told you. They're already doing double duty. I

wouldn't be in the field if the company wasn't stretched to the max. We'll have to wait for one of my supervisors to get to a place in his project that he can pass off his current work to crew foremen and come here."

He scrubbed his hand across his handsome face and Charlotte took the opportunity to simply look at him. Black overcoat, with a white shirt beneath a black suit—probably silk—and a neutral-colored tie that was definitely silk.

A thought struck her, and she had to hold back a laugh. She'd bet her last buck he'd ruined a pair of Italian loafers in the mud.

"I can't wait forever."

She leaned back farther in her chair, appearing even more accommodating. "It'll just be a couple of days."

He sucked in a breath. "You do realize I have to guard you."

"Why?" She opened her hands. "Look around you. The only thing these guys care about is my ability to get them jobs, and enough money to support their kids."

"Doesn't matter. The official word from the estate is once we find an heir that heir gets a bodyguard."

"I don't need a bodyguard."

"It's not my rule. It's the attorney's rule. And it's warranted. We had a…misstep…with the first heir we found. She was on her own in a coffee shop and somebody took pictures of her, spied on her phone, figured out who she was."

The word *misstep* caught her attention, but her brain shimmied when he said *first heir*. She sat up on her seat. "I have a sibling?"

"You don't read the papers? It was all over the news when the reporter outed her."

"I work twelve-hour days. I don't have time for tabloids, magazines or even my local paper. I read three respected online sites. They don't print gossip and most certainly don't write about celebrities. They didn't even report it when my dad died. I found out from my mom."

He shook his head, but said, "You have two siblings. We've found you and your sister. She's the youngest heir, a twenty-six-year-old social worker."

Amazement flooded her. "I have a *sister*."

"Half sister. Leni Long." He paused for a second, then said, "Didn't you ever check to see if Mark had any other kids?"

She gaped at him. "How? Look at every birth record in every state to see if his name was on any birth certificates?"

"That's how the estate found you. Mark's name was on your birth certificate."

"No kidding. I already offered up my birth certificate but apparently only DNA testing will do."

"Hey, when there's an opportunity for irrefutable proof available and we've got scam artists coming up with some really great fake birth certificates, why not use it? DNA rules out the fakes."

"I'm not a fake."

"I know that and you know that, but we're holding everybody to the same standard."

"Fabulous." She sighed with disgust but peeked over at him. "Tell me more about my sister."

"She divides her time between New York with her boyfriend, Nick Kourakis, and her small town in Kansas where she's using a chunk of her share of the estate to spruce up the place."

"She's renovating an entire town?"

"Her hometown. She's probably the nicest person I've ever met."

The thought of having a sibling washed over her. Raised in the country, with only her mom, in a huge, four-bedroom farmhouse, she'd spent a lot of lonely hours. During the day, she'd wish for someone to toss a ball with or explore the woods behind the barn. Sometimes at night, she'd pretended she was on the bottom bed of bunk beds and her sister was above her. Sometimes that sister would be older and wiser. Sometimes she'd be younger and in need of Charlotte's counsel. But no matter how she'd imagined her sister they'd been best friends.

She and Leni Long had missed having a childhood together. But what would it be like to have an adult sister? What would it be like to have someone who shared her blood, her oddball past? Someone who understood being Mark Hinton's kid wasn't a joyride.

"Sorry. That just threw me for a loop, and I needed a second."

"You could fly to New York with me today and probably have dinner with her tonight."

The thought almost made her breathless and tempted her far too much. Especially when she had a job to do.

"We're still waiting for my replacement."

He slapped his hands on his knees. "All right. Fine. Then I'll set up shop here for a few days. Where you go, I go."

As he rose from his seat, the squeak of the main door opening rippled into her office.

"Hey, Charlotte?" Aaron Birmingham entered the trailer, calling her.

Charlotte yelled, "In here, Aaron."

The front-end-loader operator clamored across the common area and into her office. Seeing Jace, he winced. "Oh, hey! I'm sorry. I didn't realize you had someone from corporate in here."

"He's not from corporate. He's…" Oh, crap. The man was dressed too well to say he was a construction worker. And he was going to be following her around. She thought for a second, but there was only one kind of person who wouldn't look suspicious following her around. She smiled.

"He's my new assistant."

Aaron's face brightened. "So, you got corporate to loosen the purse strings!"

"A lot more than I thought I could," she said, pointing at Jace. "Look at that suit."

"Yeah, buddy. You really don't want to be wearing your good clothes here. Tomorrow you should come in jeans."

Charlotte leaned back in her chair and laughed. Maybe this wouldn't be so bad, after all?

Jace scowled at her, and feminine hormones that she could usually control rose up like a tidal wave of need. She did not fault her hormones in the slightest. Jace MacDonald was tall, broad-shouldered, good-looking and every bit as cantankerous as she was. Any woman who liked a man who treated her as an equal would be attracted to him. The trick was not to let it show.

Unfortunately, she had days of him shadowing her everywhere she went. She'd have to hide the silly feelings at least eight hours a day. That was not going to be easy because he checked all the boxes of her list of things she wanted in a mate—

Her chest froze as another thought popped into her head. What if he was "The One"? He really did check all her boxes. Gorgeous. Tall. Strong. Treated her like an equal. And not intimidated by her.

Aaron snapped his fingers in front of her face. "Earth to Charlotte. I came in here to ask you about the area by the pond."

She came to attention quickly, not wanting her gorgeous bodyguard—

Oh, damn. He was her *bodyguard*—sent to her by her wealthy, uncaring, mean-spirited father's estate.

It wasn't an accident or glorious trick of fate that this handsome man had stumbled onto her jobsite. He worked for her dad—albeit via his estate. It would be a cold, frosty day in hell before she even considered getting chummy with one of her dad's employees.

She took another quick inventory of striking Jace Mac-Donald, dressed in black, looking dark and mysterious and so sexy even she could have swooned.

Too bad.

She dismissed her disappointment. Right now, she needed to get all the facts about his bodyguard duties for the next few days and come up with a plan to keep her distance, so she didn't slip up and do something foolish like flirt with him.

Because the last thing she wanted to do was get involved with someone, *anyone*, who had liked or respected the dad who had made the last twenty-eight years of her mom's life miserable.

CHAPTER TWO

JACE HEARD THE door close as Charlotte's front-end-loader operator exited the trailer. He waited two beats to make sure the kid was gone. Then he said, "I'm not your assistant."

"I couldn't think of any other way to explain you."

He sighed. He should be glad she hadn't blurted who he really was or who *she* was. Danny Manelli would kill him if another heir was exposed before they got her to New York where they could keep her hidden while they went over the details of the estate with her and waited for DNA results.

No matter how much he disliked it, Charlotte's explanation that he was her assistant was plausible. There was no sense arguing.

"All right. Fine."

She breathed a sigh of relief. She'd obviously been worried he wouldn't accept it, and, technically, his purpose in guarding her *was* to make her transition easier, not harder.

He backed off his temper a bit more.

Her gaze met his, her blue eyes wary. "I do have a couple of questions, though."

"Let's have them."

"What does a bodyguard do?"

"Generally, they protect you from getting killed, but in an instance like this my job is to keep the press away…and watch the people in your life to see if any one of them is just a tad too interested."

"Meaning?"

"Meaning I'll be scrutinizing the people around you to see if there are signs one of them has been approached by the press to spy on you."

She laughed. "That's ridiculous."

"Right now, I agree. No one knows who you are. The press doesn't realize they should be interested."

"So, you're pretty much just going to follow me around?"

"That and keep an eye on your people to make sure none of them is getting ideas."

"Where are you sleeping tonight?"

"Where are *you* sleeping tonight?"

"I have a house. A very safe house. I'm hoping you'll find a hotel."

He eased his hip on the desk, enjoying the odd shiver in her voice. She was so tall, so strong, so put together, that it was fun to unnerve her. "No such luck."

Emotion gathered on her face like a thundercloud. Fun or no fun, he'd gotten sufficient concessions out of her that teasing her was wrong. He knew firsthand what could happen if he got too friendly with a client. He had a job to do. Unlikely as it was that someone might have figured out she was a Hinton heir, he would do more than his due diligence.

"I'm not finding a hotel. I told you...where you go, I go. But I probably won't be sleeping as much as catnapping on the sofa nearest your front door."

Her face twisted as she thought that through, but her expression never reached acceptance.

"Come on. Cut me a break. The estate lawyer, Danny Manelli, is very particular. But I just have to be able to say I was in the same building as you."

"This Manelli guy calls the shots?"

"Yes. And he expects me to guard you. I don't have to be in your bedroom, watching you sleep. As long as no one gets suspicious about who you are, I can give you a fairly wide berth. But you have to let me do my job. Once your replacement is here, we can fly to New York, do the DNA and orient you to everything your dad owned, so that you'll be making an informed decision if you opt out of the estate. If you still decide you want no part of the money, then you're on your own again."

She groaned. "The things I haven't gone through because that man was my father."

"I get it. You can pick your friends, but you can't pick your relatives."

Her gaze leaped to his. "Your family is crap, too?"

He almost told her yes, just to give them something in common. But he didn't want to lie to her. He liked her no-nonsense way of dealing with things. He didn't want to lose that. He wanted her to continue being honest, so he had to be honest.

"No. My family's really cool. But I've worked for some rock stars who give 'crazy' a whole new meaning."

She laughed and tossed her pen to her desk. "Okay. It is only going to be a few days, then all this will be over. That man will finally be out of my hair."

Respect for her rose in him. She knew how to compartmentalize to get things done. "It's actually going to be more like two weeks. Your DNA sample will be sent to three labs. There'll be no mention of your name and though we'll put a rush on them all labs have different timetables. We might get one back in three days, another in a week and the third could take two weeks, but in that time you'll be briefed on everything your dad owned, including companies and investments. Even if you opt out, the estate wants to ensure you are making an informed decision."

She made a sound of disgust but said, "Okay." She sat forward on the squeaky chair. "I have work to do. And if we want to keep this charade true, your job is to answer the phone."

He squeezed his eyes shut but remembered his mission.

"Go sit at either of the two desks out there and wait for the phone to ring."

"While I watch who's coming in," he reminded.

"That, too." She grinned. "See? Look how convenient it is for you to pretend to be my assistant. There is only one way into this office and you'll be sitting in front of it."

He gave her points for that and headed to the door.

"Hey, wait, Jace… Mr. MacDonald… What do you want me to call you?"

"Jace is fine."

"Okay, Jace," she said, accenting his name in such a way that it sounded like a caress. Without the hard hat her pretty yellow hair fell to her shoulders in a nice wave. Her blue eyes sparkled.

He told his hormones to stop noticing her. He had a job to do. Nothing more. This wasn't an episode of *The Bachelor*. He'd made the mistake of getting romantically involved with a client once and only once. That ding to his reputation had not gone away easily. A wise man did not go down a bad road twice.

"The last temp we had left a bunch of magazines in one of the desks. Feel free to read them."

"Right." Like he'd spend an afternoon browsing gossip magazines. He snorted and headed out the door to the first desk. The one closest to her office.

Because his Italian loafers were already ruined, Charlotte didn't hesitate to go onto the site. But she only went out twice. Jace really did look like someone from corporate following her around, taking in everything that was going on. Except a guy from corporate would be analyzing what she was doing, how she was spending shareholders' money. Jace looked for vulnerabilities. She could see it in the way his gaze faltered when it landed on a rip in the six-foot chain-link fence. His fierce dark eyes narrowed, and she made a mental note to send John Franklin out to mend it.

No sense arguing with a bear.

And he was a bear. Good Lord. She was an inch shy of six feet tall. She towered over most people. Yet, Jace had a good four inches on her. And muscles. When he'd taken off his overcoat and suit jacket, she'd seen his shoulders and chest stretching that perfect white silk shirt of his.

She'd bet he had flat abs, too.

She stopped the pitter-patter of her heart by reminding herself he didn't just work for the father she despised, but also gorgeous guys like him didn't go after tall, tomboy women. They went after cute, sweet, lovable types.

Too bad she'd already shown him her surly side.

She shook her head to clear it. Her goal wasn't to wish for things that couldn't be. It was to forget about the possibility of anything between them. Considering that she'd just met the man that should be easy. She focused on the project—the slimy dirt, the pond that wasn't doing the job it was designed to do—and forgot all about being attracted to Jace MacDonald.

After their second trip outside, Jace scraped the mud off his shoes, shrugged out of his overcoat and took his place at the desk. She strode into her office and made the calls she'd been dreading. Before they'd gone out, she'd done a quick internet search on Waters, Waters and Montgomery and Danny Manelli. When that panned out, she'd called Danny to confirm Jace's story. When the estate lawyer parroted everything Jace had said, she knew this was real. She hadn't doubted it. She knew she was Mark Hinton's child. But she wasn't going to New York with a stranger without investigating.

Then she spent an hour looking at all the Kaiser and Barclay projects, evaluating the foremen, and made her choice. *She* was the vice president and director of operations for Kaiser and Barclay Development. She'd put herself in her current position at the jobsite because she didn't have anybody else to fill it. So, playing Rubik's cube with her foremen and projects, shifting and considering all the possibilities, she'd rearranged everything and found the best combination of people and jobs to get a replacement for herself.

"Good news, Skippy." After having made her calls, she breezed out of her office and into the main area where Jace looked like an adult sitting at a kid's desk. "I only have to finish out the week. Then we can go."

He rose. "Your boss found a replacement that quickly?"

"The director of operations is a genius," she said, motioning to him that she was ready to leave for the day.

He scowled. "*You're* the director of operations."

She laughed. "And I'm a genius."

She pointed at the door again. Jace rose and shrugged into his overcoat as she switched off the light. He walked out of the trailer in front of her, and she turned and locked the door before she led him to her big, black truck.

The sun had set long ago. The heavy equipment operators had already gone for the day. A lovely quiet had settled over the usually bustling ten acres surrounded by chain-link fence and smelling like spent diesel fuel.

He nodded once at the big truck. "Nice."

"Thanks. It was a birthday gift to myself."

He grunted. "You have good taste."

And here was another reason she usually ended up "friends" with the guys she found attractive. She loved engines. Loved speed. Loved power in a vehicle. Once she established that, men never saw her as feminine again.

But what the heck. Any minion of her dad's wasn't a potential match for her. Might as well pound a stake into the heart of her attraction to him and kill it once and for all. "What are you driving?"

He nudged his chin toward a huge SUV.

She sniffed. "Nothing says security detail like an enormous black SUV with tinted windows."

He ignored her sarcasm. "I'll follow you."

"Do you want the address in case I lose you?"

"I have the address."

His comment wasn't exactly matter-of-fact, but he wasn't angry as she expected him to be after almost six hours of just sitting, watching the trailer door and her office door. She supposed that was a bodyguard's primary duty. But the lack of movement or mental creativity would make her nuts.

She got in her truck and headed home, a midsize, midcentury modern house. She hadn't merely designed it herself; she'd supervised every inch of the construction and decorated it.

She pulled her truck into the garage and Jace parked in her driveway. But she didn't enter through the combination mud room and laundry room as she usually would have. She walked outside and guided him to the front door. No reason for him to see the two weeks' worth of dirty clothes she'd been avoiding.

As she punched the numbers on the security pad, he walked up behind her, then over to the front porch swing. Bending, he grabbed something and dragged it toward him.

Her breath caught. Had somebody figured out who she was and put a bomb under her swing?

He presented a duffel bag. "My staff had this delivered."

She put her hand on her chest. *Shoot.* She hadn't meant to act like a coward but all his talk of bodyguards and people coming after her had caused her brain to go in that direction. His fault. So, she would pretend it hadn't happened.

"Your staff is efficient. What's in there?"

"Work boots, work shirts, jeans." He shrugged. "A few notebooks and pens so I look like a real assistant, and my laptop so I can get some work done."

Impressed with his effectiveness, she smiled. "Wow."

"Oh, come on. I saw you with your staff. You say jump. They say how high. We're two peas in a pod."

She wasn't sure about being two peas in a pod, but every leader should have the ability to get his staff to do his bidding. So why did a stupid duffel bag under her front porch swing have her wanting to fan herself? She'd thought she'd killed the attraction.

So, he was competent?

Masterful.

Sort of sexy with the gruff way he made it all sound perfectly normal.

She told her brain to stop before it engaged other parts of her body, like making her breathless or stutter or—please, God, no—want to flirt.

Tossing her jacket and briefcase onto a convenient chair in the entryway, she said, "Bedrooms are back the hall to the right. Your room will be the first one. It has a private bathroom. I'm guessing you're going to want to change."

He grunted and headed down the corridor. The second his back was to her she squeezed her eyes shut.

Why did he have to be so gorgeous? And *tall*. For Pete's sake, men were rarely taller than she was. Yet, the first really tall, really good-looking guy she finds has to be one of her dad's minions.

If she didn't so desperately want to meet her sister, she'd be shipping Jace MacDonald back to where he came from. Not because she didn't like being attracted to him but because she couldn't have him.

She opened the fridge in her all-white kitchen with marble countertops and stainless-steel appliances, looking for something to make for dinner.

She absolutely refused to even be attracted to anyone who worked for her dad. And Jace probably wouldn't want her, either. She'd been sassy and smart with him because when someone was on her turf, they had to accept that she was the boss. Besides, who was she kidding? Sassy was her middle name. She prided herself on being able to lead. She liked being strong and capable.

She sighed. Boy, now that she spelled that out for herself, she saw the flaw in her thinking. She'd always felt disadvantaged by her height but there was nothing she could do about that. Did she really need to be bossy, too?

She closed the fridge and headed for the pantry. She found macaroni and cheese, grabbed two boxes and returned to the fridge, this time looking in the freezer compartment and finding hamburger meat.

Perfect. She could brown that and stir it into the macaroni and cheese, then make a salad.

It didn't take long to brown meat. With prep work, it took about ten minutes to make the pasta, and she cut up the salad veggies while the macaroni cooked.

When Jace returned from his shower she turned to casually say, "I made dinner."

But her tongue stuck to the roof of her mouth. He looked pure Scot with his wet black hair, loose T-shirt skimming broad shoulders and a stomach that was as flat as the first cake she ever baked. Sweatpants hung low on his lean hips.

She worked to loosen her tongue and finally said, "I made macaroni."

Einstein she wasn't. But at least she'd stopped standing there like a fool, drooling over him.

"I see that." He lifted the lid on the pot. "I love this stuff."

"Me, too."

He returned the pot lid. "And the salad gives it a boost into a healthy meal."

"That was the plan."

He shook his head. "I don't remember the last time someone cooked for me."

Her heart melted. She wasn't domestic. She wasn't overly feminine. Everyone called her a tomboy. But there was something elemental in having a person appreciate her bare-bones domesticity.

She stifled a groan. She had to get her thoughts out of that place, or she'd have to worry about flirting again. "You don't have a mom?"

He chuckled. "Yes, I do. But my dad's family is still in Scotland. My older brother moved there two years ago to keep an eye on our grandmother. His wife is pregnant, so Mom flies over every other month."

She leaned against the stove. No mention of a wife and no ring. Still, she couldn't come right out and ask…could she?

No! For Pete's sake. This guy worked for her dad. Plus, everybody knew bodyguards weren't supposed to get involved with their clients. *She* was his client. If she made a pass at him, he'd rebuff her, and wouldn't that be embarrassing?

She turned and retrieved plates from the cupboard. "If you don't mind, silverware is in that drawer."

"Sure."

He pulled out forks and knives and grabbed a few paper napkins from the fussy carved marble container her mom had bought for her as a housewarming gift.

Working together, they easily set the table, then took their dishes to the stove to scoop out the macaroni.

When they were both seated at her round white kitchen table with aqua chairs, he forked a bite of the mac and cheese. "Mmm… Takes me back to grade school when my mother would bribe me with this stuff to get me to do my homework."

She laughed. "Mine used it as a reward for when I'd agree to wear a dress to a dance."

"Sweet."

"It was. My mother is the sweetest, kindest person on the face of the earth." An average-size woman, she hadn't known how to handle it when her baby girl was the tallest kid in kindergarten, elementary and middle school. Happily, the boys' hormones kicked in in high school and she was only the third tallest kid in her class.

"We were lucky to have good mothers."

She nodded. "It's probably why we're both so successful."

"That and hard work."

"Only someone who's struggled a bit to become successful says that."

He thought a minute. "I did struggle. I can guard anybody. It's getting clients—the marketing and PR ends of things—that I had to learn."

She leaned her elbow on the table and studied him. "But you learned."

"Learn or die."

She stifled a laugh. Damn it. She wanted to like this guy. She *did* like this guy. But not only was he her bodyguard—somebody who common sense said wasn't allowed to get too chummy with her—he'd seen her pushy, bossy side.

He wouldn't want her even if she wasn't a client.

They finished their meal. She retreated to her office to handle some of her regular tasks that had been sitting while she managed the new project. Jace said he'd scope out the place, then watch TV.

When she was done with her work, she took some pillows and blankets to him and left him in her living room. Most of the furniture in the house was ultramodern. Metal legs on furniture with simple, clean lines on glossy hardwood floors. But she'd found a way to fit a fat, comfortable gray sofa into that decor and was glad since she'd hate to have anybody sleeping on the thin cushions of a flat sofa while he guarded her front door.

Ten minutes later, she stepped into the shower, and the reality of Jace MacDonald shimmered through her. She was naked, water spritzing over her, and there was a strange man in her living room. Sure, she'd checked him out. She'd called Waters, Waters and Montgomery and talked to Danny Manelli. So Jace was legit.

But—

Holy crap. There was a man in her house. Not to fool around with, but to *guard* her. She thought about the reporters Jace had mentioned, then thought about her sister who'd been outed as an heir. Her mom had told her that her biological father didn't come around or even admit to her existence because he was afraid for her. She'd cited kidnapping threats and even death threats that led him to his decision to hide her in plain sight.

As a child, she hadn't thought too much of it, except that her "daddy" had been big and strong and smart so that had to be right. As a teen, she'd decided it was a cop-out. Though teenagers are usually overly dramatic, that assessment stuck because it was correct. What guy abandons a woman he supposedly loves, makes her raise a child alone—so far in the country she didn't have friends? A coward or a blowhard.

She'd chosen to believe he was both. And she could easily ignore his existence. Actually, ignoring his existence had made her life normal. Sure, she was raised by a single mom, but lots of kids had been. It nudged her to work harder to get her degree and make her place in the world, and she was proud of her accomplishments.

But now—

With a bodyguard in her living room and Mark Hinton's life finally intersecting with hers—

It all seemed surreal.

If she were smart, she'd focus on the gorgeous guy in

her house, rather than why he was here, but then she'd have to deal with the damned attraction.

After one last check of her emails, she finally crawled into bed. When she closed her eyes, she realized she was going to have to tell her mom the estate had found her, and she'd be going to New York to prove she was an heir to the fortune of the man her mom had loved so much she'd never dated again. As if she hadn't grieved enough already when Mark Hinton died, this would make it so much more real for her mom.

She groaned. She'd never understood her mom's fixation with a guy who didn't want her, but, on the good side, she credited watching her mom waste her life with keeping Charlotte herself from making a fool of herself with men like Jace MacDonald.

Her mom's fixation on and pining for a man who didn't want her would keep her from even thinking about a guy who'd probably brush her off.

She settled on her pillow. She did not like being made a chump. Her biological dad had made suckers enough of both her and her mom. She'd held her head high, kept her nose clean and made something of herself. But that didn't mean that late at night, when no one was watching, she didn't feel the sting of being rejected. Her mom had adored Mark Hinton. He'd apparently also loved her mom. Things hadn't changed until Charlotte came into the picture.

She didn't think nonsensical things like her mom and Mark would have spent a happy life together if Penny hadn't gotten pregnant. She didn't blame herself for her mom losing Mark.

But she did know he hadn't wanted *her*.

Or her siblings apparently, if there were supposedly two more children, scattered around, none of whom had a clue they were an heir.

So that was on him.

But the feelings of being unwanted that she'd carried from grade school and almost the whole way through grad school had taught her that rejection was a powerful thing. It could mow down the smartest, fastest, most capable people. She'd been mowed down once, at age twelve, when she was old enough to put all the puzzle pieces of her mom's life together and realize *she* was the reason for her mom's bone-deep sadness. She wouldn't be mowed down again.

Her rationale in place, she nestled into her pillow. Having survived the greatest rejection of all—a parent who hadn't wanted her, who'd changed his life to get away from her—not getting involved with the handsome Scot sleeping on her sofa should be a piece of cake.

CHAPTER THREE

THE NEXT MORNING Charlotte woke and swore she smelled bacon. Then she remembered she had a houseguest and she pulled the covers over her head. She was a Hinton heir. In some circles that apparently made her a celebrity. So, she had a bodyguard—a flipping bodyguard—who would be following her around the jobsite, while she tried to get oodles of work done before Western Pennsylvania's epic spring rains killed her chances.

She forced herself out of bed and into jeans and a plaid work shirt and headed for her kitchen.

Dressed in a T-shirt, butt-hugging jeans and sensible work boots, her heart-stopping bodyguard stood by the counter, drinking a cup of coffee.

She pushed her feminine happiness aside and said, "Good morning."

"Want some breakfast?"

"I'm not a breakfast eater."

"Strange for a woman who has bacon in her fridge."

"I like bacon on my cheeseburgers."

He nodded. "So, you're ready to go?"

"I normally put coffee in a take-out container before I leave."

He reached into the cabinet beside the coffeemaker, grabbed a mug with a lid, filled it and handed it to her. "Then let's go."

So that was it. Simple. No nonsense.

He pointed at the door. She headed for the one that connected to the mudroom and garage since he didn't need to follow her to get to his SUV.

"Where are you going?"

"My truck is in the garage."

"Unless there are tools or something you need in your truck, we take my vehicle."

"I have to ride with you?"

"You have to *everything* with me."

Too tired from a restless night to argue, she walked to his SUV, the crisp April air making her breath mist. He walked beside her, his head moving inconspicuously from side to side as his sharp eyes took in everything.

The craziness of it got to her. "My neighbors are going to think I had a sleepover."

He opened the door for her and peered at her over his sunglasses. "You did."

Damned if her heart didn't flutter. Still, she said, "Don't flatter yourself."

"Oh, I don't have to."

She climbed inside and he slowly closed the door. She didn't need to give him directions to the jobsite. He knew them as if he had memorized them. The second the SUV stopped, she jumped out, worried that he would open the door for her in front of her men.

Chuck Carter, a crew foreman, already walked toward her. "There's water."

"Well, of course there's water. It's April. You know. April showers and that whole thing."

"So, we keep going?"

She sighed. "No. Let me look at it."

Jace rounded the hood to stand beside them. Chuck glanced from Jace to Charlotte and back again. His eyebrows rose.

"Don't get excited, Zorro," she said to the almost-forty foreman. "We just happen to live near each other."

His eyebrows rose even higher. "An assistant can afford a house in your neighborhood?"

Jace calmly said, "I married well."

If Charlotte had been drinking coffee, she would have spit it across the hood of the SUV.

Chuck headed toward the heavy equipment and guys milling around. Jace walked behind him and in front of her. Not wanting Jace to arrive before her and look like the one calling the shots, she quickly maneuvered to the head of the line, taking control again. Leading the three of them into the field, she stewed a bit. Jace was probably a top-of-the-line bodyguard, but as an assistant, he was a bit pushy. And if he kept doing things like this, she was going to have to have a talk with him.

They looked at the water and traipsed around the site a bit before Charlotte studied the topographic map again. Jace glanced at his watch. Fifteen minutes. They'd walked, they'd yacked about dirt and now they were silently studying the map.

It was going to be a long day.

Finally, she made a decision, gave an order and they tromped into the trailer. As Charlotte talked on the phone in the back office, Jace washed the old, disgusting coffeepot and pulled a packet of coffee grinds from the briefcase he'd brought. He had a packet for morning and one for afternoon. He refused to die from whatever lingered in that old pot or drink the cheap crap the company provided.

The phone rang, breaking into the silence of the trailer. With a breath, he walked over, scooped up the receiver and said, "Kaiser and Barclay."

"Is this the Riverdale jobsite?"

Well, damn. Maybe that's how he was supposed to answer? All he knew was her company name.

No harm done, though. "Sorry. Only my second day on the job. I'll get it right next time. How can I help you?"

"I need to talk to Charlotte."

"Sure." He hit the hold button and walked back to her door. "Pick up the blinking line. Some guy wants to talk to you."

"You didn't get a name?"

"You're lucky I didn't hang up on him. Your phone's an antiquated piece of junk."

"Because we're at a jobsite where new things can get ruined." She sighed, sat forward and punched the button on the ancient phone. "This is Charlotte." As the guy answered, her face lit; she leaned back on her chair comfortably.

"Hey, Jim!"

Jace's chest froze. Whoever Jim was, she clearly liked him. Maybe he was even a friend, not a coworker. Not that Jace cared. He was only here to guard her.

She motioned for him to close the door, and though the muscles in his arms bunched and hardened, he casually reached in, grabbed the knob, shut the blasted thing and went back to making his coffee.

As it brewed, he found mugs and washed them, wincing at how scummy they were. How could they have dish soap beside a faucet and not make the astounding conclusion that they should wash their mugs? And how could she stay on the line for so long with a guy who was a friend, not a coworker?

Of course, he didn't know if Jim was a coworker or a friend. He'd guessed from her gorgeous smile and the way her eyes lit that her caller was more of a friend than a coworker.

Finishing the last mug, he told himself to stop think-ing about her—

Except what if the guy was more than a friend and she'd done something foolish like tell him about Mark Hinton... or, worse, made a date?

The strange something rippled through him again, tight-ening his muscles and making his stomach feel funny.

He swore his body was wrong. He was not jealous. He had learned his lesson about being attracted to or getting involved with clients with Misha. He would not do that again. But he did have a job to do.

Mugs draining on a paper towel, he ambled to the of-fice, opened the door, walked in and sat on the chair in front of her desk.

She said a few things about Jim's house and a fix for his lawn tractor, then said, "Sorry. Gotta go. But we'll catch up soon. I promise."

She hung up the phone, then, shaking her head, she looked him in the eye. "What?"

"What you mean, what? You locked me out of a conver-sation that judging by the closed door was more personal than business. I gave you a few minutes, but I wasn't about to stay out while you made arrangements to have dinner with some guy."

"I would have let you watch. Isn't that what bodyguards do? They go to a restaurant with their client and sit at an-other table and watch."

He squirmed on his chair. She wasn't even pretending Jim wasn't a friend or hookup or something. "Yes."

"Okay, then we're good. If he calls back, I'll suggest dinner."

Annoyed with himself and her, he rose. "No! Damn it! You said we'd leave for New York at the end of the work-week. That's tomorrow. We don't have time to be squeez-ing in dates."

"It wouldn't be a date. He's married to my friend." She toyed with a pencil, looked up and smiled at him. "And just for fun, we could have gone to dinner with them and pretended you were *my* date."

The idea sizzled a bolt of electricity to the very wrong place. He took a breath, squeezed his eyes shut, prayed for strength, then popped them open again. "If you want to have dinner with a friend, pizza with the entire cast of a Broadway show or go shopping for pineapple, I don't care. I'm trained to guard you. But we have only one more day in which the most important thing is keeping people from realizing who you are. Keeping people from realizing something is different in your life. The more friends you see, the more people you talk to, the more chance you're going to slip something. Wouldn't it be easier to stay home with me?"

She sighed as if put upon. "I suppose."

"Don't 'I suppose' me. You get home at dark. You work another hour on your computer. Then you go to bed." He turned to the door. "You're just being difficult. You don't have time to socialize."

He was out the door before Charlotte could count to two. So, she stood and called, "That doesn't mean I don't want to."

She sat again, her heart stuttering and breath catching. She shouldn't goad him like that, but oh my goodness, he was glorious when he was mad.

She managed to behave herself the rest of the day. She even smiled and cordially offered to make dinner when they got home. But he insisted on cooking.

"You cooked last night."

"Macaroni."

"It was still cooking."

"All right. Fine. You can make dinner." Skepticism about

his abilities had her wincing. But most single guys could cook. So, she stifled that. "I'll go change."

Kicking off her grimy boots in the mudroom, she stripped out of her socks, work shirt and jeans and slid into her most comfortable sweatpants and a T-shirt. Feeling human again and ready for food, she ambled out of the mudroom toward the kitchen. The scent of something sweet and meaty filled the air. Charlotte's mouth watered. If she were to guess she'd say Jace had found pork chops in her freezer, defrosted them in the microwave and was now grilling them in her oven…with barbecue sauce. Sweet, tangy barbecue sauce.

Suddenly her front door opened.

Standing by the oven, which had a clear line of sight to the door, Jace stiffened; his entire body went on red alert and he reached behind him to the waistband of his jeans.

Charlotte's heart stopped.

Then her mother entered, her mid-length yellow hair styled to perfection, a soft floral blouse over jeans and stylish boots.

Jumping in before Jace had a chance to pull a gun, Charlotte said, "Mom! What a surprise!" She gave Jace a pointed look and he relaxed. "What brings you here?"

Penny Fillion held out a square plastic container of cupcakes. "I baked today."

"Ooh…cupcakes!"

Penny ambled to the center island that divided the kitchen from the dining area. "It's fabulous to have a child who can eat and not gain weight. That way when I want a cupcake, I can bake them and not worry about eating the whole batch." She smiled at Jace, even as her sharp blue eyes clearly sized him up. "And you are?"

Jace said, "Charlotte's assistant," at the same time that Charlotte said, "My bodyguard. Dad's estate found me."

Jace's mouth fell open. "What the hell are you doing? What happened to the plan?"

"This is my mother. I don't lie to my mother."

Penny laughed. "She does, however, stretch the truth."

"It doesn't matter. No one is supposed to be told about the estate, so there'll be no slipups or surprises like someone talking to the press."

"My mom knows who I am. Why hide the fact that the estate found me?" She faced her mom. "And they want me to go to New York for a couple of weeks to prove I'm an heir so I can officially relinquish my share of the inheritance."

Penny sat at one of the stools in front of the island. "It's going to take you *weeks* to prove you're an heir? Why not just show them your birth certificate?"

Charlotte slid onto the seat beside her mom. "I offered it. They want irrefutable proof."

Penny sighed. "DNA."

Jace crossed his arms on his chest and leaned against a nearby counter. "It's more than that. The will has protocols Mark wanted followed so that the real heirs are vetted the same way the fakes are so no one can take issue with how it's all done."

Penny drew in a slow breath. "If nothing else, Mark was a planner."

Jace quietly said, "I'm sorry for your loss."

Charlotte peeked at him. Aside from Charlotte, he was the first and maybe the only person who'd acknowledged her mom's loss. It was the sweetest thing she'd seen anyone do in forever. This time when her heart swelled it was with appreciation, something warmer and sweeter than mere lust.

"Thank you," Penny said. "But life goes on." She faced Charlotte. "And I won't have you throwing away your future because you didn't like your dad."

"I'm not throwing away my future. I intend to run Kaiser

and Barclay someday." She opened the cupcake container, ran her finger over the icing of the first cupcake, then licked it. "That's a future anybody can be proud of. Plus, it's all mine. I worked for it. Sacrificed for it. Got it on my own."

"Technically, you have to give your father credit for part of that. He did buy the farm and pay child support."

She gaped at her mom. "The man paid a fraction of what he'd have probably paid if he'd acknowledged me. And that farm was his idea to keep us hidden."

"Keep us *safe*."

"Potato, pa-tah-toe."

Penny looked at Jace. "I never win this argument."

Jace laughed. "I figured that out already."

"Don't let her walk away from a fortune."

"It's not my job to convince her. Only my job to protect her. Please don't tell anyone Charlotte's been found and she's being vetted as an heir. I know here in peaceful Pittsburgh it seems like second-rate news, but in New York, there are reporters who'd sell their souls for the names of any of the Hinton heirs."

Penny looked at Jace. "*Heirs?* How many kids are there?"

Jace quietly said, "Three. One older than Charlotte. One younger."

"Oh."

Charlotte's heart broke. She knew her mom liked to believe that Mark Hinton had pined for her as much as she'd pined for him. But the existence of a child *after* Charlotte was proof he'd moved on.

Jace broke the silence. "We haven't found the older one. But the younger one is Leni Long. A social worker from Kansas. Very nice woman. I know Charlotte's going to love her."

Penny perked up. "A sister! You have a sister."

Charlotte laughed. "Yes. I hope to meet her while I'm

in New York. Even if I don't take my share of the money, I'd like to get to know her."

"Well, something good did come out of this, after all." She brightened and slid off her stool. "I smell dinner cooking and I didn't come here to intrude. Just to bring the cupcakes." She kissed Charlotte's cheek. "Let me know how it goes."

Charlotte said, "I will," and walked her mom to the door.

Penny grabbed the knob but stopped midtwist and leaned in to whisper, "He's adorable."

Charlotte rolled her eyes. "He's also my bodyguard and a minion of my father's."

"You've got to get over that."

"The fact that he's a bodyguard?"

"No. Hating your dad."

"I never really hated him. What I feel for him more than anything else is irrelevance. And though you might find that sad, it works for me to have put him in a tidy little box and not need him."

With a shake of her head, Penny left. Charlotte closed the door behind her and returned to the kitchen.

"I like your mom."

"Everyone does. She's cute and sweet."

She expected Jace to laugh or mention how different she and her mom were, but he didn't. He removed the pork chops from the oven, poured a noodle side dish of some kind into a serving bowl and took heated veggies from the microwave.

They ate dinner in silence. Charlotte's mind drifted as she thought about her mom, not quite sure if she should be worried about her. Having Mark die was one thing. Hearing he'd fathered a child after their relationship might have burst the bubble of hope her mom always held on to that she was Mark's one true love.

Still, she didn't say anything to Jace. He'd made a nice

comment about her mom and she appreciated that, but he was her bodyguard, not her new friend. No matter how often what she was thinking almost spilled out of her mouth, she'd catch herself and pull back her words. Once she was vetted, Jace would be out of her life. Stupid to confide in someone who was part of a temporary arrangement.

She said good night and slipped off to her bedroom after nine.

The next morning, having another person in her house grew tiresome. She felt self-conscious showering, but the reality of being Mark Hinton's kid hit home in a way it couldn't when having Jace MacDonald around was new. He'd now insinuated himself into her work life, cooked for her, met her mom and eaten one of the cupcakes her mom had baked.

With the novelty of it seeping away, she realized this would be the rest of her life if she took her share of the estate. With a bodyguard at her side 24/7, she'd never be alone again.

She froze under the warm spray of water. She *liked* being alone.

Except—

What if she kept Jace as her bodyguard?

The mere thought of having him in her life more than temporarily kick-started her heart and sent a weird kind of happy expectation shimmying through her—

She groaned. Was she daydreaming about a guy she couldn't have?

Charlotte Fillion did not do that!

She got out of the shower and dressed, getting more and more surly.

CHAPTER FOUR

JACE WOKE IN a good mood, glad they would leave for New York at the end of her shift. Watching Charlotte work the day before had made the tedious task of following her around far too interesting. The woman was so smart that Jace understood exactly why her crew was putty in her hands. If she gave them an order, it was the correct one. He almost hated taking her away from her job, but she had to be vetted as a Hinton heir. Then she had some choices to make.

But he'd also be back on his turf where he could control everything she did. His life would get easy again, the way it had been before Mark Hinton died—

Jace squeezed his eyes shut as a suspicion entered his brain. Mark's yacht had caught fire in the Caribbean. Though Mark put out a distress call and had a lifeboat, he wasn't there when help arrived, and they'd never found the lifeboat. After a thorough search, a significant lapse of time and a boatload of protocols and legal mumbo jumbo, he was declared dead.

Some mornings when Jace was still half-asleep, the thought tiptoed into his head that it all seemed so convenient, so coincidental. Mark's yacht catches fire. His lifeboat is lost…and Mark is free.

Angry with himself for thinking about something that couldn't possibly be true—real people didn't fake their deaths—Jace rolled himself to a sitting position on the sofa.

Charlotte came out of her bedroom and his thoughts about Mark evaporated as his heart stopped.

She wore a light blue dress, fancy jewelry and high heels. Her pale hair framed her face with wide curls. The dress showed off her perfect figure.

He almost had to pound his chest to start his breathing again. "What's with the get-up?"

"You didn't think I would leave for New York for goodness knows how long without informing my boss, did you?"

He scrubbed his hand down his face. The voice coming out of the drop-dead gorgeous woman was Charlotte, but her fancy hair, makeup and high heels were throwing him. She was so damned feminine he couldn't stop staring at her, and that was trouble.

He had vowed—*vowed*—never to get involved with another client and being this attracted to one put him on a slippery slope.

"I hadn't given much thought to your boss."

She slid a sparkly earring onto her earlobe. "I'm going to have to make up a plausible explanation for my absence while you shower."

He growled. "You're going to make me wear a suit, aren't you?"

"Damned if I know. I don't even know how to explain you since it will look odd that I'm traveling to New York for personal reasons with my 'work' assistant. I haven't thought far enough ahead to get to your clothes." She straightened her dress. "Go shower."

In the end, he wore the suit he'd worn on the first day, with the black overcoat and his work boots—since his loafers had been ruined. His pants fell past his ankles. Most of the boots were hidden and the rest he'd buffed clean. But with Charlotte beside him, he doubted anyone would notice his feet.

Neither of them spoke as they drove into Pittsburgh.

Maneuvering his SUV into the parking garage, Jace automatically clicked into bodyguard mode, peering around at the typical concrete structure. Nothing unusual. Nothing to worry about. It would be a good, easy day.

Jace and Charlotte were the only two people in the elevator on the way up to the corporate office. Thick, awkward silence filled the space. It didn't bother Jace. It made him feel like things were the way they should be. Client and bodyguard. Not chatty friends. Not two attracted people. Bodyguard and *client*.

Charlotte sighed. "Your dinner last night was great."

He made a *"Pfft"* noise, as if cooking had been no big deal. He didn't want them to get close, but if she wanted to talk, he could do small talk. Ease her nerves. "Your mother's cupcakes were the showstopper. Besides, you cooked the day before."

"Yeah. Macaroni from a box." Still facing the elevator door, she gave him the side eye. "Seriously, you're a great cook. I haven't eaten a dinner so good in years."

"You know, with billions of dollars you could hire a chef who cooks like I do."

"Why don't I just hire you?"

He peered over at her. "You're thinking of taking the money?"

"No. But nice try."

"I wasn't trying to trick you into saying you wanted it. Actually, I understand why you don't." He sucked in a breath. If Mark had faked his death, this woman would hurt him. Thank God Jace really didn't believe he had. It was just a weird thought that popped into his head once in a while. He'd use his legendary discipline to even stop considering it. Because it was wrong. Pointless. Mark was dead.

"You're very good at what you do."

Surprise flitted across her pretty face, and for a second, he was caught by her beauty. High cheekbones, a strong chin, blue eyes that communicated everything she was thinking.

"Well, thank you, Jace."

The way she said his name almost had him sucking in another breath, but he stopped himself. Though her voice was like warm honey, he could not dwell on how that made him feel. Mostly because he knew she found him attractive, too. And that was trouble. Being attracted to clients wrecked careers.

He couldn't believe he had to remind himself of that. But everything she did hit him directly in the libido. He'd never been instantly, completely attracted to anyone before. Not even to Mary Beth. She was a beautiful brunette with a heart of gold, and he'd liked her before he'd loved her. Because that was how it was supposed to be. Feelings were supposed to increase over time. Not run over a guy like a freight train.

Of course, his relationship with Mary Beth had ended. Badly.

She'd broken his heart. Nearly destroyed his confidence. And the one time he'd seen her on the street, with his ex–best friend as her husband and an adorable baby girl… Well, he'd gone a little crazy, confided in a client, and they'd slept together. Years later, when Misha's dad disinherited her, she wrote a tell-all book to show her dad she could make her own money, and she'd told the whole blasted story. Except she'd embellished certain details. Details that made him look like a borderline stalker. Clients who'd trusted him suddenly looked at him differently. Clients with young wives or grown daughters fired him.

That's when Mark had taught him about PR and recruiting new business.

It's also when he'd vowed never get himself into that kind of position again.

Which sort of was his point. First, what he felt for Charlotte couldn't be anything more than hormones. Second, he had no intention of getting involved with a client again. Only an idiot made a business-killing mistake twice.

He was not an idiot. He would forget how Charlotte's simple thank-you had made him feel.

"I mean it. You're so good at what you do, no one ever questions you. Which means you have a good reputation."

"I do. I worked for it."

He sniffed a laugh. "I don't doubt that for one second. Which proves my point. You have what you need. There's no reason for you to take Mark's money."

"Exactly." She grinned. "I knew that a guy who had successfully started his own company would eventually get it."

"Good God. Was that a compliment from you…to *me*?"

She glanced at her fancy watch. "I know you're more than muscles."

His ego loved that she'd noticed his muscles. Which was silly, but who could really understand the effect of hormones on an otherwise rational human being? Luckily, he really did have legendary discipline and he could also keep his ego in line.

The elevator chugged toward the top floor. One of her fancy earrings fell from her ear. He bent to pick it up and handed it to her.

Suddenly, they were face-to-face and close. He watched her eyes sharpen and her slow intake of air as if her breathing had stalled, even as his chest tightened and his mouth watered.

"Thanks."

Her voice shook the tiniest bit, but he couldn't find fault because his limbs felt clumsy and his brain had clouded. He had the slow burn feeling he loved. Not of risky passion, but leisurely, scrupulously thorough lovemaking—

Which was wrong. And certainly not something he'd let himself dwell on.

"You're welcome. Better check the clasp to make sure it's not broken."

She turned away from him and slid off the good earring and slipped both in her purse just as the elevator pinged.

The door opened onto a busy reception area. A tall front desk stood as a barrier between the elevator and the company, but behind the receptionist were work hubs filled with people.

"Hey, April, how's it going?" Charlotte said.

The pretty redhead looked up. "Hey, Charlotte! Nice to have you here again."

"Well, I'm here but I'm not here. I have an appointment with Mr. Ferguson."

April punched a button on her phone. "Let me confirm." She spoke with the company president's assistant, then hit the button again. "You can go back."

When the receptionist pointedly looked at Jace, Charlotte easily said, "He's my assistant. New guy. I'm showing him around."

April nodded happily. "Good to see you finally got some help."

When they started down the hall, Jace said, "The whole company seems to know you didn't have an assistant."

"With computers I could handle most of my own admin. I especially like having control of my schedule."

Jace didn't doubt that for a second.

They walked through a door to an office in the back. "Good morning, Paul."

The young man in the small office in front of the bigger one nodded once. "Good morning, Charlotte. Mr. Ferguson is ready to see you."

She said, "Thanks," as they breezed past and into the fancy office behind Paul's.

Jace's eyes widened. "Wow." The room was done with

an Asian flare, complete with samurai swords and bamboo floors.

Charlotte leaned in a whispered, "I know. Reeks of money, doesn't it?"

He laughed.

A short balding man in an expensive suit entered the office from a side door. "Charlotte!" He walked over and hugged her. "And you must be the new assistant, Jace."

He shook Ferguson's hand. "That would be me."

Charlotte's boss studied him. "You look more like a truck driver."

Jace laughed, but Charlotte said, "That's because he's not really my assistant. He works for a law firm handling a legal thing for my family. Something confidential."

Though Jace wasn't sure where she was going with this, he remembered how she'd handled her mother and gave her some leeway. She hadn't said bodyguard. She hadn't said estate. And as she'd already hinted at that morning, a guy as smart as her boss would certainly question why she was going to New York for something personal with her work assistant.

Ferguson frowned, walked behind his desk and motioned for them to sit. "Sounds serious."

"It is, Brice. But it's also something that will literally be handled—totally over and done with—in two weeks. Unfortunately, it means I'm going to be in New York until it's resolved."

Again, she'd kept things vague. But also, honest. She might not be telling her boss everything, but she wasn't lying.

Brice studied her. "Are we going to be able to keep our projects moving without you?"

"I've trained my staff to work independently. Plus—" She held up her cell phone. "There's this. I'll take my laptop, of course, and be able to answer any questions, and video chat in on meetings, if need be. It'll be like I'm here in the office."

Brice bobbed his head as he thought all that through. "Okay. Sounds like you have it all worked out." He grinned. "Maybe this is our test of how well you've really trained your staff."

Charlotte laughed. "Bring it."

Jace just stared at her. The woman did not have a timid bone in her body. And if that wasn't the hottest thing he'd ever seen he didn't know what was.

He groaned. Damn it. This attraction wasn't going away.

And handling it was taking far too much of his brain power, brain power he needed to make sure she was safe.

Ten minutes later, they were out of the building, walking toward Jace's SUV.

Confusion nagged at Charlotte. She waited until they were seated in his vehicle before she said, "I thought for sure you would kick me or something when I explained why I'd be out of the office."

"You told him the truth."

"But no one's supposed to know."

He shrugged. "You didn't tell him the secret part."

"So, you didn't mind?"

"Hey, you had good reason for telling your mom last night and good reason to give your boss at least part of the truth today. What you said was perfect." He pulled out of the parking space and headed up the busy street before he peered over at her. "I like that you know how to be honest without selling the farm."

Those crazy happy hormones danced through her again. She found herself indulging in the pleasure of them and stopped them cold.

This was getting ridiculous.

She could accept that he was adorable and sexy. She

could even let herself enjoy looking at him when he didn't notice. She could also respect that he was a successful businessman, a discreet bodyguard, a good actor.

But this thing they had where they clicked? It kept throwing her.

He cooked. She loved to eat.

She recognized his good points. He saw hers.

They were so attuned that she'd had to force herself not to talk to him about her mom at dinner the night before.

Damn it. Every day he felt more like "The One" but he couldn't be! She wasn't supposed to be thinking about him that way. And he absolutely was not thinking of her that way. But every once in a while he slipped, like this morning when she'd walked out of her bedroom in the dress with her hair fixed and high heels. His eyes had sharpened and for a few seconds he'd been speechless. Or in the elevator when he'd picked up her earring. They were suddenly so close he could have kissed her, and she swore he'd been thinking about it.

She told herself to get her mind off those things. They had two weeks together in New York. His turf. And she had to be a professional about this.

"Are we leaving this morning?"

"If all your business is done here, yes." Jace got on the interstate that would take them to her suburb. "How long will you need to pack?"

"I packed last night."

"Then I'll call the pilot. We can be in the air in two hours."

The pit of her stomach pinged. She wasn't afraid to fly but she did have a thing about takeoffs and landings. Just the word *pilot* gave her a queasy, awful reminder. Still, flying was the fastest way to New York and she always handled those few minutes of heart-stopping terror. "Sounds good."

"It'll be nice to get into a pair of real shoes again."

Forgetting all about her flying phobia, she laughed. In case she'd missed it in her list of his good points, Jace also had a sense of humor. A sense of humor that matched hers.

"I have to admit I was sort of impressed by how much you value honesty."

"No. I value my reputation. All it takes is being caught in one lie to ruin everything."

He made a sound of agreement. "I know how that goes. Almost killed my entire company by making one wrong move." He glanced over at her. "How'd *you* get to be so smart?"

"Grade school."

He sniffed. "What?"

"It's the height thing." She waved one hand above her head indicating how tall she was. "When you're close to being as big as the teacher in first grade, nobody even thinks to make you their friend. So, I learned to insinuate myself into small circles of kids playing games and went along with everything and pretty soon people stopped seeing me as a threat."

For a few seconds the inside of the car was silent, then he said, "I like your height."

Of course, he did. He was "The One." She just knew it. But fate was ruining everything by having them meet when she was his client. He didn't even have to tell her it would be a conflict of interest to get involved with someone he was guarding. It was common sense.

Yet here they were…perfect for each other and not able to do a damned thing about it.

She wouldn't meet his gaze. "Yeah well, that's because you're four inches taller than I am."

He said, "Good point."

She stared out the window, thinking this through. *Come .on, Charlotte. You are a renowned planner. A strategist. If this were a job, how would you handle it? How would you get rid of something that didn't work? Fix a behavior that was wrong, wrong, wrong?*

Jace suddenly said, "You know. I never put all this together, but Mark was my height. Being tall was one of his trademarks." He frowned. "People in Pittsburgh might not notice, but reporters in New York City, the ones assigned to flushing out the Hinton heirs, could see you with me and figure out who you are."

He thought for a couple more seconds. "I should assign someone else to you when we get to New York. Maybe even someone new."

She wished he would, if only to end all this confusion. That might even be the real reason he'd suggested it. To separate them. Not working together would render their attraction irrelevant.

"But Danny won't allow that. The Hinton estate is my biggest client. And we did have the slipup with Leni. He now insists I guard the heirs."

Charlotte sucked in a breath.

He peeked over. His smile gone. His face grim. "We're stuck together for at least two weeks."

And he didn't like it any more than she did because his reputation would suffer more than hers if they slipped up and did something foolish like kiss or, God forbid, sleep together.

Yet they were both tempted.

They reached her house and without a word she got out of the SUV. She headed for her room and grabbed her suitcase packed with enough clothes for two weeks. But as she fumed at fate, destiny or whatever force thought it was funny to have her ridiculously attracted to a guy she couldn't have, the oddest thought hit her.

What if this attraction was a paper tiger?

Sure. He was good-looking and intelligent, and they

seemed to have a lot in common. But what if she kissed him and… Nothing?

She'd had this happen before. There was a guy she liked who went to the same coffee shop she did. He'd been cute and funny, and they went out on a date that was good. But when he kissed her… Nothing.

Nothing.

Despite all the signs, they hadn't had chemistry.

She and Jace could be agonizing for nothing!

Jace MacDonald might kiss like a rock!

That was her salvation. The answer. A test to see if their chemistry was real.

All she had to do was kiss him.

CHAPTER FIVE

SOMETHING WAS GOING on with Charlotte.

Jace watched her sit in one of the brown leather seats of his jet and smile.

Again. All she'd done was give him an odd, goofy grin since they'd left her house.

"Those four chairs release, so they can be turned to form a conversation grouping."

Easing the back of her chair into a more comfortable position, Charlotte said, "Nice. This is a hundred times better than our corporate jet."

"It helps when you pay the extra money to customize."

She gave him the strangest look. Her eyes were bright. Her mouth had pulled into a big, fake smile. "Absolutely."

Okay. Something was definitely wrong for her to be this nervous. He didn't think she'd be jittery meeting the attorney for her dad's multi-billion-dollar estate. She didn't want the money. Yet that was the only thing that had changed since he'd walked into her construction trailer. They'd boarded the plane that would take her to New York, where she'd jump feetfirst into squaring up her past.

Take the money or leave it; she was facing the biggest decision of her life. So, okay. Nerves happen.

Still, he could not present her to Danny Manelli when she was this jumpy. He was going to have to do something to get her back to normal.

"What do you say we play cards after we're at cruising altitude?"

"Look at you, talking all aeronautical."

"Cruising altitude is a common phrase."

"Right."

She settled back in her seat. He almost sat as far away from her as he could to give himself time to figure out how to get her back to normal before they met with the estate lawyer. But the oddest thing occurred to him.

"You're not afraid to fly, are you?"

"No! No! I'm fine."

He sat beside her. "Well, something's wrong."

"All right. Here's the truth. I'm not afraid of flying. It's the takeoffs and landings that give me the heebie-jeebies."

"Really?"

She glanced away. "Yes. I know it's an irrational fear, so I don't let it control my life. I fly all the time."

From the way she wouldn't look at him, he sensed she was either embarrassed about something she would consider a weakness, or she wasn't telling him everything. Like maybe she threw up when the plane took off.

Whatever. He'd seen that hundreds of times with clients. "If you're going to puke, there's a bag in the seat in front of you."

"I don't throw up, you goof. I just—" She pulled in a breath. "Get a little high strung."

"A little? If your mouth pulls any tighter, you're going to burst a blood vessel."

She laughed.

"That's better."

The plane shifted, then started to taxi to the runway. Luckily, on this private airstrip, everything was close. They wouldn't spend thirty minutes with her nerves winding tighter and tighter as they waited for their turn. Their take-off would be fewer than five minutes from now.

The pilot's voice came over the intercom system. "Good morning, Charlotte, Jace. It's a perfect day for flying. Our flight time is approximately ninety minutes. And we'll be in the air shortly."

"Shortly? What does that mean?"

"Did you want him to say we'll be taking off in exactly three minutes and forty-five seconds?"

"No. I just… Exact numbers make me feel in control."

Jace undid his seat belt, walked over to a cabinet and pulled out several magazines. "Here."

"What's this…? Is this payback because I told you to read magazines while you guarded the trailer door?"

"Nope. You need to amuse yourself. Shift your mind away from the takeoff, and before you know it, we'll be in the air and you said you're fine then."

"I am."

He nudged his head toward the magazine. "Then open that. Distract yourself."

She flipped the first page of the magazine. "You have some experience in this, don't you?"

"Yes. When I was barely more than a one-man operation, I did most of the traveling. Some of my clients had kids. Or they were elderly. Or they were high or drunk or both. I had to learn to deal with things."

The plane sped up, an indicator they were about to lift off.

Charlotte took a breath, flipped open the magazine and for the next three minutes read aloud about a family that was famous for being famous. "And at last rumors have been confirmed that Natasha is pregnant."

She set the magazine on her lap. "Well, good for her."

Jace laughed. The plane was in the air. Climbing, but in the air. Charlotte's nerves had clearly settled.

"All good now?"

"All good." She blew out a breath. "You do not know how much I hate being weak."

"Of course I do. I can't afford to be weak. If I'm weak at the wrong moment someone could be snatched or killed."

She leaned her elbow on the armrest and caught his gaze. "Really?"

She was a little close and the odd look was back in her eyes, even though they were in the air. "Truth be told, sometimes my job is more about having magazines, being able to get around a city and knowing how to cure a hangover."

"There's a cure for hangovers?"

"Hair of the dog."

"That's an old wives' tale."

"Not for everybody."

She pulled back, gripped the armrests with both hands and took a long, solid breath. "So, we have ninety minutes until I have the opportunity for another panic attack. What do you want to do?"

"I have cards. I have simple games." He released his seat belt and walked to another cabinet. "I like playing rummy."

"Me, too! My goodness, I used to play with my mom all the time, but I haven't played rummy in forever."

"Okay. Rummy, it is."

He got the cards and motioned for her to join him in an area in the back that had the same seats as the conversation area, except there was a table.

"Nice."

"I told you I have to be prepared for everything."

She sat as he dealt the cards. "It sounds like, in some ways, you're a babysitter."

"And usually for adults—who don't realize they need a keeper. I have to know when to butt in or when say, Do you want a magazine? Do you want to play cards? How about a drink? Or, Put down the whiskey bottle."

She considered that. "You're bossier than I am."

"I have to be."

She drew a card, added it to the seven cards she had and simultaneously discarded one as she set down her hand. "I'm out."

He gaped at her. "I didn't even get to play a card!"

She laughed with glee. "I know! I love this game."

It was her first spontaneous laugh since they'd left her house. His chest loosened with relief, which was normal when working to make a jumpy client calm. The happiness that surged was not. He squelched it. Her questions about his job had reinforced who he was and what he was supposed to be doing. No matter how talkative they got, it was still his job to protect her. Not like her. Not be curious about her. Not wonder what it would be like to kiss her, which was what had begun happening that morning. She looked pretty. Smelled better. And her honesty with her boss had made him want to grab her upper arms, yank her to him and kiss her.

Wrong on so many levels he couldn't even count them. He'd learned that lesson the hard way. But he was back to normal now and everything was fine.

They played cards until the pilot announced they would be landing in twenty minutes. Knowing the drill, Jace returned the cards to their box.

"Your choice. Stay here and buckle up or move back to the seats we were in."

"The seats we were in were lucky for our takeoff. I say let's not mess with a good thing."

He shook his head. "You're superstitious."

"No. I simply never abandon what works."

They returned to their seats and buckled in. The plane began its descent. Not a dive, but more of a layer by layer fall.

Until they hit the last layer. Then the nose pointed down and they headed for the runway.

Charlotte grabbed his hand. He turned his head to see what was going on with her. Her eyes were wide and bright with fear. He hadn't exactly forgotten her hatred of takeoffs and landings, but she'd been so calm—

"Distract yourself."

"With what! We put the magazines back in the drawer back there."

"Okay. How about this? Count to seven thousand."

"That won't help!"

"We have about thirty seconds till we're on the ground. Just do something that will occupy your mind for thirty short seconds."

"You want me to do something that will occupy my mind?"

"Yes."

"Totally occupy my mind?"

"Yes."

"Okay."

She leaned over and planted her lips on his.

The shock of it froze him. But when she eased her lips across his, tasting him, tempting him, his breath shivered and needs he'd been fighting all morning resurrected with the power of a tornado. He forgot all about diversions and conflict of interest and took command.

He took control of the kiss in a flash of heat that raced through Charlotte. The meeting of their mouths was heaven, so delicious she forgot she'd kissed him as a diversion.

Temptation rose. Urged her to take. She slid her hands to his biceps, letting her heart swoon at the strength of them before her fingers moved on, across broad shoulders to link at the back of his neck.

The fire inside her crackled. Despite her seat belt, she shifted, getting closer, and sucked in a breath when their upper bodies met. Jace deepened the kiss. The fire roared.

Vaguely, in the distance, she heard a voice. With Jace's mouth on hers, their tongues twining and volcanic heat bursting through her, the thought of caring who spoke was laughable until she remembered they were on a plane. The plane had been landing.

They were probably on the ground and that voice had probably been the pilot announcing it.

She pulled back. So did Jace. Their eyes met and for ten seconds there was nothing but silence. That hadn't been an ordinary kiss. They both knew it.

It might have been the diversion she needed for the landing, but it hadn't helped her rationale about being attracted to him. He absolutely did not kiss like a rock, and he was every bit as attracted to her as she was to him.

Part of her thrilled at the prospect. But this attraction was not a good thing. They both knew that, too. They were where they'd started. Attracted and not allowed to be.

She fell back on humor. "And that, Skippy, is how you create a diversion."

She unbuckled her seat belt and started to rise, but he caught her hand and pulled her down again.

"We're both adults here. So, let's not play games. We're ridiculously attracted to each other, and we need to talk about this—" He motioned from himself to her. "Because it's wrong. You are a client. It is a conflict of interest for me to get involved with you. But more than that, it might impair my ability to do my job."

Disappointment flooded her, even though she already knew everything he said. Their meeting and being together was business. And not just for Jace. For her. She had a chance to get the dad who hadn't wanted her out of her life for good. If she didn't play this correctly, keep her focus, she could make some bad choices.

That woke her up.

She sucked in a breath, brought herself out of her disappointment and into her normal, intelligent state. Out there in the big, wide, wonderful world there was a guy for her. Someone as tall as Jace, as smart as Jace. Her equal. She would find him and not make a mistake by getting involved with someone who wasn't right for her.

"I get it," she said as the pilot left the cockpit and headed toward them. "And for your information, I knew all that. I was just checking to see if you kissed like a rock." She faced the pilot. "Hello, there. You did a wonderful job."

The handsome fiftyish pilot laughed. "It's not every day I get a compliment." He faced Jace. They talked about a few technical things as she maneuvered her way out of her seat to the compartment where she'd stashed her purse.

By the time she was ready to deplane, Jace was by her side.

They walked down the steps, then to a waiting limo.

When the door closed and the driver headed behind the wheel, Jace turned to her. "What the hell do you mean kissed like a rock?"

She picked imaginary lint off her navy-blue coat, so she didn't have to look at him. "Some guys can't kiss. I was hoping you were one of them and the attraction would fizzle."

"If I'd known that, I would have pretended to kiss like a rock to end this."

Her gaze jumped to his. "Oh, don't do that."

"Do what?"

"Ruin my memory of a wonderful kiss."

He grinned. "That good, huh?"

"Don't go thinking you're all that."

He just kept grinning.

All of Charlotte's competitive instincts rose. "You do not want to challenge me, or you won't like the results. Whether the attraction is pointless or not, we now know we're a good kissing combination. That's not going to make ignoring it easier. What we need to do is back away. Give each other a little space."

He grunted and shook his head. "That's what we were doing and doing well until you kissed me."

"Hey, you said divert my attention and I did." She peered at him. "And I might have started the kiss, but you made it more than it needed to be."

"Maybe I wanted to see if *you* kissed like a rock."

She gaped at him. "You didn't even know what rock kissing was!"

He shrugged. "So, we use different phrasing for finding out if someone's a good kisser."

She sniffed. "I think you lost control."

"Really? Wanna try that again with me showing you what losing control looks like?"

Oh, Lord, yes. She would love to try that.

But that wasn't smart. So, she sighed and said, "No."

"Then don't press your luck."

CHAPTER SIX

As THEY HEADED to Danny's office, the limo got quiet. Charlotte wished she had that old magazine to get her mind off the thought of what it might be like to kiss Jace when he lost control. She didn't regret kissing him. That had been a necessary diversion, which nicely dovetailed into the test she'd wanted to make. But did he have to take it to the next level, tempting her to imagine what his best kiss would be like?

It didn't matter. The kiss had happened. The discussion after the kiss had fueled the fire of her imagination and she would deal with it. First, because he would. He could not get involved with her. His job depended on him being alert, sharp, and on his clients being able to trust him. She would respect that. But also, because she was on the cusp of getting her father out of her life for good. Distancing herself from him, his life, the worry, the threats, the bodyguards. It was her chance to keep the life she'd made for *herself*.

When they reached Danny's building, Jace helped her out of the limo. Stepping onto the sidewalk, she glanced from side to side, taking in structures, people, traffic. "You know, Pittsburgh is bad, but this place is crowded."

"It's one of the biggest cities in the world."

"Thanks for the geography lesson."

He chuckled, back to being a congenial bodyguard. It boggled the mind that he had better discipline than she had, and she shook her head. No one had better self-control than she had. She *would* handle this.

He led her through the building's lobby to the private elevator in the back. They got in and in seconds the doors opened onto an office.

A tall, lean, dark-haired man rose from his seat behind a huge desk. Walking to them with his hand extended to shake hers, he said, "You must be heir number two."

"Yes. I'm Charlotte Fillion. And you're Danny Manelli." She gave him her brisk, professional handshake. "We spoke on the phone the day Jace arrived on my jobsite."

"You look like your dad."

Jace winced. "That might not have been the compliment you wanted it to be."

Motioning for them to take the seats in front of his desk, Danny said, "What am I missing?"

"Charlotte's like Leni. Not sure she wants Mark's money."

Danny groaned.

Charlotte sat up, went into business professional mode. She refused to look crazy for not wanting her part of the estate. "I'm a vice president in a development company. I don't need the money of a man who didn't want me, and I certainly don't want hundreds of reporters following me all day, every day."

Danny shifted on his tall-backed office chair. "Okay. I understand that. But you have anywhere from a week to two weeks in the city. First, we'll be awaiting DNA results, which will probably stagger in, considering we're using three different labs. But the will has also deemed it part of the process for you to view the slides of all your dad's properties, and to review his business holdings and private investments, so that if you do bow out, you will know what you're refusing. It's not my job to persuade you. The decision is yours. But the will insists on full disclosure to you of everything you're turning away. If you decide against participating in the estate, I will draw up papers and you will be out."

With that confirmation in place, she said, "Perfect."

Danny nodded. "Let me suggest, though, that you keep an open mind. Leni is doing a lot of good with her share. There might be something you want to do in your life."

"I'm doing it. I'm a vice president of a company, looking to one day become president and eventually CEO. I have enough on my plate, thank you."

"Great. Then let's move on to the reason you're here." Danny buzzed his assistant, instructing her to bring in the lab tech. He swabbed Charlotte's cheek three times.

"We send three blind samples to three different labs. We put a rush on one, but not the other two. We don't want it to look like there is any collusion, so we use different labs every time. Without the rush on the second two samples, we get in line with every other sample that comes to the lab. So, it could take up to two weeks to get all the results. But we want all three for absolute proof. There's a hell of a lot of money here and people are coming out of the wood-work for a share. Even with our protocols, we know there will be lawsuits, but with our three-pronged DNA, blind sample-testing, the courts won't be able to argue if we have three people who match in all three tests and others who don't match at all."

Charlotte inclined her head. "Makes sense." She hated being away for weeks, but if this got her off the hook of Mark Hinton's hold, it would be worth it.

"In that time, you and I will have a few meetings about the estate, but primarily you'll be meeting with Nick Koura-kis."

She straightened in her chair. "My half sister's boy-friend?"

"Yes. He has the slides that show everything your dad

owned. Even if you bow out of the money end of things, you might want to take a beach house or the Jet Skis or one of his antique cars."

"Charlotte's more interested in meeting Leni."

Danny's face brightened. "Of course! That can absolutely be arranged."

"If you want, I can call Nick," Jace said, glancing at Charlotte. "We could have dinner tonight, if they're free."

Something inside her melted. She might not like her dad, but he'd given her a sister. That was the part of the estate she desperately wanted. "That would be great."

"Good," Danny said, rising from his seat. "I'll also let you be the one to set times with Nick for the days you can meet to see the slides of your father's properties."

Charlotte rose, too. "Days to see slides?"

Danny laughed. "Your dad owned *a lot* of things."

The thought that it would take so long to see everything her dad owned blew her away. "I know. But *days*?"

Danny batted a hand in dismissal. "We'll let Nick show you."

Charlotte was back to wearing the funny look that Jace didn't trust. The last time he couldn't read her expression she'd kissed him. The memory of it surged through him. Her soft mouth. The way they fit. The feelings that rose before he could stop them.

At the elevator, Danny shook her hand again. "It was a pleasure to meet you. Nick, Jace and I will do everything in our power to make your stay in New York interesting, so you aren't bored while you see the slides and get the rundown on everything the estate entails."

"I almost feel like I should go back home and let Nick send me the slides."

Danny shook his head. "No. We're working very hard to keep this from turning into a circus. We managed to do damage control after Leni's identity got out. So far, we haven't had a run of people claiming to be heirs. There are a few, but that number could double or triple if the estate gets too much attention."

"I'm putting up a building," Charlotte said with a laugh. "I'm not going to be making the circuit of late-night talk shows. My crew doesn't know who I am. I managed to sidestep the facts of why I'm in New York when I talked to my boss. My neighbors aren't interested in my comings and goings. I do not see how my returning home could be a problem."

"You act differently."

Danny and Charlotte turned to Jace.

Her face fell. "What? How?"

"When I first found you, you threatened to call the police on me. Now, we're having lunch and dinner like friends." He didn't mention that she also had a soft, sexy way of looking at him and had kissed him like a lover.

"That's because we're spending so much time together!" She rolled her eyes and faced Danny. "Sheesh! This guy. Noticing things that aren't there."

"I notice things people think they're hiding." That's why he could tell how affected she'd been by their kiss. She did a really good job of holding in her reaction. But he saw the facial cues, heard the softness in her voice.

"In any event," Danny said, interrupting them. "Go have a nice lunch. Jace is paying. He gets reimbursed by me. This time tomorrow, I will have credit cards and a bank card for you to use."

"Why?"

"It's part of the vetting process. Everyone with a legitimate claim as an heir gets a few hundred thousand dollars to spend in the two weeks they are in New York waiting for DNA results and being vetted by the estate."

Her eyes widened. "You're giving hundreds of thousands of dollars to the fakes, too?"

"Believe me, the estate doesn't miss the money. Plus, it looks good in the file that we treated you all equally, vetted Mark's real children the same way we did the group of 'potential' heirs. We're doing everything by the book."

After they'd said goodbye and the elevator doors had closed on them, Charlotte turned to Jace.

"He really does do everything by the book."

"Stickler for details," Jace said. But the elevator seemed small and she seemed awfully close. He'd felt her vulnerability in that meeting when they'd talked about her sister. Though she'd tried to be an executive with no feelings, her emotions were right there for anyone who knew what to look for. He chalked it up to her desire to meet Leni, but he'd still pay close attention. Look for shifts. Indicators that she might decide the whole process was nonsense and bolt—

Or that she might kiss him again.

God only knew what was going on in that supersmart, superanalytical brain of hers and he was going to have to manage it for two long weeks.

They got into the limo and headed for a quiet, exclusive restaurant, where the people who saw them wouldn't care if she was a Hinton heir or a member of a royal family because they themselves were heirs and heiresses, princesses, kings and billionaires.

After they ordered, she stayed quiet. He had a million topics he knew she'd respond to, but that was the problem. They were so compatible. Add that to their attraction and they were prime candidates for a misstep. All he had to do was think about that kiss and his brain shifted from work to molten need. He no longer saw her as a client and thoughts of her being his lover teased him. And that was how mistakes were made. The Hinton estate was huge, and he was responsible for her. He couldn't afford any slipups. He didn't want her found out, preyed upon, hurt.

He said the one thing he was sure would keep them on the right track and take her attention where it needed to be. "As soon as we get settled, I'll call Nick and set up dinner tonight, if he and Leni are available."

He knew that was the draw for her. The reason she hadn't just kicked him out of her office that day at her jobsite trailer and let the estate do her bidding. She wanted to meet Leni. Jace would introduce her to Leni, make her happy and keep her happy for the two weeks she was his responsibility.

After that…

He had no idea. She seemed to think she could walk away from the money and all would be well. But it wouldn't. She could run but she could never hide, and if she thought refusing the money would make her less interesting to reporters, she was sadly mistaken. The way Jace saw this, that would actually make her more interesting to reporters and curiosity seekers.

There was no walking away from this for her.

He simply didn't want to be the one to tell her.

After lunch, his limo took them to the Upper East Side and his condo. The driver came around and opened the door, but Jace helped Charlotte out. She emerged from the car, a picture-perfect blonde in her pale blue dress, with a navy-blue coat over it, and sunglasses, looking Princess Kate beautiful and Jackie Kennedy elegant.

Which made him very glad he'd decided to keep her at his condo rather than a hotel. She was too tall and too pretty. Any arbitrary photographer could look at her, assume she was a model and snap a picture. Months later, after the estate announced the heirs, that photo would be worth a small fortune.

He squeezed his eyes shut. Damn. He was going to have

to tell her that she couldn't hide from this by refusing her share. A woman could not look like Charlotte did without attracting attention. Bow out of the estate or not, she would become a curiosity to reporters and an easy mark to kidnappers because she wouldn't have the protection the other heirs had.

As the driver walked to the trunk for their suitcases, they turned to enter the sand-colored stucco building and she said, "This isn't a hotel."

"It's my condo building."

One of her eyebrows rose above her black sunglasses. "You think this is wise?"

The glass doors automatically opened, granting them entrance into the quiet lobby. The doorman, the only person in the room, saluted Jace, and he nodded once as he led Charlotte to the elevator. He pressed the button for his floor, then ran his key fob over the private security panel. His condo might be luxurious, but it wasn't the only one on the floor, so they couldn't completely lock the floor.

As the elevator zoomed upward, he asked, "Do I think what is wise?"

She turned her head. He couldn't see her eyes behind the big, black glasses. "Us staying in the same condo."

He knew what she meant. But she didn't have to worry about him or their attraction. Now that he'd figure out just how much trouble she could be in if she refused the money, there'd be no more friendly talks. No chances for them to realize how alike they were or how much they enjoyed each other's company.

"It's the safest way to do this. Besides, even if you were staying in a hotel, I'd be in the sitting room of the suite, catnapping on the sofa, watching the door."

She sighed.

He shook his head. "Come on. In those sunglasses you look like a supermodel. Some photographer scrounging for celebrities could see you and snap a picture knowing he could figure out who you were later. Then when the news broke about you being a Hinton heir, that photo could be all over the city."

The elevator doors opened. "This city must be desperate for entertainment."

He walked her to his condo door. "This city is odd. We have everybody here from Broadway stars and financial gurus to maids and garbagemen. Every man wants to be the guy who finds himself in an elevator with Jennifer Lopez and every woman wants to be the one who's suddenly standing next to a prince on the sidewalk."

She pondered that for a second. "That prince's bodyguards would be fired for letting someone get that close."

"True, but not my point." He opened the door onto the foyer of his condo. "My point is in those sunglasses you look like somebody. Better to have you here, where no one will get curious enough to take your picture." He held back a wince realizing this was his opportunity to give her the bad news about refusing her dad's money. He couldn't jump in with both feet, but this was as close of a segue as he was going to get. "And once the estate papers are filed and everybody knows you are one of Mark Hinton's kids, one of his *heirs*, if you accept the money or not that picture could be used to find you."

"I suppose." She shrugged out of her coat.

"You suppose? Do you realize how much potential danger you're in?"

She laughed. "Look at me. I'm not easy prey. Plus, I won't have any money. Reporters might find it fascinating that I refused billions of dollars, but that will fizzle in a few years when they see how boring I am. And kidnappers? Why take a normal woman?"

"Because you might not have billions, but your biological family will. A kidnapper won't call your mom. They'll call Leni…or your other sibling once we find him or her. You'll be an easy target. Which will make Leni and your other sibling's life more difficult."

"Damn." She took a breath. "You make a good case."

"Because I'm correct."

"Maybe. I'll need to think about it."

Shaking his head, he led her into the open-floor-plan living room, dining room and kitchen. Such a stubborn woman. He certainly hoped the result of her thinking was the realization that she couldn't simply walk away.

"Nice digs."

"Thanks." He glanced around at the white kitchen with stunning shiny white tile floors and black quartz countertops. "I did none of it myself."

Beyond the kitchen he had a blue love seat flanked by white chairs with a blue, beige and gray area rug. But the lure of the space was just beyond the dining room table with its four navy-blue wingback chairs. A floor-to-ceiling window curved from one side of the room to the other, displaying a breathtaking panoramic view of the Upper East Side.

After stashing her sunglasses in her purse, which she tossed on one of the chairs, she walked to the blue love seat. "Bet you don't sleep here on restless nights."

He snorted. "No."

She glanced at him. "Why so small? Why not a sofa?"

"Nobody really ever sits there. The whole living room is just for show." He motioned her to the right. "Come here."

He opened the door on what should have been a bedroom but which he'd converted into a space with a pool table and a big-screen TV.

"Now that's what I'm talking about." She faced him. "You're either into football, baseball or hockey."

"A man can watch basketball on a big screen, too."

"Agreed." She walked in reverently. "My next project is to put a room like this in my basement."

One short conversation and they were two peas in a pod again. If they could pursue this, they wouldn't merely be lovers; they'd be friends. A relationship with her would be easy, natural.

Which was the totally wrong direction for his thoughts. Forcing his brain out of that spot, he took the conversation away from how they both liked sports and comfortable rooms, and to a neutral place. "With a one-story house, your basement is probably huge."

"It is. I could hold wedding receptions and bar mitzvahs down there."

"A nice side income."

"Yeah, in another century I'd have as much money as my supposedly wealthy dad had."

He snorted. "Or you could just take your share of the estate."

"More fun to earn it on my own."

He couldn't argue that, which almost annoyed him. Why did she have to be so smart, so fun? He could imagine what making love to her would be like. She'd be involved, probably throw her whole self into it.

Picturing it, he held back a groan and led her out of the TV room. "I wanted you to see you'll be comfortable here for two weeks."

"What will you be doing?"

"Guarding you. But I also have a business to run." He guided her a little farther down the hall. "This is bedroom number three of four. Bedroom one—" he pointed beyond the open-floor-plan living area to the other side of his condo "—is a maid's quarters." He pointed a few feet in front of them. "That's the master bedroom." He grabbed the doorknob to the room beside them. "And this is where you'll be staying."

The white distressed wood bed sat on a bright yellow print rug. Yellow curtains blocked out the sun. For the first time since he'd had this place decorated, he actually noticed it. But that was because it suited her. Bright and sunny. Happy. Easy on the eyes.

Getting even more annoyed with himself, he forced his mind back to what he was supposed to be doing and motioned to a closed door. "There's a bathroom and a closet behind that. You'll be perfectly comfortable."

She caught his gaze. "Will I?"

He knew she wasn't talking about the pillows or the proximity to the bathroom. Memories of their kiss collided with all the other images he'd unwittingly been conjuring, and his hormones awoke and battled to take charge. He imagined she had the same problem and had to inhale a breath to squelch the bright light that snapped on in his ego. Though it was totally wrong, he loved that she was attracted to him.

He stomped out the images, killing the bright light of his ego. "Yes. I'm a professional."

"So you've said."

He didn't remember how they got to be standing so close. If she'd taken a step or if he'd taken a step. But they were near enough to touch without stretching, close enough to kiss again.

Warmth flooded him along with the urge to grab her, kiss her and do all the things he knew they could do together. He stared into her eyes, hoping she'd give him a look that would make him think he was imagining the attraction was mutual, but all he saw was curiosity. Would they be as hot together as their kiss hinted they would be?

If he'd known she'd been checking to see if he kissed like a rock, he could have shut this whole attraction down with one awkward, sloppy kiss. But his inner guy laughed at him. She'd taken him by surprise, lured him to wrestle for control... Did he really think he could have shut that down?

He stepped back, wanting to shake himself silly. One

taste of her had upped the temptation. And that's what killed him. Usually when he made a firm decision about anything, he was like a rock of determination.

He called on that discipline to ignore everything but his need to keep her hidden while she was in New York. "Yes. I know you're safe with me. You're a stubborn woman who I believe has made up her mind to do the right thing about our attraction."

She laughed. "Calling on my innate stubbornness to keep me in line so that all you have to worry about is yourself? That's good."

"What can I say? I've had a bit of experience in this."

Her eyes widened "You've kissed other clients?"

He cleared his throat. "Once. But I've had better reasons to learn how to keep my charges in line. Experience is experience. Some things translate."

She sniffed a laugh.

Feeling like he'd dodged a bullet when she didn't ask him to elaborate about the client he'd kissed, he said, "This is the perfect time for you to set up your laptop and check in with your jobsites. I'm going to call Nick and see if he and Leni have plans for tonight. After that, how about a few games of pool?"

"I'm not sure how long I'll be on the phone with my foremen."

Even as she said that, the doorman appeared with her luggage, including the briefcase Jace assumed held her work.

"That's fine." It would make his life a hundred percent easier if she could entertain herself until it was time to go to Nick and Leni's. "I'll let you know what Nick says about dinner tonight."

He closed the door as he left. But before walking down the hall, he stopped and sucked in a breath. For the first time since his wife cheated, he genuinely clicked with a woman. The sexual attraction was off the charts, but what he felt wasn't just lust. Charlotte was smart, interesting, funny.

And he had to walk away.

If the Hinton estate wasn't his biggest client, he would seriously consider bowing out because he truly liked her. But the Hinton estate was his best customer and he had twenty employees with kids to feed on that job alone. He couldn't lose all that for someone he'd known a couple of days.

But oh, it would be so much easier if he could give in to the temptation of her pretty eyes, luxurious hair and smoking-hot body—

Or would it?

Charlotte was a nice woman. Smart, articulate, sometimes even cutely sassy. But deep down she was good. And he'd been hurt enough to have walls the size of China around his heart. He might like her, but he'd never love her. He'd never trust his heart like that again.

And, at some point, she'd realize that and be hurt.

Did he really want to hurt Charlotte?

No. He wanted to protect her. Even from himself.

CHAPTER SEVEN

CHARLOTTE TURNED TO unpack her suitcase, but her insides quaked. That was the sexiest, nonflirty conversation she'd ever had with a man. They might have talked about not doing anything about their attraction, but the desire in his eyes told a whole different story and that clicked with something in her. It was everything she could do not to kiss him again.

It wasn't like her. She always had her stuff together. If she needed to be disciplined, she could be a rock.

Yet, no matter how hard she tried, she couldn't pull that rabbit out of her hat when she was around Jace. She'd even forgotten she hadn't checked in with her crew. Jace had had to remind her.

With a shake of her head, she set up her laptop on a small table by the window. Determined to get her mind off Jace, she busied herself with pulling up budgets, estimate sheets, labor allotments, and began calling her foremen for progress reports.

Midway through her second conversation, he appeared at her door. "Dinner tonight at Nick's penthouse. I'm not risking you and Leni out in public together."

"Just a sec, Pete," she told her foreman before she put him on hold and glanced over at Jace. "Really? We're sneaking around?" This was the one thing that could get her mind off how sexy he was. The estate's insistence that she have a bodyguard. It was overkill. Plus, take away the bodyguard, take away the attraction. Undoubtedly, Jace thought he was clever overguarding her and Leni to make his point about heirs being targets—but she didn't buy it. She hadn't bought it when Mark Hinton had said she was in danger simply by virtue of being his daughter and she didn't buy it now.

"Why don't you just change my name to Double-O-Seven?"

"Because you're not a spy. You're merely being careful for the next two weeks."

"I thought you said I'd have to be careful forever."

"If you refuse your share once DNA proves you're an heir, you won't be my problem anymore."

That simultaneously relieved her and squeezed her heart. He'd been in her life 24/7 for only three days, but it was impossible to wrap her head around never seeing him again.

She groaned internally.

Where was her legendary discipline? She'd dated at least twenty guys and had never once been dumped. She'd always seen trouble before they did, and no matter how attractive the guy, she could walk away. Around Jace she forgot all that.

He grinned. "But dinner at their penthouse also means we can wear jeans."

She couldn't let him see that just the thought of not having him in her life threw her, so she smiled as if absolutely thrilled about getting to wear jeans. "That is a plus."

"Good. I'll tell them we'll be there."

He left and she tossed her hands, annoyed with herself. Especially since she had work to do.

She took Pete off hold and settled in to hear reports and help problem solve to forget about Jace and her fire-breathing monster of an attraction.

At five-thirty she headed for the shower to get ready for dinner with her sister.

Her sister.

The other thing that could make her forget about sexy Jace.

Having a sister seemed surreal. Even the normal tasks of drying her hair, sliding into jeans and a sweater, pulling her leather jacket out of her suitcase, felt different, weightier somehow.

She wasn't an only child. Even if she decided not to participate in the estate, she and Leni Long would always be sisters.

And there was another heir. Another sister, maybe. Or perhaps a brother? She might have a *brother.*

What would that be like?

She didn't even try to make conversation in the car. Neither did Jace. Now that they weren't dancing around the attraction, he was only her bodyguard. Barely talking to her. Watching out the car window. Because she was an heiress.

Not merely a woman with a sister and a possible second sister or brother. But a woman connected to billions of dollars.

Damned if that didn't make it hard to breathe.

That's what Jace had been trying to tell her. She could bow out, but she'd always be linked to the Hintons, the money, the notoriety. A sister she didn't know, another sibling who hadn't yet been found.

What if they didn't like each other?

What if one of them was a criminal? A drug addict? A con artist?

She faced Jace. "You are coming in for dinner, right?"

Jace snorted. "Nick is a good friend of mine. Even if you weren't here, he and Leni would feed me."

"I'm just saying I'd feel weird if you sat in the car and waited for us."

"And it would also be nice to have a buffer."

She held back a sigh. Damn him and his perceptiveness. "Yes. If things get awkward between me and Leni, like if we can't think of anything to talk about, feel free to jump in with interesting conversation topics." She shook her head. "You have no idea how freaky this is. I spent my entire life as an only child. Now I'm part of a tribe."

Jace slid a glance her way. "The great Charlotte Fillion is nervous?"

"Kind of nervous but more amazed. I've wanted a sister forever."

The limo stopped. Jace got out and offered his hand to help her out. "Good. You should be amazed. I told you. Leni is a wonderful person. You are going to love her."

They walked into a building so elegant that Charlotte looked around in awe.

After Jace asked the doorman to inform their hosts that they were on their way up, she said, "I'd love to see the blueprints for this."

Leading her to a private elevator, Jace laughed. "Always working."

"Nope. Still stuck on amazed." Not to mention confused, awestruck and overwhelmed.

He punched some numbers into a keypad; the elevator door opened, and they stepped inside.

"Wow."

"Nick's family had money but when Nick took over their business it blew up. I can't even imagine their net worth now. He has a knack for finding the right investment at the right time."

"In other words, he's as wealthy as my sister."

"It makes them a good match."

She nodded. "No worry that he's dating her for her inheritance. No fights about money."

He inclined his head to the right, studying her. "You do

know that you're moving into a whole new social circle, right?"

She swiped her hand down the sleeve of her jacket, pretending to brush off dust. "I'm not moving anywhere."

"Maybe not, but every time you visit your sister, you'll be stepping into that world whether you want to or not."

She'd figured that out in the car. But that didn't mean she wouldn't seek a workaround. "We can always meet for lunch at a diner on the interstate halfway between Pittsburgh and New York."

"And she'll be bringing bodyguards."

"Who will sit at the next table." She shook her head. No matter how hard this pressed in on her, she couldn't let Jace know how confused she was, how a simple refusal of the Hinton fortune had become complicated. Their being able to talk, being so attuned to one another, was part of the attraction, and right now she was annoyed with the attraction. Annoyed with herself for having so much trouble fighting it when Jace had made it clear he wasn't interested.

"Sheesh. I thought we'd talked about this. I'm fine."

The elevator door opened onto a huge open-floor-plan space with a kitchen and seating area with pool table and bar by the wall of windows.

"Wow."

A petite brunette in jeans and a peach-colored sweater and a tall dark-haired man walked over to meet them. "Charlotte?"

"Leni?"

"Yes!" The smaller woman hugged her. "And this is Nick."

As she stepped back, Charlotte said, "You're so small!"

Leni laughed "You're so tall!"

Both Jace and Nick said, "Mark was tall."

Leni laughed again, but Charlotte gave Jace the side eye.

There was something about the way they'd said that simultaneously that gave Charlotte an odd feeling.

Leni motioned to the seating area. "Come in! Janine is making her famous beef tenderloin with shallots." She gasped. "Oh, shoot! I never thought to ask if you were a vegetarian or vegan."

"Nope. We're good," Charlotte said, staring at Leni, studying her. "I'm so amazed to have a sister."

Leni caught her hand and squeezed. "Me, too. I was an adopted only child. I was lucky, though. My parents are wonderful. I can't wait for you to meet them."

Charlotte followed Leni to an aqua sofa. "My mom's pretty cool, too."

As Leni sat, she said, "I can't wait to meet her."

"I'm sure she'll love you." Charlotte glanced around. "So, you're a social worker?"

"I trained to be. But once I sorted through everything, I saw I could put my life to better use with philanthropic work." She smiled. "And you're a vice president in a development company?"

"Yes." Clearly Leni had done her homework. "I'm angling to become president of Kaiser and Barclay, then CEO, then chairman of the board."

Leni frowned. "You're staying at your job?"

"Of course. I've been working toward this for years. College, grad school, four years of slogging through jobsites—"

"In four years, you became a vice president?"

Nick said, "Impressive."

Jace laughed. "I watched her work. She's a dynamo."

Nick rose from the sofa. "Can I get anyone a drink? Wine, maybe?"

Charlotte said, "A glass of wine would be great. Whatever you recommend. I'm not picky." And she was also desperate for something to soothe her nerves. She liked Leni.

It was hard not to like an adorable pixie. But her soul had swelled with pride when Jace said she was a dynamo. He understood her in a way no one in her life ever had. That's why she could be herself with him.

That's why she liked him. Why this attraction had latched on and wouldn't let go. Since the day she'd met him, she'd been only herself. And he still liked her—even though he wasn't supposed to. He'd all but admitted he was fighting the attraction, too. Though with much more success than she was.

"Anyway," Leni said. "I can't wait to hear everything about your childhood. I'm so happy to have a sister."

"I'm happy to have a sister, too," Charlotte said. "I'm not sure if I had an odd upbringing or a good one. My mom and I lived on a farm about five miles outside a little town near Pittsburgh. Though I had a vegetable garden, we didn't work the land. We leased it to a neighbor who even used our barn to store hay. So that was fun."

"You lived in the country! I grew up in a small town. My dad was a construction worker. My mom worked in the diner. When I turned sixteen, I waitressed there, too, to save money for university tuition."

"I was a salesclerk." Charlotte laughed. "That's how I saved for tuition."

Nick brought the wine. Charlotte accepted her glass with a smile. "Danny tells me you and I will have to get together so you can show me the slides of what Mark Hinton owned."

"He called me." After giving Jace and Leni a glass of wine, Nick sat beside Leni. "I know it probably seems like we're keeping you in New York unnecessarily, but it's important that you know everything your dad owned so that if you decide not to take anything you know what you're refusing. Name the day and hour and I'll bring the laptop to Jace's condo or you can meet me here and we'll watch in the media room."

It suddenly hit her that everybody knew every step of her life. Danny had probably called Nick about the slides. Jace had called Nick to arrange for dinner and would have mentioned Charlotte was eager to meet Leni. And she knew Leni had already gone through this process—

Of course. That's why everyone appeared overly informed. They'd been through this once.

"Danny told me it will take days just to see the slides of what he owned."

Nick chuckled. "Your dad had tons of things."

Jace said, "Nothing says love of the water like thirty sets of Jet Skis."

"Not to mention the four beach houses and two lake houses."

Charlotte's mouth fell open. "Four beach houses?"

"Every beach house is different," Jace explained. "The house in the Florida Keys was all about fishing. Fiji was where Mark hid. Hawaii's just plain beautiful. And Ocean City was where he could get lost in the crowd."

Charlotte said, "Wow." But the feeling that something was off about this discussion surged through her again. Jace was awfully familiar with her dad's things. She supposed it could be knowledge gained while guarding him, but there was something about his tone of voice that said there was more. There was an affection he couldn't hide.

Her brain caught up with reality slowly. She wasn't supposed to like or trust people who were involved with her dad. Especially someone who was as close to her dad as Jace had been. Yet, she liked Jace. Instantly. And more than she'd ever liked anyone. But his connection to her dad should have dissolved any sort of romantic feelings. Just being *similar to* her dad had caused her to knock more than one guy out of her dating pool—

Confusion made her frown. Odd disjointed memories swamped her. Breaking up with men who were overly committed to their careers—because they reminded her of her dad. Not compromising. Not investigating. Not trying things. Just a cold, hard no to men who reminded her of her father—

Looking back over the short list of men she'd dated, men she'd slept with, even men she'd thought she could love, at some point every one of them had reminded her of her dad. Or, more appropriately, her mom's situation with her dad.

The room shimmied. Her brain stalled. Her whole dating life flashed before her eyes one more time just so she could be sure she was remembering correctly.

All these years, she'd believed seeing her mom's life had been a good thing. A warning that she didn't want to get involved with someone who'd hurt her like her dad had hurt her mom. But what if her dad's desertion and her mom's devotion had actually scarred her so much that she chased *everyone* off?

Never trusted?

Never let herself fall in love?

What if her father had caused her to nitpick every man until *no one* was good enough?

Even the idea that there might be "The One," with her standards so high most men didn't reach them, might have been a way to protect herself.

The thought left her breathless and angry. Not with her dad. With herself. All this time she'd thought she was strong, smart. But what if she'd simply been too scared to take a risk?

CHAPTER EIGHT

THEY LEFT NICK and Leni's penthouse around ten. Though the dinner conversation had been lively with Leni telling Charlotte about her plans for her hometown's restoration and revitalization, and Charlotte offering development and construction tips, Jace's instincts had shifted to red alert. Charlotte was smart, obviously liked Leni and Nick, but never said another personal word about herself.

He led her into the cold April night and to the limo. After they were tucked away in the backseat and the driver had pulled into traffic, he thought about asking her if she was okay, but his mind ventured to their kiss again. The power of it. The *fun* of it.

Normally, he kept on top of his client's moods, but this client was tricky because he really liked her. If she wanted to talk, he would let her. But maybe it wasn't so smart to nudge her to open up, to take them to that place where they realized how well they got along, how much they liked each other?

He stayed silent and so did she.

In his condo, she said good night. As he punched numbers in a keypad to activate the locks and alarms, she walked directly to her room.

Jace watched her, reminding himself there was nothing wrong with that. Her saying good night and going to her room while he secured the premises was typical bodyguard stuff.

The way it should be.

The next morning, keeping them within the context of bodyguard and client, he woke first, made eggs and toast and knocked on her door to tell her breakfast had been made but she reminded him she wasn't a breakfast person.

Fine. She was an adult. She also wasn't the kind of person who liked someone looking over her shoulder or telling her what to do. Still, her tone of voice had been so cool…

He shook off the sense that she was angry with him. She couldn't be. He hadn't done anything.

Except kiss her.

No. Technically, she'd kissed him. He'd simply taken a great kiss and made it better. And they'd talked about that. They were square. She was not angry with him. He was jumpy because she was quiet, but if he left her alone it would all even out.

He went to his office space, a desk in a nook in the master bedroom, got to work and came out after an hour for coffee. He expected to see evidence that she'd at least made herself a cup, too, but everything was exactly as he'd left it.

All right. That was enough. He'd ever seen her go a morning without coffee. Something was wrong and he needed to be on top of it.

He walked back the hall again and knocked on her door. "I made coffee."

"Thanks, but I'm fine."

"If you drink tea—" She hadn't the two days they were at her house, but an unexpected desperation had settled in his chest. If she were a normal client, he'd walk into her room and ask her point-blank what was wrong. But he couldn't sashay into her bedroom. It wasn't merely invasive…it was suggestive.

This is what he got for kissing her. Now everything was confused. He couldn't do what he knew he should do.

"I have tea bags in the second counter from the right."

"No, thanks."

He battled back the guilt. Okay. Yes. She'd been a bit weird during their conversation after the kiss, but she'd also gotten details of her dad's estate and met her half sister. Any of those things could have overwhelmed her enough that she'd withdrawn.

He squeezed his eyes shut. It didn't matter why she'd pulled back, why she wouldn't even drink his coffee. She had still withdrawn. And having her not talk was as bad as getting too friendly. It might seem okay that her mind was off somewhere, stuck on things she wasn't telling him. But he needed to have her attention. He needed to know she'd hear his orders. Not get bumped or shoved or even photographed because she hadn't heard him say, "Go this way," or "Turn that way."

He had to get them back on track. Things might be fine right now, but they had to be prepared. She had to talk to him. He had to talk to her. Just not about personal stuff.

He walked back to his bedroom nook. Even before he set his coffee on the small desk, his phone rang. Caller ID indicated it was one of his best men. Oswald Patterson, a team leader who was currently guarding a pop star.

"What's up, Oz?"

"We've got a problem with Seth Simon."

"Is he drunk?"

"Stayed out all night."

"Damn."

"He wants to go for a walk around the city. Meet his fans."

"He can't do that. Not drunk, anyway. His squeaky-clean image would go straight to hell after two minutes of him slurring his words and spitting on people."

"I know. I've barely kept him here since I sneaked him back into the hotel. And his concert's tonight. I need to make sure he goes to bed and stays there. There's no way in hell I can attend our staff meeting."

Jace groaned. "I forgot about the staff meeting." He paused a second. "Tell you what. We'll have our meeting in Seth's suite."

He clicked off the call, and sent a text informing the rest of his team leaders of the change of venue for the meeting. He picked up his laptop, pretty sure it was safe to leave Charlotte alone, but a thought stopped him.

Charlotte didn't understand why she'd need a bodyguard, a real bodyguard, not someone she treated like a friend? Maybe this meeting with his staff giving reports would change that?

He knocked on her bedroom door, but didn't wait for her answer, just entered. "Hey, I have my weekly Saturday staff meeting this afternoon. Wanna come with me?"

"You're leaving?"

The lightness in her voice didn't sit well. It almost sounded like she planned to make a break for it. "Yes, but I thought you'd want to come with me."

"Why would I want to go to a staff meeting?"

"To get out of the condo? To hear some interesting stories from my guys? We're providing security for a singer who's giving a concert tonight." He shrugged. "We're actually having the meeting in his suite."

"So, I'd meet a rock star?"

"He's more pop than rock, but you could call him a rock star."

"Who is he?"

"Seth Simon."

Her eyes widened. Her mouth fell open. "Seth Simon, the cutie pie?"

"You're about to find out he's not so cute."

She laughed. "That might be even more fun."

"You just have to take a vow of silence."

She frowned. "So, I'm back to being a spy?"

"You were never a spy. Spies have missions. People who guard just watch. We don't try to steal military secrets or corporate secrets or any kind of secrets at all." He grinned. "But we do see and hear some great stuff. And you have to promise to keep it confidential."

"You know what? I'm in, anyway. It's Saturday and I'll only get reports from jobsites that are on overtime and then not until after dark." She grabbed her leather jacket. "And I'll keep Seth Simon's supposed secrets. You're his security company, responsible for him. I'm guessing you think anything he does that's outside your box is bad behavior. I'm a civilian. I understand when someone wants to have fun. The poor guy probably flushed the toilet wrong and your team jumped. I'm guessing I'll love him. The man is adorable."

He followed her to the front door, then the elevator. The doors opened and they stepped inside. "We'll see if you still think he's adorable after twenty minutes."

A laugh bubbled from her, but she caught it. Stopped it before it could fully fill the air.

His chest bunched. He hated the distance she'd put between them. He knew it was necessary, but she didn't have to be a totally different person. "It's okay to laugh."

"That was an aberration. I don't want to laugh."

"A lot happened yesterday. Danny told you things that probably blew your mind. Then you met Leni, and if meeting your sister for the first time wasn't unusual enough, you saw a lifestyle so different from your own that it might have confused you. And somehow you found a way to blame me for all of it when none of it's my fault. I'm just your bodyguard."

Their gazes connected. Confusion filled her blue eyes.

"Charlotte, we have to communicate. Out there in the big, wide, wonderful world, your life could be in jeopardy.

It's my job to see problems and avoid them. I can't do that if you won't look at me or talk to me."

She snorted. "Right. This is actually our real area of disagreement. You think I'm in danger. I think I'm perfectly safe. There are eight million people in this city. More than ten million during the day when workers commute in. I'm like a bean in a big bag of beans. Yet somehow you think I stick out."

"You do. But not in the way you think and not to everyone."

She shook her head. "You're crazy."

"Okay. I can handle you thinking I'm crazy. But we need to talk. If it helps going back to the way we were before the kiss, we could do that."

The elevator door opened. "You mean talk like friends?"

"Yeah."

"I thought that screwed up your bodyguard mojo."

"In some ways." He smiled. "But I like you. We always find interesting things to talk about."

Her eyes changed, softened, and she swallowed.

"I promise nothing will happen like that kiss again."

Her eyebrows rose.

He laughed. "Just get out of the elevator."

With a breath she stepped into the lobby, strode to the revolving door and then the limo.

He opened the door for her. "Now that we have that settled, we'll have some fun this afternoon."

Her entire countenance changed. "Yeah. Meeting a rock star. I like this part of your job."

"Just don't get in the way."

"Moi?" she asked innocently, her eyes widening comically.

He groaned. "Get in the limo."

As Charlotte expected, Seth Simon was staying in the penthouse suite of an elegant hotel. She didn't care that she wore a sweater and jeans and looked like an average fan. The man was a superstar. She didn't want to marry him. She just wanted to meet him, flirt a little, hear stories about how he came up with his beautiful, heartrending songs.

And then brag to her friends.

The thought of it made her giddy as they rode the elevator to the suite. The door opened on opulence so magnificent she had to work to catch her breath. Ultramodern furniture sat on shiny white floors. In the back, a baby grand piano stood in front of a wall of windows. She could picture Seth sitting there, a lone soul with the big city as a backdrop, singing his gut-wrenching songs about longing for real love.

Her heart fluttered.

A twentysomething kid wearing jeans and a black T-shirt with enough tattoos to be an art gallery came into the main area.

Jace said, "Charlotte, this is Oz Patterson, one of my best men. Oz, this is Charlotte Fillion, also a client."

Charlotte reached out and shook his hand. "So, you're guarding Seth Simon!"

"More like babysitting," Oz said. "Guys are in the conference room."

Charlotte looked around in awe again. "This suite has a conference room?"

"Of course."

"Wow. Where's Seth?"

"Sleeping off one hell of a night last night."

Charlotte gaped at Oz. "He was drunk?"

"As a monkey."

Jace snorted. "I told you he's not what you think."

"But he's sleeping! I came here to meet him."

"And you will. He'll be awake before you know it. He doesn't really sleep. Just catnaps." He directed her back a hall to the right. "Wait in the conference room with us."

She followed him with a sigh. "You just want me to get introduced to your crew so I'll see they're harmless and agree to let one of them guard me when I go back to Pittsburgh."

Jace laughed. "I thought you didn't want a guard."

"I don't!"

They stepped into the conference room area where pots of coffee in silver carafes sat spaced apart in a line on the long table.

Jace's five team leaders rose as Charlotte entered the room, but she stopped dead in her tracks. Two tall, handsome men wore suits. One guy and the woman to his right wore jeans. The woman wore a sweater with hers. The guy had on a plaid work shirt. The fifth guy looked like he'd pulled his clothes out of a ragbag.

Jace walked to the head of the table. "This is Charlotte Fillion, a client. I thought she'd enjoy sitting in on a meeting and meeting Seth Simon."

All five groaned.

Charlotte ambled to a chair at the far end of the table. "He can't be that bad."

One of the guys in a suit rolled his eyes. "He's Satan."

Charlotte laughed. "No. He's not. He's cute and honest and likable."

Opening his laptop, Jace said, "His songs are cute and honest and likable. He is not."

"So, the whole thing he does onstage, with finding a girl and singing to her and making space for kids in wheelchairs…that's just an act."

The men laughed. The woman snorted in disgust.

"Wow."

Jace introduced people as he pointed at them. "Elizabeth Nelson, Carter Davis, Blake Regan, Isaac Tanner and you met Oz."

Charlotte politely said, "Nice to meet you all," even

though she expected to be bored and was totally annoyed that her reason for coming here was asleep.

Jace opened the meeting. "This week's assignments are on your phones. Each of your team members will get their schedules tonight with your squad leaders getting them about an hour before in case they have questions or problems."

Confused, Charlotte held up her hand and said, "Wait. These five people are your team leaders."

One of Jace's eyebrows rose. She wasn't sure if he was angry that she had a question or angry that she'd interrupted. She kept going, anyway.

"Then each of you supervises a group of squad leaders," she said, pointing at the five people sitting at the table. "And they supervisor your basic bodyguards?"

They all said, "Yes," or "Exactly," or some form of affirmation.

She peered up at Jace at the far, far end of the very long table. "Just how many people do you employ?"

"Probably as many as you supervise."

"I have hundreds of people under me!"

"So do I." He gestured to Elizabeth. "Liz has almost two hundred in her group alone."

"We do 24/7 protection for a large New England family. Five guards on the compound grounds, two watching monitors, three shifts a day, drivers and personal guards when they travel," Liz said proudly. "And that's just one client."

"That's also because they have a big family," Jace said. "Grandparents, parents, six kids and their husbands or wives and babies."

Impressed, Charlotte sat back. "Okay, then."

She let him proceed with his business because he had her attention. She watched him discuss strategy, hear reports on the progress of new hires and engage in a lively debate with Carter over his choice of route through the city for yet another rock star.

"Excuse me," she interrupted again. "You have more than one rock star client?"

Jace looked at her. "Word gets around that we're good."

She leaned her elbow on the table, studying him. The devil in her wanted to say, "I'll bet you are." But there was more than one meaning to that and she wasn't entirely sure which one she meant. She'd thought it was masterful that he'd gotten the right clothes to her house for working on the jobsite? Watching him plan, critique and engage his employees almost made her breathless.

This was the point when her brain always shimmied. Told her to run. Reminded her that she couldn't or shouldn't like someone who was in any way, shape or form similar to or connected to her father. For the first time in her adult life she recognized the fear that eased its way into her thoughts, made her want to find a fault, pick Jace apart and back away.

But this time she didn't have to. Jace didn't want her.

Maybe that was why she could see her own side of things so clearly. Every other relationship, she was the one doing the rejecting. This time, Jace had rejected her.

A funny feeling filled her chest. It was equal parts of odd and amazing to be seeing her behavior so clearly. But it was also incredibly sad that he didn't want to follow through with what they felt.

But if he did, if he'd been the one to kiss her, would she be backing off, finding fault, looking for the fastest way to get away from him?

It angered her to think about it but being angry with herself was foolish. Once a person recognized a bad behavior it was smarter to fix it than indulge useless emotions.

But how could she fix this? She couldn't go after a man who didn't want her.

An hour into the meeting, the conference room door opened. Seth Simon walked in—naked.

"I need a burrito."

Without looking up, Jace said, "You need pants."

Oz pulled out his phone. "I'll call room service."

Jace said, "Get a half dozen bottles of water, too. It's time he started hydrating so he'll have a voice tonight."

The naked rock star standing no more than twenty feet away should have had her full attention. Instead, she stared at Jace. His instincts were so good he didn't even have to glance at Seth Simon to know he was naked.

"I hate water."

Jace shook his head. "Fine. Have dry vocal cords. Disappoint your fans. None of that would surprise me."

"You suck as a security service."

"No, we don't, or you'd fire us." Jace nodded to Oz. "Order the burrito and the water, then get him back to bed."

Oz rose. Seth Simon sighed but he spotted Charlotte and his face lit as he walked toward her. "And who is this? My new guard?"

She should have gasped with joy. Maybe even fought a giggle. But her favorite singer was naked. And being a pain in the ass.

Giving Oz a pointed look, Jace said only, "No. Charlotte is not your new guard."

"She's tall enough and looks sturdy."

Charlotte gaped at him, all thoughts of being impressed by him gone. Being crude was bad enough. But calling her sturdy? That was nineteenth-century insulting. "What am I? A horse?"

"And I love her sense of humor! Please, please, please can I have her?"

"Have me?" She stood up and towered over him. "This isn't the Old West. Men don't choose a woman and run off with her."

Looking confused and wobbly, he stared at her. Oz came over, grabbed his arm and guided him out of the room.

Charlotte watched them leave. "I guess it's true what they say about meeting your idols."

All four of Jace's remaining supervisors laughed.

Jace closed his laptop. "We're done, anyway. Anybody else want a burrito?"

Liz had a lunch meeting with the mother of one of her clients. Carter, Blake and Isaac scrambled to the door with various excuses and were in the elevator in what seemed to be seconds.

"A client like Seth is potential poison," Jace said as he rose from his seat. "That's why they all jetted out of here."

"Poison?"

"Sure. No one wants him to remember their names. He's going to fire us eventually in one of his tantrums and I probably won't argue. I'll gather my guys and leave."

"How's that poison?"

"He'll bad-mouth us." He stopped her before she headed up the hall. "Everybody has the same opinion of him you had before you met him. His songs make everyone think he's a great guy. So, when he tries to ruin our reputation on social media most people will believe him."

"Then why take him as a client?"

"He needs us."

Skeptical, she narrowed her eyes. "Really? That's why you're here?"

"I'd guard him forever, keep him hydrated and his reputation intact because deep down he really is the lost soul he sings about. He overcompensates by being a jackass. But pretty soon, he's going to get in a mood and dump us. Then at least I'll know I did what I could for him."

Her heart softened. "You're a nice guy." She should have realized it when he extended condolences to her mother on Mark's death, but it only fully hit her now.

Jace laughed. "I'm a nice guy to a point. No matter how much I want to protect him, I won't let him hurt us. I've planned for the inevitable social media war."

Charlotte tilted her head and studied him. It was no wonder she liked him. He wasn't just muscles, sex appeal and bossy. He was a genuinely good person.

He shrugged. "You would plan for it, too."

She would. If she and Jace ever started a business together, they would be invincible.

If they started a romance, they'd be red hot and fierce.

She had to stop thinking that way. Because for the first time in her life, someone she was interested in didn't want her—

It was confusing and annoying. Mostly because she knew she shouldn't start something with a man who was only trying to do his job.

She pulled in a breath, clueless about what all this meant. She was twenty-eight, had never been dumped, had always been the one to break things off. Under normal circumstances, she'd think life was telling her she should break the cycle with Jace—

But he was her bodyguard.

And didn't want her.

They walked up the hall. Room service arrived with a bucket of bottles of water on ice and what looked like a mountain of burritos.

Wearing a robe now, Seth lounged on the sofa. He gave Charlotte the killer smile he was famous for, the one that made him look sexy in an innocent boy-next-door way.

"Sorry about the whole no-clothes thing." He laughed. "I sometimes like to rattle the team."

His voice had softened. His face appeared almost angelic. She'd think she was crazy, that she'd somehow misinterpreted what had happened when he'd stepped into the conference room, if she hadn't witnessed it for herself and didn't trust Jace enough to believe everything he said.

Her breath caught. Dear God. She *trusted* Jace?

Yeah. Of course she did. Actually, that was the missing link. The reason she couldn't shake the attraction the way she'd shaken off her attractions before this.

She didn't merely like him. She wasn't just attracted to him. She trusted him.

None of which mattered. He wasn't interested.

"I'd love it if you'd join me for lunch."

Seth Simon's angelic voice, the voice that sounded like it came from heaven, interrupted her thoughts.

She glanced at Jace, who gave her a nod telling her the decision was hers. The comparison that resulted was almost comical. Next to strong, smart, disciplined, masterful Jace, Seth Simon was…weird.

"Sorry, Seth." She gave him *her* best smile. The one that fooled wayward employees and subcontractors into thinking they weren't on thin ice with her. "But I have to get back to my suite to make some calls."

"Too bad." His eyes shadowed.

He could certainly pull out the charm when he needed it.

Seth snapped his fingers. "I know! Come to my show tonight." He pushed off the sofa and headed for the piano by the wall of window. Grabbing two tickets from the bench seat, he turned to her. "You and Jace."

The guy might be a fake. But she did love his music. "You know what? I'd like that."

Seth said, "Those tickets come with backstage passes that you'll get at the door."

Truly touched, she took the tickets. "Thank you."

Genuine, innocent, he nodded. "You're welcome."

Jace pressed the button for the elevator door to open. "Go eat your burrito and drink that water."

Seth laughed. "Will do, boss."

Jace snorted as the elevator door opened. Charlotte stepped inside and even gave Seth a little wave as the doors closed.

"Are you sure he's more evil than good?"

"The good is an act. Trust me."

She pulled in an uncomfortable breath. There was that word again. Trust. Realizing they were back to being friendly, and that she was facing an attraction to a man in a totally different way than she ever had, her chest tightened. Without the crutch of comparing him to her dad, being able to walk away before she got hurt, she was shaky, vulnerable.

Jace shook his head. "Such an act, giving you backstage passes."

"I thought it was a nice way for him to make up for being an ass at first."

Jace peered at her. "I run his security team. I print those backstage passes."

"Oh." Yet he hadn't embarrassed Seth when he'd made what he'd thought was a grand gesture. He also hadn't yelled at him for being naked. He'd told him to put on pants. And he worried about his performance that night… reminding him to hydrate.

Jace MacDonald was an interesting, complicated man, and the thought of spending more time with him, actually being in a relationship with him, was equal parts frightening and wonderful.

But for once in her life, she wasn't calling the shots. He was. And he was saying no to anything happening between them.

CHAPTER NINE

CHARLOTTE DRESSED FOR the concert in a pair of skinny jeans and her leather jacket, looking as she always did, tall and sleek with a splash of cool when she put on her sunglasses. Jace directed her to the door of his condo without breaking out of bodyguard mode, though his heart stuttered. She was sexy as hell.

For the first time since he'd chosen his profession, he felt out of step with it. He'd never been as attracted to or as in tune with a client and every instinct he had was screaming that it was wrong that he couldn't touch her. Couldn't laugh with her. Couldn't talk about anything but her dad, the estate, how she would need protection.

Because protecting her was his job.

Nothing else.

And that felt wrong, too.

They arrived twenty minutes before the show. As Jace's crew handled Seth, Jace stayed with Charlotte. She might not stand out at a concert, but she was still his responsibility.

The opening act finished. Seth took the stage. He didn't have a big band behind him. No special effects. Just himself, a guitar and that sweet angelic face of his that had made him millions.

He sat on the tall stool, strummed the guitar to tune it, made friends with the audience who clapped and cheered and yelled, "We love you, Seth!"

Jace watched it all, not sure if he was proud of Seth for using his talent or confused about how someone could be one way onstage and exactly the opposite in real life.

Two of the guys from the opening act walked over to Jace and Charlotte, who stood just out of the sight lines off the stage. One cracked open a beer. The other had a whiskey bottle in his hand.

Still in costume—baggy shirts and low-riding print pants with wide legs—they looked like refugees from a hair band in the 1990s.

The first one said, "Evening, mates."

Jace nodded. "Evening."

Charlotte smiled.

The tall one with perfect teeth faced Charlotte. "So, what agency are you with?"

Seth's soft mellow music in the background didn't preclude conversation so Jace wasn't surprised when she answered.

"I'm not sure what you mean."

"You model, right?"

Charlotte laughed. "No. I'm a vice president in a development company."

He grinned. "A big shot."

She laughed again.

Seth finished one song and started another, but he stopped abruptly after only a few chords. "You know what? This is such an emotional song for me, I think I want to be closer to you all. Let me move this stool up a few feet."

The audience cheer sounded like a roar of thunder. Feet stomped. Whistles sounded.

He slid off the seat, but his foot caught, and he fell forward. Jace was on the stage and in front of him in seconds. He didn't prevent his fall, but he was there in time to help him up and ensure he was okay.

* * *

Charlotte watched it all, her heart in her throat. She'd developed a theory about Seth. That he was a lost soul and he needed someone like Jace. With every fiber of his being Jace was a protector. Happy to help him.

"So, while that simpleton's melting his way into women's panties by pretending to be wounded, what do you say we go back to the dressing room and unpack the hard stuff?"

Charlotte turned to the member of the opening act who had spoken. "What? Hard stuff?" She shook her head. "Guys, I drink a beer now and again. Maybe have a glass of wine. But that's as far as I go."

Band member number one caught her arm. "Come on. That's nonsense. Everybody likes to party."

"Not me," she said, yanking on her arm, but his grip was firm. She didn't like this guy or his smarmy friend. With their scarf headbands and wide-leg printed pants they looked like they shopped at Steven Tyler's garage sale. For once, she was glad to be under Jace's care. "Besides, I'm with Jace."

"That old stick in the mud?" He laughed. "You need to spend some time with a real man. See what fun is."

The obvious direction of his thoughts made her stomach turn. His pupils were dilated. His breath stank of whiskey. But his grip was almost superhuman.

Behind her the crowd broke into applause. The creep tightened his hold on her arm and shoved her to the right. "Let's go."

She tried to stand her ground, but her feet slid in the direction he dragged her. "No!"

His friend came around to the side, caught her other arm and all but lifted her off the floor.

"Jace!"

She screamed his name but knew her voice would be

swallowed by the noise of the crowd. Close to the back now, almost at the elevator, they weren't even in a position that Jace could see her.

Jace returned from the stage, shaking his head, laughing at how smoothly Seth had gotten beyond his fall by introducing Jace and making him take a bow for helping him.

He began to say, "Did you see—?"

But Charlotte was nowhere in sight. Panic rose from his stomach to fill his chest. He raced to the side, pushing his way through the small crowd of roadies, press and people who'd been granted backstage passes, and saw her with the musicians from the opening act. Each held one of her arms and she was struggling.

He took off running and caught them just before they reached the lift to the lower area and the dressing rooms. He yanked the skinny lead singer away from her and would have punched the guitarist, but his eyes widened, and he dropped her arm.

He faced the lead singer. "What the hell are you doing?"

"Just trying to have some fun, mate."

"The lady didn't want to go with you."

He looked affronted. "I planned on convincing her." A drunken grin lifted his lips. "I can be very persuasive."

Jace fought the urge to haul off and hit him. "You can be a piece of crap. You know that?"

He caught Charlotte close. "And for God's sake, get a stylist. The '90s are over."

He headed toward the stage. "Are you okay?"

"I'm fine. They rattled me. But I'm fine."

She didn't look fine. Her face was pasty white. Her eyes were shiny and confused.

He tapped his earpiece. "Oz, I'm leaving with Charlotte. Get someone back here pronto. And alert security about the opening act. Tell them they tried to accost a woman and we want them off-site. Also call Seth's manager and tell him that Seth never works with these two again."

The word "Affirmative" came through his com.

He motioned for Charlotte to turn right and walk with him. They went down the back stairs and made their way through a maze of corridors and tunnels before they reached the door, walked outside and to Jace's limo.

They got in and he told the driver to take them to his condo.

Charlotte leaned back on the seat and closed her eyes. After about ten minutes, she said, "That was stupid."

"Which part?"

"Their behavior." She sat up again. "The fact that I couldn't get away from them. Both." She made a sound of disgust. "I'm a very strong person. They should not have been able to outmaneuver me that way."

"You have the strength," Jace said, his heart finally settling down now that they were close to home. "But not the moves."

She narrowed her eyes at him. "Moves? What are we? Dancing?"

He laughed. Her face was no longer pasty. Her humor was back. "In a way."

She sniffed.

"Seriously. If you know the right moves, you can get yourself out of situations like that."

"And here I thought you'd be glad something had happened to show me that I needed a bodyguard."

"You say you don't want one."

"I don't."

"And in my world the customer is the boss." He met the gaze of her pretty blue eyes. "But that doesn't mean I won't worry about you."

He could tell she almost said something about being fine. But they both knew she wasn't. The incident had shaken her. Only a fool would pretend otherwise. Charlotte wasn't a fool.

But he saw more. Her eyes softened when he'd said he'd worry about her. It hit him oddly too. They'd only been together a few days, and in another few days they'd part. Maybe never to see each other again.

The mere thought did funny things to his heart. He told it to settle down and brought the conversation back on track, to the real problem they needed to discuss.

"Since what you say goes, and you're walking away from protection, I think we should use some of your time with me teaching you a few easy defensive moves."

She inclined her head in agreement. "Maybe it wouldn't be a bad idea for you to teach me a few of the difficult moves, too."

Her voice held a slight quaver that told him she'd been a little more upset than she'd wanted him to believe. That caused the funny floating feeling in his heart again. If he let himself picture her being accosted when he wasn't around, his brain would explode.

"Okay, as soon as we get inside, we'll both change into sweats and a T-shirt and I'll show you some really effective moves."

She nodded. "Sounds good."

They reached his condo building and were quiet as they entered the lobby and rode the elevator. They walked back to their rooms and in less than five minutes both were standing in the center of his living area, dressed for the lessons.

Looking antsy, she said, "It's so tidy here. I'm afraid we'll break a lamp."

"What do you think we're going to do?"

"Aren't you going to show me how to lob someone over my shoulder while yelling, *Hy-ya!*"

He laughed. "No. But there is some movement." He

glanced around. "I'll tell you what. There's a big open space in the master bedroom. Let's go there."

She followed him back to his room and they walked inside. "Nice. Very horror film decor."

He flicked on a few extra lights. "I work back here. The darkness makes me feel like it's totally private."

"The fact that you're thirty stories up and only have one other tenant on your floor should actually manage that."

She looked lean and supple in her yoga pants and white T-shirt. Very bendy. Like someone who could karate kick you in the face, then step back and do fifty squats. She should be extremely easy to teach.

He guided them to stand in the center of an area rug he'd always thought had no purpose until just now. It was large enough and thick enough to act like a mat.

"Fine. Whatever. Do you want to learn or not?"

She raised her hands in surrender. "I'm ready."

"Okay, first order of business. Less is more. If you can kick your assailant in the nuts and disable him…run. That's your best defense."

"I'm a good runner." She held out a leg. "Long legs. A benefit of being tall."

With her slender form outlined in the tight clothes, he saw other benefits, but quickly shifted his mind elsewhere.

"If you don't get a chance to kick him in the privates, or if he or she is coming at you, there are a few moves to protect yourself." He took a defensive stance. "For instance, if someone punches you, grab the elbow of the arm coming toward you—" He caught her elbow with one hand and made a fist with the other. "Then use your free hand to punch them in the stomach."

She made an awkward attempt at mimicking what he'd shown her.

"That's pretty good. But the trick is to use your whole arm. Your whole upper body."

He took the stance again. "Okay. Let's try something else. If someone comes toward you to grab you like this—" he reached toward her with both arms "—you catch their hands and flip them down…as you kick them in the nuts."

She laughed. "So, what you're consistently saying is I have to do two things at once."

He didn't see anything funny in anything he'd said. "Yes. They'll be expecting one move. You do two. Plus, flipping down their hands is more of a distraction, so they don't notice you're about to kick them."

He held out his hands. "Let's try. Grab my hands, then do the initial movements of the kick, but don't actually kick me."

She swallowed back a laugh. "Yeah. I'm glad you set some boundaries because I did not want to kick you there."

She caught his hands, turned them down to shove them away, then did a partial kick.

"That wasn't bad."

She danced around like a prizefighter. "Show me something else."

"Let's try the thing where you block the punch, but this time use your shoulder to knock them back."

She nodded eagerly. He faked a punch. She blocked it, but her shoulder knock was weak.

"Try again."

She did and was equally unsuccessful.

He walked behind her. "Here's the deal. When people are struggling, their instinct is to use their hands. Block. Shove. Push. All they think of is hands."

She nodded.

"Raise your right arm."

She did.

"Bend it at the elbow."

She bent it.

He lifted his hand to her fingers. "This is what you

have at your disposal. Fingers to jab in someone's eye. Hands to slap. Forearms to block." His hands followed his words, drifting from her fingers to her wrist to her forearm. "Elbow. Great again for jabs. Upper arms, stronger than forearms. And shoulders." He'd been following the inside of her smooth, silky arm, not realizing he wouldn't end up at her shoulder but right above her breast. He moved his hand quickly to her shoulder, but instinct wanted him to slide down along the sides of her breasts to her ribs to her stomach to the soft flare of her hips.

His breath stuttered. His bedroom grew silent.

His *bedroom*. What the hell had he been thinking, bringing her here? Sure, there was more space. But—

He cleared his throat. "Anyway, let's practice some of that."

He stepped away and walked in front of her again, but when he turned to face her, her eyes were bright, her lips parted.

Damn. He shouldn't have touched her—

But his ego puffed a little. His innocent touches had her breathing funny, too—

Not important.

"So, what you need to learn is to use your upper body like a weapon."

Eyes serious and confused, she nodded.

"Do you think you can barrel into me with a shoulder?"

She nodded.

He took the stance. "Okay, so I'm a kidnapper. You're on your way to a restaurant, reading a text from the person you're meeting. You look up and here I am, ready to grab you and toss you into this van."

He pointed to the right where he wanted her to imagine a van. Her gaze ambled over and one eyebrow rose.

She should have made a smart remark about the pretend van. Instead, her shiny blue eyes met his.

He swallowed. He'd just invited her to plow into him, when the feel of her skin had him about crazy. He had no idea what would happen when her entire body bumped into his.

He pointed at his rib cage. "Your goal is to hit me here." He motioned to the top of his stomach. "Or here."

She started her prizefighter dance again. "With my shoulder."

"Yes. Hit me really hard with this part of your shoulder." He grabbed the bony part of his own shoulder. "Hard enough that I will grunt and be caught off guard."

She nodded again.

"Okay. You're on your way into a restaurant, looking at your phone, you glance up and there I am. Bend, shift your shoulder to the front and ram into me."

She did as he asked but the hit was weak.

He brought her out of her bent posture. "You need to focus your power from here…" He motioned from her stomach, up her chest. His hands were centimeters away from her belly, her ribs, her breasts.

He swallowed. "To here."

She blinked at him.

Time spun out with them inches away from each other, holding their breaths, just wanting to touch the forbidden fruit that was always in front of them, always tormenting them.

She took a step toward him.

He took a step toward her.

He wasn't entirely sure who made the first move but the next thing he knew they were kissing.

CHAPTER TEN

FAMILIAR FEAR RACED through Charlotte. The fear that he was just using her. The fear that he'd leave her. But she stopped it. There was no place for fear in what she felt for Jace. Even if this was a one-night stand, she wanted it. It was time to change the way she felt about everything. Time to let go of the past. Time to stop thinking of everything in terms of her dad. Fight the fear. And live her life.

She reached for the bottom of Jace's shirt and yanked it up, shifting away from their kiss only long enough to pull it over his head and toss it away.

"Charlotte—"

"Stop. Don't talk us out of this. I like you. You like me. We both want this." And for once she wanted to be rid of the fear, to look it in the eye and tell it it didn't matter. That she'd survive a little pain because the pleasure would be worth it.

She must have convinced him because he kissed her again. His mouth moved over hers hungrily and she responded equally greedily. Terrible reminders of being abandoned flitted through her brain. She blocked them. Her entire life had been spent being worried about the future. She desperately needed to live in the moment.

He grabbed the hem of her T-shirt and yanked it up as she stepped back far enough that he could pull it over her head. When they were breast to chest, her eyes drifted shut.

With only the thin lace of her bra between them, the sensations passing through her stole her breath. She'd made love with men before but never one she was so attracted to. Never someone she wanted so much, even though she knew this wasn't permanent. In a few days or weeks, he'd be out of her life.

But that was the point. Not everything had to last forever. Some things were short-term. For enjoyment.

He reached behind her and unhooked her bra. Their gazes caught as if each gave the other one last chance to back away. But neither moved until Jace slid his hand around her neck, pulled her close and kissed her as if he'd been starving for her his entire life.

Everything after that happened in a rush. A riot of touches and tastes, smooth caresses and kisses so long and deep she could have drowned in them. His silky soft burgundy-colored sheets added to the pleasure and she forgot all about her life, her fears, and lived in the sinfully sexy moment with the strongest yet somehow nicest man she'd ever met.

Jace woke the next morning wrapped around Charlotte. He gave himself thirty seconds to enjoy it—to soak in the feeling of her sleek shape pressed against his—then he squeezed his eyes shut.

He'd slept with a client. He'd done that only once before to devastating consequences. Charlotte wasn't the kind of woman to write a tell-all book. But sleeping with a client was against rule number one for security people. No matter how good, no matter how much they'd both wanted this to happen, it had been wrong.

His instinct was to rain kisses from her shoulders to her hips, to flip her over and do everything they'd done the night before, this time in the light when he could fully appreciate her.

His brain told him to get up, get a shower and go to the kitchen…all without waking her because he had to do damage control and he needed to think this through.

He managed to slide out of bed without disturbing her. He did allow himself a sigh of regret when he looked at her, her beautiful yellow hair spread out on his pillow, her creamy shoulders a stark contrast to his wine-colored sheets. After those sixty seconds, though, he headed for the master bath.

He showered but left his hair wet so he didn't have to run the hair dryer, which sounded like a jet engine and would wake her. He found sweats and a T-shirt in the walk-in closet/dressing room and tiptoed out into the hall.

The night before, they'd been cocooned in a world so private everything that happened between them had felt sacred, right. He'd been terrified when he hadn't seen her when he came off the stage from helping Seth Simon. He'd thought teaching her self-defense would ease the pounding of his heart and his worry over how easily something could happen to her. It hadn't. He'd never felt that kind of fear for a client, and when they'd started touching and her soft skin had been a reminder that she was safe, the relief had nearly overwhelmed him. It had certainly blotted out his better judgment.

In the kitchen, he made a pot of coffee and drank two cups before she finally found him. Dressed in her sweats and T-shirt from the day before, she rounded the island that bridged the living area and kitchen, slid her arms around his neck and kissed him.

Oh, God. It was the best kiss he'd had in years. Maybe decades. His body woke. His mind flooded with good ideas. But his left brain cleared its throat and reminded him that his entire life had been invested in his security company and he couldn't lose it all because he had the hots for a client.

He pulled back. She smiled at him. "Good morning, stud."

Even as his ego puffed out its chest, he winced. "Don't call me that. We shouldn't have slept together. You're a client."

Her forehead bunched. "Seriously? I mean, I know you said before that we shouldn't get involved. But this whole thing between us is different. I'm not your ordinary client."

He pulled back, away from her. "No kidding. Except you not being an ordinary client isn't because we like each other. Do you have any idea how much this estate is worth? I'm not just responsible for the heirs. My company is responsible for security systems in houses and vehicles, for security checks twice a month to make sure alarms are working and twice a year to make sure nothing has gone missing. We guarded your dad, his jobsites, his offices…"

She studied him a second. "So, combining what I saw yesterday with your supervisors to what you just said, I'm going to guess my dad's property is half your work."

"Yes."

"If you lose the estate as a client, your company loses half its value."

"In the snap of one person's fingers."

Her head tilted. "What does that have to do with you and me?"

"You're a client." He said it weakly. Because she already knew it. But it was still the crux of why sleeping with her had been the stupidest thing he'd ever done, even though it had also been the most wonderful.

He took a breath. "I'm your bodyguard. The great big, general guiding principle, first rule of bodyguards, is that you don't sleep with a client."

"Humph. I thought you would say the first rule is not to get personally involved because that would include all genders and ages."

He put his attention on the coffeepot and off her sweet butt. "You know I have to get personally involved."

"Just not too personally involved."

He peeked at her. "There has to be a line drawn in the sand."

"I'm not sure I understand why. If sleeping together makes me happy, keeps me from being bored, predisposes me to following your orders because I now think you're adorable when you boss me around…how is that bad?"

"Because I can't be distracted."

She laughed. "Are you saying you're blinded by my beauty?"

He groaned. "It's more than that. It's more like being with you pulls me out of a mind-set I need, away from the focus I need." He took a breath. "But if you want to make this personal, there are other very good reasons why us messing around is wrong. For one, you don't know me."

"Because we've only been in each other's lives a few days. I'm sure we'll—"

"I'm divorced."

That stopped her. "Oh."

"And my wife cheated with my best friend."

"Oh."

That "oh" was longer, and her tone of voice told him she understood the depth of that kind of betrayal.

She considered that for a second before she said, "A relationship for you wouldn't be a simple, easy thing."

"No. But there's more." He pulled in a quiet breath. "I ran into my ex and former best friend—the guy she ultimately married—about two years later, right when my business was exploding. I was guarding the extremely spoiled thirty-year-old daughter of a client, and when we ran into my ex, Misha figured out what was going on pretty quickly."

Charlotte leaned against a cabinet. "That sounds like a good thing."

"I thought it was, too, because she slid her arm under mine and pretended that we were an item. There she was— gorgeous, obviously wealthy—with me in my suit and silk tie, and we looked like the kind of couple that ends up in a magazine."

She sniffed a laugh.

"When we got back in the limo, we kept up the game that we were dating. Laughing because it sure as hell had been good for my ego to be with someone when I ran into my ex, her new husband and their baby. But then we took the game too far."

"So, you didn't just kiss a client before. You slept with her."

"Only once. I learned my lesson when her dad disinherited her, and she decided to make money by writing a tell-all book."

Charlotte winced. "Ouch."

"We slept together only that one time, but she exaggerated. The way she wrote about it I was the aggressor and it took some..." He cleared his throat. "Coaxing for her to give in." He pulled in another breath. "Those couple of pages in her book rocked the trust of most of my best clients. I lost some. Sleeping with someone you're guarding isn't just an oops. It's a breach of trust."

"How can it be a breach of trust for us when I was as involved as you were?"

"Things change. Feelings change. What seemed like a good idea last night might someday seem like the stupidest thing you ever did."

"Or I might need the scintillating situation to perk up my tell-all book."

"Yes."

She gaped at him. "Seriously? I look like the kind of person to write a tell-all book?"

"It doesn't matter. My job is to protect you."

"And you've been attracted to me all along and still done a great job." She tilted her head as she studied him. "Our situation is different."

Her cell phone rang.

"Damn it!" She yanked it from the back pocket of her sweats, mumbling, "A building better have fallen down overnight for a foreman to call me this early." She frowned. "It's not one of my guys." She glanced at Jace. "It's my mom. I have to take it."

Jace said, "Sure. Absolutely." But when she left the room, he called himself all kinds of names. Most of what she'd said was true. She was different. And he hadn't neglected his duties up to now, even though he'd been ridiculously attracted to her. In fact, what he felt for her sent a whoosh of supercharged desire to make sure nothing happened to her.

But those also felt like excuses. He'd lost control the night before because he'd been so afraid for her.

And that loss of control *was* a direct result of being attracted to her, liking her, connecting to her on a level he didn't with other clients.

She popped out of the hall and into the open area, looking as confused as he felt. "My mother is at LaGuardia."

"The airport?"

"You know another LaGuardia?"

"Does she have a ride?"

"She said she could catch a cab, but I told her to stay put. You'd probably send a limo."

He grabbed his phone and started texting. "Did she give you flight info?"

"Yes." She rattled off her mom's flight and which baggage claim area she was in.

Jace texted that to one of his drivers. "Someone will be there in thirty minutes or so, depending on traffic. Text her and tell her to get some coffee or something but be at her baggage claim area in thirty minutes."

"Great." She winced, looking sheepish. "Apparently in our last phone conversation, I gave her the impression I was bored. So, she decided this would make a good girls' trip."

His heart stuttered, even as his left brain sighed with relief that her mother would be around to send them both to neutral corners, no more long glances, no teasing, no kissing and absolutely no way they could sleep together. Maybe with that distance, the next time he got an opportunity to talk to her, she would actually hear what he was saying. That being attracted might be natural but acting on it was wrong.

"I think having your mom here is a good thing."

"Sure. It's particularly good to have my mom here if you insist that we're sticking to your plan of going back to bodyguard and newly found heiress and not following through on something I considered three steps above great."

"I'm insisting. Charlotte. I know you don't understand how much danger you are in, but anyone could be a fanatic with a gun, a kidnapper looking for quick money, an extortionist. I can't be distracted. I need to protect you. So, everything personal has to be off-limits."

She said, "Fantastic," but she didn't sound like she meant it.

He shook his head. "I can't be noticing how beautiful you are when I should be watching your surroundings. I can't be laughing with you when anyone around us could be a threat. I can't be silly with happiness and forget who you are, what you represent, how many people want a piece of what you're inheriting. Even if it means hurting you. Some people will stop at nothing to get to you."

She studied him. "I think you see problems where there are none."

"And I think you've led such a quiet life that you forget who you are. But I know who you are, what's at stake. And I will do my job."

She held his gaze for a good minute, but finally shook her head. "All right. I understand."

"Do you?"

She sucked in a breath. "Yes. I'm not sure I'm a hundred percent in agreement. But I can see that's what you believe. So, I respect it."

She turned to leave, and he almost collapsed with relief that he'd won—

Won?

Really? He was going to call it a win that he'd never get to touch her again. Never get to feel the length of her body beneath his.

He cursed. How the hell could he be conflicted when he knew the stakes? She was an incredibly wealthy woman. Even if she refused the estate money, predators would come out of the woodwork. And from here on out if he were to talk about anything personal with her, *that* was what he should be telling her.

That was what he had a responsibility to tell her.

Because for the first time in his life he was genuinely afraid for one of his clients. The estate had been reasonably quiet. Danny was keeping the frauds and fakes in line. But there were a million what-ifs. And if she returned to Pittsburgh alone, opting out of the estate, she'd be a sitting duck.

He shouldn't be teaching her defensive moves.

He shouldn't be telling her he was divorced and had been burned by a client he'd slept with.

He *should* be telling her she needed him—him and his entire staff—to watch her world so no one hurt her.

Just the thought of her alone, even in Pittsburgh, at her

jobsite, in her beautiful house, scared him silly. Because she didn't understand the stakes or the risks. And she didn't seem to believe him when he told her.

She headed down the hall to her bedroom. "I think I'll call Leni, see if she wants to go shopping with us. She'd mentioned a boutique where some woman named Iris is very helpful. And my mother loves to shop. This will be a great way to introduce her to Leni, if she's free."

Jace said, "Okay. Sounds good."

She turned and gave him a weak smile. "Yeah. It's super."

She walked away, disappointment shimmering from her, but whether she knew it or not, their world was righting itself.

She needed him.

Especially if her father hadn't died the day his fishing boat caught fire so far out in the ocean everyone *believed* his life raft had drifted into the vast open sea never to be found. *Believed* being the operative word. Without a body how could anyone know for sure?

Jace cursed. Told himself that was nonsense. Crazy thoughts. The ruminations of a guy who overthought everything. Was suspicious of everything. Mark's disappearance had been investigated by professionals.

He could not be alive.

But Jace also knew why the thought had popped into his head. It was better to ponder something ridiculous than endure the upset of knowing he'd hurt Charlotte.

By the time Leni arrived, Charlotte's mom was already at Jace's condo. Penny Fillion walked with Charlotte to the door when Leni's bodyguard opened it.

Charlotte made the round of introductions and her mom stared at Leni. "You are not what I expected."

Her petite half sister smiled as she tucked a strand of

her long brown hair behind her ear. "I'm guessing my biological mom was really short."

The three women laughed. Jace did not. He was back to only being her bodyguard.

Disappointment and confusion rippled through Charlotte. Sleeping with Jace was supposed to have been a declaration of independence of a sort. She'd forced herself not to think about a future with him, not to worry that he'd leave her the way her dad had left her mom. At first, it had been terrifying, but she'd stayed in the moment, enjoyed every second, being herself, not feeling the fear, and it had been magnificent.

He had perfect muscles, perfect form and stamina the likes of which she'd never seen. Just thinking about him hovering over her made her want to fan herself.

God, she liked him. She really liked him. But he took his job seriously—and he'd had some bad experiences.

She had, too. Not with other lovers or romantic relationships. With her parents. She should want to be as cautious as he was. After all, this relationship was not going to end in happily-ever-after.

So maybe one night was all she needed? The first step toward overcoming her fears and stepping into the real world.

Maybe, now that she understood what had been happening, why she'd frozen with fear, jumped to conclusions, kicked every guy she'd ever dated to the curb, she really would find "The One."

The three women and two bodyguards rode down in the elevator. They piled into the back of the limo with the chitchat of Charlotte's mom and Leni filling the air. The three women sat on the bench seat facing front. Leni's bodyguard sat with the driver. Jace sat on the seat across from Charlotte, Penny and Leni.

Her mom kept the elevator conversation going, talking about Charlotte's childhood, comparing it to Leni's.

Charlotte sneaked a peek at Jace. He looked out the window, but not like a tourist or someone staring because of boredom. He was truly watching the traffic, watching the street outside the limo when they stopped at a light.

He was so gorgeous, so kind to the people he guarded, that it was hard to imagine a woman hurting him. She must have been a piece of work—

Which was exactly the problem. His marriage had ended in the worst possible way. If that hadn't caused him to never trust again, having a client write a tell-all book had probably sealed the deal.

But she wasn't looking for forever. She sure wasn't going to write a book. And she didn't want to stop what they'd started the night before. She wanted more. She wanted practice with living in the moment, not expecting something she couldn't have.

She wanted a sizzling hot, ridiculously romantic fling, not a one-night stand.

They pulled up in front of a cluster of first-floor shops in what looked to be a part of the financial district, despite the trees, a deli and a coffee shop—Caffeine Burst—on the first floor of the tall buildings. Leni's bodyguard opened the door. Charlotte, her mom and Leni exited, then Jace. Their little train of people entered the store.

Charlotte could have dwelt on the ridiculousness of it, but when the door of the store opened and she saw the white walls and black woodwork, chandeliers and sophisticated dresses, slacks and blouses on the mannequins, she gasped.

"Oh, my gosh! Have we found heaven?"

Leni slid her arm beneath Charlotte's. "No, but it sure as heck feels like it sometimes."

Charlotte's pretty blonde mom reverently said, "I hope I brought all my credit cards."

Charlotte put her hand on her mom's to prevent her from

getting her wallet. "Put your cards away, Mom. This trip is on my dad."

Penny's forehead wrinkled. "What?"

"I got an allowance for these two weeks I'm being vetted. Danny Manelli couriered bank cards to Jace's condo yesterday afternoon. I can't think of a better way to spend my portion than on pretty clothes we can take back to Pittsburgh with us."

Her mom chuckled. "I would like a new dress for Andi Petrunak's wedding."

Leni said, "And there's a fundraiser ball in Scotland next week. If you're staying, why not come with us?"

Penny pressed her hands to her chest. "A ball in Scotland? I'd go to Scotland?"

Leni laughed. "Sure. It's a beautiful event held in a Scottish castle." She nudged her head toward Jace. "It was his family's idea. They put together the event to benefit the children's wing of their local hospital."

Charlotte glanced at Jace. *His family hosted a fundraiser?*

His expression didn't change.

"He won't say it," Leni whispered. "But I think it's his parents' way of getting him to remember his life is with them…and not always with his clients."

"Ah."

"You should come, too," Leni said. "It's a smallish event, though formal. It would be a great way to introduce you around."

"I'm not supposed to be outed yet," Charlotte reminded her. "I haven't been fully vetted, shown the slides or gotten my DNA results back."

Leni shrugged. "So, I'll simply tell people you're my friend. It'll make it even more comfortable for you. That way, when the news breaks, you won't suddenly be thrust into things. Your toes will already be in the pool."

Though she didn't want to be in the pool at all, Charlotte had figured out she wasn't going to be one of Mark Hinton's kids and be totally uninvolved.

She took a breath. "Okay. That makes sense." Facing her mom, she waved her hand over the racks of dresses. "The sky's the limit. We'll add formal dresses to our list."

Leni clapped with glee as a tall, slender woman came down the stairs, wearing pearls that fell to her waist over a black pantsuit with no shirt under the jacket, exposing the upper swell of her breasts.

"That's Iris. She'll find the right dresses for your mom and you, too."

They spent the next hour exploring the shop, with Iris on a mission to find the perfect cocktail dress and gown for Penny.

After discovering two work dresses and trousers with a matching silk blouse, Charlotte moved to the second floor to browse the evening dresses. Jace followed her. While a pretty girl who looked to be in her twenties—Francine—rounded up gowns for her to try on she peeked over at him.

She could brood over his declaration that they'd only have a one-night stand or sigh over how good-looking he was, except now that he'd told her about his divorce and the tell-all book, she saw a little deeper.

He was careful with his clients, went the extra mile for them, because he understood that life wasn't easy. He'd survived the worst kind of breakup of his marriage and the result of his only other one-night stand with a client that nearly wrecked his business. His clients might not go through the exact same things he did, but they didn't have to. He understood pain, heartbreak, embarrassment, loss.

He was one strong, smart, determined guy.

That's why she couldn't be mad at him for laying down the law this morning. She understood him, too.

The first three dresses Francine brought over were good,

but the fourth was a formfitting white gown and Charlotte's heart stuttered. She knew what she'd look like in the gown. She didn't even have to try it on.

She glanced at Jace again. If his family was hosting the charity ball, he'd be going. And not as a bodyguard. As a member of the family hosting it.

Wouldn't it be nice to knock his socks off? Especially at an event where he'd just be himself...not the man assigned to protect her?

She could picture it and for the first time realized how unequal their relationship had been from the beginning. She'd thought their stubborn personalities and bossiness made them the same, but in truth he'd been doing his job.

What would it be like if he were just himself?

Would he be charming, kind, sweet, honest?

What would he be like...what would *they* be like—if they were allowed to flirt, laugh, talk, dance—

Without the worry that she was his client or he had responsibilities, they would probably have the best time of their lives and he'd see beyond the ridiculous excuse that she was his client to the real her, the way she'd been seeing the real him since he'd told her about his divorce and his troubles with the tell-all book.

She and Jace needed that ball where they would both be themselves, so he could see they were a good fit.

She might not want forever. But she was done running from good things because she was afraid of the future. She wanted to live her life without fear, without demands. She wanted the chance to be herself.

With Jace.

Francine's phone pinged. She glanced at it, then said, "Your mom is upstairs with Iris. She wants your opinion on a dress. I'll be happy to take that to the register for you."

Caught in a daydream of possibilities about Jace, Charlotte handed her the white gown. "Third floor, right?"

The young clerk smiled. "Third floor."

She made her way up the stairs. Jace discreetly followed her. She snickered. Oh, he was in for a surprise when they went to that ball in Scotland.

But when she reached the top of the stairs, she forgot all about Jace. Her mother stood on a raised platform, wearing a red dress so stunning Charlotte stopped walking.

She had on shiny silver shoes and Iris or Leni had pinned her hair into a loose updo to mimic what she'd look like at Andi's wedding.

She grinned. "What do you think?"

"I think you're beautiful." She suddenly saw what an up-and-coming rich guy might have seen in her mom, twenty-nine years ago. It flashed through her brain that her mom should have spent her life in boutiques like this, buying pretty clothes, attending fancy parties with her dad—

Except her dad hadn't wanted them.

No, he hadn't wanted *her*.

Her mom had pined for him, chatted about him for the first ten years of Charlotte's life as if one day he'd pop into their world again, live on the farm with them, be a real husband and father.

The next ten years, her mom stopped wishing out loud, but she hadn't lost the spark of hope in her eyes. The past few years, the spark had been gone.

Her mother had literally wasted her life over a man who hadn't wanted her.

She glanced at Jace, Not moving. Looking like a statue.

Her heart swelled in her chest. She felt what her mother must have felt all those years ago. That weird hope. The ridiculous hope that someday he'd see she was what he needed, the woman he wanted—

The night before she'd thought she was declaring her independence, being bold, striking out on her own. But she really liked Jace. Deep down she wanted their relationship to be more than a fling.

Last night, that subconscious expectation had been okay. This morning? Knowing he'd been married and his wife had cheated?

It was wrong.

If there had been one thing her mom had taught her, without words, without actual lessons, it had been that no smart woman ever longed for a man who didn't want her.

No matter how good-looking.

No matter how kind.

No matter how sexy, how gorgeous, how wonderful he was in bed, a smart woman did not get involved with a man who flat out told her he didn't want her.

Not when she really liked him.

Not if she was only kidding herself thinking she could keep anything between them casual.

CHAPTER ELEVEN

THE LIMO DROPPED Leni and her bodyguard at Nick's Park Avenue penthouse. Her cute, sprite-like sister all but skipped into the fancy building.

"She wasn't always like that."

Both Charlotte and her mom looked at Jace. The man hadn't spoken in hours, but suddenly he'd found his voice.

Charlotte glanced back to the building doors closing behind Leni and said, "You mean happy?"

"I mean comfortable with the estate, the money. She didn't merely learn to live with it. She found a way to use it. To make the world a better place."

"Are you hinting that's what I should do?"

He shifted on his seat. "Just reminding you of options. You had fun with her today. She likes you. You like her. You are family now. You should bond."

"Well, look at you going all pop psychologist on us."

"Don't be snarky. This is serious."

"Serious enough for you to break your code of silence..." She faltered, suddenly recognizing what he was doing. He was treating her like a client. He might not have to tell her to put on pants as he had with Seth Simon, but he was clearly guiding her.

Insult flared inside her until she remembered that he ran a huge security firm that needed the business of Mark Hinton's estate. And that he didn't want her romantically.

He'd chosen his company over her, after less than a week of knowing each other, after a night of making love.

She tried not to be insulted. She worked not to think she'd done something wrong. She knew she hadn't. Their night together had been perfect.

But he was choosing his job.

The irony of it was, the first time she'd let herself go out on a limb, do what she wanted, forget her fear of being dumped the way her mom had been…she picked a guy just like her father. A man who chose his job, his work, over her, the way Mark Hinton had with her mother.

Her mom spoke into the silence of the limo. "Your dad would have wanted you and Leni to be friends."

She snorted. "My dad obviously kept us apart for *decades*."

"Maybe he regretted that?"

She gaped at unexpectedly chatty Jace, remembering he'd been close to her dad.

"He told you that?"

"Yeah, he did. Actually, he regretted a couple of things." Jace's gaze slid to her mom and his eyebrows rose.

Oblivious, Penny said, "I think my hotel's right in Times Square."

Charlotte and Jace's gazes bounced to her.

Charlotte said, "Hotel? Aren't you staying with us?"

Jace added, "There's plenty of room in my condo."

Penny laughed and shook her head. "Oh, no, thank you, Jace. I need my space."

Charlotte squeezed her eyes shut. "Don't argue. I spent my childhood on twenty-five acres with the nearest neighbor being a mile away. When she says she likes her space, she means it."

After Jace informed the driver, Charlotte grew angrier and angrier as they drove to her mom's hotel. Jace knew something about Mark Hinton's feelings for her mom. He knew why Mark had kept her and her siblings apart.

They found Penny's hotel, got her checked in and settled in her quiet, comfortable suite and headed back to Jace's condo with Charlotte fuming.

She decided it was a joke of the universe that she should be stuck with a million questions about her dad and the bodyguard who knew him better than anyone. She didn't *want* to have questions about Mark Hinton. She didn't *want* to know about him, didn't *want* to empathize or sympathize. She liked hating him. It put that part of her life into a manageable box. Especially since she didn't need her dad or his money. She was a vice president. Self-sufficient. Independent.

Still…

She'd always wondered if her dad had disliked the idea of being a parent so much that he'd abandoned the love of his life. She'd wondered what would have happened if Penny hadn't gotten pregnant… Would they have been together when Mark died?

And Jace knew.

It gnawed on her brain the rest of the limo ride, in the elevator and as she stormed to her room to—

She didn't know what. They'd had lunch but shopping in one overstocked boutique had taken hours, so it could be time for dinner. She'd laughed with Leni and her mom, feeling like a part of a clique of girls. Two sisters and a mom. And it had been fun.

So fun that she wanted to shake the man silly who'd kept her from it. But he wasn't around. He'd never be around. Sailing off into the afterlife, he avoided all the repercussions of his decisions. But one of his friends was right down the hall. And the temptation to get answers, wrong as it was, overwhelmed her.

She raced from her bedroom, down the hall to the master suite, and punched open the door.

"How dare you tell me things that make me think about my dad! He didn't want me. He didn't want my mom. He kept me from Leni! All this might seem trivial to you, but it wasn't trivial to a little girl being raised away from people because apparently my dad had insisted on that. It wasn't trivial to a little girl who longed for a sister! It wasn't trivial to a mom who'd cried herself to sleep every night for at least ten years! I managed to get myself beyond the questions. Beyond caring. And a few comments from you has me curious about him. So damned curious because the way the math lines up, he left my mom when she got pregnant. Which means *I* was the catalyst for him leaving!"

She stopped. Her lungs pooled with air so heavy it made her eyes tingle, then fill with tears.

"You were but not for the reasons you think. Your dad knew his being around you, living with you, even marrying your mom, put you in danger."

"So, you're sticking with his story that he was protecting us."

"He was!" Jace sighed. "Charlotte, having tons of money wasn't just the issue. He did some wheeling and dealing and not always in the nicest possible way. He made enemies in the '80s. Lots of enemies. Some of them were mobbed up. Some of them were connected to cartels. Most of them are dead now, but when your mom got pregnant, he was getting a death threat every week. He really believed hiding you was the best thing."

"Don't make excuses for him deserting us!" She plopped down onto the bed. "Don't you see? No matter how you slice this, my mom and I were alone. If one of his enemies had found us, we would have been helpless. What you just told me makes it even worse that he deserted us!" She sucked in a breath as tears fell. "How is that the best thing?"

* * *

Jace's chest froze. He'd never seen her so vulnerable. He'd never seen anyone so vulnerable. The raw pain in her eyes tore at him, ravaged his soul. He realized it was the same kind of pain he'd felt when his wife cheated with his best friend. Raw, broken, he'd lashed out when he simply wanted…no, *needed*…someone to explain. No one could.

He couldn't stand back and watch her struggle. Not when he knew the pain was different, worse, than anything she'd ever felt.

He sat beside her on the bed, wrapped his arm around her and pulled her close. "I'm sorry. I'll keep my mouth shut from here on."

She shoved back. "I'm not sure I want that, either. It's like I'm finding things out that hurt but I need to know them. I feel like I have to know…like I'm on the edge of something."

"You are. You're on the edge of a new life. A whole new life as a wealthy woman who can do anything she wants."

He thought that would soothe her, but her eyes filled with tears again.

"Leni and I could have been best friends."

"You still can."

She nodded, looking as if she was hitting the place of acceptance, but he saw a softness in her face that made his heart hurt and his limbs weak. The instinct that it was his job to comfort her morphed into something more. An ache to love her, to soothe her by showing her how special she was.

He told himself not to kiss her. He moved closer, anyway. How could he resist her when she needed comfort, needed to know that she mattered? His mouth drifted over hers in a touch as light as a hummingbird's wings. But that only fueled the fire of desire, igniting his own need. His lips pressed. She responded by opening hers to him, and almost in a trance of yearning, he deepened the kiss. Keeping his wits but allowing himself the simple pleasure that would calm her wounded soul.

She wrapped her arms around his neck, and he let her melt into him. Degree by degree, what began as comfort shifted into something sweet, but scorching.

She'd worn a simple T-shirt and jeans to meet Leni, and as his hand drifted over the soft material, the longing to feel the velvety skin beneath it raced through him like a brushfire.

And why shouldn't he? This relationship was a non-starter. After their talk this morning, they both knew it. Neither one of them would get ideas of forever.

But they also both felt something incomprehensible in each other's arms. They'd found a unique peace the night before. He genuinely believed she needed to feel that again. To get the comfort or the grounding or maybe simply a night away from the stress, the worry, of everything her life was about to become.

Still kissing her, he slid his fingers under the hem of her T-shirt and lifted it over her head. They pulled apart to accommodate the shirt, and when he popped it off, their gazes met.

He answered the curiosity in her eyes by leaning in to kiss her, softly, slowly. This was no ordinary woman, no ordinary act. Had he met her before Mary Beth, Charlotte might have been the love of his life.

No. She was definitely the love of his life. So, he made love to her that way. With a respect that manifested his simple awe. Awe that she was so smart, so beautiful and, for at least the next few hours, *his*.

The word turned over in his head, flicked a switch of something purely male inside him. Possessiveness merged with the hormones currently ruling his brain and caused him to take greedily.

But she surprised him, pushing him down on the bed and standing long enough to remove her jeans. Realizing what a great idea that was, he rid himself of his clothes, and when she crawled on the bed to straddle him, they were naked. Flesh to flesh, the way he truly believed they were supposed to be.

The rest happened in a blur. One minute she was in control, the next he wrestled it away from her. He might have considered it a competition, except he loved her strength, fed off her power over him until a tidal wave of release rumbled through them both, stealing his breath and hers.

He squeezed his eyes shut, allowed himself one quick burst of anger that fate would bring her into his life when he couldn't have her, then he rolled them together on the bed. She snuggled against him and sighed with contentment but didn't speak. For which he was grateful. He wanted the next five minutes to simply enjoy the feel of her.

But his thoughts wouldn't give him the luxury of peace. They crowded him, mocked him. Though he'd gotten past the worry that she was a client, he couldn't stop the knowledge that she was a woman on the edge of an enormous life, the likes of which she couldn't even imagine.

He'd thought making love to her would help her relax enough to come to terms with some of it…

But he hadn't expected to have feelings again.

Or to want something he couldn't have.

He wasn't good at things like intimacy or relationships. But he could keep people safe. And Charlotte, brave, strong, honest-to-a-fault Charlotte, needed a relationship. Someone to show her the love she'd been denied—

He could not be that man.

There was no easy answer, so he let himself fall asleep with her in his arms.

CHAPTER TWELVE

CHARLOTTE'S PACKAGES WERE sitting on the kitchen island with the doorman's card tidily attached to the top of one of the boxes. Jace had fallen asleep and she'd had to carefully slide out of bed to keep from waking him. She might be hungry, but she knew exhaustion when she saw it, so she let him sleep and found her way to the kitchen.

She grabbed her purchases and hung them in her closet. She stopped when she came to the expensive shimmery white gown. Not taken off the rack, but something pulled from a private showroom. Something special. Something unique.

Almost a physical symbol of her segue from one kind of life into another.

She'd gone to Jace's room to confront him. Instead, he'd comforted her. There'd be repercussions. He had probably mentally lambasted himself for allowing himself to make love again.

But she didn't regret it. Not one bit. This time she'd kept the thought in her head that he didn't want her forever and she didn't want him forever. But she did want what they had. They couldn't help getting close. They were together all day, every day. He saw everything going on in her life. And she genuinely believed fate had tossed them together to show her that she could be involved in a temporary relationship and not die, or wither, or fall into a deep depression, when it ended.

Because it would end. He was divorced. His wife had cheated. That kind of wound left scars. And she wasn't arrogant enough to think she could heal them.

She made a ham sandwich and grabbed a bottle of water from the refrigerator and walked to the TV room.

So, they had what they had.

And what if that was what life was all about?

Accepting the good things that came your way and not expecting perfection.

She thought about how she'd always searched for "The One," and shook her head. Maybe it was time to get rid of that notion, too.

She heard noises outside the TV room and knew Jace was awake. She wouldn't run out to the kitchen, scramble after him like a lovesick pup. Charlotte wasn't a chaser, and she didn't think Jace was the kind of guy who liked to be chased. This was about a mutual attraction. They could fight something that felt as natural as breathing or enjoy it.

She chose to enjoy it.

The question was…would he?

"I see you don't need dinner."

She turned to the door. He looked rumpled and well loved. If she were a woman predisposed to pride, she would have grinned. "I eat a lot of sandwiches in my world."

He ambled into the room and plopped on the sofa beside her. As he slid one arm around her, he picked up the television remote with the other and turned on the Yankees baseball game, muting the sound.

"Are you a fan?"

"Half the population of the United States are fans."

She shrugged. "I like the Pittsburgh Pirates."

He laughed. "Then you're loyal."

Funny that he should mention loyalty since that seemed to be the one trait he valued most. "They have their years."

"Not many." He glanced at her from his peripheral vision. "Which makes your loyalty extremely rare."

"What can I say? I'm special that way." And she suddenly sensed they weren't talking about baseball anymore.

"Loyalty is a good trait."

"It's an essential trait. It's the kind of trait that keeps a lover from writing a tell-all book."

He laughed.

She snuggled closer, though she reminded herself she wasn't going to push him into continuing their affair. She would let it be his choice.

"This is nice."

Her heart lifted a bit, but an icy fear filled her chest. She might not want forever but she hated leaving it all up to chance. She at least wanted him to say what they had could continue. "Yeah. It is."

"You know, we can't pretend that we fell into bed this afternoon. I had a few chances to back out. So did you. We also can't pretend that won't happen again."

The iceberg in her chest melted a bit. He wasn't telling her they had to stop. Maybe he'd figured out some things about them, too?

"Nope. No such pretending will be done by me."

"We can't pretend I won't do this when we're alone." He drew her forward and kissed her thoroughly.

She smiled at him as he pulled away. The kiss had been hot enough to totally melt her iceberg of fear. "I think I like where this conversation is going."

"Every minute I'm with you, I want to talk, I want to touch, I want to kiss you."

"I really like where this conversation is going."

"Yeah, well. You don't know everything about me."

"There's more than a divorce and crappy affair?"

* * *

Jace took a quiet breath. Common sense precluded him from even trying to pretend they wouldn't sleep together again, but he also couldn't go on with what was happening between them unless he was sure she understood this wouldn't lead anywhere.

And not just because he couldn't trust. Because he didn't want to hurt her.

"That's the worst of it."

She frowned. "So, what you would be springing on me now are bad habits and goofy things you did in high school?"

He shook his head, feeling clumsy and out of his element. A man accustomed to one-night stands, he usually didn't have to talk about his feelings. "Probably. I guess what I'm trying to say is I love what we have. I don't want it to end, but it's going to."

"Okay."

He sighed. She was not cutting him any slack. She was going to make him say it. "But if we're both on the same page, there's no reason we can't continue."

"What about your bodyguard duties?"

He wouldn't tell her that getting so close to her would make him crazy vigilant. He hadn't yet worked out if that was good or bad.

"Aren't you the one who said that getting involved made you think my bossiness was sexy?"

She laughed. "Yes."

"You paying attention to me is fifty percent of the battle when I guard you. We'll work as a team and everything will be fine."

"I still say I'm not in any danger and you see a witch under every wisteria."

He shook his head. "Whatever." Having said his piece and content they were in agreement, he distracted her by sliding his hand to her nape and under her glorious hair. "Did you get something to wear to the ball in Scotland?"

"Yes. I did. And I think you're going to love it."

He probably would. He loved everything she did.

When he didn't answer right away, her eyes clouded. "You are going to the ball, aren't you?"

"Are you kidding? This is my grandmother's baby. She'd skin me alive if I tried to skip out."

Her face brightened. "So, you won't be going as a bodyguard?"

"I'm visiting my family, going to a fundraiser they host. Plus, Scotland is a fairly safe place for you and Leni. No one cares about the Hinton heirs there. I'll bet if we asked people on the street in Scotland nobody would even know there were Hinton heirs. Actually, while we're there, pretending we're dating would keep me close enough to do my job, and maybe we could have some fun."

Her face contorted. A smart woman, she never took anything at face value. "So, you're pretending it's okay for you to like me so that when we go to Scotland it will be a great way to guard me?"

"No. I'm saying going to Scotland is a perk. A bonus." He met her gaze. "I can't pretend I don't like you."

Her eyes grew soft and dewy. "I can't pretend I don't like you, either. It seems a shame that our lives are eventually going to force us apart."

"Yeah, but we have right now." He drew her close, kissed her. That was another thing he loved about her. Her logic. He broke the kiss and whispered in her ear, "Let's go back to bed and see what happens."

She laughed. He rose, took her hand and led her to his master suite.

They woke together the next morning. She gave him a sleepy smile and that was all his hormones needed. After slow, easy lovemaking they showered together and laughed as she tried to wear a pair of his sweatpants and a T-shirt so they could go to the kitchen to get breakfast.

"I have a better idea. Let's go out to eat."

"You're letting me out among people?"

"You were out with people yesterday."

"Yeah, right. Iris kept us hidden."

He laughed. "It's why we love her. But I was thinking we should do something fun like take your mom to Junior's. It's a restaurant in Times Square. Near her hotel and she will love it."

Her eyes widened. "Seriously?"

"Sure. Put on your best jeans and get ready for heaven. Their cheesecake is to die for."

"So, we're not just going out for breakfast? We're going to be bad and eat cheesecake for breakfast?"

"Oh, honey, we passed bad a long time ago."

She snickered. "Yeah, we did."

"Call your mom and tell her to be ready in forty minutes. I'll touch base with Nick and arrange for you to see some of the slides this afternoon."

She turned to head back to her bedroom to dress. "Sounds like a plan."

Charlotte's mom glowed like a lamp. Happy to be out with her daughter, she chatted the whole time they were at Junior's. Charlotte was thrilled to see her so bubbly. The cheesecake was a wonderful, decadent breakfast and Charlotte felt like she was floating.

In his T-shirt and jeans, with a black leather jacket, Jace looked like sex on a spoon. She saw women giving him sideways glances and some even sighing.

She wanted to say, "Hey, eyes on your own paper," as happy possessiveness overwhelmed her. Except he wasn't really hers. They both understood that once she'd seen the slides of what her dad owned and her DNA results came back, decisions would have to be made, but sheesh. Look at him. All gorgeous and manly, drinking his coffee and polishing off his cheesecake. She'd known this relationship wouldn't last forever, but sometimes, like right now…she wished it would…wished it *could.*

But neither one of them could promise tomorrow. Charlotte was finally beginning to understand she had no idea what would happen in her future. Whether she took the money or not, her life would change.

As they rose from the table, she said, "You know, Mom, you could come to Nick and Leni's with us to see the slides of things my father owned."

Her mom kept her attention on her purse as she pulled it from the back of her chair and slid the strap up her arm.

"Maybe another time." She glanced around, taking a long breath. "I feel like sightseeing."

Jace went for his phone. "I'll get you a driver."

Penny stopped him by putting her hand on his before it reached his pocket. "I want to walk."

"It would still be better if you had someone with you."

Penny smiled. "Maybe yes. Maybe no."

Jace scowled.

Realizing how much she'd love the opportunity to explore on her own, Charlotte said, "She's fine."

"You're damned right I'm fine." Penny laughed. "No one cares about a woman who looks like an average tourist." Heading out of the restaurant, she slid on her sunglasses. "Besides I have mace."

She walked up the street, away from them, toward the M&M store, and Charlotte laughed.

"She'll be fine."

Jace got his phone. "I'm having someone follow her, anyway."

She shook her head. "Just can't leave bodyguard mode, can you?"

"If you saw an iffy spot in the blueprints for one of your company's buildings, would you walk away without mentioning it?"

She sighed. "No."

"Okay, then."

Deciding to forget about his job and just enjoy the day, she shook her head. "You know. It might be fun for *us* to do a few touristy things." She inched closer, linked her arm with his. "See a Broadway play. Have dinner somewhere fancy." She peeked at him. "You know, since we figured out that pretending to date makes it less obvious that I have a bodyguard."

"It does work."

She grinned. "Let's go get tickets."

In the limo driving to Nick's, Jace went online and bought tickets for a show that evening.

They entered Nick's condo to find Leni in the kitchen, wearing an apron.

"I'm making cookies," she called to them as they stepped inside and removed their coats.

Nick took their jackets to a nearby closet. "I love cookies."

Leni came over and gave Nick a quick, smacking kiss. "It was a batch of Christmas cookies that won him over."

Charlotte laughed. "I know there's a story in there somewhere."

"A good one actually." The stove timer pinged, and Leni raced back to the kitchen area. Calling over her shoulder, she said, "But you're going to need days to see all these slides, so we'll save that discussion for another time."

They walked to a back room where Nick had pulled the drapes closed and synced his computer with a huge television. The picture of a white stone mansion filled the screen.

Nick sat on the chair by the computer. "That's your dad's primary residence. A mansion in Ohio."

Charlotte slowly lowered herself to the sofa. Jace leaned against the doorjamb watching. The first few slides showed the rooms of the house, and her mouth fell open slightly.

The place dripped with luxury.

The next house was equally gorgeous. A huge cabin in Denver. The next house was in Aspen.

"Why two houses in Colorado?"

"Well, Aspen's an hour drive from Denver and your dad liked to ski."

"Oh. Okay." She sat back and got comfortable. By the time they got up to his seventeenth house, Charlotte's brain was mush.

"Did he even remember he had all these houses?"

Nick laughed. "No. That's part of my company's duties for him. We don't just manage his money. We keep track of his *things*." He flicked to the next slide. "Now, we start on beach houses."

The four Jace had mentioned the night she'd met Nick and Leni were first. Then two smaller lake houses came on the screen.

Then a spotless little house on an island.

Seeing the tiny, inconspicuous house, Jace pushed away from the wall. His mouth fell open. His eyes narrowed. His breath stalled.

Damn it!

That house might not be beside the scene of Mark's boating accident, but it was close enough Mark could have gotten there if he got his lifeboat to shore.

He didn't even bother to excuse himself. He opened the door and left the room. Racing to the main living area of the condo, Jace looked for Leni. When he found her in the kitchen, he said, "Is there someplace private that I could use to make a call?"

"Nick's office." She led him down the hall and opened a door on a compact space. "There's a desk and chair, even a computer if you need it."

"Thanks."

She said, "You're welcome," closing the door behind her as she left him alone.

So angry he could barely speak, Jace checked for listening devices and cameras. When he found nothing, he pulled out his cell phone and dialed the number for Mark's international phone.

He let it ring fourteen times. It didn't go to voice mail, simply disconnected, so he called again. Again, it rang fourteen times, then disconnected.

He scrubbed his hand across his mouth. Not sure if he should feel foolish for his suspicion or relieved that no one had answered Mark's phone, he wasn't quite ready to go back to the room with Charlotte. Instead, he touched base with his supervisors, put out a few fires, then returned to the media room where Charlotte and Nick were still watching slides.

The sight of Mark Hinton's properties and possessions gave Jace an odd feeling. Sadness poured through him as he remembered being with Mark in his cars or riding on Jet Skis. He suddenly wondered if his suspicion wasn't simply a part of grief. The denial part. Maybe thinking Mark had faked his death was easier than the reality that he'd never see his friend again.

Out of sorts and not in the mood to look at slides of houses and cars and eight tons of furniture, he walked to the kitchen where Leni was putting white icing on sugar cookies. Little bottles of red, blue and yellow sprinkles sat at the ready, waiting to add color.

Leni handed him one. "You look like you could use something sweet."

He wasn't sure what he needed, but he took the cookie, bit into it and groaned. "So good."

"I love to bake," she said, smiling as she iced another cookie. "My mom taught me."

"Well, she did a good job."

"Hey." Charlotte entered the kitchen. "Oh! Cookies are done!"

Laughing, Leni handed her one. "All finished with day one of the slides?"

Charlotte rolled her eyes. "Two hours was all I could take."

Icing cookies, Leni said, "That's why the estate allows a few days to look at everything."

"I can hardly wait to get to the Ming vases. How can one person keep track of so much crap?"

Jace reached for another cookie. "He couldn't. That's why Nick keeps the lists and the slides."

Charlotte sighed. "So he said."

Nick brought their jackets. "So, I guess you'll be back tomorrow?"

"Only if I can't think of a good excuse to bow out."

Nick laughed. "I know. It's boring. But your dad's will insists that you see all the slides."

Jace laughed, but he also remembered how desperately Mark had wanted his kids to be introduced to his life, his lifestyle.

Putting it into his will that his kids had to look at all the slides suddenly seemed very convenient.

He stomped out his suspicions. He was grieving Mark. That was all this was. Denial. He was going to have to get to the point of acceptance soon or he'd say or do something that would make everyone think he was crazy.

Or make Charlotte run away. She already believed her dad was a mean-spirited con man. If she discovered Jace was having these weird suspicions, she'd be furious.

CHAPTER THIRTEEN

THE WEEK PASSED quickly for Charlotte. The Broadway play she and Jace saw was funny. Dinner afterward was romantic. She spent most mornings with Nick, looking at slides, but in the afternoon, she shopped with her mom, who loved being in New York. She had a glow about her that Charlotte had never seen. But she still liked her private time. Stayed in the hotel. Noticed the bodyguard Jace had assigned to her, and when she couldn't lose him, she sent him home.

Which made Charlotte laugh. Pretending to be dating, she and Jace had gone out like a couple, returned to his condo to sleep together and brought each other coffee every morning, depending on who woke first.

It was the perfect week. So, the evening they left for Scotland, on Jace's big plane, with Nick and Leni to arrive the next day in his jet, it seemed odd to Charlotte that Jace was uncharacteristically nervous.

"I'm the one who doesn't like takeoffs and landings," she reminded him, plopping down on the seat she'd been in the first time they'd flown. Though she had a carry-on with pajamas for sleeping through the long flight, her luggage had been taken by the driver in their condo and she'd comfortably accepted that she wouldn't see it again until they got to Jace's grandmother's home.

Noting that her mother was busy exploring the plane, she said, "Why are you nervous?"

Jace shook his head at her. "You and I have more or less agreed this is a short-term thing between us—"

She'd argue that. Whatever was between them was strong. And though it might not last forever, she sincerely doubted it was short-term.

Still, a good poker player didn't show her hand. She played it. She trusted her gut that she'd know when to quit. Until then she planned to make the most of every minute they had together.

"And I'm about to introduce you to my family."

She laughed. "You're afraid that after they meet me and see what a great person I am, they'll trounce you when you dump me."

He sat beside her. When he caught her gaze, his eyes were oddly serious. "What makes you think I'll dump you? What if you dump me?"

"Then you'll get their sympathy. Because I am quite a catch."

He snorted.

The plane taxied to the runway and Jace took her hand. "Not gonna kiss me this time, are you?"

She glanced back at her mom, who had her nose in a book. "Let's see how it goes."

His brow furrowed. "You don't want to kiss me in front of your mom?"

"I don't think I've ever kissed a man in front of my mom."

"There's a first time for everything..."

But the private plane had already found the runway and was shooting into the sky. Charlotte's heart skipped a beat. Her chest tightened to the point that she wasn't sure she could breathe, and she began counting in her head to distract herself.

Then it was over. They were airborne.

"You're beginning to get beyond your fear."

She relaxed. He had no idea how many fears she'd been conquering with him. "I think I am."

"If you participate in the estate, you'll fly like this all the time and pretty soon you'll grow so accustomed to takeoffs and landings they'll be nothing for you."

It was the first he'd mentioned the estate in days and she almost hated that he had. The real test of their relationship would be if she took her share of the money. Figuring out what to do with it, she'd enter a new phase of her life. She guessed that would require travel, meeting people, investigating charities…

Jace could still be her bodyguard but that seemed tacky. She'd be the cliché heiress sleeping with her bodyguard. If she had to have someone following her around, it would be better for it to be a neutral party.

But then she and Jace would never see each other.

She tried to think that through but there were no easy answers. He was busy. She would be, too. And if she decided not to take her share of the money, she'd go back to Pittsburgh. Unless he found time to make a special trip to her city—or if she flew to New York—their time together would be over.

Either way, her acceptance or refusal of her dad's money would end them.

Not wanting to think about that anymore, she unbuckled her seat belt and walked to the back of the jet to get the cards. She suggested to her mom that a good start to the flight would be a few games of rummy before they hunkered down and got some sleep.

Her mom closed her book. "I'd like that. We haven't played rummy since you built that fancy house of yours."

"Then come on over to the table."

They played cards for two hours before her mom yawned. A gentleman, Jace gave the bedroom to Charlotte and Penny. As he settled into one of the reclining seats to sleep, she and her mom went to the back of the plane to the little room with the big bed.

Behind the closed door, her mom said, "You like him."

"A lot. But cool your jets. The man was burned by a really bad marriage."

Penny slid into her pajamas. "Aww. You don't think it's going to last."

"Actually, we've agreed that it's not going to last."

"Oh, no." Her mom's face saddened. "I see what's happening. You're protecting yourself because of what happened with your dad."

"No!" But she had been. Jace was the first guy with whom she wasn't protecting herself. The first time she was letting nature take its course, and not worrying about the inevitable ending.

Her mom sighed. "Not every relationship ends in goodbye and even the ones that do are sometimes worth the trouble. Worth the memories. Worth the good times."

Charlotte shook her head. That had been her rationale about sleeping with Jace. Which she did not want to discuss with her mom.

Penny sat on the bed, tucked her legs beneath her. "I remember meeting your dad." She sighed. "He was so tall and so good-looking. Our first date he took me to Italy for spaghetti." She laughed and shook her head. "The first time we slept together he took me to Paris for breakfast. We ice skated, fished, rode horses, skied in Switzerland. The three years we were together he made my life rich. Fun. But also important. He needed me. He said I grounded him, gave him strength. He also said losing me was the hardest thing he'd ever endured."

Seeing the love in her mom's eyes, Charlotte's eyes filled with tears. "You never told me any of this stuff before."

Penny inclined her head. "I wasn't about to tell my ten-year-old daughter intimate details about her mom and dad."

"True. But you could have told me about Italy and the spaghetti. When I got older you could have told me some of the other stuff."

"And you would have liked hearing those things about him?"

Charlotte winced. "I don't know."

"I do," Penny said firmly. "You hated your dad. Didn't want to hear his good points." She smiled. "And he really did have his good points. Like he was funny. And generous. Unfortunately, he was also ruthless when it came to a business deal."

Charlotte pulled in a breath for the first time in her life picturing her dad making a deal, being sharp, being determined—

A little too much like herself for Charlotte's comfort.

"Well, he certainly had to have been a good businessman to amass his fortune."

Penny smiled. "You're a lot like him that way."

She squeezed her eyes shut, not wanting the comparison, but it wasn't as revolting as it might have been. Since getting involved with Jace she hadn't just sloughed off her own fears, she'd begun understanding her mother's love for Mark.

Though Charlotte wouldn't wait almost thirty years for a man, she could understand the love her mother had felt for the reclusive billionaire.

"I'm starting to see you thought he was pretty special."

"He was." She laughed. "But he was a bit crazy, too. Paranoid, yet somehow easygoing. Ruthless but generous." Penny crawled to the head of the bed and pulled back the covers. "Everybody's complicated, Charlotte."

"I hadn't thought I was until this week."

Her mom peeked up at her. "What happened?"

She slid under the blankets of the queen-size bed and plopped onto the pillow. She wasn't about to tell her mom that she'd just figured out she dumped every guy she'd dated because she didn't want to get hurt the way her mom had. Penny deserved the good memories she had of Mark Hinton. She'd certainly earned them with over twenty-eight years of devotion.

"Meeting Leni, thinking about being an heiress." She laughed. "That one's like a punch in the gut."

"You could do so much good with that money."

"Probably. But now's not the time to think about it. We're lucky to have a long enough flight to get some sleep because it will be morning in Scotland when we get there."

She closed her eyes, indicating to her mom that she was too sleepy to keep talking, but her mind rolled on and on. She thought about how lucky Mark had been to have her mom and it warmed her heart. Her mother never disputed that her dad was a tad crazy, but she'd loved him because he needed someone to love him.

Maybe like Jace?

She always thought of her life in terms of goals. Meeting Jace she'd learned to live in the moment. Now she had to wonder…

Her mother had sacrificed her entire life for Mark Hinton, raised his child, lived alone.

Jace didn't need her to sacrifice her life, but he did need her unconditional love. Not the love of someone who enjoyed his company but the love of someone who gave him the benefit of the doubt, put his needs before her own…

That was stupid. They were equal. Neither one had to put the other's needs ahead of their own.

Plus continuing what they had didn't work. The man had been burned. He didn't want a relationship.

And she did want a relationship. Someday.

She'd find a nice guy, maybe someone who was also in construction and development, and they'd have a normal courtship and marry under the big oak in her mom's back-yard, have kids—

The thought of living her life with anyone other than Jace squeezed her chest, brought tears to her eyes. The display of emotion concerned her more than the thought of living her life without Jace.

She'd worked all this out. Until she'd heard that wonderful softness in her mom's voice. The happiness that made no sense. The emotion that could only be described as real love.

She wanted that real love so bad that her heart hurt, but even as she thought that she pictured Jace. Thought about what they had. Thought about how she felt with him and the heart squeeze that resulted shook her to her core—

Surely, she hadn't fallen in love with Jace in less than two weeks?

She flopped over on her pillow. No. She couldn't. She'd known all along her relationship with Jace was just about fun. She wouldn't even let herself consider the possibility that she'd fallen in love with someone she couldn't have.

But what if she had?

Her mom fell asleep almost immediately. Charlotte slept restlessly. She woke before her mom, checked the time and slipped into jeans and a sweater before going out to the main section of the plane.

Jace slept soundly.

She inched her way to the seat about two feet away from his, sat on the arm and watched him. The first nights at her house, he hadn't more than catnapped. Once they began sleeping together, he'd eased into deep, restful sleep. As if everything in his world was okay when she was beside him.

Their connection was so strong it was hard to believe they weren't a happily-ever-after couple. But they weren't. He did not want to commit, and she was testing the waters of a casual relationship, something she'd never done. For once, she wasn't looking for "The One," wasn't putting that burden on someone.

Except he was so kind, so sexy, so wonderful, the temptation was strong to believe—

One of his eyes opened. "Am I drooling or something?"

She laughed and rose from the seat's arm. "No. But if my calculations are correct, we should be landing in about half an hour."

He yawned and stretched. "Good. Go wake your mom."

Her mother woke slowly and grumpily, and once she was out of bed, Charlotte left her alone to dress. A few minutes later, Penny sat on the seat across the aisle from the two seats Jace and Charlotte were in.

Jace said, "Good morning."

Penny mustered a smile.

Then the plane began to descend. Charlotte squeezed Jace's hand when the wheels bounced onto the runway, but otherwise she was fine.

Jace gave her a quick, sloppy kiss of praise, and when they realized he'd kissed her in front of her mom, they both laughed. The night before her mom had guessed they'd started something…no point in not kissing. But there was something about coming out, letting other people know they'd started a romance, that almost made her giddy.

She shook her head to clear it. No matter how many people they told, how happy they were together, how sad it would be not to spend the rest of her life with him—it would end. And if she didn't stop longing for things that weren't going to happen, she'd miss the last few days of fun she had with him.

They gathered jackets and carry-ons and headed to the waiting limo. The drive was longer than she expected and by the time they reached the MacDonald family home— which was more of an estate—Charlotte was starving.

A man and woman about the same age as Penny raced

out of the main house, a huge stone dwelling that Charlotte could tell was not only at least a hundred years old, it had to have six bedrooms, maybe eight.

"Mom," Jace said as he hugged the dark-haired woman, then the tall man with hair that had begun to gray at the temples.

He faced Charlotte. "Mom and Dad, this is Charlotte Fillion and her mom, Penny."

Charlotte went to shake hands and instead was enveloped in a huge hug first by Jace's mom, then his dad.

A light laugh escaped. "Well, it's nice to meet you, too."

"You can call me Lorraine," Jace's mom said as she looped her arm through Penny's. "And my husband is Bill."

Charlotte nodded, noting the lack of Scottish accent and remembering that Jace's parents lived in the United States. His brother and sister-in-law were living with his aging grandmother, but their home was also in the States.

There was something sweet about the way the whole family clearly considered Scotland and this estate their roots, their home base.

Lorraine led Penny toward the front door. A newish garage built to look like an old-fashioned carriage house was off to the left. Three other structures made a semicircle to the right. A barn sat in the distance. Morning dew covered the lawn. Crisp, clean air filled her nostrils.

Charlotte glanced around. "Reminds me of being ten and taking my breakfast outside so I could gobble it down on the way to the barn to get my bike for a morning ride."

Jace's stomach growled. "Speaking of breakfast." He laughed and put his arm across her shoulders. "Let's go inside."

Charlotte nodded. Little things like that—incidental, wonderful things like the easy way he put his arm around her—sent her mind in that bad direction again. The one where she could see their future. See their lives intersecting and how they could help each other. See their kids. A beach house for weekends.

Craziness. All of it. They'd stated their intentions, and as far as Charlotte was concerned, that was a verbal contract. She wouldn't break it with new demands. No matter how much the squishy feeling in her stomach meshed with the softness in her mom's voice when she talked about Mark Hinton, Charlotte refused to believe she'd fallen in love.

They headed up a cobblestone path to the house, which was lovely. Modern furniture had been supplemented with heavy cupboards and side tables that were clearly antique.

In the kitchen, where a long table had been set for seven, a younger version of Jace and a sunny, dark-haired, clearly pregnant woman stood by the counter, filling platters with eggs, sausage, bacon and toast.

Jace nudged her. "That's my brother, Oliver, and his wife, Emily."

She smiled at the pair as she and Jace sat. "Nice to meet you."

Jace said, "This is Charlotte."

Walking to the table, his brother and sister-in-law both said, "Nice to meet you."

It was odd that no one questioned her presence, or razzed Jace about having a girlfriend, but she suspected Jace had told them not to make a big deal. Which was kind of cute and funny, even as it was sad. They probably thought Jace didn't want to be embarrassed, when the truth was Charlotte would be disappearing from their lives.

After Emily and Oliver sat, Jace's mom started the platter of eggs around the circle of people. His dad picked up the platter of sausage links, snagged three and passed it around.

Charlotte filled her plate.

Jace said, "I thought you didn't like breakfast."

"Maybe it's the air," she said as she reached for toast. "But I'm starving."

Emily said, "It's chilly this morning. That always makes me hungry."

The conversation went on like that naturally and easily. When Charlotte asked about Jace's grandmother, Emily laughed and said, "She sleeps till ten."

That began a lively discussion about the seventy-eight-year-old MacDonald matriarch, who still kept chickens, a cow and a few goats. Even as Charlotte enjoyed the easy camaraderie of family, she also felt the sting of having been raised alone. She now had Leni, but other than that, she only had her mom. Though she would try to see her half sister often—

Actually, if she took her share of the estate, maybe she and Leni could team up, looking for charities and benefits and ways to put their father's money to good use.

It was an excellent plan, but sitting in the country kitchen, enjoying Jace's family, it somehow seemed hollow. She and Leni had missed so much it was hard to believe they could form this kind of solid, easy bond.

When breakfast was finished and everyone was talked out, Lorraine and Bill led their visitors upstairs where their driver had taken their suitcases. The last one on the stairs, Charlotte paused to watch Emily and Oliver work together to gather the dishes and tidy the kitchen.

There was something about the pair that tugged on her heartstrings. Maybe it was because they were expecting their first baby. Maybe it was because they were young and starting out together with nothing but each other.

But something about them got to her. They were so easily in love. So natural with each other. So loving. So committed—

Her head tilted as she studied them. She'd bet her bottom dollar that Emily never wondered if Oliver would commit to her. She'd bet her last cent that Oliver hadn't played hard to get or warned Emily that he would never trust enough to have another relationship. She'd bet everything she had that they'd taken one look at each other, blushed and flirted, and from that moment on, they'd been inseparable.

Nothing like the way she and Jace had sparred and tried to hold back from flirting. Nothing like the way he'd warned her he wouldn't ever commit again, and how they'd settled for what they could get, both too afraid to take a real step—

She shook her head to clear it.

She was not too afraid. Being with Jace was her way of proving she *wasn't* afraid.

She had to stop overthinking this. What she and Jace had was like a verbal agreement and she wasn't allowed to redefine it—

No matter how much she wished she could.

With a groan, she started down the hall to the room she would share with Jace. No one else had a problem with them as a couple. And if she hadn't seen his sister-in-law's pregnant belly and his brother's glowing eyes, she wouldn't, either.

Would she?

Her heart melted in her chest. She'd always wanted kids. Always wanted a home like this one filled with love and camaraderie. No matter how hard she tried to pretend the thought hadn't entered her head, Jace was the guy she kept putting in the picture of her future.

He was strong and smart and sexy and would be a great dad—

She had to stop. She'd begun this relationship knowing it would end. Changing the rules wasn't fair. Not to Jace or herself.

Planning a future that wasn't going to happen was how people got hurt.

* * *

The first day of their visit, Jace took Charlotte and her mom to see the sights. His grandmother let Penny feed her chickens, which was equal parts of funny and sweet. Jace didn't think he'd ever laughed so hard at someone doing barnyard chores.

The following morning they lazed around on the back porch, reading and in general relaxing. That afternoon, Lorraine took Penny and Charlotte to a beauty shop in town to get their hair done for the ball. Jace employed the driver of the limo that took them into town and knew neither his mom nor Charlotte would be surprised when he came into the shop and discreetly watched the door.

Though Penny had her hair fancied up in some sort of hairdo that swept her blond locks into looping curls, Charlotte's hair looked as it had the day she'd gone to work to tell her boss she'd be away for a few weeks.

The way Jace liked it.

Memories of that morning trickled through him. Picking up her earring in the elevator, feeling things he hadn't ever felt. Not even with Mary Beth. And now here they were, lovers.

He put on his tux, struggling with the bow tie as she dressed in the bathroom off their bedroom. He heard the door open and automatically turned, the instinct of a bodyguard always taking charge. When she stepped out, wearing the slinky white gown, her curves outlined, her height somehow accented instead of downplayed, his heart stuttered.

"You look amazing."

She twirled once. "I do, don't I? I saw this gown at Iris's boutique and knew it was the one."

She stopped abruptly as if something about her words had surprised her, but she shook her head, laughed a bit and walked over to him, shimmering all the way.

"You look long and sleek, like a dangerous jungle cat."

"I like that." She eased his hands away from his bow tie and made short order of tying it. "Jungle cat. Maybe that can be your private pet name for me."

Everything seemed perfectly normal, perfectly logical, except for that one hiccup when she'd talked about her dress being the one. Yet he knew something was wrong. Her voice wasn't different. Her sense of humor was on target. She looked fabulous. She smelled even better...

But there was something in her eyes. A shadow. As if she were sad or maybe thinking too much.

"Are you okay?"

She grabbed a sparkly white handbag from the corner of their bed. "Never better."

He caught her hand and prevented her from leaving their room. "You would tell me if something was wrong, right?"

"When have I ever been able to keep my mouth shut?"

That was certainly true. She was the most honest woman he knew. It was why he loved her...

His brain stopped. Froze. A hundred happy moments with her raced through his mind. His heart swelled. His throat tightened with emotion—

No! He was not supposed to love her. That was not their deal.

Or was it? Couldn't he love someone he was having an affair with?

Maybe.

Wasn't that the reason they couldn't keep their hands off each other? The emotion that connected them?

He stifled a groan. The plan had not been to fall in love with her. He couldn't commit. Someday she'd need a commitment. They got along, but they did not mesh. He couldn't trust. She needed that closeness. Plus, she would be entering a whole new world. He had to stay where he was. They'd both known it from day one.

But he loved her.

Just the thought filled his chest with warmth and his brain with wonder.

He loved her.

She headed for their bedroom door and he followed her out, his heart thundering in his chest. They were going to part someday. That was the only reason he'd let them indulge their feelings. He knew there was a natural end to this, so they might as well enjoy what they had and at least have memories.

But it had backfired. Instead of enjoying the time they had together, enjoying her, he'd fallen in love.

He paused at the top of the stairs, not sure if he should be confused by the way things turned out or angry with himself. Finding no answer, he forced himself down the steps. He knew the drill. There was a difficult, confusing side to everything. Questions. Troubles. Work. Endings that weren't always happy.

Plus, all along he'd known they couldn't be together forever. So rather than panic, maybe this was simply phase two of enjoying what they had for as long as they had it.

Maybe that was it? Sure, he "loved" her. Why wouldn't he? She was funny and lovable. And for as long as their lives fit, he could enjoy the feeling.

That had to be it.

Because he wasn't the settling down kind. And he wouldn't hurt her by telling her he loved her, then letting the relationship end.

They rode to the event venue, a castle near a moor. His grandmother being the sponsor of the event, she and his parents had gone an hour before and were probably standing in a receiving line near the ballroom entrance.

Limousines cruised up the circular drive, deposited their passengers and drove away. Jace got out first, helped Penny, then Charlotte.

Touching her hand, loving the way she looked in the long, smooth, shiny dress, he swallowed back a torrent of feelings. How right she was for him. How much he loved having her in his life. How different his vision of his old age became when he imagined her in it.

He stopped the last thought. Stomped it out with a ferocity that scared him. He'd had a vision of the future with another woman. He'd had a best friend. They had betrayed him. Mostly, Mary Beth had told him, because she'd moved on. What they'd had had been great, but it had a shelf life. *A shelf life.* As if he were a can of creamed corn.

But he understood what she meant. That was how life was. People changed, moved on. No matter how strong his feelings for Charlotte, they'd ebb. They'd mellow. And pretty soon they'd be gone.

So would Charlotte's.

Refusing to analyze why that thought made him impossibly sad, he took her hand and led her into the foyer and to the circular ballroom. Crowded with people, the black-and-white floors were nearly invisible. Waiters in white shirts and waistcoats over dark trousers served champagne. He took a glass for himself and one for Charlotte.

She glanced around. "Where did my mom go?"

"I heard her phone ring just as we got in the castle."

Charlotte sniffed a laugh. "Modern technology. Can't even go to a ball without somebody finding you."

He gripped her hand, turned her to face him. "Let's not worry about modern technology. Let's just have fun tonight."

"That was the plan, Skippy."

And she was back. His Charlotte. The one who made jokes while she looked at him the way Emily looked at Oliver. As if he was smarter, funnier, more interesting than he really was.

His chest tightened. Longing washed through him. The

urge to trust her, to believe in something he was sure didn't last, rolled though him—

He ignored all of it. "Let's go find our seats."

They skirted conversation groups with him needing to stop periodically to talk to people who recognized him. He saw the family table, in the front of the room, with Leni and Nick and Nick's parents already seated at the table beside it. The table where Charlotte's mom would sit.

"You know, you never really told me that you came from money."

He stopped walking. "Does it matter?"

"You led me to believe you were a working stiff, just like me."

"I am a working stiff just like you."

"No. You're someone who works, even though he doesn't have to."

"I still work. And if you take your dad's money, you'll be wealthier than I'll ever be…and I'll bet you'll still work."

One of her eyebrows rose.

Not sure what that meant, he said, "We're not rare. Every life needs a purpose."

"True."

"Which also means your dad's money doesn't have to stop you from being who you are. Except that you might look at your life as having a bigger purpose."

She glanced around again. Jace's heart melted. She was more beautiful than any woman there, more accomplished, too, and somebody ninety percent of the people in the room would admire.

"I have actually been thinking along those lines. Maybe working with Leni to figure out how to dole out our dad's money so it does the most good."

His soul filled with hope for her. "Really?"

"Yes. All along I fought the obvious conclusion. Money changes things. But I didn't want to change, so I bucked a little. But now…" She caught his gaze. "Now I see how it all fits together."

It was clear from the expression in her eyes that she also saw *him* slightly differently. She understood his business better. Understood he wasn't ruled by needing to make a profit but by a desire to keep people safe. And made the connection that with her new wealth that was how she should live her life, too.

He felt the click again. The knowledge that they weren't merely right for each other. They were like interconnecting pieces of a puzzle.

And suddenly he didn't want to fight it. Dear God. He wanted this. He wanted what Oliver and Emily had. He wanted a home, this wonderful woman, any children they might have…and a life.

His breath stuttered as the truth of that hit him. The past years, maybe even as far back as Afghanistan, he hadn't had life. He'd simply been living. Waiting to come home to Mary Beth, then totally submerged in pain when he returned to find her with someone else.

And now, Charlotte had awoken him. Made him see what he wanted. Showed him how he—how *they*—could have it.

"Excuse me, Mr. MacDonald."

The waiter brought him out of his reverie. "Yes?"

"There's a call for you in the white room."

"A *call* for me?"

"Yes, sir. Can I show you the way?"

"No. I'm fine. I know the way."

The waiter left and he turned to Charlotte. "I have no idea who would be calling me here instead of on my cell."

"Maybe Seth Simon."

He laughed, then impulsively kissed her, filled with something he could neither define nor describe. Cautious, but curious. Wondering if he should tell her his conclusions or wait a few days or weeks to let everything settle.

"I'll keep it short."

"I'll go chat with Leni and Nick."

"Good idea."

He circumvented the crowds by walking to the back of the room and through a nearly invisible door used by staff. He strode down one hall, then another to the white room, a room in an area of the castle not available to the public.

He opened the door and froze. There on a Queen Anne chair, his head shaved and wearing dark-framed glasses, making him unrecognizable to anybody but someone who knew him very well, was Mark Hinton.

"I'm ready to announce to the world that I'm alive."

CHAPTER FOURTEEN

CHARLOTTE CHATTED WITH Leni and Nick for fifteen minutes, meeting his parents, who had flown to Scotland with them for the ball. When Bill and Lorraine led Jace's grandma, Jean, to the main table, she realized dinner was about to start and she needed to get to the main table with Jace's family.

Panic fluttered through her. Her mom had disappeared and now Jace was gone, too. She didn't want to miss whatever Scottish delicacy was about to be served, but she also couldn't let dinner start without her mom and the host's grandson.

She turned to Leni. "I'll be right back."

"Better hurry. Looks like things are about to get under way."

"I know. But Jace was going to the white room." She shook her head. "A waiter told him he had a call."

Leni's brow puckered. "A call? Who wouldn't call his cell?"

Ill at ease, Charlotte rose. "I know."

Nick rose. "Let me come with you."

Charlotte shook her head. "No. You stay. If everything's about to start, we shouldn't both miss it."

"Are you sure?"

"Yes. I'm fine. Jace probably doesn't realize the time."

Stopping to ask one of the staff for directions, she made

her way to the white room. Her tight dress kept her from taking long strides and she could almost hear dinner being served without her, making her stomach protest.

Finally, she found the room. A tastefully etched plaque marked it as the White Room. The closed door gave her a moment of pause as she considered that perhaps Jace had finished his call and wasn't there anymore.

Still, rather than walk down the hall a second time, she opened the door and found Jace sitting with a tall, bald man. Black framed glasses sat on the round table in front of them. And when the man turned at the sound of the door opening, she saw his face.

His aristocratic nose, high cheekbones, strong chin. He might have shaved off his hair, but she'd seen enough pictures in her lifetime to recognize her father.

Her lungs stopped taking in air. Her mouth fell open.

Jace rose. "It's not what you think."

"I don't think anything." She'd been having kind thoughts about Mark Hinton since her talk with her mom. And suddenly here he was. Head shaved, glasses probably disguising his identity enough that he could use a fake name and fly anywhere he wanted in a private plane that landed on a private airstrip.

Son of a bitch. Her self-centered, selfish, mean-spirited father had faked his own death.

As confusion became anger, she turned to leave the room, needing to get the hell out of there before she said something she'd regret. Or, worse, *her father* would try to explain why he was alive when he was supposed to be dead.

Jace caught her arm. "You can't leave until you hear the whole story."

"Why? So I'll keep my mouth shut? The way I have to keep everything I see with you a secret?" She shook her head, then looked at the ceiling. "I am such an idiot."

"You're not an idiot. This is a complicated situation."

She glanced at her father, wearing a tux, obviously intending to attend the ball, as if nothing was wrong, as if nothing was off or amiss or weird about him disappearing for months.

"Complicated situation, my ass. He—" she nodded at her dad "—wanted something so he set things in motion to get it. And you—" she looked back at Jace "—obviously helped him."

"No! I didn't know. I suspected and called his private cell but he didn't answer. So, I told myself I was just imagining things."

"But you suspected?"

Jace ran his hand along his forehead as if warding off a headache. "I suspect a lot of things. I'm a bodyguard. That's part of my job."

"He didn't know." Her dad rose and approached her. "And I'm sorry I put everybody through this, but the real point is, I made a mistake not being in your life, the lives of all three of my kids. But I needed an opening, a way to ease the three of you into my world. I knew if I just walked into your life, asking for a chance to have a relationship, you'd reject me, and even if you didn't, you'd be overwhelmed by the money, the press, the bodyguards. This way, with you thinking you were inheriting instead of meeting me, you—"

"No!" She rounded on him. "I don't want to hear it. You abandoned me. Now, you've made a fool of me. And my mom." She stopped as a new area of concern hit her. "My God! What is my mom going to say!"

Then she remembered that her mom had been missing since they'd arrived. She'd gotten a phone call and disappeared. She'd insisted on staying at a hotel in New York, entertaining herself, being by herself—

She squeezed her eyes shut. "She knows, doesn't she?"

"Yes. I told her after Jace took you to New York. She met me there."

She faced Jace. He spread his hands helplessly. "I did not tell him we were in New York! I don't know how he knew."

Her father said, "I love your mother and I want her back in my life, too…"

She pressed her fingers to her temple. "Oh, my God. I can't even take this in."

She whirled around and raced toward the door.

Jace said, "Wait, Charlotte!"

She whipped around again. "No. You knew how I felt about my father. How could you have kept your suspicions to yourself? You didn't even give me a chance to consider that he might be alive, to mentally prepare for this—" She pointed at her dad. "I think that's proof where your loyalties lie and it's not with me."

She headed out of the room again, moving faster this time. She didn't care if she pulled the seams of her beautiful white gown. She just wanted the hell out of there without the pain of having to hear any more from her dad. Or Jace. No wonder he wouldn't even consider a real relationship. Deep down inside he probably knew her dad would show up and she'd be gobsmacked.

At the entrance, she told the doorman that she was with Jace MacDonald's party, leaving early, and would he please summon her car. Happy to help, he called Jace's driver.

She waited ten minutes, afraid Jace would catch her, then suddenly realizing he wouldn't. Like Seth Simon, her father was a lost soul. Taking care of him was part of the job Jace was so good at. Fixing awkward situations, helping lost souls, was what he did best.

He wouldn't come after her. She wasn't that important. She was a temporary fling.

The limo drove her to Grandma Jean's estate. In fifteen minutes, she'd packed and was in the backseat again, her luggage in the trunk. Instructing the driver to take her to the airport, she sat back against the seat, too angry to cry. She got a commercial flight to New York, stayed awake most of the trip and took a cab from the airport to Jace's condo.

She packed again, taking the clothes she'd brought from Pittsburgh and leaving everything she'd bought at Iris's on Jace's bed.

Then she headed to Pittsburgh. It wasn't until she was home, in her own shower, that she let herself cry.

But not for long. Angry with her father, she wouldn't cry over him. Accustomed to her mom loving her crazy, selfish father, she'd almost accepted that her mom probably didn't see the craziness of this whole mess.

And Jace…

She couldn't believe she'd trusted him.

Jace ran after Charlotte until he saw the family limo driving away and realized he'd never catch her. He threw his head back and groaned, watching her drive off. Then he made his way back to the white room.

He had an enormous PR problem on his hands.

"Do you really think you're just going to walk into that ballroom, dance with Penny and pretend the past few months haven't happened?"

"I don't see why not. I have a reputation for being quirky. I've also spent all those months on an island not calling anyone, not using the internet, just staying in the house I typically hide in. I'm done. I want to be among people again."

"I thought you said you needed this charade to get your kids together."

"I did."

"Yeah, well, your charade pretty much cost you Charlotte. She's never going to recover from this."

"Or trust you."

"What happens with me is irrelevant." Even as he said the words, he knew they weren't true. His ex might have done a number on him, but *he'd* hurt Charlotte. A woman he loved so much he hadn't even realized it was happening.

"Is it?"

That might be a good question, but this was none of Mark's business. "My job is to protect you and right now my instincts are screaming that you're announcing yourself the wrong way. I don't think Charlotte will call the press and tell them you're alive, but if she does…then what?"

"Then I hold a press conference."

"And what about the third heir? Exactly how to do you expect to have a conversation with the child we haven't yet found, with him or her knowing you faked your death?"

Mark ran his hands down his face. "There are complications that would arise and make that impossible."

"Make what impossible? A conversation?" Furious now, Jace said, "For once, why don't you tell me everything. Not pretend, not hint, not insinuate. Flat out tell me. So maybe I can help you."

Mark squeezed his eyes shut. "Because Danny Manelli is my son."

Jace fell to the chair behind him. "Oh, hell." He let his breath out in a long, slow stream, then said, "Why the devil did you make him the attorney for your estate?"

"I wanted him to see everything, to meet his sisters, to know everything before I popped into his life and told him one of his one-night stands resulted in a child."

"What?"

"My son has a child that he doesn't know about." Mark pulled in a long breath. "That's really what started this. I found out Danny had a child and absolutely couldn't let him go through life not knowing his own son the way I hadn't known mine."

Jace rose. "You'd better get your ass to New York tonight and set up a meeting with the partners at Waters,

Waters and Montgomery as soon as you get there to explain all of this."

"What are you going to do?"

"As involved as I am with the estate, now that I've seen you and talked to you in person, I'm pretty sure I have to at least tell Danny, as attorney for the estate, that you're alive. I might also be duty bound to tell the authorities that you're alive. But I'll give you a day." Thinking it through, he took a long breath. "Because I shouldn't have to do any of that. You should. You should call Waters, Waters and Montgomery and let them tell you how you can announce you're alive without getting arrested for fraud or whatever law you broke faking your death."

"Jace, I didn't even go online the whole time I was supposedly lost. I could claim I didn't know the world assumed I was dead. If there are fines or costs, I'll pay them. Don't worry. I set it up so I won't get in trouble."

"You'd better hope."

Mark nodded. "I'm more concerned about my kids." After a brief pause, he said, "And what about Charlotte?"

"That's something you're going to have to figure out on your own."

"I'm not talking about me. I'm talking about you. She loves you."

Jace sniffed a laugh. "Yeah. She does. And I realized tonight I probably love her, too. But right now, she undoubtedly hates me."

"She needs you."

Jace slammed his hand on the table. "Do you listen to anything anybody tells you? This little charade of yours made it so she won't ever trust me again."

"But you are trustworthy, Jace. You always have been. You just need to talk to her, explain things."

Jace gaped at him. "Are you kidding me? She's not even going to let me in her door!"

"Go, anyway."

Jace squeezed his eyes shut. He wanted to. He could not see a future without her in it. But worse, he hated having her think he'd betrayed her. He hadn't. He *wouldn't*.

The news was filled with the astounding discovery that Mark Hinton was alive. At her desk in her office in Pittsburgh on Monday morning, Charlotte scoured every article to see if her name was mentioned.

Not once did she show up.

In the process of searching for her name, making sure she was being kept out of this mess, she unintentionally read her dad's explanation. His boat had wrecked. He'd gotten to an island. Not a lie. He'd stayed on the island where he had a tiny home, enjoying the privacy. Also not a lie because his nearest neighbor was miles away. Most didn't know who owned his house, or even that there was a house that far up the mountain.

He'd stayed off the internet. Didn't watch the news and in general simply did not know the world thought he was dead.

When asked how he felt about his heirs dipping into the estate, he'd happily announced that he was thrilled to have his children back in his life. That the unfortunate belief that he was dead had brought his family together and he was ecstatic. Anything he owned, they owned. There would be no more separation.

The partners at Waters, Waters and Montgomery had issued a statement that they were happy Mark was alive, but Danny Manelli had been unavailable for comment.

She stared at the paper, beside the stack of tabloids she'd read, for the first time in her life totally adrift. Her mom had called her and she'd made peace with the fact that she was in Mark's life for good. It had been what her mom wanted Charlotte's entire life. She'd be pretty selfish not to be happy for her mom and wish her well.

She groaned thinking about holidays. No matter what kind of idiot Mark Hinton was…she would be eating Christmas dinner with him.

But none of the articles or interviews had talked about Jace.

Why would they? He was an employee. The background guy.

Such a weird combination of absolute loyalty for his clients and distance with everyone else.

She didn't want to miss him. But she did.

Didn't want to long for him, but Sunday night she'd ached for him.

She looked at the picture of her mom and Mark on the front page of the paper and shook her head. Her mom had waited forever for Mark to come to his senses. With no guarantees. No idea he'd one day change his mind. Just a strong, unmovable hope.

She'd say Jace didn't deserve that kind of hope. But Mark Hinton hadn't deserved it, either.

Still, her mother wasn't a world-class executive. She hadn't put her heart and soul into her career. She'd put them into Mark.

All her life, Charlotte had considered her mom a chump of sorts. And Charlotte didn't want to be a chump, waiting forever for a man who didn't know he wanted her.

But a part of her, the part that had loved Jace's wit, his strength, the way he let her be herself… That part of her wept and mourned, though it seemed crazy to pine for a guy who'd kept reminding her what they had was temporary.

But she did.

Every damned hour of every damned day.

Still, one morning she knew she'd wake up and he wouldn't be the first thing she thought of. He wouldn't cross her mind when she got into her truck or pulled up to a jobsite. She wouldn't remember him following her around, pretending to be her assistant, the dinners he'd made or the Broadway shows they'd seen.

She'd be Charlotte again. Single executive, looking for "The One," even though she was fairly certain she'd found him, and he hadn't wanted her.

CHAPTER FIFTEEN

JACE HAD HIS cleaning service change his sheets when he got home on Monday night, but he still smelled Charlotte on his pillow.

He'd thought and thought about everything she'd said the night of the ball in Scotland. He knew she believed he'd had a bigger part in Mark's charade than he had. Though he should be able to explain, the truth was he wasn't sure how. He'd never told her he loved her. He'd never given her any reason to believe he ever would. Now, suddenly, after her dad shows up and Jace *needed* her forgiveness, he was going to tell her he loved her? And think she would believe that he'd realized it ten minutes before Mark showed up and their world had exploded?

He'd spent Sunday working to ensure her name didn't appear in any of the press releases Waters, Waters and Montgomery issued and that Mark didn't mention her name at his press conference.

He managed the one thing Charlotte had always wanted but he'd believed she could have. He'd given her her life back.

At least for the past two days.

Tuesday morning, he walked into his office suite—a reception room, two offices used by whichever of his team leaders needed space, one long, utilitarian conference room and his huge office.

"Good morning, Patty."

"Good morning, Mr. MacDonald."

He picked up the mail. "I've told you repeatedly to call me Jace."

She perked up even more, though Jace wasn't sure how that was possible. "I like the formality of calling you Mr. MacDonald. You're the boss, the guy in charge, owner of everything we survey…"

"Patty, I can see the whole of Manhattan from the window behind you. I don't own everything I can survey."

She laughed. "Such a kidder."

He sighed and headed for his office. She meant well. And he was a grouch. Might as well own it.

"Wait, Mr. MacDonald—"

He closed his eyes, took a breath and said, "What?"

"There's a man in your office."

He faced her. "You probably should have told me that first."

She giggled. "Yeah. Probably. It's Mark Hinton."

He held back a groan. "This day just keeps getting better and better."

He strode into his office with ultramodern furniture in shades of beige and coral, and uncomfortable visitors' chairs so no one stayed too long. "What did you break now, Mark?"

Mark rose from one of the coral-colored chairs shaped like a scoop. "I've broken nothing. And, in fact, I think I'm finally beginning to fix things. Leni and her parents have totally accepted me."

On his way to his desk, he leafed through his mail. "Only because they are nice people. Charlotte hates you. Danny is humiliated. He thought he'd earned the position as attorney for your estate. To find out he was your son and being bamboozled mortified him."

"He'll come around. I have a plan."

Jace groaned. "I don't want to hear any more of your plans."

"That's fine. I'm not here to talk about Danny. I'm here to talk about Charlotte."

Jace sat. "I have a guy keeping an eye on her. No one in her face, but men investigating the people who come and go in her life." He looked Mark in the eye, communicating that he'd better not argue. "That's the best we can do without her noticing us."

To Jace's horror, Mark laughed. "Oh, if you're nebbing into her business, she's noticing. She simply hasn't pounced yet." He shook his head. "She's a pistol. I adore her."

Jace stared at him. "You're crazy. You know that?"

"Of course I know that. But I'm not crazy as much as eccentric. And maybe forced to do things that seem wrong because I had to protect myself and my family." He sat back and tried to get comfortable in the scoop chair designed to make him say his piece and get the hell out. "But now I have you. Your team is top-notch. You know when to step in or when to step back. Your guys guard without getting in the way." He smiled. "Which makes you also sort of responsible for me feeling it's okay to come out into the world again."

"Peachy." He stifled the urge to sigh heavily. "My staff and I are thrilled. Unless there's something specific you need, I'm busy."

"Well, there is a little something that I need to talk to you about."

Jace leaned back in his chair. *Here we go.*

"I hate what you did to Charlotte."

Jace bounced forward and almost across the desk. "What *I* did to Charlotte? You have got to be kidding."

"Not kidding. I know I was the perpetuator of the whole fake-my-death thing that infuriated her. But I didn't lure her to trust me, romance her and then drop her like a hot potato when things got tough."

"I didn't do that." But he had. Sort of. Not intentionally. And not so damned cut and dry. "It might have seemed like that, but that's not how it went." He'd been on the verge of telling Charlotte he loved her, wanted her in his life, when Mark had shown up.

Mark growled. "I don't care how it went. I want you to apologize to her. I want you to somehow make it right."

"There's nothing I can do to make it right. Everything I say to her is going to look like I made it up to get myself off the hook for not telling her I suspected you were still alive."

Mark finally rose. "Say it, anyway. Tell her the truth and she'll believe you."

He headed for the door. Jace stood up. "No, she's too much of an overthinker. She won't buy it."

Mark didn't even bother to turn around. "Yes. She will."

Little pinpricks of annoyance ran along Jace's skin. As if there was anything he could do...anything he could say... to make up for—

What?

He hadn't really deceived her. He'd simply not told her that he suspected her dad was alive. But he hadn't been in on Mark Hinton's plan.

And that night he would have told her he loved her—

He did love her. He missed her so much he ached for her.

And she wasn't the kind of woman to throw her lot in with someone she didn't truly care for. So right now, she was hurting, too.

And why?

Why?

He knew she loved him. And he loved her.

He was more than willing to trust her with everything— his life, his money, his heart...

And he knew that deep down she'd always trusted him.

But a trickle of fear ran through his veins. He thought of Mary Beth, thought of how clueless he'd been that she hadn't wanted him in her life anymore. What he and Charlotte had had been deep and profound, but also new and fragile.

He could blame Mark for ruining it, but his inbred honesty knew that was a copout. The emotion of the moment in Scotland would have carried him along, would have allowed him to say, *I love you*, and then bumble his way into what came next.

In the cold light of day, he loved her so much that he wasn't sure he wouldn't have lost her even if Mark hadn't shown up. Blaming Mark allowed him to skirt his real issues. What if everything they felt was smoke and mirrors, a temporary thing that would wither like the grass in winter?

Could he lose the real love of his life and survive? Or was it better to pretend Mark had ruined everything and not have to face the misery of hearing Charlotte tell him it was fun while it lasted but she wasn't as interested as she'd thought she was?

The knowledge that he was a coward washed through him. He sucked in a breath, squeezed his eyes shut.

How could he fall in love with someone after such a short time?

How could he think that love would last?

But the bigger question dwarfed both of those…

How would he survive this loss if he never tried to talk to her, to say his piece, to win her back?

Wednesday morning, at her desk, happily ripping apart the budget of a newbie, Charlotte heard a commotion up the hall, but she paid no attention. That wasn't her job. If the receptionist had an iffy visitor, she was to call security—

Crap! Why did she have to think the word *security*? Now, her brain would whip off into one of those tangents about Jace. At first, she'd think good riddance. Then she'd remember how silly he could be, how fun, how sexy.

And from there it was a short trip to remembering—

"Tell your receptionist it's okay for me to be here."

She blinked. That was his voice—

She looked up. And that was him, standing in her open doorway.

After the train of her thoughts she wouldn't be surprised if she'd conjured him or summoned him. Or maybe her thoughts had turned to him because he'd been in the building, on his way up the elevator, and her sixth sense about him had kicked in.

She automatically said, "It's okay, April. I know this guy."

But as April shook her head and walked off in a huff, Charlotte's spunk returned.

"If you're here to tell me my dad wants to see me, get out. We had a chat. I'm pretending he's the new guy my mom is dating. We may never fix the other stuff but at least I can be civil to him if my mom has a Memorial Day picnic."

"I'm not here to get you to see your dad."

"Okay, then, if you're here to tell me I need a bodyguard, you can save your breath. As you can see, I'm fine."

"You're fine because your name hasn't leaked. Right now, in New York somewhere, there's a smart reporter who is looking into everything there is to know about your mom because she and Mark are clearly an item. Nine chances out of ten, that reporter has already found you. She's just trying to figure out if there was a connection between Mark and your mom around the time of your conception. It's only going to take one credit card receipt for you to be outed."

"If she's got a suspicion, I'm surprised she hasn't published yet."

"A tabloid would have. This smart cookie probably works for the *Times*. She'll have all her ducks in a row and when she writes the story there will be no turning back for you."

She huffed, but her insides quaked. She wasn't afraid of a reporter. Wasn't afraid of the world discovering she was Mark Hinton's daughter. The man was a nut case. Most people who found out would feel sorry for her.

Jace caused her trembling. He looked gorgeously masculine in his jeans and T-shirt. No leather jacket on this warm May day. And boots. The man wasn't a cowboy, but he could wear a boot.

Unfortunately, he was here for her father. Or the family…whatever. There wasn't an estate anymore. There was just money and a crazy dad who clearly needed someone like Jace to organize for him.

She returned her attention to the really bad budget of the newbie. "Okay. I get it. I've been warned. You can go."

He stayed lounging in one of the two comfortable chairs in front of her desk.

He said nothing for so long that she growled. "What!"

"I miss you."

Her heart leaped but her brain shifted into fifth gear with reminders of how he'd kept her out of the loop about her dad, always told her he wasn't the settling down kind. She had three long days of getting over him under her belt. Did she want to let one arbitrary comment destroy all that?

"Get out."

He stayed put.

"I'm serious."

"I'm serious, too. I love you. I think I loved you from the second you tried to give me the heave-ho out of your construction trailer."

The memory rose, swift and clear. As if it was yesterday, she saw him in the black overcoat and mud-covered Italian loafers. It hurt her heart especially because he'd slid in the

I love you. The words she'd longed to hear when they were together. The words she kept telling herself weren't coming.

"If the first time you say you love someone is in the middle of trying to get her back, it doesn't count. It could be a tactic."

He sighed. "Always thinking."

"It was not thinking that got me into this mess."

"Oh, we did a lot of thinking. A lot of wondering what it would be like to kiss and touch and finally make love. The way I see it, thinking got us into this mess."

"Okay. You agree it's a mess."

"What about life isn't a mess? Life's a complicated roller coaster. Things go our way sometimes. Things don't go our way others. It's up and down and crazy. That's why I want someone I can trust with me for every second of it."

Oh, he knew how to get to her. He'd made her picture it.

She stared at the budget screen, not seeing a word or a number. "You may be able to trust me. But as we both witnessed, I can't trust you."

"I'm here to tell you that you can."

She laughed, still refusing to look at him. She didn't want to see those dark sexy eyes. Didn't want them to lure her into something that was oh-so-wrong for her.

"Well, I say I can't trust you. And I'm ordering you out. If you don't leave, I'll call security."

To her disappointment, he sighed and rose. "Okay, I'll leave."

Her heart stuttered. She really, really did not want him to go. She wanted every word he said to be true. She wanted him to love her and she wanted to be able to trust him the way she had when they were in New York—

Her usually intelligent brain told her to call him back. To tell him she loved him, too. And wanted him in her life, which was so much better than needing him.

But she stared at the computer screen, her eyes filling

with tears of confusion. How could she love a man who'd kept secrets? Who betrayed her?

Call him back.

Call him back.

No.

She said no in her brain, even as she glanced sideways at the door, but he wasn't on his way to the door. He was heading to her desk. He rounded it, caught the top of her chair and spun it around so she faced him. Then he slid one arm under her legs and the other around her back and lifted her out of her seat.

Her breath hitched. A laugh bubbled but couldn't come out over the screech of her protest. "What are you doing?"

"I'm taking you somewhere we can talk. Somewhere that you can't threaten to call security."

"Jace!"

He walked out the door, up the hall, into reception.

Everywhere he carried her, people rose from their desks, craned their necks, followed them, confused but also curious.

"Stop. You're making a spectacle."

"I don't care. I love you. We're talking this out."

April all but swooned.

Charlotte's heart did a little melting itself. Still, she was supposed to be angry with him...wasn't she?

He hit the down button for the elevator. The employees of Kaiser and Barclay stared at them.

"Isn't one of you going to save me?"

An accountant stepped forward. Jace laughed. "Seriously? I'm like three times your size." He caught Charlotte's gaze. "And I'll fight for my woman."

The melting of her heart became like a warm puddle of happiness.

The elevator came. They stepped in.

Someone yelled, "Security is on their way."

Jace said, "Tell them not to waste time coming up here. We'll be on the first floor before they get up this far."

The door closed. "You can put me down."

"Nope."

The feeling of being held by him, her arms looped around his neck—for safety, not because they wanted to be there—the scent of him invading her space, all hit her at once.

"This isn't funny."

"Of course it is. But that's how we are. I could have sent you eight million roses and you wouldn't have cared. You wanted me to make a big move? I've made it. I showed your entire company that I love you and will go to great measures to keep you. If you want to talk about trust, that's a conversation I'm willing to have. Maybe ground rules would help."

She laughed and playfully slapped his shoulder. "If we have to have ground rules to have a conversation, that's the definition of distrust."

He caught her gaze. "So, you admit there's an us?"

Her soul got on its knees and begged her not to throw this away. To take the olive branch. To love him and trust he would love her.

"There's always been an us."

The elevator doors opened. Three blue-shirted security officers greeted them.

"Stand down," Charlotte said. "He's with me."

All three frowned.

"I'm her bodyguard," Jace said, grinning.

She shook her head. "I'm one of the Hinton heirs. My dad's the jackass who let everybody think he was dead."

Jace laughed.

"There. Let that little reporter from the *Times* chew on that."

"You're accepting who you are?"

"If I want you to be honest, I have to be honest, too. Especially if we're going to start something."

"Oh, we started something a long time ago," Jace said, stepping out of the elevator.

The security guards parted and made a way for them. One shook his head and headed off to the left. The other two gave them puzzled frowns.

"You can put me down."

"No, I think I like holding you."

"I think you like showing off your muscles."

"That, too."

She laughed. The automatic doors opened. Everybody in the lobby watched them go through and out onto the street. His SUV, black with tinted windows, was right outside the door.

"I see you brought the security mobile."

"Not denying who I am, either."

He set her down, opened the door for her. But she didn't slide inside. She studied his face for a few seconds, saw the sincerity, but also her guy. The One.

Her future suddenly stretched out before her, different, better than anything she'd ever imagined...even if Mark Hinton was her dad.

Her lips twitched, then rose. Then she leaned in and kissed Jace.

When she pulled back, he said, "A smart woman would have led with that."

She threw her head back and laughed. "This is going to be fun."

She got into the SUV, and as he closed her door, Jace said, "Count on it."

EPILOGUE

THAT CHRISTMAS EVE Jace and Charlotte walked down the Main Street of Leni's hometown—Mannington, Kansas—arm in arm, their boots kicking the fat fluffy flakes of snow piling up on the sidewalk.

"I feel like I'm in a Norman Rockwell painting."

Jace glanced around. Everything in his life was perfect. He had plenty of work for his crew. He'd learned how to relax. And he had the woman of his dreams. The right woman this time. Charlotte was wonderfully honest. And beautiful. And fun.

"Or maybe one of those Christmas movies."

She took a long drink of the crisp air. "My sister is a dynamo."

"That she is."

"Do you know she and Nick are building a skating rink?"

He laughed. "Doesn't surprise me. Nick's a pretty good skater. Leni actually competed."

"Nothing about Leni surprises me."

"She did get the whole family to *her* hometown for Christmas."

Charlotte's voice lowered to a whisper. "Not Danny."

"Not yet, but Christmas isn't actually until tomorrow," Jace corrected. Still, Danny had always been the wild card, the one whose life Mark had felt needed fixing enough that it was worth bringing all three of his kids out of hiding. The one who hated Mark meddling in his life.

But Leni and Charlotte had also started out disliking him. Charlotte still kept her distance, though she'd had some good times with Mark that summer when Jace talked her into going out with him and her mom on his fishing boat.

The whole family was learning that life wasn't black and white, good or bad.

It was what you made it.

And Charlotte loved what she was making of hers with Jace.

Big, strong, handsome Jace. Absolutely positively The One.

* * * * *

FORTUNE'S GREATEST RISK

MARIE FERRARELLA

To Charlie
Whose Kisses Still Make the World Fade Away.

Prologue

If anyone would have said to him seven months ago that twenty-nine was far too old for someone to actually feel homesick, Dillon Fortune would have laughed them off. In his opinion, being homesick was an emotion associated with preteens who were spending a month or so away from home surrounded by a bunch of strangers at a sleepaway camp for the very first time.

And yet, here he was, a grown man, feeling a deep, penetrating wave of homesickness.

Granted, he had been in Texas for more like seven months. And, yes, instead of being alone amid a bunch of strangers, he'd come out here with two of his brothers, Callum and Steven, as well as one of his sisters, Stephanie. But, when all things were considered, he had to admit, if only to himself, that he was most definitely homesick.

Very homesick.

Yes, Rambling Rose, Texas, was a beautiful place as well as an up-and-coming, flourishing town. A town that he and his brothers were heavily involved in building up, thanks to the construction company that the three of them owned. But if anyone would have asked him, Dillon would have had to say that his heart was back in Fort Lauderdale, Florida.

Dillon wished that the rest of him could be back there, as well.

But he had always been raised to believe that commitments, especially to family, came first and he couldn't very well just take off for Fort Lauderdale now, even though he really wanted to. He was committed to these various projects. His brothers were counting on him and he knew he couldn't just leave before all the projects were completed and up and running.

Granted, the new pediatric center and the veterinary clinic were now both open and successful. The pediatric center had even been christened, so to speak, on its very first day. A pregnant woman—Laurel, last name unknown—had gone into labor during the clinic's ribbon-cutting ceremony. She was quickly rushed to a hospital in San Antonio with a NICU just in time, and gave birth there.

But the same success story couldn't be written about The Shoppes at Rambling Rose, a collection of high-end stores which were built on the site of what had once been the town's five-and-dime.

Not that any of the shops had failed—it was too soon to say something like that—but so far, they hadn't been able to find their dedicated audience yet, people who could be seen as a loyal clientele. He had no doubts that that would happen—Callum had a knack for picking places that were just *waiting* to become successes. But Dillon had no desire to remain here waiting for that magical moment to transpire.

This part, he thought, could easily go on without him.

Yet here he was, sitting in his car outside of the town's newly renovated wellness spa, another one of Fortune Brothers Construction's projects. Paz Spa was going to be opening its doors for the first time this week. Somehow, his brothers had managed to talk him into coming here today for a final walk-through. That way, they said, he could make sure that the spa was all set to go full speed right out of the starting gate. Reluctantly, because he had never been able to say no to his brothers, he had agreed, even though this wasn't his kind of thing. He was more of a design guy, not a people person. Nevertheless, here he was, trying to get himself to leave the shelter of his vehicle and walk into the spa.

If the spa faltered for some reason, then that might adversely affect their biggest project. The new town hotel—their company's pride and joy— was still on the drawing board. So many factors could get in the way of it becoming a reality.

Again.

There were two different ways of thinking regarding all these new projects he and his brothers had undertaken. The town's older local residents weren't very gung ho when it came to building this new hotel, but the newest segment of the population, the millionaires who had taken up residence within the gated community of Rambling Rose Estates, were definitely all for it. Truthfully, The Shoppes had been built with these people in mind, in the hopes that eventually, with enough prodding, the locals would grudgingly come around. At least they seemed interested in Ashley, Nicole and Megan's farm-to-table restaurant, Provisions,

which was set to open within the next few weeks—
barring any unforeseen complications.

His brothers were totally convinced that they
could get the locals to change their minds, but as
for him, well, Dillon had never viewed things in the
same sort of positive light that Callum and Steven
did. His take on the matter was that the construction company had done all it could here and they
should move on to another town.

Preferably one in Florida.

But then, Dillon supposed he had never been as
dynamic or optimistic as either Callum or Steven
were. Truth be told, Dillon would have been the
first to admit that he had always had a far more
cautious view of life.

However, he was a Fortune and his brothers
made it clear that they were depending on his clear
eye to make sure that all systems were "go" before
the spa's grand opening.

In other words, they had faith in him.

All things considered, Dillon thought, he would
rather have a root canal than face what he was
about to endure now.

Well, it wasn't going to get any better or any
easier to face with him just sitting here, Dillon
thought, finally opening his door.

Swinging out his long legs, he let his boots hit

the ground and he got out of his car. The ache he felt in his shoulders reminded him that he hadn't been exercising lately the way he was accustomed to doing. This project had caused him to let a lot of things in his life slide lately. That was going to have to change.

Closing the car door behind him, he locked it. As he walked toward the entrance of Paz Spa, a line out of an old Tennyson poem he'd once read way back in elementary school suddenly popped up in his head.

"Into the Valley of Death / Rode the six hundred."

Given the challenge of the task ahead, it certainly seemed to capture his mood appropriately enough.

Chapter One

Yup, those were definitely butterflies in her stomach, Hailey Miller decided. They were not only flapping their wings, they were also multiplying like crazy.

Not that she anticipated anything going wrong, the petite spa manager thought, nervously combing her fingers through her long blond hair and pushing the wayward strands away from her face and off to one side. She was just focusing on everything going exactly right for this tour. This was her first time in the role of manager, and she wanted it to be perfect.

That was the reason she had dressed with such

care this morning instead of throwing on a pair of jeans, a comfortable shirt with the spa's logo on it and, like as not, a pair of her favorite boots the way she had done these last few weeks. No, today was special and that was why she had put on a flowing pastel blue dress and a pair of strappy high heels, the ones that flattered her legs. In her opinion, her legs were her best feature and she needed all the help she could get to look her best this morning.

Because this morning she was showing Dillon Fortune around the spa and Dillon Fortune was the man to please, Hailey thought.

The spa, located across the street from the Shoppes, had been his special project and he was the contractor responsible for the spa's newly renovated look. In addition, the man was jaw-droppingly good-looking if the photographs she had seen of him on the internet were any indication. Hailey had a feeling that someone who looked like that was accustomed to being surrounded with beautiful, intelligent women. She definitely didn't want the man to feel as if he was slumming when he conducted his tour through here.

Get a grip, Hailey. He's not going to care what you're wearing, or what you look like. The man's coming here to see what you've done to highlight all the work that was done on the spa.

Just as she pressed her hand against her turbulent stomach, Candace Allen, her new assistant, came hurrying toward her.

"He's here, Hailey," Candace breathlessly announced. "Dillon Fortune!"

Okay, showtime! Hailey took in one last big breath to steady her nerves.

She turned toward her assistant and in that moment saw probably the handsomest man in her near recollection walking in her direction.

Instantly she felt those butterflies of hers revving up for one massive, uncoordinated takeoff.

Even at a distance, she could see that Dillon Fortune looked far more handsome in person than his photographs had made him out to be—and that had been pretty damn near perfect.

Okay, Hailey, you can do this. This is nothing more than a courtesy walk-through for the guy who made all this possible.

So why did part of her suddenly feel as if she were trying to make her way across hot coals?

As Dillon Fortune drew closer, she decided that her fresh wave of nerves had to be due to the look on the man's lean, handsome face. The contractor looked distracted, as if he didn't really want to be here.

Why? Was there something wrong?

Walking up to Dillon and meeting him part of the way, Hailey put out her hand and gave him her widest, most welcoming smile. "Mr. Fortune, I'm Hailey Miller, Paz Spa's manager. I'll be the one giving you a tour of this lovely facility this morning."

Just for a moment, Dillon was caught off guard by the very attractive, animated woman standing before him. For such a petite woman, she had the largest, most expressive blue eyes he had ever seen. He found them almost hypnotic and just for a second, he forgot how much he didn't want to be here.

But then it all came back to him. His intense homesickness, how all of this—the touring, the glad-handing—just felt like such a waste of precious time.

His precious time.

Still, he knew he couldn't be rude. It wasn't this woman's fault that he was halfway across the country from where he wanted to be. And he could see that this perky manager was eager to show the place off to him. A place he felt it prudent not to point out that he was already familiar with, thanks to the fact that he had been the one who had drawn up the initial blueprints and then designed the spa's look from top to bottom.

He offered the petite blonde what he hoped passed for a smile.

"I guess you were the one who wound up drawing the short straw," Dillon told her. Belatedly, he remembered to shake the hand she was still holding out to him.

Hailey could only stare at the contractor. She had no idea what he was saying to her—or why. What short straw? "Excuse me, Mr. Fortune?"

Dillon didn't think he had said anything particularly mysterious. "Well, you obviously have better things to do three days before the spa's grand opening than dropping everything to give one of the people who renovated this place a tour of the exact same area."

Put that way, she didn't know if he resented having her show him around his own work, or if there was something else going on.

"Not really," Hailey answered uncertainly. "We all thought that you might like to see how the ideas all came together to create this rather inviting haven. Everyone here is very eager to have the spa's doors finally open so that our clients can come in and enjoy all the amenities that this place has to offer." If nothing else, she thought, she could be a saleswoman with the best of them.

"As you can see," Hailey continued, gesturing

around the wide-open reception area, "this was all finished with reclaimed wood and other natural materials. It's all extremely pleasing to the eye," she pointed out with pride.

"Now if you'll come this way," Hailey urged as she began to lead the way farther into the spa, "I'll show you some of the inner rooms that will be enjoyed by our clients."

She opened a door that led into a room with a massage table. A mural of a peaceful forest scene on the far wall added to the feeling of tranquility. "We offer various kinds of massage therapy to help our clients relieve some of the stress they've built up during their week. As I'm sure you know, a tense body causes mental stress and may often be responsible for sleeplessness, gastrointestinal distress and headaches, to mention just a few things. The right sort of massage therapy will allow our clients to de-stress and rejuvenate."

Hailey continued talking as she brought Dillon to another room painted in different colors. The main piece of equipment here was the same as in the first room. It all centered around a massage table, except here, there were two tables for the couples looking to reduce their stress levels together.

"I'm sure you'll agree that in this fast-paced life

we all lead, we could certainly use a little revitalization, not to mention a small precious island of
time where we can step back from our incredibly
busy lives and just take a deep breath and relax.

"And did you know that a good massage can
also improve your circulation? That means no
more cold hands and feet—if you have them, that
is," she quickly added in case he thought she was
insinuating that this was his problem. "Think how
good that would feel," Hailey added with another
bright smile. "Massage therapy can also help improve your flexibility, strengthen your muscles and
reduce your pain levels by releasing endorphins."

Her hand on his elbow, she gently guided Dillon toward yet another area.

"Now, right over here, Mr. Fortune, is where
we decided to put…"

Hailey continued with what turned out to be a
monologue for another good half hour, opening
various doors and explaining in vivid, glowing
detail what each area was for, be it a sauna, a tan-
ning salon or the aforementioned massage tables.
There were also large rooms where various classes
would be conducted.

"Giving massages is my specialty," she told the
contractor. "I actually began working in the wellness field as a masseuse."

She turned around to see how her one-man audience had received that piece of information. Looking at Dillon, she stopped talking for a moment, wondering if he had heard a single word she had said. He certainly didn't act as if he had. He hadn't made a single comment or said anything at all during the entire tour she had just conducted.

In fact, if she were to hazard a guess, Dillon Fortune was acting as if he would rather be *anywhere* else other than here.

Oh, he was being polite, she'd give him that, but the man was also being distant. *Extremely* distant.

And just like that, without any warning, she was five years old all over again. Five years old and desperately trying to engage her father by attempting to show him the new hairstyles she had so painstakingly fashioned for her favorite dolls. He'd been a workaholic who had never had time for her. All she wanted was just a little of his attention, but he was always too busy being successful to notice her. Eventually, she gave up trying.

Her father had had that same distant, removed look on his face that was now gracing Dillon Fortune's ruggedly handsome face.

Well, handsome or not, it wasn't good enough as far as she was concerned. Mentally resolved, Hailey decided to give it one last try. She was determined to engage Dillon Fortune on some level so she wouldn't feel as if she were talking to a wall.

Or to a man who just didn't hear her.

"You might have noticed," Hailey started again brightly, "but everything here at the spa has this really good smell about it."

Checking his phone for what felt like the tenth time since he'd arrived, Dillon looked up at his incredibly chipper tour guide. Had she just said something about smelling good, or was that just his imagination?

She was looking at him as if she expected some sort of a reaction from him. "Excuse me?"

"Scent," she repeated. "There's a really good scent here at the spa. That's not by accident," she assured him. "Finding just the right scent is all part of the experience here at Paz. We find that the right scent helps not just soothe our clients but it also invigorates them. We're planning to use some of these scents as part of our aromatherapy massages."

Hailey found herself talking fast now, trying not to lose his attention. To that end, she began showing him all the different bottles of the various scents that the spa had stocked up on.

"Care to take a whiff?" Hailey offered, uncorking one of the bottles. It was jasmine and was her personal favorite.

Dillon shook his head. "No, that's all right."

He was resisting, she thought and took it as a challenge. She was determined to use this latest example of therapy to get through to this man. These scents were meant to soothe a client, to help that person relax, and if there was ever an uptight person who needed to relax, it was definitely Dillon Fortune.

"C'mon," Hailey coaxed, "you can take one whiff, can't you?" She raised the bottle up for Dillon to get a better sense of what was in it. "Go ahead. Try it."

Seeing that she wasn't going to back off until he did as she urged, Dillon said, "Okay, fine, let me smell it." If he didn't breathe in too deeply, he'd be all right, he told himself. And then maybe she'd terminate this tour and let him leave.

Hailey held the open bottle up to his face and Dillon took a deep breath of the scent.

Perhaps a little too deep because the next thing he knew, he was sneezing.

A lot.

Waving Hailey back away from him, he accidentally hit the bottle she was holding up to him.

That in turn sent the entire contents of the bottle flying out and all over his shirt.

And just like that, Dillon found himself utterly drenched in jasmine oil.

Horror stricken by the unfortunate chain of events that had brought about this present dilemma, Hailey could only stare at the drenched man, wide-eyed.

"Oh, my Lord, I am *so* sorry, Mr. Fortune," she cried, embarrassed.

Dillon couldn't comment on her apology at first. Not because he was so angry but because he just couldn't stop sneezing.

Finally, all but wiped out thanks to his sneezing, Dillon could only hold his hand up, silently indicating that she had to stop saying she was sorry.

Damn it, Dillon thought, he smelled like a damn flower garden. Not exactly the scent he was going for, he thought.

He should have known better than to let this woman anywhere near him with that bottle. He wasn't normally prone to allergies, but there were certain scents that could just set him off. He had never investigated the matter or found out which particular scents affected him, but he was aware that there were some that could be devastating to him. So he normally steered clear of all of them.

He realized he should have stuck to that instead of allowing himself to be overwhelmed by a rapid-fire motor mouth.

Dillon waved the petite woman away.

Stunned and embarrassed, as well as somewhat annoyed, she moved back. She was still clutching the bottle. It was obviously empty now, but who knew, maybe whatever traces of the scent that could be left coating the sides of the bottle might still be affecting him.

As if reading his mind, Hailey tossed the bottle into a trash can on the other side of the room.

When she quickly rejoined him, Dillon was still sneezing, although not nearly as violently as before. Hailey realized that he was sneezing because the scent was still around him, thanks to the fact that it had soaked his shirt and was now probably on his chest.

Hailey instantly felt just awful. It was clear that Dillon was suffering.

"Again, I am so sorry," she apologized with feeling. "I didn't know you were allergic to the oils we used. Why didn't you say something?" she wanted to know.

It took Dillon a moment to clear his throat enough to be able to answer her. "Because I'm not allergic to oils," he informed her almost indignantly. And then he was forced to add, "I just have this reaction sometimes when I pass by a department store perfume counter... I mean, not that I go around inhaling perfumes, it's just that sometimes there are these overly zealous sales people spraying perfumes into the air and—"

Dillon had to abruptly stop because he'd started sneezing again.

Hailey saw only one solution to end the man's misery. "You're going to have to take off your shirt," she told him.

Her declaration caught Dillon totally by surprise. He stared at the spa manager, certain that he had misheard her. "Say what?"

"Your shirt. It's soaked," she pointed out in case he had somehow missed that. "Take it off," she instructed. It was half a request, half an order. "I can wash it for you."

The hell she could, he thought. He wasn't about to strip off his shirt.

"No, that's all right," he said as he began backing away. "I can just—"

"What, walk out of here smelling like a flower garden on steroids?" she asked him. There was a skeptical expression on her face. "I don't think so. At the very least, you might wind up attracting bees and being attacked by them. Besides," she said, pausing as Dillon sneezed again, "you're probably not going to stop sneezing until you're separated from that scent. It's clearly all over you, and in your case, apparently a little bit goes a long way. So don't argue with me, Mr. Fortune. Give!" she told Dillon, holding out her hand. "We have a small dedicated laundry area here at the spa. That's how we get our spa robes so clean and fluffy."

Dillon still looked really hesitant about surrendering his shirt.

"That's too much trouble," Dillon told her. "I can just—"

"Oh, I know what the problem is," she told him, realizing why he was hesitating so much—or at least she thought she knew why he wasn't taking his shirt off. After all, he was the spa's contractor. He didn't exactly want to be standing around in his semi-bare glory. The man looked as if he had hard muscles rippling under that shirt of his. Still, being shirtless would undoubtedly prove to be somewhat embarrassing for him. She could understand that.

"Oh?" Despite himself, Dillon's curiosity was aroused by what this woman *thought* she knew.

"Yes," Hailey answered enthusiastically. "You need something to put on," she declared as if she had the inside path to his mind. "Wait right here.

I'm going to go find something for you," she promised, rushing off.

"No, really," Dillon called after her, "you don't
have to go to any more trouble."

Especially since she had managed to cause all
this trouble just by taking him on a harmless tour
of the place to begin with.

But Dillon found he was talking to himself. Hailey Miller, eager beaver par excellence, had rushed
off in search of something for him to wear.

Dillon was about to cut his losses and just get
out of here before something else went wrong. But
his dearly savored escape was quickly aborted
when Hailey came hurrying back less than a minute and a half after she had left him standing there
dripping.

Instead of a T-shirt with the spa's logo splashed
across the front as Dillon would have anticipated,
she came back carrying something white and
fluffy.

"Here," she announced, holding up what looked
like one of the spa robes. "It's the best I could
come up with on such short notice—and it does
cover everything up." Although, she caught herself thinking, the man did have a really nice set
of muscles on him.

Looking at the robe, Dillon suppressed a groan.

Chapter Two

The next second, Dillon's mind did a complete 180 degree turn regarding what he was about to do. Although the bubbly manager was holding out the white robe for him to put on, Dillon decided he wasn't about to put it on.

"No, that's all right," he told Hailey, shaking his head. "I'll just take a pass on putting that on, thanks." He spared one final look at the offered garment, a disapproving expression on his face. "It's not exactly my style." He was rather conservative and the idea of stripping his shirt off in front of a total stranger left him with a bad taste in his mouth.

For a second, Hailey was puzzled. She looked at the robe she was holding out as if she'd never seen it before and reevaluated it.

And then it suddenly dawned on her.

"I didn't mean that you'd have to wear this when you leave," she clarified. "This is just something for you to put on temporarily while I'm getting that overwhelming scent washed out of your shirt. C'mon," she urged, taking a step toward him, holding out the robe again. "The sooner I take the shirt and get started, the sooner you'll get it back."

Dillon took a step back, and then another and another. For her part, Hailey just continued coming toward him. He felt like he was being stalked, while for her part, Hailey felt he was being unduly shy. She was only trying to help.

"No, I said it's okay. Really," he stressed. He didn't know how to make his position any clearer to her.

"But it's *not* okay," Hailey insisted. "I can't have you leaving here like this, with your first impression of the spa being the place where you wound up smelling like a garden full of jasmine on steroids. Consciously or unconsciously, you'll wind up hating the place. And who could blame you?" she told Dillon. "No, you need to take your shirt off so I can wash it," Hailey repeated, more force-fully this time.

He made one last attempt to beg off, but it was becoming very obvious to him that the woman didn't know how to take no for an answer. He opened his mouth to protest again, but before he could say a word, Hailey was already talking.

"Look, Mr. Fortune, I need your shirt," Hailey stated in a friendly but firm tone.

With every step that this persistent petite woman had taken toward him, Dillon had taken an equal step back. But now his back was against the wall—literally—and he had nowhere to go.

The only way he could get her to stop was to raise his voice and tell her to back off, although that really wasn't his style. However, as a last resort, he was willing to change his tactics.

And he was just about to, when the slender, vivacious spa manager cut him off at the knees. She raised up those big beautiful eyes of hers, aimed them directly at his and then fired the winning salvo.

Hailey said, "Please?"

And just like that, Dillon felt as if he'd been completely disarmed.

With a loud sigh, he conceded that he had lost the battle.

But how was he going to remove the shirt without feeling like a male stripper?

Hailey had always been blessed with the ability to somehow intuit what was going on in a person's mind. She applied that ability to the situation she found herself in at the moment. When she did it, she was able to see exactly why Dillon was still hesitating to give her the shirt.

For some reason, he was embarrassed. Dillon was obviously well built, but apparently he was not one of those men who was comfortable about flaunting it.

"Tell you what," she proposed. "There's no one around here so you can take your shirt off now. I'll even turn around to give you your privacy," Hailey offered, then smiled brightly at him. "You can't really do better than that, Mr. Fortune."

"Oh, I don't know about that," he countered, contemplating whether or not to tell her exactly *how* he could have done better. He could have passed up on this royal pain of a tour altogether, he thought. But saying that out loud sounded cruel to him, so he decided to let it go.

Rather than argue with him, Hailey deliberately turned her back on the man she was determined to impress.

"Any time you're ready," she cheerfully announced, holding the robe out to the side.

Keeping her back to him, Hailey took a single step backward toward the contractor so that the robe would be more accessible for him.

As she did so, because of the angle where he was standing, Hailey realized that she could see his naked upper torso. It was reflected in the side mirror near him and that image was ricocheted back to her via the larger mirror that ran the length of the left wall.

The end result was that she was able to see exactly what he undoubtedly hadn't wanted her to see—Dillon in all of his exceptionally sculpted glory.

Hailey's mouth suddenly went very dry. It became clear to her that she wasn't really able to swallow even if her life depended on it.

Dear Lord, the man was *magnificent*!

It was all Hailey could do not to utter the word out loud.

Belatedly, she realized that she had given herself away because in that first unguarded, unprepared moment, she had sucked in her breath the way someone sitting in the first car of a roller-coaster ride might do just as that car started to take its first plunge down the steep incline.

No matter how prepared she might have thought she was for the sight of this good-looking male, she was not *that* prepared. Seeing all those muscles, all those incredibly hard ridges, even secondhand because she was seeing them all reflected in the mirror, she was totally *un*prepared for the effect that gorgeous body had on her.

Maybe he hadn't heard her, Hailey thought, crossing her fingers.

The next moment, her hopes were dashed. She could see from the raised eyebrows in his reflection that he'd heard her. Moreover, he probably knew that she knew.

Dillon, however, made the decision to carry on the charade and pretend that he *hadn't* heard her sharp intake of breath. It was far safer that way. This way there would be no need to talk about anything.

Ignorance created a welcomed cloak that draped helpfully over everything, he thought as he thrust the shirt in the direction of Hailey's waiting outstretched hand. "Here's my shirt."

"I can tell," she answered, smiling to herself as her fingers closed over the surrendered article. Without turning around—she could tell by the sound that he was just shrugging into the robe she'd given him—Hailey started to hurry off. "I'll get this started. Your shirt will be the only thing in the washing machine so it should be done in no time flat."

It wouldn't be done fast enough for him, Dillon thought.

When Hailey returned to the area several minutes later, Dillon saw that her hands were empty. Still, he couldn't help asking her, "Is the shirt ready yet?"

"The spa's washing machine is the very latest model on the market," Hailey proudly told him. "But it's not *that* fast," she politely pointed out. "Again, I am *so* sorry about all this."

Had he been one of those spiteful people willing to blame everyone else for anything he had to put up with, Dillon would have let her continue beating herself up for dousing his shirt and causing him to practically sneeze his brains out. But to do so wouldn't have been right, or fair and he had too much of a conscience to indulge in that sort of behavior.

"It's not your fault," he told her. "The fault is mine. I wasn't paying close enough attention to what was going on. Like I said, sometimes I have an allergic reaction to certain scents. If I had been paying closer attention to what you were trying to show me, I would have realized that."

Hailey felt his admission opened up a door, leaving her free to talk. Maybe some good could come out of all of this, after all.

"You know, you did look a little preoccupied when I was taking you on that tour," she told him. Actually, he had looked a *lot* preoccupied, but saying that might have sounded as if she were criticizing him, so she left it at her initial statement. Instead, she diplomatically approached the subject she was attempting to broach. "Maybe you could stand to avail yourself of one of the spa treatments we offer here at Paz." Her enthusiasm grew as she continued, "I could personally set up an appointment for you and then—"

Dillon immediately stopped her before she could get carried away. "No. No, thank you. I'm good," he assured her.

The man was good-looking, but he definitely wasn't "good" in the sense he was trying to convey. He needed prodding, she thought.

"Are you sure? Because these treatments can be really helpful, Mr. Fortune. They're designed for the busy executive like yourself. Tell you what," Hailey continued eagerly. "If you feel a little uncomfortable about getting one of our special tailored massages, I would be more than happy to be the one who—"

"Nope, I'm fine," Dillon insisted, cutting her off. "It's all good, really. Thanks, but no thanks," he repeated, leaving the woman absolutely no wiggle room to talk him into anything.

The truth of the matter was he sensed that he could easily be attracted to this woman. The very last thing he needed—or wanted—was for that feeling to escalate. And *that* would be exactly what would happen if she put her hands on his back and torso to work the kinks out of his stiff, sore muscles.

"Okay," Hailey replied compliantly, "if you say so. But I want you to know that if you should decide to change your mind, the offer stands open anytime that you feel the need to try our method of—"

"Thanks, but I won't be changing my mind," Dillon informed her, cutting her off. "Don't worry about it," he stressed rather forcefully. "The only thing I want from you is—"

"Your shirt, yes, I am well aware of that," Hailey said, anticipating what he was about to tell her. She really didn't have to be a mind reader in order to know that.

"Well, yes, that, too," Dillon readily agreed.

"But what I was about to say is that I'd also like you to promise me that you won't mention this incident to my brothers. I doubt if the topic will come up," he added, stating the fact before she had an opportunity to, "but on the outside chance that it might, I'd really rather that they didn't find out about this unfortunate incident."

"Yes, of course. I won't say a word to anyone," Hailey promised him. "Your secret's definitely safe with me, Mr. Fortune."

Dillon laughed despite himself. "Considering everything that has just happened between us, I think you can call me Dillon," he told her.

A smile rose to her lips, so warm in scope that it fascinated him for a couple of moments.

"I'd like that," Hailey told him, then added his name, making what she said sound infinitely more personal. "Dillon."

He caught himself thinking that his name sounded almost lyrical as it came from her lips.

Wow, he was really getting carried away, Dillon upbraided himself. At best this was just a business meeting that had gone wrong, nothing more. Besides, as Hailey had already pointed out, his mind had been elsewhere, not here.

"Would your brothers really give you a hard time if they knew about this?" she asked, curious.

Hailey immediately backtracked when she saw Dillon's brow go up. She didn't want him getting the wrong idea. "Not that I'd ever mention any of this," she quickly added, trying her best to reassure him. "Because I'd never say a word. To anyone," she emphasized once again. "Really," Hailey stressed. "I just asked you that because I was curious about what it was like, having all those siblings around. People who you know you can always lean on, no matter what." That sounded like heaven to her. "How many siblings do you have again?" she asked, cocking her head.

He was doing his best not to get distracted again. There was something about this woman that tended to do that to him. Anyway, why would she want to know that? he couldn't help wondering.

"I have seven," he finally answered. He kept the fact that some were half siblings to himself. Continuing to remain cautious, Dillon watched the woman's face as he asked, "Why?"

Hailey shrugged. "No reason. I was just thinking that it had to be nice, having that many siblings around. You always have someone to talk to, someone to turn to for advice. I just have one sister," she told him. "And I have to admit that I always thought it would have been really great to come from a large family."

Dillon shrugged, thinking of the people who comprised his family and of some of the incidents that had occurred while he was growing up.

"It has its moments, I suppose," he admitted somewhat reluctantly.

"Like what?" she asked, her tone encouraging him to elaborate.

Damn, it was happening again. He was getting distracted. Why did this woman have that effect on him? She seemed so guileless...

He had to snap out of it! He really needed to be on his way.

Dillon glanced at his watch again, then at her. "Could you check to see if my shirt's ready yet?"

The man looked as if he were ready to jump out of his skin at any second, Hailey observed. She wondered if she'd said something to set him off.

His question had her snapping to attention. "Oh, right. Sorry, I guess I forgot about that," she confessed. "But you obviously didn't," she added with a smile. She could feel herself growing nervous again. "How could you, standing there in that robe?" she asked. "I didn't mean to go on like that," she apologized for what felt like the dozenth time since he had arrived at the spa. "I'll go right now and see if it's ready." She hurried off.

It wouldn't be ready, he thought. Not unless the

shirt somehow "knew" it had to dry itself after it had finished washing.

He glanced at his watch again. How much longer was he going to have to hang around this place waiting for his shirt to dry?

Not that being with this woman was any sort of actual hardship, he amended in all honesty. Under any other set of circumstances, he might have even welcomed the excuse.

But right now, he felt like a total idiot and standing around in this long fluffy robe just seemed to intensify that reaction.

It also upped the chances of someone coming in and seeing him looking like this.

He *really* wanted to get out of here.

Now.

Chapter Three

A while later, the dryer Hailey had put Dillon's newly washed shirt into was still running.

To check, Hailey pressed the pause button on the oversized machine and it tumbled to a noisy halt.

Opening the door, she fished out Dillon's shirt, ran her hand over the material and frowned. It still felt a bit damp. Not dripping, she conceded, but definitely damp. If given a choice, she knew that she wouldn't have wanted to put it on. The damp material would feel clammy against her skin.

Against *his* skin, Hailey corrected herself.

She was about to put the shirt back into the

dryer when she heard Dillon's deep voice coming from directly behind her.

"Is it ready yet?"

Surprised, she turned around. He'd followed her. She wouldn't have thought that he would. The laundry room wasn't all that hard to find, but coming here necessitated walking out into the hallway wearing that long, flowing fluffy robe—and being *seen* wearing it, something she'd gotten the very strong impression that he wanted to avoid.

The man *really* had to be anxious to get out of here, she thought.

Even so, Hailey felt she had to be honest with him. "No, not really." She looked down at the shirt as she spoke, and when her eyes raised, she noticed Dillon had crossed the floor and was now standing right beside her.

For some reason, being alone in the room with Dillon and envisioning him naked from the waist up beneath the spa robe made the hairs along her arms all stand up, almost at attention.

You're not being very professional, Hailey. You've had undraped men on your massage table before and it's never affected you.

Still, the appealing vision of Dillon Fortune that had popped up was a difficult one to banish from her brain.

"Let me see it," Dillon was saying. He put his hand out expectantly, waiting for his shirt.

"Okay." Hailey held the blue silk shirt out to him. "Go ahead, touch it," she coaxed.

The moment the words were out of her mouth, she realized how they must have sounded to him. They sounded like an invitation. Embarrassed, she cleared her throat. "I mean, you can see that it's still pretty damp," she told Dillon, avoiding his eyes. "If you give it a few more minutes—"

"That's all right," Dillon said, overriding the woman's protest. At this point, in order to be on his way, Dillon would have worn the shirt even if it were completely sopping wet.

His urge to bolt was so strong that he allowed the robe to drop off his shoulders. It fell to the floor as he slipped on his shirt. He was so intent on putting it on, he didn't see the startled look, immediately followed by an appreciative one, passing over Hailey's face. But she was very aware of it as she caught her reflection in the dryer door.

Damn, she'd already seen the man's sculpted torso, but seeing its reflection completely paled to viewing the man up close and personal like this. Hailey felt a wave of intense heat pass over her and it was all she could do to keep her knees from buckling.

How was this man walking around unattached and without legions of starry-eyed, eager women following him around, desperate for his attention? It made no sense to her.

Breathe, Hailey, breathe. He isn't interested in you that way. His desire to make a hasty exit makes that perfectly clear. Don't complicate matters by drooling on him.

Meanwhile, Dillon was still getting dressed. It was a little tricky, pushing his arms into the damp sleeves, but it was amazing what a man could do when pressured by a sense of urgency.

"The main thing," he told her, "is that that smell is gone."

As if to test his statement, Hailey leaned in toward his chest and took a deep breath. She wrinkled her nose a little.

"Well, actually, there's still a trace of it left," she told him. Wait. What was she doing, stepping so close to him and smelling him? Had she lost all sense of professionalism?

After a moment's hesitation, Dillon leaned back. "I—" He stopped, then started again, regaining his thoughts. With her so close, it wasn't easy. "It's good enough," he finally declared. "As long as it doesn't attract a swarm of bees, I'm ahead of the game."

"But if you just give it a few more minutes, Mr. Fortune…" she tactfully protested. In light of his obvious anxiousness to flee, she had reverted back to his surname, feeling that to call him *Dillon* was far too familiar right now.

"I'm already late for…something," Dillon said evasively.

That would explain his constantly looking at his watch and his phone while she had been taking him on the tour, she thought. The pang that went through her was involuntary. Did he have a hot date waiting for him? Or maybe he was going to be meeting up with his next conquest?

It was none of her business, Hailey silently told herself. Whoever it was, the person was obviously enough to distract him.

Hailey bent over to pick up the fallen robe and slung it over her arm as he finished buttoning his still damp shirt. It seemed to cling to every ridge, every ripple, she couldn't help noticing.

Keeping her face forward, Hailey fell into place beside him as Dillon started walking toward the front exit.

"Will we be seeing you at the grand opening?" she asked.

Focused on making his retreat, as well as on what time it was, Dillon hadn't heard her. But by the look he saw on her face, the woman was obviously waiting for some sort of response from him.

"What?" he asked, still walking as he tucked his shirt into his slacks.

"The grand opening, it's in a few days," Hailey prompted. "Will we be seeing you there?"

"Oh. Right. Yes, of course. Wouldn't miss it," he assured her a second before he made good his escape.

"I don't know about that," Hailey murmured under her breath as she watched him hurrying down the front steps. "You seemed to have missed the tour, even though you were physically here for it."

With a sigh, Hailey turned away from the spa's large double-glass doors.

"So? How did it go?" Candace asked.

Hailey's assistant seemed to materialize directly behind her the moment that the contractor had walked out of the building.

"It went," was all that Hailey allowed herself to say.

Candace frowned. "Well, that doesn't sound very good."

Hailey tactfully walked back her initial assessment. "It could have gone better," she amended. "I got the impression that Mr. Fortune's mind was elsewhere during most of the tour."

"His mind was probably on his next project," the young woman guessed.

Or his next conquest by the looks of it, Hailey thought. She had seen men preoccupied with the women in their lives, or the women they were about to have in their lives. Dillon had all the signs.

But, for the sake of the spa and things moving forward on that front, Hailey decided to agree with her assistant. "You're probably right. He was undoubtedly thinking about his next project. I guess I'm being just a little bit edgy."

Still, despite her pep talk to herself to the contrary, Hailey couldn't help being curious about who the person on the other end of Dillon Fortune's phone had been. Whoever it was was wreaking havoc in what otherwise seemed like Dillon Fortune's orderly world.

To her way of thinking, the butterflies that Hailey had experienced at the beginning of the week while she had waited to give the handsome contractor a tour of the spa were just a dry run for what she assumed she would be experiencing today, at the spa's official grand opening ceremony.

But oddly enough, she turned out to be wrong. To Hailey's surprise, when the big day came, she was completely calm.

Hailey had spent the days between then and now overseeing every single detail involved in the grand opening, then going over them twice, from the festive decorations to the extensive array of catered food. She'd even easily handled the last-minute shipments of some equipment. Mercifully, nothing rattled her.

She survived it all and when the big day finally did arrive, she was ready hours ahead of time. To her relief, the butterflies in her stomach seemed to remain subdued.

One of the first people to arrive to the festivities was Ellie Fortune Hernandez, Rambling Rose's mayor and Steven Fortune's recent blushing bride. As expected, Steven was at her side.

The mayor was scheduled to make an appropriate speech about how the spa was one of the projects that were already revitalizing the town and how she anticipated that this feeling would be on the upswing in the weeks to come, thanks to other projects that were in the works.

Waiting for the official ribbon-cutting ceremony to take place, everyone meandered around the front of the spa, availing themselves of the refreshments that were set up on tables before the front doors. Hailey was there to play hostess to the gathering crowd.

The slender dark-haired mayor and her six-foot-tall husband were still practically newlyweds. The striking couple definitely looked the part. Anyone looking at them could see that they still had that newlywed glow about them, although Hailey was willing to bet part of that glow was due to the fact that Ellie Hernandez was also pregnant. Her condition was just now beginning to show and no matter what the young mayor talked about, she seemed to be literally beaming.

Hailey found that she was both very happy for Ellie as well as just a little bit envious of the woman. Hailey could only imagine what it had to be like to be that in love with someone and to be that loved in return. In Hailey's estimation, anticipating the birth of a baby only added to that perfect scenario, increasing happiness by a hundredfold.

She sincerely doubted that it would ever happen for her.

Don't bite off more than you can chew, Hailey.

Just as she was about to say something to Ellie, the mayor beat her to it. Ellie came up to her, gestured about the immediate area and said, "So I see congratulations are in order."

Hailey's eyes dipped down to the mayor's waist. It was still very trim looking, but Hailey could see that it was just beginning to widen in order to accommodate its new little boarder.

"I hear the same can be said to you and your husband, Madam Mayor," Hailey responded, looking over Ellie's shoulder and catching a glimpse of Steven who was talking to someone.

Ellie offered her a serene smile, the kind that was so commonly seen gracing the faces of expectant mothers.

"Thank you," Ellie responded, her eyes shining. The next moment, the mayor's husband came up to join them. He rested his hand protectively on Ellie's shoulder.

"Don't you think you should be sitting down?" he tactfully asked her.

"I feel fine," Ellie assured him. "Really." Looking at Hailey, the mayor decided she needed to explain her husband's display of concern. He wasn't just being a typical nervous husband. "I had a touch of morning sickness earlier, but it's gone now. Really," she repeated, underscoring the word for her husband's benefit. "I'm not a fragile little flower, ready to wilt at the slightest provocation," Ellie insisted. "I never have been."

"Well, between you and me, Ms. Miller, my wife wouldn't say a word even if she was at death's door," Steven confided to Hailey.

Ellie laughed, waving away her husband's obvious concern.

"Luckily, I'm not," she insisted. "I—" She pulled up short as she pointed at two men who'd just arrived. "Steven, look. Aren't those your cousins?" she asked.

Hailey and the mayor's husband both turned to see who the mayor was referring to. The two men who had just walked up the spa's front steps definitely bore a striking resemblance to not only Steven but to several other Fortunes, as well.

But while the two men looked vaguely familiar to Hailey, Steven recognized the duo almost immediately.

"You're right," he agreed. "That's Adam and Kane Fortune. They're my Uncle Gary's two oldest sons," he said for Hailey's benefit since he knew she wasn't as up on the Fortune family tree as he and his wife were.

"Are they in the construction business, too?" Hailey asked, making what seemed like a logical assumption to her.

Steven laughed under his breath. "I think they probably think they are."

Hailey was trying to follow what Steven was saying. "So they're *not* part of your construction company?" she asked the mayor's husband.

She knew that Steven as well as Callum were both part of the same company that Dillon was part of. All of them had helped make the spa and several other new projects in Rambling Rose a reality in the last few months. The Fortune brothers were responsible for breathing life into the fading town.

"No," Steven said with feeling. "They're most definitely *not* part of the company. They're recently in from New York, but I think they're here to get the lay of the land and they either plan to eventually ask to join up with our company, or to form one of their own. To be honest," he confessed, "it's not exactly clear to any of us yet." And by *us*, Hailey knew he was referring to Callum, Dillon and himself.

The next second, Adam and Kane came up to join them.

"Hey, you guys did a great job here," Adam announced in a loud voice. "Too bad we didn't arrive here sooner so we could have gotten in on the ground floor with all this."

"There'll be more projects," Steven answered vaguely. "Right, Dillon?" he asked, looking over his cousin's shoulder toward his brother.

The latter had just arrived and was silently taking all this in.

Ellie turned around to face her brother-in-law.

"When did you get here? I don't remember seeing you when we got here a few minutes ago."

"That's because I just arrived," Dillon answered. For some reason, he felt it prudent to avoid Hailey's eyes. Instead, he nodded at his two cousins. "Kane. Adam."

"They were just saying how much they regret not having arrived in Rambling Rose sooner, that way they would have been here to help work on the various construction projects that are either going up or being renovated. Seems that they think this is a good place to invest in and build up," Steven told his brother pointedly.

Ellie picked up on her husband's tone and looked from him to his brother. "Am I missing something here, boys?"

Steven smiled. "Dillon's the family Cassandra," he explained. He continued despite the frown on Dillon's face. "You know, the woman in Greek mythology who always foresaw all the bad things that were going to happen."

"I didn't say something bad was going to happen," Dillon insisted. "I just don't wear the same rose-colored glasses that you and Callum do," he said flatly.

Hailey was trying to follow what was being

said. "You didn't want to renovate this spa?" she asked him.

Rather than attempt to deny the statement, Dillon tried to explain his thinking. "I just didn't think the town was ready for it. The bottom line was profit and I just didn't think that there was going to be that much profit to be made here, not the way my brothers did," he explained.

"Let me put it this way," Steven responded. "Callum and I see the glass half full and getting fuller by the minute, while Dillon here—" he glanced at his brother with an affectionate smile "—well, his glass is always half empty. Not only that, but the glass is leaking, as well. Am I right, Dillon?"

Dillon didn't believe in washing dirty laundry in public. And even if he did, this wasn't the time to do that or to argue, not at an important grand opening ceremony and definitely not in front of his cousins and a stranger, even a very attractive, sexy one. He decided to let the topic go. Any actual discussions he needed to undertake would be conducted with his brothers in private.

Smiling at his brother, Dillon inclined his head. "Close enough, brother," he said to Steven.

Chapter Four

Steven Fortune inclined his head in close to his wife's ear and whispered, "Looks like it's time, Madam Mayor." When Ellie turned her head to look up at him, he asked, "Are you ready, or do you need a little more time? I can stall if you'd like." Taking nothing for granted, Steven was concerned that, even now, his wife might be battling another wave of morning sickness.

Her husband's thoughtfulness touched her each and every time he displayed it. Once again, Ellie thought how very lucky she was that the two of them had found one another. When she thought of the odds against that happening, against her finding her soul mate, especially when she was already carrying another man's child, Ellie was nothing if not humbled.

Grateful, Ellie squeezed her husband's hand. "I'm fine," she told him.

Taking her at her word, Steven moved over toward Dillon and gave his brother a thumbs-up sign.

"Looks like it's time," he told his brother in a quiet voice.

Watching them interact, Dillon found himself envying their closeness, and wishing he could find someone to love him who loved him back the way Steven had.

Ordinarily, Dillon didn't welcome being in the spotlight. However, Ellie would be the one with all eyes on her and he knew his brother's new wife thrived on the favorable attention.

"Everyone," Dillon said, raising his voice as he addressed the people in front of the wellness spa. "If I could have your attention for a moment, please," he began.

Slowly, more and more people turned to look in Dillon Fortune's direction, their conversations halting until relative silence reigned.

"I want to welcome all of you here today and thank you for coming," Dillon said, addressing the gathering. With that, he turned the proceedings over to the town's mayor. "Madam Mayor, they're all yours," Dillon told her.

All eyes turned toward Ellie, waiting for her to cut the white ribbon and officially open up the spa to make it become a part of the townspeople's lives.

"I'm not going to bore you with a long, fancy speech or a lot of rhetoric," Ellie began warmly. "We all know why we're here."

"Yeah, for the refreshments," someone in the back of the crowd called out.

Laughter rippled through the crowd.

"Exactly," Ellie agreed. "Refreshments for our bodies as well as for our souls, which is exactly what this spa with all its new techniques and amenities promises to deliver," the mayor told her constituents. "Paz Spa brings what all of us would agree is a much needed shot in the arm to the residents of Rambling Rose. I for one can't thank the Fortune family enough for having traveled here and bringing their ideas and their revitalizing energy to our heretofore sleepy little town. Though in the beginning, some of us weren't quite convinced about the merits of this undertaking, you," she said, pausing to smile at her husband and at Dillon, "have shown us the error of our thinking. Believe me when I tell you that you have earned our undying gratitude many times over.

"In the famous words of Humphrey Bogart at

the end of the classic film *Casablanca,* 'I think this is the beginning of a beautiful friendship.' And I can say that we are all looking forward to watching that *friendship* unfold and thrive.

"So now, without any further ado," Ellie declared, taking hold of the over-sized scissors that Dillon had handed to her, "let me cut this ribbon and declare Paz Spa officially open for business!"

With that, holding onto the two large halves of the scissors, one in each hand, the young mayor cut through the fabric. The two severed white halves of ribbon fluttered to the floor amid enthusiastic cheers.

Steven put his arm around Ellie's shoulders as he pressed a kiss to her temple. "Well done, Madam Mayor," he told her with a pleased laugh.

"Actually, holding onto those two ends and getting them to cut through the ribbon isn't all that challenging," Ellie cracked.

"Well, you pulled it off with grace, the way everyone knew you would." Hailey knew that some women had a tough time coordinating the demands of their jobs with pregnancy. But Ellie seemed to sail right through things, unaffected.

"I wasn't worried," Ellie said, glancing over her shoulder toward her husband. And then her dark eyes twinkled. "I had a backup waiting in the wings."

"Everyone, please, there's a lot of food waiting for you to do justice to it. So eat, drink and—well, you all know the rest of that saying. Now go do it!" Hailey instructed, waving the crowded gathering to move into the spa's reception area where a buffet had been set up.

There were all sorts of sandwiches as well as several kinds of tortillas to choose from. Alongside that were different cuts of fried chicken. They were sitting next to french fries, pizza slices and so many different kinds of pastries, Dillon lost count when he'd tried to catalog them. There were also a selection of salads, smoothies and fresh fruit for the dedicated purists.

When he'd instructed the spa's manager to spare no expense for this celebration, he hadn't thought that much of his words, but she had obviously taken them to heart.

Coming up to Hailey, Dillon felt that he had to tell her what he thought of the tempting array.

"You certainly do know how to put on an inviting spread."

Hailey turned toward the sound of the deep male voice and smiled warmly up at Dillon. She appreciated him telling her that.

"Thank you, I'm glad you approve. I wasn't sure exactly what you had in mind," she confessed, "so

I figured that if I got a little of everything, I'd wind up covering it."

"Yes, I noticed," he said with a laugh. "If we get locked in here for a week for some reason, we certainly wouldn't starve," Dillon commented. "By the way, I didn't see a bill for all this." He felt he had to bring that up because he didn't want her getting stuck footing the bill for this celebration. From what he gathered, she wasn't being paid enough for that.

"That's because I haven't forward it to you yet," Hailey told him.

She had been so completely immersed in all the preparations there'd been no time to pull the tab together. But it was nice of him to make that point.

"Well, just make sure you do," Dillon told her. He looked around the huge salon again with all the people milling around, enjoying themselves. "Everything really looks great, Hailey," he repeated with feeling, as well as an element of approval.

Hailey could feel that same warm sensation spread out all through her again. "Thank you, Mr. Fortune."

Dillon looked surprised that she had used his surname. "I thought we decided you were going to call me by my given name," he reminded her.

"Sorry, I forgot." She hadn't, but by the time he'd left the spa last time, wearing his not-quite-dry shirt and hurrying off to his car, Hailey felt that their relationship had reverted back to its previous formal standing.

"Well, call me Dillon," he instructed.

The next moment, someone else was calling out his name. It turned out to be one of his cousins and Hailey got the impression that he didn't look all that anxious to respond.

"I guess this is a case of careful what you wish for," she said, taking a chance that her observation wouldn't sound too familiar.

Rather than take offense, Dillon laughed softly to himself.

"You can sure say that again." He sighed. He could see that his cousin was *not* going away. "I'd better go see what Adam wants."

Judging by the expression on his face, Hailey had a feeling that he already knew exactly what his cousin wanted to see him about. Adam and Kane Fortune had made no secret of the fact that they wanted to get into the "family" business, not because they harbored any desires to expand Rambling Rose commercially—or to expand any other town that way for that matter. What the cousins seemed to want to be part of were the resulting profits that would be coming down the pike.

Very soon, they hoped.

Hailey watched as Dillon made his way over to his cousin Adam. One minute the contractor had been smiling at her, the next he was withdrawing, as if folding his tent and all but disappearing into the night.

Not again, she thought.

She honestly didn't know what to make of the man, but she did know that she really wanted the opportunity to be able to get to know him better so she could make an intelligent decision about him. That way she could see if they had anything in common outside of those sparks she'd felt the other day, as well as today. Some sparks fizzled while others, if fanned, could turn into a roaring fire.

But first, of course, she needed to get the man to stand still in one place long enough for her to make up her mind about him.

And this was not the right time.

Right now, she needed to mingle and promote the spa's many services. This seemed like the perfect opportunity, while everyone was in a festive, receptive mood and the spa was brand new and at its most appealing.

In her new mindset, the first person Hailey came across was Ellie Hernandez who, for once, wasn't surrounded by a gaggle of people. And the mayor's husband seemed to be otherwise occupied, as well.

She had the woman all to herself.

"That was a very nice opening speech, Madam Mayor," Hailey said, coming closer to the young woman.

"Thank you. It was impromptu," Ellie confessed to Hailey.

"It didn't sound as if it was," Hailey told the woman in all honesty.

"Normally I prepare in advance," she explained and then confided, "but I'm afraid this pregnancy is taking a toll on me and wearing me down more than I'd like to admit."

"Really?" Hailey asked, her interest really piqued now. "Well, lucky for you, I just might have the answer for that." Nothing gave her more pleasure than helping someone *and* advancing the spa's clientele.

"The answer?" the mayor questioned. "I don't think I understand."

Hailey smiled. "Well, Paz Spa offers prenatal massages. They're specially tailored to the particular difficulties that the mother-to-be—meaning you—might be experiencing. These sessions are guaranteed to make a brand new, relaxed woman out of you instead of having you feel as if you were hauling around increasingly heavier, not to mention exceedingly uncooperative, large cargo."

"Right now, making a new woman out of me

sounds like heaven," Ellie told her with a deep appreciative sigh. "Where do I sign up?" she asked enthusiastically.

Was she kidding, Hailey wondered. Or didn't she know? "For you, Madam Mayor—and especially seeing that you have this marital connection to the contractor—all the sessions would be free."

Ellie looked surprised as she shook her head, turning down the offer.

"Nonsense, absolutely not. I'm not going to take advantage of my so-called *connection* to the Fortune family. Besides, how is the spa going to make any money if I do something like that?" the mayor wanted to know.

"Well, I am planning to have at least a few more clients than just you," Hailey said with a laugh. "Not to mention that if you enjoy your sessions and, more importantly, find that they really help you, maybe you can pass the word along. You know, tell your friends. Word-of-mouth is a very good way to advertise the spa," Hailey told her.

"Oh, I'm sure the sessions will help and I can definitely spread the word about the spa," the woman agreed.

Hailey's eyes sparkled as she put out her hand to the mayor. "Wonderful. In that case, I believe we have ourselves a deal," she said, enthusiastically shaking the woman's hand.

Just then, out of the corner of her eye, Hailey saw Dillon go by. He was talking to his other cousin now. For a second, Hailey's attention shifted to the contractor and she temporarily lost her train of thought.

The man did have a way of getting to her, even when she wasn't expecting it, Hailey thought ruefully. She was going to have to watch that.

When she looked back at Ellie, the woman had an amused expression on her face.

"Something on your mind, Hailey?"

For a second, Hailey debated asking the question and then she decided, why not? She really didn't have anything to lose and maybe, just maybe, there might be something to be gained.

"Well," Hailey began cautiously in a lowered voice, "as a matter of fact, since you are married to Steven Fortune..."

"Yes?" Ellie asked, her tone nothing if not encouraging.

Hailey gathered her courage to her and forced herself to push on. Friendly though she was, this wasn't easy for her.

"I thought that you might know what his brother's status is."

"I'm sure I do," Ellie agreed. "Which brother is it?"

Idiot. Her husband's got more than one brother.

"Dillon. The contractor who renovated this spa," she qualified, making it sound as if it was the all-important connection rather than her own reaction to the man.

"Well, Dillon's unattached," Ellie told her. "But…" Her voice trailed off, sounding uncertain.

Although distant alarms went off in Hailey's head, for some reason the mayor's words only aroused Hailey's curiosity even more. "But what?"

"To be honest," Ellie confessed, "I don't know if Dillon's really in the market for anyone."

That was an odd way to put it, Hailey thought. "Do you mean at the moment, or ever?"

Ellie glanced toward her brother-in-law and then sighed. That in itself wound up raising far more questions than it could possibly answer.

"I really don't think I should be the one to answer that, Hailey," the mayor admitted. "I'm afraid that you're going to have to ask Dillon that question." And then Ellie squeezed her hand. "Now, if you'll excuse me, I'm afraid that I'm required to mingle with the good citizens of Rambling Rose or they won't feel as if they've gotten their full nickel's worth."

Hailey laughed as she stepped back, clearing a

path for the mayor. "I had no idea you were charging admission to this."

Ellie smiled in response. "If I did, it would be a great deal more than just a nickel," she told Hailey, winking at her.

Left alone, Hailey caught herself intrigued by and thinking about what Ellie had just told her.

Was what the mayor said true? *Was* there some reason that Dillon Fortune had withdrawn from the dating field? But if that was the case, why had he kept checking his phone so often the other day when she'd been trying to give him a tour of the place? A man who wasn't interested in interacting with potential dating candidates didn't "half" dabble in the field. He was either in or he was out.

And if he was "in," well then, the game was on, wasn't it? And that in turn meant that she was going to have to buckle down and give this her all.

Hailey made up her mind.

She was well aware that she might regret this path she was contemplating taking, but she still wanted to see where it would lead her.

It was settled.

She was definitely in.

Chapter Five

Hours later, after the spa had emptied out and all the well-wishers had gone home, Hailey joined some of the members of her staff to clean up the party area. She wasn't the kind of boss who delegated tasks and then just stood back while they were done. She firmly believed in working alongside her people. And right now, the wellness spa needed to be ready for business bright and early the following morning.

Her problem, Hailey thought as she was working next to her assistant and one of the other instructors, was that she had always allowed her heart to rule her head. This kind of thinking, she readily admitted, left her open to new experiences, allowed her to easily make new friends and, in some cases, find new loves.

As far as that last part went, Hailey was willing to acknowledge that thinking this way had also gotten her into trouble on more than one occasion. If she were being honest, she would be forced to admit that she'd had a series of what her parents had once told her they considered *unsuitable* boyfriends.

But, to her credit, Hailey thought, she had bounced back each and every time. Thanks to her positive frame of mind, she had remained relatively unscarred and more than willing to take yet another plunge into the swirling, turbulent waters of romantic encounters.

And that in turn was all thanks to her personal philosophy. Hailey made no secret of the fact that she firmly believed that life was too short to hang back warily regarding the waters that were up ahead, too afraid to test them.

Her way of looking at things was all because of Janelle.

Sweet and funny, Janelle Walters had been her best friend all throughout elementary school and high school. She and Janelle had been completely inseparable during all those years, sharing secrets, making plans for the future. They were both determined to do great things once they graduated from school and, acting as each other's cheering squad, they always encouraged each other.

The world, they both felt, was at their feet, just waiting for them to dive right into it.

Of the two of them, Janelle had always been the bolder one, the one who didn't back away no matter how great the challenge confronting her. On the rare occasions that Hailey hesitated, Janelle would always be there to urge her along, to tell her that the only thing she had to be afraid of was *not* trying.

Hailey had worshipped her. In Hailey's eyes, Janelle had seemed utterly invincible, a bright shining light in a sometimes darker world, who was always willing to do anything, try anything.

It seemed to Hailey that there wasn't *anything* that Janelle couldn't do.

And then her friend got sick.

Really sick.

Janelle merely shrugged it off, saying it was nothing, that she just needed to eat better, or take some vitamins. No big deal. But eventually, even Janelle couldn't ignore her weakening state.

Alarmed, Janelle's mother finally all but dragged her friend to see a doctor. And then another doctor. And another. They all said the same terrible words that caused the light to go out for Hailey.

Pancreatic cancer.

When she first heard the diagnosis, Hailey had felt completely devastated. But Janelle, her incredible, ever upbeat friend, refused to accept the diagnosis, refused to give up or surrender to the ever-encroaching disease that was, for all intents and purposes, a death sentence. Instead, Janelle fought the good fight, behaving as if "forever" was still in front of both of them and that she would triumph over this so-called "obstacle" and move on.

Right up until the end.

And when the end finally came, just before Janelle finally lost her brave fight, her friend had turned to her and whispered, "Now you have to live for both of us. Promise me you'll live for both of us." Weak, she had tried to tighten her fingers around Hailey's and implored, "Promise me."

Hailey vividly recalled that she could hardly speak because of all the tears that had filled her throat, but somehow, she managed to make the promise to her dearest friend.

Janelle died several hours later. There had actually been a smile on her friend's face as she passed from one world to the next.

Hailey had been utterly inconsolable at first, grieving over the life that had been so cruelly cut short. But then, at her lowest point, she could have sworn she heard Janelle's voice whispering to her, reminding her of her promise.

Drying her eyes, Hailey resolved to honor her promise to her best friend, to live for both of them. Committed, she never looked back.

Janelle was also the reason why Hailey was so totally dedicated to furthering the wellness spa's agenda. She felt it was her own small way of honoring Janelle's memory.

And, of course, Janelle was also the reason why she was so determined to live life to the fullest. She had learned firsthand that life could be incredibly fleeting. For that reason, it needed to be enjoyed to the fullest before it suddenly disappeared.

And that was why she knew she had made the right decision today. She had to seek out Dillon Fortune and see if there was something there.

Hailey didn't realize it then, but spending time cleaning up the discarded plates and cups turned out to be the last peaceful moments she would spend. The very next day, as soon as the spa's doors were opened, the pace was keenly ramped up to almost an insane level.

It seemed as if everyone who had attended the opening ceremony was now eager to find out just what the wellness spa had to offer in the way of improving their lives.

Because of that, business was immediately robust. It remained that way, not just for a few hours but for the remainder of the day, and it had all the signs of continuing at this stride without letting up.

Hailey was determined to do her part to make it continue. She was everywhere at once, answering questions, conducting a variety of demonstration sessions, welcoming new clients. She kept this pace up from the moment the doors opened until they closed again for the night that evening.

Two days later, happily exhausted, Hailey knew a lot of people would have said that it was too soon to think of the wellness spa as a success. The situation could change drastically once the spa's novelty had worn off. But Hailey had never been someone to wallow in sobering thoughts, nor was she someone who prudently restrained and tempered her enthusiasm.

As a result, her enthusiasm knew absolutely no bounds.

So anyone within close proximity could see that she was thrilled by this onslaught of clients and prospective clients crowding into the various classes.

By the fourth day, as she continued taking all this in, Hailey didn't even bother to attempt to hide her wide smile. As if it had a life of its own, the smile spread out from ear to ear.

Silently congratulating herself on her part on

this achievement, she felt as if it looked like the wellness spa was a rip-roaring success.

We did it again, Janelle. We're a success. And I couldn't have done it without you!

Ever alert, Hailey had taken note of the fact that over the last few days several members of the Fortune family had dropped by to check things out. They had all come away looking as if they were well pleased.

At the last minute, just before the spa had had its official grand opening, Hailey had felt inspired and had added an additional class to the roster. A yoga class specifically designed for mothers and their babies, although an asterisk to the left of the listing in the brochure told any interested parties that fathers were welcome to the class, as well.

When the first day for the class arrived, Hailey was delighted that one of the enrollees was Callum Fortune's new wife, Becky. A former widow and a nurse at the new pediatric center, Becky was the mother of very lively one-year-old twin girls, Luna and Sasha. She brought them with her to class. The girls gave the impression of barely contained little rockets who were ready to go off at any second.

The slim dark-haired nurse was holding her own at the moment, but it looked as if that situation was touch and go and liable to change at any given moment.

Although she had been the one to come up with the class in the first place, Hailey wasn't scheduled to teach it herself. However she had decided to hang around the class in case she was needed to offer help or some advice. Seeing Becky and her girls, Hailey was glad that she made this decision.

Taking leave of the woman she had just been talking to, Hailey made her way over toward the slightly frazzled-looking young woman who appeared to be struggling mightily to hold onto her daughters and keep them both in the same area.

"Hi," Hailey said brightly, greeting Callum's wife. She ran her hand over Sasha's—or was it Luna's—hair. "Looks like you've really got your hands full, Becky." Hailey smiled at the two upturned faces that were presently regarding her with unbridled curiosity. "If you don't mind my saying so, you're pretty brave, taking on this class by yourself with both your little girls at the same time."

"Oh, I'm not alone," Becky told her as one of the twins attempted to tug away from her. Becky managed to hold onto her—for now. "At least, I won't be for long." She suppressed a rather deep sigh. "Callum said he was coming to lend not just his support but his two hands, as well." Her smile wasn't forced, but it did seem just a wee bit weak around the edges as she held the potential runaway closer to her body. "I don't think I can manage this all by myself, at least not the first few times," she confided. "They just have too much energy!"

Because of all the various interactions that she had experienced these last couple of weeks, Hailey was beginning to feel as if she were actually part of the family, even though her only real connection to the Fortunes was this wellness spa that the brothers had built. But Hailey had always had the ability to make friends easily and the men's spouses had been quick to open up to her. They'd talked to her as if she were one of them almost from the start, and Hailey had responded in kind, welcoming the bonding experience.

"Tell you what," Hailey suggested, slipping her fingers around one of the twins' small hands. "Why don't I just hang around a bit and help out until your husband arrives with his own set of very capable hands?"

Although Becky looked grateful at the offer, she felt it only right to respond with a protest at first. "I wouldn't feel right about taking you away from all your other commitments."

"Oh, you're not," Hailey was quick to assure the woman. She wasn't just being polite. She genuinely liked the nurse and wanted to do whatever she could to allow Becky to take full advantage of the class. "Everything that happens here is all part of my *commitment*," she told Callum's wife. Looking down at the perpetually moving duo, she couldn't help smiling. "Your girls are beautiful, by the way."

Becky laughed. "I'm kind of partial to them myself," she responded. "I just wish they'd slow down a little bit. They're into *everything*—usually at the same time and in opposite directions. For a while Sasha was the quiet one, but now there's absolutely no difference between them. If anything, she's seems to be trying to make up for lost time."

"Well, this class might just take a tiny bit of the edge off their energy and hopefully tire them both out enough for you to be able to recharge your batteries," Hailey told her. And then she reconsidered her words. "Or at least to catch your breath."

"Oh, if only," Becky said wistfully with a heartfelt sigh. "But by then, I'll have to be back at work," she confided.

Just then, the entrance to the Mommy and Me class opened. As if on cue, Becky and Hailey both turned toward the door. Each was expecting to see Callum come walking into the room.

The next second, Hailey felt her pulse leap a little. Instead of Callum, she saw Dillon coming in.

Hailey immediately regretted that she hadn't worn her more attractive athletic attire. Thinking only of mobility and comfort, she'd put on an outfit that she had to admit had seen better days. The only consoling thought here was that the light blue outfit she had on had come to look this way because she had worn it while doing one of her many workouts. For the spa's first month, she wanted to look like a hands-on manager who used the facilities herself. She felt that this made her look more approachable, as if she, her staff and her patrons were all one big family.

"Dillon," Becky said the moment her brother-in-law had joined them. "What are you doing here?"

The second he had reached them, Sasha and Luna began to climb all over him as if he was a living, breathing jungle gym.

Moving carefully so as not to dislodge his tiny climbing monkeys, Dillon dropped down beside the nurse that his brother had had the good fortune of marrying. "I'm here to tell you that Callum sends his regrets but he's been unavoidably detained at a building site. He sent me to temporarily take his place until he's able to get here himself."

Becky looked at her brother-in-law a little skeptically. "Are you sure that you know what you're in for?"

Placing a protective hand on the twin who had managed to climb up onto his forearm, he gently guided the little girl back to the floor. "Haven't a clue," he confessed. "Callum said something about this being a gym class for toddlers. How hard can it be?" he asked, although he was beginning to see that maybe he had underestimated the assignment.

"It's not a gym class," Hailey told him, flashing a smile as she stepped in to greet him. "It's a yoga class for moms and their kids."

"Moms?" Dillon repeated. That wasn't what Callum had told him. "Then why am I here?" he asked, confused.

"It's also for dads," Hailey quickly told him.

Dillon still looked a little skeptical. That didn't sound right to him. "Yoga for dads?"

"Yes. It's really very beneficial," Hailey assured him. She was trying hard not to laugh. Not at his stance, which admittedly was a bit awkward, but at the way his nieces seemed to regard him as a piece of equipment. "Yoga has been found to really help you relax. I don't mean you specifically," she quickly corrected herself. "I mean people in general."

Out of the corner of her eyes, she could see the rather amused expression on Becky's face. She couldn't help wondering if that was in response to Dillon looking like a fish out of water, or if there was another reason for the woman's amusement.

She had to admit that having the little girls climbing all over him did look pretty funny. The fact that he endured it without protest spoke well of him.

"And Callum knew this?" Dillon asked, looking at his sister-in-law. "That this was a yoga class?"

"He did," Becky confirmed, doing her best to try to maintain a straight face.

Dillon sighed, resigned. "Well then, I guess I can give this a shot."

"Good for you," Hailey said, pleased as she tried to cheer him on.

Dillon's expression indicated that he wasn't all that sure about what was about to happen, but he had committed himself to this and he wasn't about to backtrack, at least not in front of witnesses.

Because he'd been somewhat forewarned about the nature of this class, Dillon had stopped in the locker area to change out of his suit and into a pair of shorts, a comfortable pullover and a pair of sneakers. He definitely didn't look at home in any of it.

Apparently he noticed the way Hailey was looking at his foot attire.

"Callum said I needed to wear something other than boots," he explained.

"Ah, so you made the ultimate sacrifice for your nieces," Hailey concluded. Her smile was wide as her eyes sparkled. "Very noble of you."

Coming from someone else, Dillon would have

taken it as sarcasm. But there was something about the way the woman smiled when she talked that softened everything and pulled him in. He couldn't take offense.

Shrugging, he told her, "I didn't want to scuff up your floors."

Hailey inclined her head by way of acknowledgement. "The floors and I thank you." She looked over toward the instructor in the center of the room. "Looks like you're about to get started," she warned Becky and Dillon.

Becky and her brother-in-law each took a twin's hand. The girl that Becky was holding onto looked disappointed to have her connection to her uncle broken.

"I really appreciate this, Dillon," Becky told him.

He shrugged off Becky's thanks. "Don't mention it."

He slurred the statement a little because Luna, having shimmed up his leg, was now trying to stick her fingers into his mouth.

Apparently, Hailey judged, the little girl was plucking at her uncle's face, trying to make her uncle's smile wider.

"Luna, honey, Uncle Dillon doesn't want to smile right now," Becky prompted.

The little girl looked up at him questioningly,

then pushed even harder at Dillon's mouth, determined to make him grin as Becky tried to entangle the twin from her brother-in-law.

Hailey tried her best not to laugh, but it wasn't easy. "I'd say you definitely have your hands full," she said as she began to back away.

"You're going?" Becky asked, sounding just a touch distressed.

"Unless you'd like me to stay," Hailey told her. She had gotten the impression that Dillon would have rather that she wasn't around to witness what he was about to go through.

"Please," Becky said.

The hopeful look on Becky's face overrode what she assumed might be Dillon's wishes in the matter. After all, he hadn't said anything.

"Then I'll stay," Hailey replied.

Glancing in his direction, Hailey couldn't tell if Dillon took her decision in stride, or if her presence put him on edge.

She supposed she would find that out soon enough.

Chapter Six

She had learned something today, Hailey thought, smiling to herself. She had learned that, without a shadow of a doubt, Dillon Fortune was an incredibly patient man.

She had been watching Sasha and Luna's *Unca Dilly* contort his body into all sorts of really awkward, uncomfortable positions for the last half hour, simply to entertain his sister-in-law's two little girls.

Some of the movements he'd attempted, like virtually making a pretzel of himself, could *not* have been easy for him. Hailey was fairly certain that at least half the moves he attempted had to have really hurt.

In her opinion, the movements he was doing would have been challenging for an accomplished yoga instructor to execute.

But Dillon had gamely tried each and every one of them as they came up. Some movements he'd attempted had come with accompanying sound effects. Those too had been for the girls' gleeful benefit. The twins had lapped it all up like hungry little puppies. Entertained, they had giggled to the point that they had fallen down—and then they had giggled some more.

It was clearly obvious to anyone who was watching that Sasha and Luna really loved their uncle.

They weren't the only ones, Hailey thought. She found herself thinking that the contractor was just adorable, willingly doing all this just to keep the twins entertained.

If it hadn't been for the twins, Hailey was fairly sure that she would have never been privy to this kinder, sillier side of the handsome contractor. While she was attracted to the former, she found *this* Dillon Fortune to be utterly endearing.

Her only problem was that she kept staring too much.

But she really couldn't help it. Every time she tried to look away, Dillon did something else to make his nieces laugh and she found she just couldn't take her eyes off him.

When she managed to avert her eyes, she noticed that Becky looked a great deal more relaxed now than she had when she had first walked in.

The man was definitely a miracle worker, Hailey thought, even though she suspected that, if he was human, he just *had* to be counting the minutes until the class was finally over.

And then, inevitably, it was.

The moment Linda Hathaway, the woman who was running the class, declared, "That's it for today, Moms and Dads. See you all on Friday." Dillon, already on the floor because of the last exercise he had attempted to do, completely collapsed and seemed to all but press his exhausted body flat, practically sinking into the exercise mat he was on.

"Oh, thank God," he murmured, barely audible. "If I had to contort myself into one more position, I think I would've wound up breaking up into a hundred pieces," he groaned for the benefit of his pint-sized captive audience.

Sasha and Luna might not have understood all the words, but they did understand that *Unca Dilly* was out of oomph. The little girls gathered around him on either side, giggling, and then they finally lay down next to him, curling up against him.

"I really appreciate you doing all this for Sasha and Luna," Becky told her brother-in-law. She gently tried to prod the twins to get them up. "C'mon, girls, your uncle's exhausted. You need to give Uncle Dillon a little breathing room."

But the girls stubbornly remained where they were, apparently content to be lying next to their beloved, funny uncle forever.

"That's all right, Becky. Don't worry about it. Leave them where they are right now. I can breathe," Dillon told her.

Even so, Dillon did sit up, although he made no attempt to rise to his feet and move away from the little girls.

"You certainly have the patience of Job," Becky marveled, making no effort to hide how very impressed she was with her brother-in-law.

"The girls are very lucky to have someone like you around," Hailey remarked, adding her praise to Becky's. "You're really a natural born father," she told him with enthusiasm.

Dillon looked at her sharply. Rather than take her words as a compliment, the way she had intended, she saw Dillon's face darken in response. Not only that, but he seemed to withdraw and totally shut down right before her eyes.

Hailey's comment had hit far too close to home,

Dillon thought. And just like that, it had brought with it all sorts of thoughts, not to mention regrets, that he was trying his best to at least bury temporarily, at least until he was able to do something about the situation.

But right now, given this resurrected frame of mind, he needed to leave. Otherwise, he was afraid he'd wind up bringing the little girls down and that was the last thing he wanted to do.

Hailey saw the change in Dillon immediately.

Stunned, Hailey could only wonder what had triggered it.

For heaven's sake, she had given the man a compliment, not verbally filleted him, she thought, at a loss.

Confused, when Hailey looked at Dillon's sister-in-law for some sort of an explanation or enlightenment, Becky only shook her head, a blank, bewildered expression on her face.

Obviously Becky didn't understand his reaction any more than she did.

She was on the verge of asking Dillon what she'd said that was so wrong, but now that the class over, he gave her the impression that he was going to leave.

Immediately.

His next words, addressed to Becky, confirmed her impression.

"I've got to get going, Becky," he told his sister-in-law. "You'll be okay?"

"Yes, of course," she told Dillon with a weary smile.

But his nieces, it seemed, had another opinion on the matter. Each little girl grabbed hold of one of Dillon's arms clinging like limpets to keep him from leaving.

Although he clearly doted on the girls, Dillon looked resolved. He was leaving.

Bending down to the point that he appeared to be folding up his large frame, Dillon kissed the top of each twin's head.

"I'm afraid I have to go, girls. But I'll be back," Dillon promised. Taking hold of one of the girls' hands, he gently tried to extricate himself from his tiny rabid fan club.

As he made progress with one, the other little girl would grab onto him, giggling as if this was a fine new game she and her sister were playing.

"C'mon, girls, let go of your uncle," Becky said a bit more forcefully than the way Dillon had expressed his feelings. "He'll be back soon. Won't you, Uncle Dillon?" she asked, looking at her brother-in-law for his confirmation.

"You bet," Dillon responded. But even so, when

he tried to pull his hands away, his nieces continued to hold onto him for dear life.

Hailey sensed that she had to come to the rescue to keep this from ending with the little girls in tears.

"Hey, how would you girls like some ice cream?" Hailey asked, saying the word *ice cream* as if it were the most wonderful treat imaginable and theirs exclusively to enjoy.

That seemed to do the trick. Letting go of their uncle's hands, the twins eagerly gathered around Hailey, their eyes huge with anticipation.

"Well, you're in luck. I just happen to know where we can find some." Hailey glanced over toward Becky. "Is it okay, Mom?"

Becky laughed. "How could I say no?"

"Well then, come on. Let's go get these hardworking little ladies some well-deserved ice cream," Hailey coaxed for the twins' benefit.

As she herded the girls toward the spa's designated kitchen area, she glanced over her shoulder toward Dillon. She expected to see him watching them.

Hailey was disappointed to see that he had used the opportunity to make good his escape. He was clearly anxious to get away, and although it could all very well be connected to his business, she couldn't shake the feeling that it had something to do with what she'd said.

But how could what she had clearly meant to be a compliment have had such an adverse effect on Dillon?

And why? What did he think she meant by it?

Hailey suppressed a sigh as she led the little girls and their mother into the kitchen. It just made absolutely no sense to her.

But she intended to find out, she promised herself. Her curiosity had been aroused and she wasn't one of those people who was content to just let things go. She wasn't going to be happy or know any peace until she had an answer.

She began by asking Becky.

"Do you have any idea what made your brother-in-law suddenly turn tail and run like that?" Hailey asked as soon as she had handed ice-cream cups to Becky's daughters after first carefully pulling off the tops. She also presented each little girl with a small spoon and armed herself with a lot of napkins for the cleanup she knew would be ahead.

"Well, he didn't exactly run," Becky tactfully pointed out. "And he did say that he had to be getting back, probably for the same reason that Callum couldn't make it here in the first place," Becky surmised.

Hailey thought about letting the matter drop, but her curiosity just wouldn't let her.

That was why, in the next moment, she heard herself asking, "Do you really think that?"

Becky neatly turned the words around without appearing to be argumentative. "You don't?"

"I'm not really sure what to think," Hailey confessed honestly. "One minute, Dillon is all but cavorting with your kids, acting like just another big kid himself. The next minute, he's acting like a dark rain cloud about to let loose with a deluge, all because I paid him a compliment." She rolled what she'd said over in her mind, searching for what might have offended him about the words she'd used.

Coming up empty, she decided to say her comment out loud, hoping that might trigger something for Becky. "I said that he had the makings of a really great father. Why would that upset him? It's obvious that Dillon likes acting the part."

Hailey looked at Becky, waiting, but the latter only shook her head helplessly. "I'm afraid I have no idea. I really don't know very much about Dillon." She smiled ruefully at Hailey. "I'm still learning things about Callum," she confessed.

Hailey felt guilty about prodding the woman. Heaven knew Becky had more than enough to deal with between her job, her new marriage and her little girls.

"I'm sorry, you're right. I have no business playing twenty questions with you about Dillon. He probably misunderstood what I was saying to him." She waved away the whole thing as if she could literally erase it with her hand. "Forget I said anything," she told the new Mrs. Fortune.

Getting up from the small snack table, Hailey handed Becky the fistful of napkins she'd grabbed earlier. "For cleanup," she explained, nodding at the twins. "Although it does look like they managed to get a little bit of ice cream into their mouths," she deadpanned.

Becky laughed, wiping the mouth of the twin who was closest to her.

"That's better than they usually manage to do," she told Hailey. "I'm just glad you gave them vanilla instead of chocolate. It always looks so much messier with chocolate ice cream. I can't wait until they grow out of this phase and they can eat like normal people without creating such an awful mess."

Hailey nodded as she took possession of the used napkins that Becky was discarding. "I understand, but I also know that according to some more seasoned mothers I've talked to, you are going to look back someday and miss this."

Becky sighed as she rose, taking each semi-cleaned twin by the hand. "I know that you're probably right. But I sure would like the chance to find that out for myself," she said, then tagged on the word, "Soon."

"The next Mommy and Me class is the same time on Friday," Hailey said, calling after the departing woman.

Looking over her shoulder, Becky promised, "I'll be here."

Hailey couldn't help wondering if that meant that Dillon would be coming with Becky, as well. Or had her comment about fatherhood scared him away from here permanently?

Get over yourself, Hailey. If the man doesn't show up, it's because his brother was able to take his place. Or rather, take his own rightful place. Callum's the one who married Becky, the one who adopted the twins. Not Dillon.

Hailey sighed as she walked away, heading to another part of the spa. There was no doubt about it. She could all but hear Janelle's voice in her head, telling her that she was spending much too much time thinking about Dillon. It was energy that was better spent elsewhere.

But that being true or not, Hailey couldn't help thinking and wondering about the elusive Fortune brother. She still didn't know very much about him other than the general information that was available about all the Fortune brothers who were currently working hard renovating and building up the town of Rambling Rose.

She knew that Dillon hailed from Florida, a good place, in her opinion, to be *from*, if for no other reason than the place was rumored to have mosquitoes you could put a saddle on and ride.

She also knew that he was part of a far larger family than the seven siblings he had mentioned, although it seemed to her that having seven siblings was definitely large enough for anyone. He was involved in the construction company with his brothers, but unlike Steven and Callum, she didn't have a clue what the man's marital status was,

Was his family covering for Dillon for some reason?

No, that didn't seem possible. Ellie didn't strike her as being a devious person.

Neither, for that matter, did Becky. If her gut impression meant anything, neither were Steven and Callum. They seemed to be rather genuine if she had to make an assessment of the men.

So what was Dillon's big secret—if there *was* a secret?

And if there was no secret, why had Ellie intimated that he might not be in the market for a woman at this time? Was he recovering from a bad relationship?

More importantly, why had he suddenly grown so quiet and all but run away when she had said that harmless comment about him having the makings of being a good father?

She chewed on her lower lip, feeling confused and bewildered.

None of it made any sense to her.

But that didn't mean that she was going to just let it lay there, waiting for someone to say something in passing that would wind up clearing it up for her some time down the line.

No, Hailey told herself, she fully accepted the challenge of unscrambling this mystery, of getting to the bottom of it and making sense of the situation.

Now.

For some reason, what she had said to Dillon about his making a good father had definitely not sat well with the man. That either meant that he secretly wanted to be a father or he already was one and had made what he probably considered to be a horrible, irreversible mess of the situation.

There was a third, sadder alternative to that. He already had become a father but no longer was one because the child had either died or been whisked away by his or her mother, not to be found again.

But if that were the case, wouldn't one of his brothers have known about that? And if one knew, wouldn't he have shared that piece of information with his wife?

The logical answer to that was yes, but Hailey had a feeling that there was absolutely nothing logical about this case.

Which meant that she wasn't going to have any peace until she was able to find out what the big mystery surrounding Dillon was.

And she fully intended to.

Chapter Seven

Despite her best efforts to focus on all the hundred and one details she had to see to in order to keep the spa in top running condition, Hailey still found herself looking forward to Friday and, specifically, the Mommy and Me class.

And Dillon.

Though part of her knew she wasn't being very realistic, she was hoping that Dillon would once again be at the class, filling in for Callum the way he had initially.

But when Friday rolled around, not only wasn't Dillon there but neither was Becky. In their place, looking very much like a fish out of water, was

Callum. Dillon's older brother arrived a few minutes before the class was scheduled to begin, flanked on either side by one of the twins and doing his best to look as if he was actually up to this challenge.

This was a man who had helmed the purchase of large plots of commercial properties within and around Rambling Rose. Blessed with astute business acumen, Callum had gotten in on the ground floor of what he and some members of his family referred to as the town's "gold rush." He was a contractor accustomed to juggling several projects at the same time, but even with all that going for him, he still appeared to be no match for Luna and Sasha, the two little girls he had adopted when he had married Becky.

One look at the man and Hailey could see that he clearly needed help.

With effort, Hailey put her disappointment at Dillon's absence aside and made her way over to his harried looking older brother.

"You look like you're a little overwhelmed here," she observed with a smile. "Would you like a hand with your energetic twosome?"

He flashed a sheepish smile at the spa's manager and said, "I'd be very grateful for any help you can possibly offer."

Hailey's smile widened. "My pleasure." She turned her attention to the twins. Today they were dressed in matching turquoise leotards. "Hi, girls, welcome back." She tousled one of the girl's hair. "Remember me?"

Two identical heads enthusiastically bobbed up and down.

"Is it okay if I help your dad?" she asked solemnly, addressing each of the twins. "He might not know what to do since he wasn't here last time." Again both little girls nodded. They obviously didn't absorb all the words, but they looked very pleased to be consulted. "Thank you," Hailey said, "I appreciate that." And then, sitting down next to Sasha— she silently congratulated herself at getting better at telling the girls apart—Hailey asked their father, "Where's Becky today? Why didn't she come with you?"

Considering the nurse's busy schedule, Hailey thought that the Mommy and Me class would have been something Becky would have looked forward to as a break in her hectic routine.

"Linus's father, Eric, turned up with Linus at the pediatric clinic this morning," Callum told her, making a grab for Luna who was about to escape and fraternize with a little boy in the row behind them.

Hailey was surprised to hear about Linus's return. Barely four months old, Linus was regarded as quite the celebrity in Rambling Rose since, his mother, Laurel, had gone into premature labor at the opening of the pediatric clinic. Becky and Dr. Green had tended to her before transferring her to the hospital in San Antonio to give birth. From all indications, that would have been the end of the story if Laurel hadn't suddenly reappeared weeks later, only to leave Linus on the doorstep of the clinic.

Stephanie Fortune—Dillon, Callum and Steven's sister—had stepped up to temporarily become the abandoned baby's foster mother. Stephanie had grown very fond of the infant when Laurel's old boyfriend, Eric Johnson, had abruptly turned up to claim the boy as his son.

That had been a couple of months ago and Stephanie, according to what Becky had told her, still missed the infant terribly.

"I thought Eric left town with the baby," Hailey said, looking at Callum.

"He did, but he came back to talk to Dr. Green. Eric's worried about Linus because he doesn't think the baby's growing at the proper rate he should. Becky said that Eric thought it might be because the baby had been born several weeks prematurely, but the baby's father wanted to be sure that there was nothing else wrong so he brought Linus back to be checked out."

Hailey could certainly understand that. "Better safe than sorry," she agreed. Since Callum hadn't mentioned it, she thought she'd ask. "I take it that there's been no word about Laurel's current whereabouts?"

"Nobody's seen Laurel since the day she left Linus at the pediatric center."

When that had happened, it had seemed to Hailey as well as several others that events had come full circle. Or, better yet, that poetic justice was involved. Leaving Linus on the doorstep of the new pediatric center seemed like echoes of the past because the center had been built on the foundation of what had once been the Fortune's Foundling Hospital.

Callum was about to say something else to Hailey, but whatever he intended to say, she never got a chance to hear it. Luna, anxious for his undivided attention, had suddenly pulled on his arm. Caught off guard, because he had been leaning on that arm, Callum almost fell over.

Hailey managed to suppress her urge to laugh at what looked like a comical scene. Instead, she said seriously, "You have to be careful. These little girls of yours are really fast," she warned him. "And they do outnumber you."

"Tell me about it," he said, shaking his head. "I don't know how Becky does it, working all day and then coming home to these two live wires." With one arm around each twin, he hugged both of the girls. "I get worn out just thinking about it."

Hailey laughed. "From what I've heard, moms come with permanently rechargeable batteries," she told Callum. "And don't feel like you need to keep up with Linda, either," she said, indicating the instructor who had just walked into the room. "She's been doing this sort of thing for a few years now. Just do what you can," she advised. "The key thing to remember is to have a good time bonding with your girls."

Callum smiled at Hailey as he nodded. "Good advice," he said just as the class officially began.

She was full of good advice, Hailey thought, settling in to help Callum with his daughters. Too bad she couldn't seem to take her own to heart and stop thinking about Dillon.

But she found that it was hard to stop thinking about the man when their paths kept crossing. Or almost kept crossing. By the time the weekend rolled around, she had just barely missed running into Dillon a number of times.

Just two ships passing one another in the night, Hailey thought philosophically.

She felt frustrated. There had to be some way they could travel in the same direction, at least for a little while, she thought.

"I could sure use a little help here, Janelle," Hailey murmured under her breath the following Saturday morning as she drove to Mariana's weekly flea market. "I'm trying my best to grab onto life with both hands just the way you always told me to," she told the memory of her best friend, "but so far, life seems to just be slipping through my fingers. At least when it comes to Dillon."

She sighed as she continued making her way to the flea market.

Maybe she was being too impatient. Janelle had always said if something was meant to be, it would happen, usually when you were just about ready to completely give up.

"Sure hope you're right about that," Hailey silently said to her friend, "because I'm pretty close to giving up on that hunky cowboy-hyphen-construction guru."

Yes, she wanted to find out what his secret was

and why he had suddenly withdrawn when she had told him he had the makings of being a great dad. But there was a fine line between determination and stalking, and there was absolutely no way that she wanted to accidentally blunder into *that* category.

Okay, she told herself as she reached her destination, she had very little free time to herself these days and there didn't seem to be a letup coming anywhere in the near future. Which of course was a good thing as far as the spa went. But this was an island of time she had managed to cut out for herself and she needed it. She was going to use that time to see what treasures she could find at Mariana's.

Specifically, the treasures she was on the look-out for were frog figurines, something she had started collecting way back in her early teens. Every few weeks, she would hit the flea market, Rambling Rose's very own treasure trove, to see if there were any new figurines there waiting to be added to her personal collection.

Searching through the hastily assembled tables that seemed to go on for endless row after row was both her hobby and her diversion. Just looking through all these things was its own reward, and whenever she actually found a figurine, it was a little like Christmas morning when she was a kid all over again.

She parked her car in the lot that stretched out along the fairground's perimeter. Getting out and eager to get started, she was completely focused on the hunt before her. For the first time in a while, she wasn't even thinking about Dillon.

Which was probably why she didn't see the man until she was practically right on top of him.

Actually, she *was* on top of him, having walked right into someone without even realizing it.

Their bodies collided and it was all she could do to keep from falling down. The only reason she regained her balance at all was because the person she had walked into grabbed her hard by her shoulders in an effort to keep her upright.

Hailey began to apologize before she realized whom she had walked into.

"Oh, I'm so sorry, I didn't mean to—Dillon," she exclaimed, practically doing a double take. Hailey tried to back up and found she couldn't.

Belatedly, Dillon realized he was holding onto her. Not only that, but it took him a second to release his hands from her shoulders. Electricity shot through him, as if holding her like that felt right somehow.

He was going to have to watch that.

"I didn't realize you would be here," she cried, feeling genuinely flustered and more than a little tongue-tied, which was highly unusual for her. "Sorry," she apologized again. "I didn't mean to walk into you like that."

Rather than be standoffish, which was what she half expected, since she'd gotten the impression that he was avoiding her, Dillon looked amused.

"Who did you mean to walk into?" he asked Hailey.

"What?" And then she realized that he was teasing her. She laughed, some of her nervousness leaving her. "Nobody. I was just trying to get my bearings. The people who bring their things to Mariana's Market never seem to be in the same place twice. They're always switching around so it's like a brand new treasure hunt each and every time."

Dillon looked at it from the point of view of a businessman. "They do that so they can try to catch your eye with something new, something you didn't even know you were looking for until you see it."

Hailey looked impressed. She wouldn't have thought a flea market would have any allure for him. "You sound as if you're talking from experience."

"I am. Secondhand experience, actually," he readily admitted. "But still valid in this context.

Steven came here just last month and found this really cool scrapbook while he was browsing one of the stands."

"Oh?" He'd caught her attention even as she continued weaving in and out of the rows, looking at what the various sellers had on display. "What made it so cool?" She couldn't help being curious about what Dillon and his brothers might have found appealing at a flea market.

"It was filled with old articles about the town, you know, the way it was back when it was first built," he told her, following Hailey as she turned down another row. "There was even an article about the old Foundling Hospital—except it wasn't old at the time."

"That sounds really interesting. I'd love to see the scrapbook sometime," she told him in all sincerity.

"Okay, I'll ask Steven about it and see if I can get him to lend it to you." The next row was rather crowded so it took him a moment of weaving in and out before he could continue talking. "He seems pretty taken with the scrapbook himself. Looking through it is like looking into a passageway between the past and the present. I could almost see the wheels in his head turning as he was making more plans for future projects."

Dillon realized that he was going on and on, monopolizing the conversation and not giving Hailey a chance to talk. He supposed that was because of his nerves. He found himself being really interested in her despite all his attempts not to be. "So, what brought you here?" he asked.

Hailey was intently searching for one of the sellers she had connected with the last time she was here. So far, she hadn't been able to find the woman. Preoccupied, she answered, "Frogs."

Dillon abruptly stopped walking and looked at Hailey. "Excuse me?"

She turned to look at him over her shoulder. He looked so stunned that she had to laugh. And quickly followed that with an apology. "I'm sorry, I didn't mean to laugh like that. I'm not laughing at you," she added. "I'm laughing with you."

"But I'm not laughing," Dillon deadpanned.

He looked so serious for a second that she became flustered again. She really didn't want to mess up this rare opportunity, especially since he seemed to be in a good mood and they were hitting it off.

"I'm sorry, Dillon. I didn't mean to imply—"

"It's okay, Hailey, I'm just messing with you," he told her, waving away her apology. "But seriously, you're here looking for frogs?" he repeated. He wouldn't have thought she was the kind who would have wanted a pet frog. She struck him as more of a pet puppy person.

"Frog *figurines*," she clarified. "I come here to Mariana's flea market every few weeks, hoping to find another figurine to add to my collection."

She sounded serious, he thought. "How big is your collection?" Dillon asked.

"Not very big," she admitted. She was familiar with the people in the next row and knew there were no figurines to be found at their tables. Pausing, she looked up at Dillon and answered his question. "At last count, I had almost twenty figurines, all different," she specified, since that was important to her. And then she laughed softly. "You'd be surprised how many of these things there are out there once you start looking."

Intrigued, he asked, "Why did you?"

She didn't quite follow him. "Why did I what?"

"Start looking for figurines of frogs?" he said, supplying the rest of his question. "I mean, it's not something that is typically collected—at least, I wouldn't think so," he amended. He didn't want her to think he thought her hobby was odd—just maybe a little unusual.

Hailey shrugged. "I guess it goes back to when I was a little girl. I always loved the story about *The Frog Prince*. I must have made my mother read that story to me at least a hundred times before I finally learned to read it for myself."

"The Frog Prince," Dillon repeated, still trying to understand the reason behind her fascination. "As in you have to kiss a lot of frogs before you meet your prince?" he asked.

She blushed a little, something that he found instantly endearing. "Something like that," she admitted.

"And did you?" Dillon wanted to know. "Did you meet your prince?"

"No," she admitted, thinking of some of the wrong choices she had made in her life. "Not yet."

"Well, I guess I know how that is," he said, commiserating with her. "Kissing your share of frogs, I mean." When she looked at him curiously, Dillon quickly explained, "I've probably kissed my share of… What's the female equivalent of frogs? Froggettes?" he asked, testing the word out.

For some reason, the word he had come up with really struck her as funny. Hailey started to laugh, really laugh. Hard.

Listening to her, Dillon found himself captivated by the sound of her laughter. So much so that he could feel himself wanting her.

Really wanting her.

Chapter Eight

"You know," Dillon heard himself saying quietly so that no one could overhear them, "I wouldn't mind being one of your frogs." The moment the words had come out of his mouth, he was afraid that they could be misconstrued, or, at the very least, they didn't come out quite right. He didn't want Hailey to think he had lost his mind. Or that he was putting moves on her. That would be too crass. "I mean..."

At a loss, he wasn't sure just how to finish his sentence.

He was shy, Hailey realized, delighted by the very idea. Who would have ever thought that someone as incredibly sexy and good-looking, not to mention talented, as Dillon Fortune could actually be shy?

She smiled at him, doing her best to encourage Dillon to continue his thought—and to act on it.

"I think I know what you mean," she told him.

Was it his imagination, or did Hailey seem to move closer to him without actually taking a single step? Or maybe he had somehow just willed the distance between them to disappear?

Whatever the reason and however it happened, one moment he was looking down into her upturned face, the next moment Dillon was kissing her.

He wasn't the kind of man who believed in engaging in public displays of affection. On the contrary, Dillon had trained himself to behave like an extremely private person, keeping his thoughts as well as his feelings tightly under wraps.

But this was different. He didn't know why it was, he only knew that it was.

So very different.

He had caught himself thinking about kissing Hailey since that first day when she had uncorked that unfortunate bottle of jasmine and wound up christening his shirt with it. That act alone, even though it was unintentional, should have made him extremely wary of her—but it hadn't.

To be honest, nothing she had done had driven him away, even though, under normal circumstances, it would have.

Kissing her now was a totally intoxicating experience.

Damn but she tasted heavenly. Her lips were sweet, like strawberries that had been picked just at the right moment. Not too sweet, not too tart, just incredibly arousing.

Desire shot through Dillon's veins as he deepened the kiss.

Hailey felt herself getting lost in his kiss.

Lord, but he was making her head spin. This was even better than she could have possibly imagined. Her blood was rushing through her body, making her aware of just the moment, just the man and nothing more.

Ordinarily, Hailey was always aware of her surroundings, always aware of everything and everyone around her, no matter what. But this time, Dillon had no sooner kissed her than everything else around them had just managed to vanish, becoming one with the universe as it slipped away into the mist.

Leaving just the two of them.

All she was aware of was this incredible surge within her, this incredible desire to slip away with him somewhere and explore all these wonderful, delicious feelings that she was experiencing. The feelings that were racing through her body, making her want him. Making her want to *be* with him.

And then, finally, because he sensed that they had to undoubtedly be attracting attention to themselves, Dillon reluctantly drew back his head.

He smiled into Hailey's mesmerizing blue eyes. "I take it that's a yes?" he asked the moment his lips were no longer on hers.

Hailey returned his gaze, feeling a little dazed, unable to form a coherent thought or even follow what he was saying to her.

She blinked, struggling to focus her brain. "A yes?" she repeated uncertainly.

Unable to resist, he ran his fingers through her hair, marveling at how very silky it felt to the touch. "To my kissing you."

And then her mind caught up to the rest of her. Hailey smiled at him, the smile unfurling like the first flower of spring raising up its petals to the rays of the warm sun.

Captivated by the sight, Dillon found he couldn't draw his eyes away from her enticingly sexy mouth.

"I wouldn't have kissed you if I didn't want to," Hailey told him.

"Just to be sure you know, you can always say no. That's your prerogative."

"Good to know," Hailey told him. She remained rooted to the spot, hoping for a repeat performance. "Then I choose *not* to say no."

He felt heartened, although there were distant alarms going off in his head, warning him not to take this any further even as he heard himself say, "Would you mind if I asked to see you again?"

"You mean other than here right now?" she asked, her smile growing deeper.

"Yes, other than that," he told her with an amused laugh.

"I'd mind if you *didn't* ask," Hailey told him honestly. "Yes, you can ask to see me again. Just name the time and the place and then we'll coordinate our very busy schedules," she teased.

Then, before Dillon could answer, she surprised him by slipping her hand into his and lightly tugging on it, getting him to come along with her. She was back to weaving her way through the various rows of tables displaying merchandise.

"Are we still looking for those frog figurines for you?" he asked. He wanted to be clear what she wanted him to search for.

"We are," she confirmed. She knew he was thinking about the kiss and how it might very well have been a signal that her days of kissing frogs were over.

Time would only tell if it was. But her days of collecting figurines were still ongoing.

She smiled at him. "I can't very well put you on my shelf, now can I?"

"Well, for one thing, I don't think I'd fit," he deadpanned.

Hailey's eyes slid over his robust body. She felt herself growing warm. "No, you definitely would not. Besides, you have work to do and so do I. That kind of stationary life is not right for either one of us." Her smile went all the way up to her eyes as she told him, "I'd like to think that's something that we have in common."

When he didn't say anything in response, Hailey wondered if he had even heard her. From the expression on his face, his attention was apparently focused on something else.

"Dillon?" she said, raising her voice, but to no avail. He still wasn't looking at her.

Maybe he was having second thoughts about their getting together, she thought. Maybe she had gone too fast, assumed too much.

Maybe—

"There," Dillon said, pointing to something she couldn't see because there were a cluster of people in the way, blocking her line of vision. He was tall enough to see over them.

"There?" Hailey repeated, still mystified. She had no idea what Dillon could be referring to. She didn't see anything around that might be considered out of the ordinary.

Rather than explain what it was that had caught his eye, Dillon suddenly picked her up in his arms and then put her on his shoulders as easily as he would a child.

It was all she could do not to squeal. Hailey struggled to contain her surprise.

"One row over," he told her, then added more specifically. "Look at the display three tables from the end."

Still confused, Hailey looked in the direction he had pointed out, vaguely aware that the milling crowds of shoppers and browsers around her appeared to be mildly entertained by their balancing act.

"What am I—?"

No sooner had Hailey started to ask him what exactly she was supposed to be looking for when she saw it. Stunned, she could only marvel at how she might have missed seeing it if it weren't for Dillon and his high vantage point.

"Oh!" she cried, utterly mesmerized.

"You see it," Dillon concluded, pleased.

Now that she was looking at it, she couldn't understand how she could have possibly *not* seen it. It was a figurine of a frog, all right. Dressed in a black tie, formal black jacket—referred to as tails, she recalled—the frog also had on a black top hat and he was leaning on a striking black walking cane. It looked so vivid, the little frog seemed as if he were about to start dancing at any moment. And if she listened, she could almost swear she could hear the dapper little frog about to break into a song.

"Oh, yes, I see it," she told Dillon with enthusiasm. When the light hit the figurine just the right way, she was certain that the jacket and top hat sparkled thanks to a sprinkling of sequins.

Belatedly, Hailey suddenly realized that he was still holding her up on his shoulders.

"I've got to be getting heavy for you," she said self-consciously. "You can put me down now."

Kneeling, Dillon carefully guided Hailey down from his shoulders, even though he denied the assumption she had made.

"You're not getting heavy at all," he insisted. "Believe me, I've hauled sacks of concrete that weighed a great deal more than you weigh. I put you up on my shoulders because I figured that was the fastest way to get you to catch a glimpse of that frog," Dillon explained to her. "I wanted you to see it before someone else bought it."

"And I really appreciate that," Hailey told him.

As if to prove it, the second her feet made contact with the ground, Hailey immediately rushed between shoppers, making her way over to the next row so she could purchase the figurine.

Dillon made no attempt to stop her or to tell her to slow down. Instead, he just followed in Hailey's wake.

She could move really fast. But then, why shouldn't she? he asked himself. Hailey obviously kept that body of hers in excellent shape with those exercise classes she had put together. He had a feeling that she didn't just stand back and let the instructors do the heavy lifting. She was the type to be there every step of the way, he thought.

By the time he had caught up to her and was at her side, Hailey had concluded negotiating with the older woman who was selling the figurine. The dapper figurine was nestled in with a number of other "treasures" that the woman had brought to the flea market in an attempt to sell.

"Can I interest you in this ancient cameo?" the woman asked, holding the necklace up and waving it slightly before her face.

"No, thank you. All I want is the figurine," Hailey assured her.

"Are you sure?" the woman asked, unconvinced. "After all, a girl can always use another piece of jewelry," the woman told her. She held up the necklace again, as if the second time was the charm.

"Yes, I'm sure. I'm only interested in the frog figurine," Hailey told her. "Now, if you have any others…"

"No, Froggie here is one of a kind," the woman informed her. Her face lit up and as she smiled, it made some of her more prominent wrinkles look as if they were receding and fading away. She gave Dillon a long appreciative look, her brown eyes sliding up and down his body. "Kind of like your fella, here," she told Hailey.

Not wanting Dillon to feel embarrassed or uncomfortable, Hailey quickly denied the woman's assumption.

"Oh, he's not my *fella*. We just ran into one another here this morning."

The older woman's eyes lit up as they gave Dillon a second, even longer appreciative survey. "Then could he be mine?" she asked with genuine interest.

The woman was probably about twenty years

older than they were, possibly more, and behind
the smile there was definitely something about
her that reminded Hailey of a determined preda-
tor. She could almost envision the seller's appetite
causing her to all but devour Dillon in a couple of
well-placed bites.

Just in case she was right, Hailey decided an
ounce of prevention might be called for.

"On second thought, I spoke too soon," Hailey told the woman as she shelled out the money
for the figurine. Sparing Dillon a quick wink, she
added, "He is my *fella*."

Rather than be annoyed, the woman smiled
knowingly as she nodded her head.

"Yes, I thought you might change your mind
once you had a chance to think about it," the seller
said knowingly.

That had Hailey wondering if she had just been
played.

Well, it didn't matter. She had gotten what she
wanted: a one-of-a-kind frog figurine in good condition.

After taking her money, the seller carefully deposited the stylish frog into a paper bag. The bag
was too small to properly house the frog, but it
did manage to cover his legs all the way up to his
waist. It also covered up his cane.

"You're good luck for me," Hailey declared with a bright, pleased smile as she looked at Dillon.

"Glad I could help."

He gave the area a quick, final cursory look. "Are we done here?" he asked hopefully, then tagged on "Or—?"

"Or," she told him without any hesitation. "I want to look around a little more and see if I can locate any more frog figurines. And besides," she glanced back at him and his hands, "you're still empty-handed," she pointed out.

"Oh, I wouldn't exactly say that," Dillon responded, his eyes drifting over in her direction.

"Well, I know what I'm looking for," she said by way of conversation. "What are *you* looking for?"

"I think it's a case of I'll know it when I see it," Dillon told her.

Hailey smiled at him with a knowing smile. "In other words, you haven't the slightest idea what you're looking for."

Dillon laughed lightly as he moved his shoulders up and down in an evasive shrug. The shrug told her beyond a shadow of a doubt that she had certainly guessed correctly.

"All right, then," Hailey told him gamely, threading her free hand through his. She glanced at her watch. "I've got another forty-five minutes before I have to get back to the spa. Let's see if we can make the most of that time."

"What happens in forty-five minutes?" Dillon wanted to know, allowing himself to be led around by his shapely tour guide.

"I turn into a pumpkin," Hailey answered him with a wink.

"*That* I'd like to see," Dillon told her, a smile curving his mouth as it seemed to snake its way up to his eyes, as well.

"Stick around long enough and you just might get to witness it," she answered.

"Promises, promises," Dillon responded with a quick wink.

Hailey felt the wink burrow its way directly into her stomach, creating its own little tidal wave as it came to rest there. No doubt about it, the man had a way of stealing her breath away.

Chapter Nine

It seemed nothing short of a minor miracle to Hailey just how she managed to move around the spa for the rest of the day, seeing as how her feet didn't actually make any contact with the floor beneath them.

She really was floating on air.

She had a date with Dillon.

Each and every time she thought of that, her stomach would do a little dance, completely throwing off her equilibrium, not to mention that her stomach wound up tying itself all up in knots. Granted the date wasn't until the end of the week—Friday—but it was a date. An official date that had absolutely nothing to do with her work or his.

At the time, just before they went their separate ways from the flea market, it had taken her a few minutes to realize he was asking her out. Dillon had adorably stumbled through the invitation and at first she hadn't been sure if he was asking her if she liked eating at the restaurant in town, the one he and his brothers were currently involved in renovating, or if he was asking her to eat at Osteria Oliva, the Italian restaurant that had recently opened at the far end of the shopping center. Maybe he wanted a layperson's point of view on the work that had been done.

When Hailey finally unscrambled his words—no easy feat—Dillon had looked almost as surprised as she was at the invitation. It was almost as if the invitation had come out of his mouth of its own accord. But what counted was that it *had* come.

Hailey smiled to herself. The man was definitely *not* a smooth talker, but she liked that about him. The last few men in her life had all been silver-tongued bad boys who, she had found out later in each relationship, had a penchant for juggling more than one woman at a time in their lives.

It had gotten to the point that she had started to think—unhappily—that she had a type, and not a good one. Or, at the very least, that she was prey for a certain type of male.

Her smile deepened as she relived the moment

he had asked her out. When Dillon had finally gotten out the invitation, he would have made the "aw, shucks, ma'am" Gary Cooper type very, very proud.

Hailey found his shyness extremely sweet. It was refreshing. At least she knew when he said something he meant it and wasn't just spouting empty words in an attempt to win her over and talk his way into her bed.

That in itself was more tempting than she would have thought possible. Dillon's utter awkwardness was exceedingly seductive.

But she was getting ahead of herself. She needed to pace herself, to go slow instead of just diving headlong into the waters. Despite all her warnings, though, Hailey could feel her pulse racing each and every time she thought of spending time with Dillon.

Hailey sighed. It was going to be a long, *long* week, she thought.

She was right. It *was* a long week and time just seemed to dribble by one excruciatingly elongated moment at a time.

But finally, *finally* after what seemed like an eternity, it was Friday.

Hailey made plans to leave the spa early in order to give herself plenty of time to get ready for her date. But life, as it was wont to do, had other plans for her, starting with two of her yoga instructors waylaying her just as she was about to leave the building.

It seemed that the instructors were teaching classes with conflicting time slots.

So, with her mind already at home, going through her closet for the perfect outfit to wear tonight, Hailey had to get her thoughts in gear so that she could reschedule the two classes. Once that had been taken care of, she found herself on the phone, calling each one of the prospective clients who had eagerly signed up for the classes.

Hailey was well aware that it was a task that could have easily been delegated to someone else to handle, but since the wellness spa was still in its infancy stage, she felt that it better if she personally expressed her regret to each client. She assured each and every one of them that something like this wouldn't happen again.

In addition, to make sure that everyone involved had their ruffled feathers smoothed, she had given the women who had signed up a discount. It had been an arbitrary last-minute decision on her part and it seemed to have done the trick.

The moment she had finished the calls, she left her office and dashed to her car. Gunning her engine, she glanced at her watch. She was going to be cutting it close, Hailey thought. The relaxing bubble bath she had promised herself had to—out of necessity—turn into a very quick shower.

She still hadn't settled on what to wear, but that too was going to have to be a quick decision rather than one painstakingly arrived at after trying on a variety of different outfits.

She did her best to calm her ever-growing nerves, reminding herself that Dillon wasn't taking her outfit to dinner, he was taking the woman *in* the outfit to dinner. Namely *her.* She had a feeling he would only notice the outfit unfavorably if she came wearing a shapeless burlap sack and a used one at that.

No, she amended, Dillon Fortune would only have an unfavorable reaction to something she was wearing if that outfit had been dipped in a bathtub filled with jasmine oil.

With that in mind, Hailey showered using unscented body wash. She also was careful not to use any colognes or lotions after her shower that had any sort of scent to them. She wanted to take absolutely no chances. The last thing she wanted was for those baby blue eyes of his to suddenly become bloodshot or blurry because of something she had unconsciously put on, washed with or accidentally applied to her skin.

The only thing she wanted to do when the night ended was leave Dillon wanting more.

She hurried through dressing, keeping her eyes on the bedside clock. Dillon struck her as the type of man who arrived early for an appointment, not late.

And, as it turned out, she was right.

Hailey had just finished getting ready by the skin of her teeth. She was in the process of slipping on her high heels when she heard her doorbell ring. Hoping she didn't look like something the cat had dragged in, she hurried to the front door and opened it.

Dillon was standing on her doorstep, looking breathtakingly handsome in jeans, a crisp shirt as blue as his eyes and a pair of tooled riding boots that looked more than broken in.

"You're early," she remarked, trying to cover up the fact that she was staring at him. Belatedly, she remembered to take a step back so that Dillon could come in.

His eyes traveled over the length of her, obviously enjoying the journey. "And you're sensational. I mean…" He found himself at a loss for words.

She grinned, relieved Dillon didn't seem to have noticed her breathless reaction to him.

"No need to correct yourself," she quickly told him. "You can stop right there. It's been a really rough week and an even rougher afternoon and your compliment is more than welcomed," she assured him with feeling. And then she smiled. "Thank you."

"I meant it," Dillon told her. "You *do* look nothing short of sensational." When he saw her reaching for it, he took her shawl in his hands and helped her slip it over her shoulders. "I kind of feel bad that I'm only taking you to the local steakhouse," he confessed. "If I was back in Fort Lauderdale, I could take you to a really classy place, but here…"

He shrugged as his voice trailed off, indicating that he felt at a disadvantage at the shortage of upscale restaurants to choose from.

Picking up her purse, Hailey led the way out. She was eager to put Dillon at ease.

"Well, this really isn't about the food, is it? It's about two people going out so that they can get to know each other better." She smiled at him as she locked her front door. "Right now, all I know about you is that you're part of a construction firm that is busy building and renovating Rambling Rose and that you have very strong shoulders," she added with a laugh.

"Not that strong," Dillon corrected. "You're not exactly heavy."

"Still, that was a very impressive move at the flea market," she told him as they walked to his car. "Speaking of which, I love my frog," she said with genuine enthusiasm. "He's officially the best piece in my collection and if it hadn't been for you, I might have missed him entirely."

Dillon nodded, really pleased by her reaction. "Glad I could help," he responded.

The drive to the restaurant was a short one. Too short to get embroiled in any sort of meaningful conversation.

Dillon seemed to be fine with that. As a matter of fact, Hailey got the distinct impression that he preferred it that way.

But then, she told herself, she was probably reading too much into the stretch of silence that occurred between them.

When they were seated and the server handed them their menus, Hailey noted with a shade of minor distress that all the meals appeared to be centered around either beef or chicken.

Noticing her frown as she skimmed the menu, Dillon asked, "Anything wrong?"

She raised her eyes to his. "Hmm? No, everything's fine," she assured him, wanting their first outing to remain positive. "Would you know if this place offers any vegetable platters?"

He looked at her as if her question didn't make any sense to him. "A vegetable platter?" he repeated, a little mystified. "This is Texas. Everything's about meat here, isn't it?"

"Not necessarily," she told him. When she saw that he looked somewhat dismayed by her reaction, she did her best to quickly try to cover it up. "That's all right. I just asked because I was in the mood for something light." She didn't dare tell him she was a vegetarian.

He thought for a second. "Why don't you try the grilled chicken? I hear that's light enough to float right off your plate."

"Well, now you've piqued my curiosity. Okay, I'll give the grilled chicken a try," she said, closing her menu and putting it down beside her silverware.

Pleased that he had solved her problem, he looked back at the menu to double check something, then put it down, as well.

"Well, I know what I'm having." He saw her raise an eyebrow, waiting for him to tell her. "The porterhouse steak. Rare," he added. "With a serving of mashed potatoes and gravy."

"No vegetables?" she couldn't help asking him.

Dillon shook his head. "They'll only take room away from the steak."

It was on the tip of her tongue to say that the vegetables were healthier and if he had his heart set on the steak, he could at least offset his choice with a side of vegetables, but she refrained. The last thing a man on his first date with a woman wanted to hear was a lecture about his food choices.

Instead, Hailey just allowed herself to make a comment about the way he liked his food prepared. "Rare, huh?"

Dillon nodded, blissfully oblivious to her subtle meaning. "Rare," he repeated, then added, "I like my steak barely passed over the flames."

She thought of all the lectures she had attended regarding the health factors of cooking red meat, and wondered whether she ought to suggest to Dillon that he reconsider and have his steak cooked a little more. Well, at least a little more! But she didn't want to come across as lecturing him, and besides, that could be a conversation for another time, in the future.

If they wound up having a future, she silently added.

"So, tell me, what made you want to become a contractor?" she asked once the server had taken their orders and retreated.

Dillon didn't really have to think before giving her an answer. "I guess I like taking old places and bringing them back to life," he told her. "Besides, it was something my brothers were into whole-heartedly." He smiled, remembering. "They have a tendency to jump in with both feet and I'm the one who stops to look at all the possible angles, all the ways something could go wrong. I suppose," he went on as he buttered one of the rolls that the server had left, "you could say that I'm their anchor and my brothers are the ones who buoy me up. In other words," he concluded just before he took a bite of his roll, "we make a good team."

"In *any* words you make a good team," Hailey countered. "But that kind of work has to be rather stressful for you," she said after thinking it over. "If it ever gets to be too much, you might want to look into taking some yoga classes."

His experience at the spa was limited to the Mommy and Me class—and that was really enough in his opinion. Dillon had to laugh. "I think bending into a pretzel would turn out to be more stressful than beneficial for me," he told Hailey. Dillon thought that his response would bring an end to the discussion.

"There's more to yoga than that," she tactfully pointed out.

He shrugged off the point she was attempting

to impress on him. "I'll just take your word for it," he told her.

She eagerly jumped at the opening he'd inadvertently created. "Well, if you'd like to make an appointment, I could personally show you how taking yoga lessons can help you."

He looked at her with surprise. "You think I need help?"

Seeing her error, she quickly restructured her statement. "I think in this fast-paced world, if we're out in it, we all need help."

"Okay," he agreed, gracefully bowing out of what could wind up being a rather lengthy, uncomfortable discussion. "I'll think about it and let you know."

"Can't ask for more than that," Hailey said cheerfully. She could, she added silently, but that wouldn't get her anywhere and the idea was for them to get to know one another, not to antagonize one another. She had a feeling that if she pushed too much, she just might drive Dillon away instead of get closer to him.

She had noticed that when they'd sat down, Dillon had placed his phone on the table right next to his plate instead of tucking it away. Not only that, but she saw that his eyes kept straying to it. He must have done that several times so far and they hadn't even been served yet.

"Expecting a call?" she couldn't help asking.

He hadn't realized that he was being so obvious. "No," he denied. "I just want to be ready in case a call does come in. In this business, you never know," he told her evasively. "Nothing more frustrating than fumbling around, trying to locate a ringing cell phone," he added in an attempt to sweep the subject under a rug. "But if it makes you feel better, I can put my cell phone into my pocket so it doesn't interfere with our dinner," he told her, going through the motions of picking the phone up, even though he was hoping she would say no to his offer. "How's that?"

"Very understanding of you, but if you'd rather keep closer tabs on your phone, please, feel free to do so." She smiled at him warmly. "I take it you can multitask?"

"With the best of them," Dillon told her with a laugh, checking the screen again in case he had accidentally turned down his phone so he couldn't hear it when it was ringing.

But according to the information, there were no missed calls and no text messages, either.

Dillon tried not to show his disappointment.

Chapter Ten

During the course of the meal, as she did her best to draw Dillon out, Hailey discovered that they were more different than they were alike.

Dillon, she found, was a dyed-in-the-wool carnivore who for the most part was a workaholic and he had a tight rein on his emotions. She, on the other hand, was a vegetarian who, while dedicated to her job, was outgoing and liked to live within the moment, getting everything from life it had to offer. She also found out that he liked spending evenings alone while she enjoyed unwinding with friends. She liked reading mysteries while he tended to read architectural books.

No doubt about it, she thought by the end of the evening, they were oil and water. However, she had to admit that they did have one very big thing going for them.

Chemistry. Really hot chemistry.

There was no denying that she was extremely attracted to Dillon and she had the definite impression that he felt the same way.

She felt this even more so when they finally left the restaurant because when Dillon brought her home, he seemed reluctant to leave and have the evening come to an end.

Hailey debated inviting him in for a nightcap and seeing where that led. She really wanted to, but at the same time, she didn't want Dillon getting the wrong impression about her, didn't want him thinking that this was the usual way she did things.

There was nothing "usual" about the way she felt about Dillon. Which was why, despite her promise to herself to the contrary, Hailey was on the verge of inviting him inside when he surprised her by suddenly asking, "Would you like to come and see my ranch next weekend?"

Hailey felt her mouth curving in amusement. "Is that anything like asking me to come and see your etchings?" she asked.

Confused, Dillon looked at her blankly. "What?"

She laughed at his bewildered expression and shook her head. *Definitely from two different worlds*, she thought.

"Never mind," Hailey said, waving away her question. "I didn't realize you bought a ranch."

"Well, technically, I didn't. Not exactly." He searched for the right words. "When we first came out to Rambling Rose to check things out, Callum felt we'd feel as if we all had more at stake and in common with the township if we actually lived here, so we bought The Fame and Fortune Ranch. Jointly," he added. "It belongs to all of us. Callum, Steven, me and Stephanie," Dillon explained when she didn't say anything.

"How do you not get in each other's way living in the same house like that?"

He began to laugh, then realized she might be thinking that he was laughing at her and quickly explained, "I think once you see the place, you won't think that."

"Big?" Hailey asked, assuming that it probably had to be, given that it belonged to the Fortunes.

He was honest with her. "It would have to be downsized for that description to fit." And then he stopped abruptly. "I'm sorry, did that sound like I was bragging?" He didn't want her thinking that he was one of those wealthy men who enjoyed rubbing other people's noses in his wealth.

Hailey laughed again. She couldn't help thinking the man was adorable.

"If anyone else had said that, maybe," she told him honestly. "But coming from you, no. You were just stating a fact for my benefit." Taking a breath, she looked up at him, all sorts of warm feelings rushing through her. "And to answer your initial question, yes, I'd loved to come and see your ranch." She thought about all the work they had done since they had arrived in Rambling Rose. "Did you and your brothers build the ranch, as well?"

"Actually, we didn't," Dillon answered seriously, "although it is brand new. The original owner built it for himself and his fiancée."

"But?" Hailey prodded, then explained, "I sense there's a *but* coming."

"Very intuitive of you," Dillon commented. "They broke up before they ever had a chance to move in together. According to Callum, who handled the transaction, the guy was anxious to get rid of the place and move on, so for the mansion that it is, the cost was relatively inexpensive."

"Mansion?" Hailey repeated, allowing the full import of the word to sink in. If Dillon referred to it as a mansion, the place had to be absolutely *huge*.

Dillon nodded, wondering if he'd said the wrong thing again.

"That's the best way to describe it," he confessed. "There's enough space in the place for each of us to have the privacy we want and not wind up stumbling across the other three if we don't want to." He smiled as he envisioned the ranch. "Not to mention that there are also two guesthouses on the property. And, while the place isn't a working ranch, at least not at the present time, there is a stable on the premises."

"And horses?" she asked, allowing a touch of eagerness to seep through.

He looked down at her, amused. "What's a stable without horses?"

"Empty," Hailey answered automatically.

"Well, rest assured, our stable isn't empty," he told her. "So, now that I've given you a quick history, are you still interested in coming out and seeing it?" he asked, wanting to make sure that he wasn't reading what he wanted to hear into her answer.

"Well, that depends," Hailey told him, doing her best to maintain a straight face.

What sort of a condition could she be putting on this? he wondered. "On what?"

"On whether or not we go horseback riding," she answered simply.

Hailey didn't add that this would flesh out the fantasy she had when she'd first laid her eyes on him and couldn't help thinking of him as the embodiment of a magnificent cowboy.

"Would you like to? Go horseback riding, I mean. Next Saturday," he added. He had planned to build his way up to that slowly once he got her out to the ranch, but since she had brought up the subject now, he figured he'd ask.

"Absolutely," she told him. There was no mistaking her enthusiasm.

"Then it's a date," Dillon told her happily. Eager now, he began making plans in his head. "How early can I come by to pick you up?"

"How early did you have in mind?" she asked. Then, in case he was going to temper his answer because he felt she was the type who liked to sleep in whenever the opportunity arose, Hailey told Dillon, "I'm an early riser."

He broached the hour slowly, not wanting to scare her away. "Is eight too early?"

"Only if I were a slug—and I'm not," she added quickly in case he wasn't certain.

"All right, you pick the time," he told her. He decided it was safer if she got to pick.

"I can be ready by six," she told him, then added, "Earlier if you need me to be."

"No, six is plenty early enough." He rolled the time over in his head. "Tell you what, make it six-thirty in case the horses want to sleep in."

He did have a sense of humor, she thought, relieved as she grinned at him.

"Six-thirty it is," she told Dillon. She decided she needed to wrap this up just in case he wanted to be on his way. "I had a great time tonight," she added.

Dillon smiled at her. "No, you didn't," he said knowingly. "I should have asked you what sort of restaurant you wanted to go to. I guess it never crossed my mind you might be a vegetarian."

Because he apologized, she felt her heart swelling. The men she was used to dating would have blustered through it, saying something about the fact that they thought she was odd rather than apologizing for possibly making her feel uncomfortable. Dillon and she might not have the same tastes, but where it really counted, they were the same. She found that very comforting.

The corners of her mouth curved. He really was very, very sweet. "You're forgiven if I'm forgiven."

Dillon didn't understand what she was saying. "For what?"

"For making you uncomfortable," she explained.

But that didn't really clarify anything for him.

"I'm not uncomfortable," he protested. Then, because he felt as if the woman who had gone out with him tonight could see through him, he added, "Now."

She looked up at him, feeling so very moved that she could hardly stand it.

"Good," she whispered as she stood there, willing him to kiss her.

The next moment, she found that she had the gift of mental telepathy because he did.

Dillon kissed her.

And this time, it was even better than it had been the first time. There were no outside sounds to block, no extraneous noises to filter out. No milling people to ignore.

They could have easily been the only two people in the whole world because, at this moment in time, they really were.

The moment his lips touched hers, her head instantly began to spin, raising her body temperature and accelerating her heart rate.

Sinking into the velvety kiss, Hailey leaned into him, twining her arms around Dillon's neck and wishing with all her heart that she could invite him in.

But for all intents and purposes, this was their first date and she didn't want him to think that this was the way all of her first dates went.

Because they didn't.

Damn, Dillon thought, but she was making things really difficult. Without any apparent effort on her part, she had breached all his barriers, leaped over all of his well-placed walls. One second she was on the other side and then, wham, she was right there, nestling in through a crack he hadn't even been aware existed.

If he weren't careful, he was in danger of allowing her to get in far closer than he wanted her to be.

Even as he reasoned with himself, he had to fight the very real desire to lead her inside and take this date to its natural conclusion.

But just as he felt that he was about to capitulate and lose the battle with himself, Dillon felt his cell phone suddenly begin to vibrate, demanding his exclusive attention.

Without looking at the screen, he knew who was calling.

It had to be her.

Dillon forced himself to return back to earth. Taking a deep breath, he drew his lips away from Hailey's.

"I'd better get going before it's tomorrow," he told her.

But even as he said this, Dillon could feel himself being trapped between a reluctance to leave and the need to go.

Hailey nodded, drawing back.

"Can't have that," she agreed, although she didn't sound all that convinced.

But maybe he was just reading into her reaction, Dillon thought, branding her actions with his own reluctance. He took a deep breath. He needed to stop vacillating and just go before he did something that they were both going to regret for very different reasons.

He began to walk away from her, then turned back and caught her up in his arms for one last deep quick kiss. When she looked at him, stunned because she thought he'd changed his mind about leaving again, Dillon told her, "One more for the road."

And then he was gone.

Forcing herself to move, Hailey slipped inside her house, then closed the door. Once she flipped the lock, she leaned her back against the door and slid down to the floor.

"You are definitely not what I'm used to, Dillon Fortune," she murmured into the darkness.

He definitely *wasn't* what she was used to. But she was really looking forward to finding out what he *was* like.

* * *

The rest of the week spread out before her like an obstacle course to be maneuvered through and conquered with the prize being the man on the other side of that week. Dillon Fortune and his ranch.

She couldn't wait to go riding with him. Couldn't wait to see Dillon looking all masculine and incredibly sexy on top of a horse.

Couldn't wait to see *him*.

Suddenly, every minute was precious to her as it went by because it was one less minute she had to live through before she could finally get to go horseback riding with Dillon.

Telling herself that she was behaving like some smitten teenager didn't make her change her behavior, other than force her to bury it—but only while she was at work.

And even then, some of her clients, the ones who knew her before the wellness spa had ever opened its doors, detected a difference in her behavior, a certain lightness about her manner.

"Someone new in your life?" Maryanne Edwards asked her.

Maryanne had known Hailey since they were both in their senior year in high school. Although not anywhere as close to her as Janelle had been, Maryanne had still witnessed Hailey going through several relationships over the years. She had also seen them all crash and burn for one reason or another.

"Lots of new someones lately, Maryanne," Hailey had answered.

"Let me be more specific," the other woman said, trying again. "Are you juggling two guys at once?" Maryanne asked enviously.

"No, it's more like juggling forty or fifty at the same time," Hailey answered.

When her friend could only stare at her, speechless, Hailey had to laugh.

Taking pity on the woman, Hailey said, "Clients, Maryanne. I'm talking about clients at the spa. I'm juggling forty or fifty clients at a time—and ready to juggle more."

Maryanne frowned, disappointed. "You know what I mean."

"Yes, I do," Hailey replied. "And if you're asking me if I'm juggling a guy, I can assure you that the answer is no, I'm not. Besides," she continued with feeling, "when would I possibly have time for a new guy when I've got so much work to keep me busy? I have to schedule breathing these days."

"I know you, Hailey," the woman told her. "If you like the guy, you would definitely find a way to fit him into your schedule."

"Ah, you give me too much credit, Maryanne," Hailey told the woman as she began to briskly walk away from her friend.

"Do I?" Maryanne called after her.

Hailey didn't answer her. But she smiled as she kept on walking.

One hour closer to her target.

Chapter Eleven

She had told Dillon that she would be ready at 6:30 a.m. Although she was carefree to a fault, Hailey had made it a point never to keep anyone waiting. Which was why the next morning she was ready by 5:30 a.m.

The last thing she wanted to do was take a chance on having Dillon arrive early, then decide to leave because he didn't want to wait around while she was getting dressed. Not that Dillon struck her as being the impatient type, but the truth of it was, Hailey was not all that sure exactly *what* he was.

While she had to admit that Dillon seemed to be acting less like he was carrying around the weight of the world on his shoulders than when she had first met him, she still sensed that there was something reticent about him. Like he was deliberately holding something back.

But as to what, she didn't even have a clue.

Hailey decided that the easiest explanation was probably that he had been burnt in a relationship by some self-centered, unfeeling woman. As a result, Dillon behaved far more guarded about his emotions than the men she'd known in the past.

But, she concluded, all that did was present her with a challenge. A challenge she was more than happy to take on and vanquish.

If that meant getting up slightly before any self-respecting rooster woke up, well so be it. It was a small sacrifice to make.

To keep her mind off how terribly early it actually was and how much she really wanted to go back to bed, after she showered and dressed for the day at Dillon's family ranch, Hailey busied herself preparing breakfast for the two of them.

Not just a simple breakfast, but one that she felt confident any diner on the East Coast would have been more than happy to put on their counter. She was motivated by his apparent attachment to the state where he had originated from: Florida.

To that end, Hailey made scrambled eggs, toast,

bacon and sausage. She also made pancakes and waf-
fles. By the time she finished, there was definitely
enough on the table to feed a small army. She willingly admitted that she had indulged in overkill, but
she had done it to give Dillon his choice of anything
he might have wanted for the first meal of the day.

In order to ensure that it all kept hot, she put everything on a warming tray that she usually kept
tucked away for use during the holidays.

Hailey had just finished arranging the pancake
stacks on two different platters when she heard
the doorbell ring. She automatically glanced at
her watch.

Surprisingly, Dillon was ten minutes late.

Putting the platters where she wanted them, she
hurried over to the front door.

Then, taking a deep breath and bracing herself,
she smiled and threw the door open.

"Hi," she said, greeting him. "You're later than
you said you'd be. I thought that maybe you had
changed your mind."

"I would have called if I'd changed my mind,"
he assured her. "I just thought I'd let you sleep in
a few extra minutes." He laughed softly to himself, acknowledging his mistake. "I guess I should
have known better."

And then he stopped, taking in a deep breath

and inhaling a number of different aromas, all delicious. He looked at Hailey quizzically.

"Am I interrupting something? What is that fantastic smell?" he wanted to know.

Pleased by his reaction, she smiled. "Breakfast. Come," Hailey coaxed, beckoning for him to follow her as she led the way into the kitchen.

"You made breakfast?" he asked, surprised. He hadn't expected her to do that. He had just thought he was coming by to pick her up.

"I had to," she answered, then deadpanned, "The elves have gone on strike."

He wasn't prepared to see all the food that was laid out on the counter. Dillon was clearly caught off guard. For a moment, he didn't know what to say. And then, when he found his tongue, he told her, "You didn't have to do all this."

"Well, once I got started, I kind of did," she told him. "I wasn't sure what you'd like to eat and I thought it safer just to give you a wide choice." She gestured toward the counter. "Take your pick," she invited, pleased by the stunned expression on his face.

The sight of all that food really did catch him by surprise, especially in light of what he said in answer to her invitation.

"I usually just have coffee," he told her.

"Oh." Hailey struggled not to sound as disappointed as she felt. However, Dillon could clearly hear it in her tone.

Thinking of all the effort she had put into this breakfast—effort she had obviously exerted because of him—Dillon quickly backtracked. "But everything looks so good, I can't just walk away from it." He looked at her, giving her a wide smile. "I'll have to taste everything."

She didn't want him forcing himself to eat on her account. "That's all right, you don't have to."

"Oh, but I want to," he insisted.

Dillon felt that although he might not be up on his dating etiquette, he was definitely up on his manners. He was convinced that it would be bad form to have her go to all this trouble and then have him just take a pass on all of it. Besides, even though he wasn't hungry to begin with, he had to admit that this food did smell pretty damn tempting. He would have had to be dead not to have that aroma arouse his appetite.

Dillon's eyes met hers. "Join me?" he asked.

Hailey flashed a smile at him as she picked up two plates. She handed him one and took the other.

"I'd love to," she told him, turning her attention to the extensive array. "I know there's a trend to skip breakfast these days, but I always felt that a healthy breakfast laid the groundwork for a productive day."

Hailey took a little of everything so that, when she was finished, what was on her plate just equaled a normal sized serving of breakfast. Dillon followed suit right behind her.

"Oh." Hailey had barely sat down when she realized that she had forgotten something.

"What is it?" Dillon asked as he saw her getting up again.

"I forgot all about putting out some dry cereal," she explained. "I didn't know if maybe you would prefer that to this." She nodded at the table.

She really did know how to overwhelm a man, Dillon thought. But then, he had a feeling that this wasn't her first time for that. Any man she would have gone out with would have been overwhelmed in her presence.

He put her mind at ease. "Dry cereal never smelled this good." He nodded at her chair. "Please sit and enjoy this with me."

Hailey liked the way he had put that. She did as Dillon suggested, sinking back down in her chair. She really was hungry at this point.

They ate in silence for about a minute, and then he had to ask, "Do you always go this overboard?"

He nodded at all the food that was still left on the warming tray.

"Only when I'm not sure of my audience," Hailey told him truthfully.

"I thought that maybe your plan was to get me so full I couldn't move," he said, breaking off another strip of bacon and eating it.

"No," she laughed, "No plan. I just prepared everything I could think of."

He wasn't in the habit of overeating, but everything tasted so good, it was hard to get himself to stop. "I guarantee you that once I finish even half of this," he said, glancing down at his plate, "my horse is going to go on strike when I try to mount him."

She had a sudden image of that and found herself grinning. "I highly doubt that."

"I don't," Dillon countered, finishing another piece of toast. "Rawhide has a mind of his own, and whatever is on it, he makes sure you know about it."

"Rawhide?" Hailey repeated quizzically.

"My horse," Dillon told her.

He was volunteering details and she eagerly soaked them up.

"What kind of a horse do you have?" Hailey wanted to know. Then, before Dillon could answer, she held up her hand, stopping him. "Wait, let me guess." She thought for a second, picturing Dillon on his horse. "A black stallion, right?"

"I'm afraid that Zorro claimed that one," Dillon deadpanned.

She ate the last of her scrambled eggs. "All right, what *do* you ride?" Hailey asked.

"A dapple gray."

She had to admit she felt a little disappointed by the image that sprang up in her mind. "Named Rawhide?" she questioned.

"That's the name he answers to," Dillon told her. "Why? Something wrong?" he asked. She had a disillusioned expression on her face.

She lifted her shoulders in a shrug. "His name doesn't suit his appearance."

Her answer amused him. He never thought about the horse's name one way or another. "Well, you can tell him that yourself when we go out riding later today," he teased.

"I didn't mean to sound as if I was being critical." She felt she owed him an explanation for her reaction. "It's just when you said his name was Rawhide, I got this image of a jet-black stallion dramatically rearing up on his hind legs."

Finishing his coffee, Dillon set down his cup. "I don't know about the rearing part, but Rawhide runs a fast mile and he has to be one of the smartest horses I've ever come across."

"Well, I'd really love to meet him," Hailey told him, hoping that she hadn't ruined anything by allowing her fantasy to get the better of her.

"You will," he assured her. Damn, but he felt full, he thought. He shouldn't have eaten as much as he had. "Along with Delilah."

"Delilah?" she echoed.

"Your horse," Dillon told her. "At least she is for today. You did want to go riding today, right?" he asked, realizing that maybe he had assumed too much.

"Oh, yes," she told him. The dapple gray might not be living up to the image she had projected for Dillon, but the bottom line was that they were going to go riding together and that was what she really wanted. "What color is my horse?" she asked, then quickly added, "No expectations. I'm just curious."

Dillon smiled. He was getting a real kick out of this woman. "Tell me, does a palomino work for you?"

Her face lit up with anticipation. "Very much so," she answered with feeling.

Dillon took a deep breath as he looked down at what was left on his plate. He had eaten more than he had thought he could. It had all been exceptionally tasty, but there was only so much he could consume without the risk of exploding.

He raised his eyes and looked at her. "Would you be very insulted if I didn't finish everything?"

She laughed softly. "I'd be surprised if you did. I told you, I didn't intend for you to eat everything. I just wanted to give you a variety to choose from."

"Well, you certainly did that," Dillon told her. He rose, picking up his plate and cup and heading for the sink. "You ready to go?"

"Since five-thirty this morning," she told him. Suddenly realizing what he was doing, she said, "You don't have to do that." Hailey began to take his plate from him, intending to put it on top of her own and bring them both to the sink.

But he raised his plate up out of her reach. "My mother made a point of teaching us all to clean up after ourselves. I might be a Fortune, but that doesn't mean I think I'm entitled to special privileges."

Despite their different tastes and approaches to things, she was beginning to really like Dillon and the way he thought.

"Just put your dishes into the sink. I'll wash them when I get home," she told him. Turning her back on him, she unplugged the warming tray and deposited what was left of breakfast into plastic containers and put those into the refrigerator.

When she turned back around to face Dillon, Hailey saw that he hadn't listened to her. He had not only brought the plates over to the sink, but he had washed said plates and was now putting them on the rack to dry off.

"You know, I could get used to this. You're spoiling me," she told him.

In her opinion, the smile that curved the corners of his mouth was positively sexy. "I could say the same thing about you making all that breakfast for us this morning," he said.

She gave him a look. "It's not the same thing. I like to cook," she emphasized. "And if you tell me that you like to wash dishes, I'm going to have to fight a very strong urge to tell you that you're lying."

Dillon grinned, clearly tickled. "Then I won't say it."

Time to change the subject, she decided. "I believe you said something about your ranch and us going horseback riding?" she prompted.

His grin widened as he dried his hands on a nearby dish towel. "I believe I did, yes," he agreed.

She took off the apron she'd had on and draped it on the back of a chair. "Then let's get to it," she urged. "I can't wait to meet Delilah."

"Okay, then let's not keep her—or you—waiting," he said, ushering her toward the door.

* * *

Hailey wasn't prepared for the ranch. She thought she was, but when she actually was able to see it, she realized that the sprawling house exceeded her wildest expectations.

As they came closer, she let out a low whistle. "You people really live in that?" she asked in awe.

"Yes, why?" he asked, amused by her reaction.

This was bigger than huge, she couldn't help thinking. "What happens when you forget to bring your GPS with you?" she wanted to know.

Dillon began to laugh. "It's not *that* big," he told her.

"No?" she questioned. "In comparison to what? New York City?"

Still laughing, he shook his head. "You're exaggerating."

"Not by much," she countered. "Don't get me wrong, I'm sure it's gorgeous on the inside. I'm just used to something a little homier. Something I wouldn't wind up getting lost in," she added.

"Do you do that a lot?"

"Not until now," she answered, looking at the mansion again.

"Then let me take you on a tour of my wing," Dillon offered.

She didn't bother hiding the stunned look on her face. "You have a wing," she marveled.

"Well, it's more like a suite, but yeah. We each do," he told her. "Remember, I told you that when I said we bought the ranch," he reminded her.

She did remember his saying something to that effect. "I guess maybe I didn't really take you literally," she told him.

He didn't understand why she wouldn't. "I don't make things up," he told her.

"I'm beginning to learn that," she said. "Tell me more," she urged.

Because he didn't know when she would want to go back home, he left his car parked in the circular driveway and then got out.

"I will. On the tour," he promised. Rounding the hood, he came up to her door on the passenger side and then opened it without any fanfare. As she began to get out, he offered her his arm.

She had assumed that his formal politeness would fade after he had gotten used to her, but apparently she was wrong. His behavior gave every appearance of continuing indefinitely.

Heaven help her, but she had to admit that she rather liked that.

Chapter Twelve

The outside of the main house that Dillon brought her to was breathtakingly huge, but that still did not prepare Hailey for what she saw on the inside.

Stepping through the massive doorway into the biggest ranch house she had ever seen.

"Wow." The word seemed to escape her lips of its own accord as she looked all around her, taking her surroundings in. It was hard not to be overwhelmed.

As he began to take her on a tour, Dillon tried to see the house he had been living in for the last few months through Hailey's eyes.

He had to admit that he envied her being able to

feel such awe. He tried to remember the last time he had felt anything remotely akin to that.

Maybe when he was a kid?

But probably not even then, he decided. Dillon was fairly certain that what he had felt was nothing like what Hailey was experiencing, judging by the expression on her face.

"I take it your *wow* means that you like it?" he asked, amused.

Hailey drew in a deep breath, and then another when the first breath didn't seem sufficient enough to help her put her thoughts into words.

When she finally spoke, it was to tell him, "I don't think *like* begins to even remotely describe something like this. I mean I've never thought of myself as being sheltered, but this—" she turned around slowly, taking in as much as she could of the expansive area "—this is a completely different world than anything I've ever known." Looking around again, she tried to envision her own home nestled in here. "I think I could fit my whole house—and then some—into what you refer to as a *wing*."

Amused, Dillon laughed. "You're exaggerating," he told her.

"No. I'm not," she insisted. "You grew up in a house like this?" she asked as they continued on their tour, passing a massive bedroom and an equally sized game room followed by a den.

"I grew up in a house," he said vaguely. "With my family." He deliberately stressed what they had in common, not their differences. "And now I am going to take a lovely spa manager—"

"I don't know about the lovely part," she murmured, embarrassed.

"I do," he assured her. "And I'm still taking you horseback riding—unless you'd rather continue the house tour."

"Definitely horseback riding," Hailey declared. "I pick horseback riding."

Dillon laughed, nodding. "Good choice. All right, let's head over to the stables. Are you game to walk over there, or would you rather we drive?" he wanted to know, giving Hailey a choice.

When they approached the property, she hadn't noticed where the stables were. Since everything on the property appeared to be so sprawling, she didn't want to bite off more than she could chew right from the beginning.

"Just how far away are the stables?" she tactfully asked.

He thought for a moment. "About a half a mile," he judged. "Maybe a little more."

She gave him a look that seemed to ask if he thought she was some sort of fragile flower. She could do that distance with one leg tied behind her back, she thought.

"I'll try not to be insulted—and we'll walk," she informed him.

Dillon's smile spread across his lips. "Whatever you say," he told her.

"There's no sense in letting a beautiful day like today go to waste," she said, as if that was what had made her decide on walking there.

He grinned. "Ah, a lady after my own heart," he responded.

Oh, if you only knew.

Like his house, the stable turned out to be massive, as well. So far, it was only half filled with horses. But from what she could see, it looked as if there were no two horses that were alike.

"Are all these yours?" she asked Dillon in awe as she moved around the well-maintained stable.

"Yes," Dillon answered, "the horses belong to all of us in the family. And we keep some on hand for company."

Hailey was impressed. That was happening a lot lately, she realized. "Do you ride a different horse every day?"

"I hardly have time to ride every day. In fact, I don't ride nearly as much as I'd like," he confessed. "This is actually a treat for me. Nothing makes you forget your troubles faster than being on the back of a horse, feeling the wind in your hair, the sun in your face and, riding with no particular destination in mind, just to enjoy the ride."

He really sounded as if he meant that, she thought. Apparently there was something that he really enjoyed doing outside of making the structures that he drew on paper come to life. She liked that, she thought. It made him seem more human somehow.

Her eyes fell on the dapple gray stallion. Her heart beating hard, she crossed over to his stall. Because the horse didn't really know her, Hailey approached the animal slowly. She raised her hand very carefully toward his muzzle, and then, when the stallion didn't pull back, she petted him. She was really pleased that he didn't move his head back but accepted the contact.

"So who rides all these other horses?" she wanted to know.

"My brothers and sister. And their friends—or spouses," Dillon said, correcting himself. He had to admit that at times it was still hard for him to get used to the idea that both Callum and Steven were married now. And Stephanie was engaged and living with Acton on his ranch. Not only that, but Stephanie was ten weeks pregnant, as well. It felt as his life was just galloping passed him.

Dillon focused on his stallion. "I think Rawhide likes you," he noted with genuine pleasure.

"Of course he does," Hailey responded, running her hand along Rawhide's muzzle. "I'm very likeable."

She wasn't bragging. She had always made a genuine effort to try to get along with everyone, and felt that her attitude just naturally radiated toward everyone, animals included.

Dillon was standing directly behind her. From his vantage point, he could breathe in the natural fragrance of her hair. Despite the fact that he had promised himself that this outing was going to be purely platonic, there was no denying that standing this close to Hailey stirred him.

His thoughts went beyond just taking a simple ride on his favorite horse with a pleasant companion. Moved, he was exceedingly tempted to slip his arms around Hailey's waist and hold her against him.

Not the way to go, Dillon. You can't afford to get involved at this point. Maybe later, when things are all ironed out, but not now. You know that.

For one thing, he wasn't free to get involved with someone here when all he had been thinking about ever since he had arrived in Rambling Rose seven months ago was getting back to Fort Lauderdale.

He constantly had to remind himself of that when he was around this woman. He looked down at her as she patted Rawhide's velvety muzzle, imagining those hands on him.

"He's beautiful," she said as she looked up at Dillon.

"Handsome," Dillon corrected her. "I think Rawhide would prefer being called handsome," he said with a wide grin. "He's a male."

"Sorry, boy, didn't mean to insult your manhood," Hailey told the stallion, playing along. For his part, Rawhide seemed to accept the apology. Hailey smiled, continuing to pet the horse. "I think he forgives me," she told Dillon, pleased.

Who wouldn't?

Dillon wasn't aware that he'd said the words out loud until Hailey turned around to look at him in surprise.

"That's a very sweet thing to say," she told him.

"I didn't—I mean…" Dillon flushed, his tongue feeling thick and cumbersome as thoughts went shooting through his head with the speed of a comet.

Feeling his best bet was to change the subject, Dillon cleared his throat and asked, "Would you like to meet your mare?"

"I would *love* to meet her," Hailey told him. Stepping away from the stallion, she looked around. "Which way to her stall?"

"Delilah is right over here," Dillon answered,

leading Hailey over to another stall. This one was located at the far side of the stables.

The second she saw Delilah, Hailey fell in love.

"Oh, she is beautiful," she exclaimed in awe. Holding herself in check, Hailey carefully went through the same process she'd used with Rawhide in order to get close to and pet this new horse. She grinned at Dillon, looking at him over her shoulder. "And since Delilah's a girl, I can say that," she added, pleased.

"Yes, you can," he agreed. He found himself being charmed despite all his best efforts to remain detached and distant. There was no denying that the woman was getting to him. "Let me know whenever you're ready to go riding," he told her, although for his part, he would have been content just to continue watching Hailey pet her mount.

Hailey's eyes sparkled as she turned them toward Dillon.

"Now. I'm ready now," she informed him with enthusiasm.

"All right, then I'll get them saddled up and we can get going," he told her as he went to get the equipment.

Hailey watched as Dillon returned with a saddle, a blanket and a bridle, setting them down in the stall. Then he did the same for Rawhide. The man did keep surprising her, Hailey thought, leaving Delilah's stall and making her way over toward Dillon's stallion.

"You saddle your own horse?" she asked.

He laughed at the expression on her face. To him there was nothing unusual about what he was doing.

"It's part of the total experience. Why?" he asked. "What were you expecting?"

Hailey shrugged as she petted Dillon's horse. "I thought you'd have one of your stable hands saddle up the horses," she confessed.

He didn't bother to hide his amusement. "In case you hadn't noticed, despite our last name, we like to get our hands dirty," he said as he slipped a bridle on the stallion.

Once he did that, he put a blanket on Rawhide's back, then placed his prized hand-tooled saddle onto the blanket. Securing the saddle in place, he checked each cinch in turn, making sure none was too tight or too loose.

"Okay, Rawhide's ready to go," he announced, hitching the stallion's reins onto a post in the stall. "Now let's get Delilah ready."

"You're going to have to walk me through this," she told Dillon, following him into the mare's stall. "I've never saddled a horse before."

Surprised, Dillon turned around to look at her. "But you have gone riding before, right?" he asked, realizing that he had taken some things for granted.

"I have, but they always saddled the horse for me at the stable. I don't own my own horse," she interjected, in case he had gotten the wrong impression.

"Well, don't worry. I was planning on saddling your horse for you, too," he told her.

"Thanks, but I'd rather you just showed me how to do it," she said. When he looked at her, she added, "This way I'll know how to do it the next time."

She was planning on a *next time*, he realized. As for him, he wasn't planning on anything beyond this afternoon that they were going to be spending together.

For a second, he thought of saying something to make her understand that there was nothing long term in the making here. But for some reason, he just couldn't get himself to say the words. Part of him felt that it would wind up terminating this ride before it even happened.

So instead, he just said, "Sure. If that's what you really want, I can show you how to saddle Delilah."

With the same equipment ready—a bridle, blanket and saddle—he got started. Gently holding the mare's head so that it remained still, Dillon talked Hailey through all the steps. As he guided her, she slipped the bridle over the mare's muzzle and ears. Putting a blanket on the mare's back was simple enough, but when it came to positioning Delilah's saddle, that turned out to be a little trickier.

When she first slipped the saddle's strap in through the cinch, she wound up not tightening it enough and the saddle slid when Dillon tested it.

"No, it needs to be tighter," he told her. "Don't worry, you're not going to hurt her," he said, second-guessing what Hailey was thinking.

Getting in behind her, Dillon placed his hands over hers and told her, "This is how it's done." With that, he carefully showed her exactly what she needed to do.

Hailey was independent and preferred doing things for herself, but even so, she could really get used to this, she thought, her eyes slipping closed for a second as she absorbed the moment and the feeling of Dillon's hands on hers.

The close contact generated a warm feeling in the pit of her stomach.

Hailey released the breath she realized she had been holding and then drew in another. "I think I have it," she told Dillon, looking at him over her shoulder.

Her mouth was so close to his, for a split second Dillon was really tempted to give in to the desire that even now was growing more and more demanding.

And he probably would have if a ranch hand hadn't picked that exact moment to stick his head into the stall to look in on them.

"Is everything okay here, Mr. Fortune?" Manny Salazar, the caretaker at the ranch, asked, peering into the stall. "Do you need anything?" He smiled politely at the woman with his boss. "Can I get you anything?"

The answer to the man's first question was yes. The answer to his second one was no. Without his knowing it, the ranch hand had managed to rescue him from making another mistake, Dillon thought.

"No, we're good to go, Manny," he assured the man. "Thanks for asking." He looked at Hailey. "Are you ready to get into the saddle?" he asked, holding the mare's reins in his hand.

"That part I know how to do," Hailey answered with a smile. The next second, she swung herself into the saddle and then took the reins from Dillon. "Now all I need is you—to get on your horse," she added, realizing that her pause, coming where it did, had made for a very awkward moment. Even though what she'd said was true. All she did need was Dillon, away from his obligations, away from all the things that distracted him.

That went for the phone that even now he kept

checking, as if he were expecting some sort of earthshaking notification to come across its screen.

Dillon swung himself into his saddle without bothering to even put his foot into the stirrup. As he leaned over to pick up his horse's reins, Hailey couldn't help thinking that he looked nothing short of magnificent astride the stallion like that. The only thing that could have improved the image he cut, Hailey mused, was if his dapple gray had been a midnight black stallion instead of the color it was.

But even so, she couldn't help thinking, Dillon really was nothing short of magnificent.

And, she thought, as they exited the stable, for the next few hours or so, Dillon Fortune was all hers.

"Ready?" he asked one last time, his entire body poised for the ride.

"Ready," Hailey declared, anticipating the ride ahead of them.

"Then let's go!" Dillon said, kicking his heels into Rawhide's flanks.

Horse and rider took off.

Hailey followed suit, doing exactly as Dillon just had. Within seconds, she happily went flying, right alongside of Dillon.

Chapter Thirteen

Hailey found that the next two and a half hours were absolutely exhilarating. The truth of it was she hadn't been on a horse for at least six months—probably longer—and she was a little nervous about being up to it at the outset. But she had always been naturally agile and happily, the whole thing came back to her within a few minutes.

When she glanced toward Dillon, he didn't look as if he thought anything was amiss about her riding. As with the house, he was involved with acting as her tour guide, showing her the acreage of the entire ranch. That included pointing out the two guesthouses as well as the various stretches of empty land in the vicinity that were just *begging* for something to be built on them.

Hailey made no secret of the fact that she was duly impressed by all of it. But what interested her the most was Dillon's role here and just what his plans were for the future.

"Given all this empty space, does that mean that you plan to build your own place here someday?" she wanted to know.

They were looking down on a particularly lush and coincidentally isolated area of the ranch that looked as if it was just perfect for a ranch house, one that wasn't ripe for the label *mansion* but a place where regular people—people like her, she couldn't help thinking—could live.

Dillon appeared surprised by her question. "No, I'm not planning on staying here," Dillon answered matter-of-factly.

Hailey told herself that his response shouldn't have made her feel as if she'd been squarely hit by a Mack truck—but there was no getting away from the fact that it did.

Doing her best to sound nonchalant, Hailey asked, "Oh? You're not?"

"No." He had always thought of his move here as being just temporary because of what he had left behind in Florida. "Once our construction projects here are finalized, I'm going to be moving back to Fort Lauderdale."

The question rose to her lips before she could think to stop herself. "What's in Fort Lauderdale?"

Dillon glanced at her. He'd already said too much, he thought. Consequently, his answer was evasive. "It's my home."

His home. He lived there. That should have been the end of it for her. But Hailey was nothing if not stubborn and she wasn't ready to just let the subject go. "Maybe you'll change your mind."

Dillon didn't want to encourage Hailey, especially since what he had just said was essentially his game plan. He just wanted to finish up here, however long it took, and then move back to Florida. But then, on the other hand, it didn't seem right to flatly rule out the possibility, however minutely slim, that he'd be staying on here in Rambling Rose indefinitely.

Technically, indefinitely was different from permanently, right? he reasoned, slanting another look at the woman beside him.

So he shrugged and said, "Anything is possible."

The smile she flashed him made his wavering definitely feel worth it. Heaven help him, but looking at her made him feel as if the sun had suddenly lit up all his insides.

When he and Hailey finally turned their horses back toward the stable another hour later, Dillon had to admit that he was impressed by Hailey's stamina. She had kept up with him the entire time and she never once made any noises about going back or being too tired to go on. He, on the other hand, had begun to feel himself flagging. He blamed it on the fast pace he'd been keeping up, but whatever the reason, it did bother him a little that he was the one who decided to call an end to their horseback-riding adventure instead of Hailey.

"You might have a little trouble walking when we bring the horses back to the stable," Dillon warned her.

Hailey looked at him, confused. "Trouble walking? What do you mean by trouble?"

"Well, you made it sound like you don't go riding very often and you did just spend almost three hours in the saddle. All I'm saying is it's all right if, when you get off and you find everything aching, you want to complain about it," he told her.

"I don't believe in complaining," she answered truthfully. "Complaining about something is non-productive. Better to put that energy into something useful. Something that could make the situation better."

Dillon looked at her uncertainly. "Are you usually this utilitarian?"

She laughed softly. "No, you caught me on a good day. Most of the time I'm just being annoyingly upbeat—or so I've been accused by grumpy people."

Her answer amused him. "I'd say that compared to you, most people would seem to come across as grumpy," he speculated.

Maybe it was the way the sun was lighting up the area, but Dillon could have sworn her eyes were literally sparkling as she told him, "You'd be surprised. And, just in case you're right about my legs being shaky, why don't you stay close when I dismount? That way, if I am wobbly, you can keep me from falling down flat on my...pride?" she said, substituting the word *pride* at the last minute for the one she really meant.

Dillon nodded, game. "You've got a deal," he told her.

And he kept his word. When they reached the stable, he dismounted first and was right there beside her horse as Hailey prepared to get off Delilah.

Swinging her leg over the mare's flanks, Hailey dismounted the horse in a single fluid motion.

With her feet firmly on the ground, she let go of the breath she was holding.

"See, my legs are perfectly steady," she told Dillon, turning toward him. However, as she began to take a step, she suddenly felt herself all but sink to the ground.

Or she would have if a pair of very strong arms hadn't instantly closed around her and managed to keep her upright.

"Maybe not so perfectly," Dillon judged, his breath ruffling her hair and grazing her cheek as he spoke. "Your legs seem to be a little wobbly," he observed.

Hailey could feel her heart racing again, but definitely in a good way, she thought, grinning up at the man holding her up.

"I guess I stand corrected," she admitted. "My legs don't exactly feel weak so much as they feel... bowlegged," she finally said, describing what she felt to the best of her ability.

"That's because you had them wrapped around the flanks of a horse for a lot longer than you were probably accustomed to." He realized that he could go on holding her like this indefinitely as he smiled down into her face. "Nothing to be ashamed of," he added.

"I'm not ashamed," Hailey protested, then qualified her initial response. "Well, maybe I *am* a little embarrassed."

His smile widened. "Don't worry, your secret's safe with me," he promised.

Then, because he was still holding her far too close than he reasoned was safe for either one of them, Dillon told himself he needed to release her.

And he had every intention of doing just that.

But for some reason, his arms remained exactly where they were. The only thing that did move was his head. He inclined it, causing his lips to be just close enough to Hailey's so that he could do exactly what he had promised himself he wasn't going to do today—or at all in the foreseeable future.

He kissed Hailey.

Dillon told himself that he only meant to brush his lips against hers. But he quickly learned that the best-laid plans often didn't go the way they were meant to. Because once his lips made contact with hers, he really had no choice but to deepen the kiss.

Deepen it to the point that he felt himself getting lost in it.

Getting lost in her.

It took everything Dillon had not to allow himself to sink so far into this kiss that there would be no coming back. No course to take but the in-evitable one.

He wasn't that kind of a man, Dillon told him-self. He never had been. That meant that he didn't believe in just availing himself of carelessly going the "love 'em and leave 'em" route. He was far too decent a man to take what in his heart he knew could so easily be his. Especially since he intended to ultimately walk away from Hailey. Things being the way they were, he had no choice but to do that.

So, with effort, Dillon forced himself to draw back. To take a breath and tell himself that what he was doing was for the best.

"So," he finally said when he was able to speak coherently without running the risk of swallowing his own tongue. "Want to test those legs again?" he suggested.

What had just happened here, Hailey couldn't help wondering. One second she was certain that he was going to take her right here in the horse's stall—was she crazy or was there something in-credibly sexy about that?—the next he was mak-ing noises as if he'd turned into a prim Sunday school teacher.

Had she done something wrong? Was there something in her body language that had put him off at the last moment, or was there some other reason he had backed off the way he had?

She felt so confused that her head began to ache.

Don't overthink it, just go with it and play it cool. She'd figure all this out eventually.

So Hailey pretended to look down at her legs, as if she was passing judgment on their condition. And then she proceeded to take a guarded step forward.

And then another, a little less hesitant this time. The third step was a normal one.

"Well, whatever was wrong with them before seems to have cleared up," she informed him. Her smile was warm as she looked at him. "Thanks for catching me before I fell on my face."

"My pleasure," he told her. And then Dillon roused himself. Time for things to get back to normal, he silently insisted. "Once I get the saddles off these horses and rub them down, I'll drive you home."

Hailey was determined to make the best of the time they had left on this date and not ask any questions. "Okay, as long as you let me help." When he didn't reply, she added, "I take it that unsaddling the horses and giving them a rub down afterward is all part of riding them."

"Well yes, it is, but I can't ask you to do that."

He couldn't picture her doing anything other than standing there, looking beautiful.

"You're *not* asking me," she pointed out with a smile that went straight to his gut, even though he was trying his best to block it. "I'm volunteering to do my part," she pointed out. "Now do you want to stand here arguing about it—an argument that you're not going to win, by the way," she pointed out, "while the horses stand around, getting even more overheated? Or do you want to accept my offer to help and get to it? The faster you do, the faster you can take me home."

She had guessed right, she thought. The idea of getting her home seemed to spur him on. She tried not to let it bother her.

He shook his head. "You do have a way with words," he told her.

Confident that she had managed to win him over, Hailey flashed another grin at him, one that he found he was becoming increasingly more susceptible to, and said, "Then let's get to this, shall we?"

That grin of hers was really undoing him. Dillon found that it took everything he had not to sweep her back into his arms and kiss her again. But he was well aware of what would happen if he did that and he already knew how dangerous following that path could be. Each time he was near her like this, his immunity to her took another hit and it was becoming in dangerously low supply at this point.

Playing it safe, he took a step back, then he nodded his head and said, "All right."

Hailey found that unsaddling Delilah took a lot less time than saddling her had.

It was the rubdown that took up most of the time. Still, that was over much too soon in her estimation. Then, before she knew it, she was back in the passenger seat of Dillon's car and he was driving her home.

She told herself that she wasn't going to ask Dillon about his sudden change of heart.

As it turned out, she contained her curiosity longer than she thought she would. The drive back to her house was filled with trivial topics she introduced just to fill the air. Topics she definitely wasn't interested in and that she didn't pay any attention to even as he was talking about them.

Before she knew it, he was parking his vehicle in front of her house. And then Dillon walked her to her door.

Adding insult to injury, after refraining from kissing her goodbye, Dillon turned on his heel and began to walk away.

This time, Hailey lost the debate she was having with herself to refrain from asking questions.

"What happened, Dillon?"

She asked the question so softly, for a second, Dillon thought he had only imagined hearing her voice and only imagined hearing the question she'd asked. But then he realized that she *had* asked because, in her place, he would have wanted to know the same thing.

He would have wanted to know why.

Taking a deep breath, Dillon turned around slowly and looked at her. He was keenly aware that he owed her an explanation. But he was a private man and there were parts of himself that he couldn't share, at least not readily.

But that didn't change the fact that he *did* owe her an explanation. So he gave her one. Or at least a partial one.

"I knew that if I continued kissing you, it wouldn't stop there. And you're too nice a person to have me do that to you. I didn't want to compromise you," he added. "It wouldn't be right."

Was that it? Really? If he was telling the truth, she couldn't begin to describe the relief that washed over her. He was being noble.

But she didn't want him to be noble. She wanted

him to be himself, a man with needs. Needs that she could satisfy.

"Maybe I don't see it as being compromised," she told him gently.

"Be that as it may, I did. I do," he corrected, even as he felt himself losing ground.

"Tell you what, why don't you come inside for some coffee, or a beer," she added, thinking that might appeal to him more than just a simple cup of coffee. "And we can talk about it."

He was tempted. Very tempted, which was why taking her up on her suggestion was not a good idea. They would both regret it for different reasons. "No." He shook his head. "I'd better go."

She cocked her head, looking at him. "Why?" she asked, her voice soft and inviting. "I don't bite," she promised. "And I'd really like to understand your reasoning."

"Trust me, it's really better this way," he told her.

"Better for who?" she wanted to know. When he didn't answer her right away, she told him, "I'm open to being persuaded." Hailey smiled at him, doing her best to win him over. "And besides, I'd like to express my thanks to you for taking the time to give me a really great day I'll remember for a long time."

She could see that he was wavering so she continued to press, "You can leave at any time. I promise I won't handcuff you to anything that you can't drag in your wake. But seriously, I'd feel a lot better if you'd at least let me offer you that beer.

"It's still early," she pointed out, and then elaborated, "Too late to do anything productive, but too early just to call it a day."

He looked torn, but underneath his resolve, he knew he was slowly giving in because he really wanted to agree with her.

It was a short debate. "Okay, you win," he told her, following Hailey in.

"I'd like to think that we both win," she said as she closed the door behind them.

Chapter Fourteen

Once inside, Hailey went to the refrigerator and opened it.

"I can offer you the aforementioned beer or coffee, some tea, or I forgot I still have a partial bottle of wine from the spa's grand opening." Still holding the refrigerator door open, she turned her head to look at Dillon. "What would you like to have?"

You.

The thought flashed through his head. *Heaven help me, I'd like to have you.*

"Dillon? Did you hear me?"

Realizing he hadn't replied, he quickly answered, "Um, yes."

Hailey thought he hadn't heard her, since his answer made no sense. Not wanting to embarrass him, she gave it another shot. "Well, just to review, I can offer you two kinds of beer. Light and real beer," she said with a smile, then continued enumerating what drinks she had available. "Red wine. Coffee or tea. Those are your choices." She waited for him to pick one.

There was another choice, Dillon thought. One that neither one of them was mentioning. One that, if he remained much longer, he had a feeling would be made for him.

Dillon's eyes met hers.

She felt as if he were looking straight into her soul. And the electricity between them was so strong, she was surprised that one of them wasn't shooting off sparks from their fingertips.

Hailey took a breath, doing her best to stabilize herself.

"Tell you what," she suggested, possibly a bit too cheerfully. "Why don't I pour you a glass of wine since the bottle is already open? It would be a shame to let it go to waste."

As she talked, Hailey took out two wine glasses from the cupboard overhead. Putting them on the counter, she took the bottle out of the refrigerator, removed the cork and proceeded to pour two glasses. She brought the glasses over to the coffee table and placed one in front of Dillon as she sat down on the sofa with the other.

"To the continuing success of all your projects," she said, raising her glass in a toast. "You are all to be commended. You and your brothers have brought fresh life to this sleepy little town." She smiled warmly at him over the rim of her partially filled glass. "Thank you for all you've done."

"It was Callum's doing, really," Dillon told her quite honestly just before taking a sip of wine. He put his glass down. "He's the one with the vision," he said. "I just came along for the ride."

"You're being incredibly modest," she told him. "Don't forget, I saw what the spa building looked like *before* you worked your magic on it, transforming it into an absolute work of art in comparison." It was, she thought with pride, the first thing that new clients commented on.

"I'd hardly call it magic," Dillon protested uncomfortably.

"Maybe you wouldn't, but I would," she told him. Hailey moved closer to him without being aware of it. "You managed to take an ordinary, lackluster building and transform it into a work of art that offers its clients hope—not to mention a variety of classes to help get them achieve their goals and get into shape.

"Which reminds me," she said, her enthusiasm for her subject growing by leaps and bounds as she talked, "I've decided to add a couple of new classes to the roster. One of the classes focuses entirely on yoga and the other is a beauty treatment oriented for every inch of your body. Well, not *your* body," she corrected, her eyes traveling over him. "Your body's definitely firm enough." Realizing that she had gotten carried away, she cleared her throat. "So, what do you think?"

He didn't want to tell her what he was really thinking. That way only led to trouble. So instead, he played it safe and said, "I think that the term *spa* typically leads people to think that they're going to be lying around and getting massages and toning treatments."

"Oh, we still offer that, too," she assured him. "But the massages aren't nearly as exciting to the clients as the other things we're putting together. We're approaching wellness from all different angles." She smiled like a proud parent showing off her brand new baby. Hailey's eyes sparkled as she asked Dillon, "So what do you think?"

It wasn't up to him to approve or disapprove, but he liked her asking his opinion he thought, taking one last sip of wine, then setting down his empty glass on the coffee table. "You're the manager, not me," he told Hailey. "I'm just the guy who designed the building and oversaw the work."

"Oh, I think you did a little more than just that," she assured him. "Tell me, is your modesty a congenital thing, or is it something that you grew into gradually?"

"I was raised to think that bragging was wrong."

"And I appreciate that," she told him. "But there is a difference between bragging and accepting your due. Don't get me wrong," she added quickly, "I find your modesty charming and very sweet," she told him truthfully. "I just want you to know how good you really are, that's all.

"Sometimes," she continued, "with everything that's going on, simple things—like words of appreciation—tend to get lost and I thought you needed to hear it, at least once in a while."

Humor curved his mouth. He couldn't help thinking again how this woman was something else. "You did, did you?"

"I did," Hailey replied in all seriousness.

By this point, egged on by her enthusiasm, there was very little space left between the two of them. So little that there was only enough room to fit in a piece of paper between their bodies. A very thin piece of paper at that.

"Well then, allow me to thank you," he said, completely mesmerized by her lips with every movement they made.

"You're welcome."

Her words came out in a low sultry whisper that in any other situation might have been referred to as the beginning of a siren's song.

Dillon would have liked to have blamed it on the wine, but he had only had a couple of sips. And even if he had downed the whole glass and then the rest of what was in the bottle after that, wine wasn't nearly as potent or intoxicating as the woman sitting so close to him.

One moment he was allowing himself to be mesmerized by watching her lips move as she spoke, the very next moment he was kissing those same lips, leaving himself utterly open and vulnerable to their magic.

The last two times he had given in and kissed Hailey, he had somehow managed to be smart enough to anchor his thoughts to something, so that he could stop himself before he got too swept away.

But this time, there was no anchor to keep him from being pulled in. This time he knew he was lost the second his lips came in contact with hers. Because doing this, making love with Hailey, had been on his mind ever since he had helped her find that frog figurine at Mariana's flea market.

Ever since he'd caught himself wanting to be a frog kissed by a princess.

Almost immediately, he could all but hear his mind frantically crying out, *Mayday!* But even as it did, he sensed that it was already too late.

He knew that he didn't have a prayer of being able to bail out. At this particular time and place, he was a goner. And, heaven help him, a part of him reveled in that.

Just like that, a sense of urgency filled him. He wanted to make love with this woman before his better instincts made a reappearance and prevailed upon his sense of decency, his desire to do the right thing by everyone, including Hailey.

Maybe most of all by Hailey.

That meant walking away from her. But heaven help him, he didn't want to.

As Dillon's adrenaline rushed through his veins, making him feel like a man who was attempting to skydive without a parachute, he could feel her lips curving against his.

She was smiling.

Confused and curious, Dillon drew his head back to look at her. "What?"

"Nothing. I'm just happy," she told him simply. And then, placing a finger to his lips, she said, "No more talking."

She was right, he thought. No more talking. This wasn't the time for that. If he talked, he might just wind up stopping what he was about to do and Lord help him, he didn't want to. What he wanted to do was make love with this woman. He wanted to finish leaping out of the plane without that parachute, because even with everything that had been going on in his life—*was* going on in his life—he had *never* felt as exhilaratingly alive as he did at this very moment in time.

Dillon found himself wanting to literally devour the moment. Devour *her.* And there was nothing he could do to stop it.

Hailey could feel her head start spinning again, but this time her head felt as if it were going so fast, she could barely catch her breath.

She had come very close to giving up hope that Dillon would respond to her. Even today, there were times that she felt as if she was getting through to him, and other times she felt as if he was literally pulling away from her.

For the life of her, Hailey couldn't make sense out of his reluctance. They'd gotten along well, and when he kissed her those two other times, he hadn't been just a man taking advantage of the moment or the situation. He was right there, totally committed. And he wanted her. Not just another conquest, not just a warm body for an interlude, but *her*.

He wanted her.

Which was why, each time he drew away, throwing up that force field between them, she couldn't understand why he was doing it. Couldn't understand why this sort of rejection was happening.

But now, as they kissed over and over again with their bodies heating up, creating something between them that was theirs alone. The rest of the world just slipped away into an abyss.

Hailey had her answer.

He *wanted* her.

And for her part, she was determined he wasn't going to regret his choice.

Dillon didn't remember undressing her. Didn't remember if she had undressed him or if he had shed his own clothing in a frenzied desire to get closer to her. All he knew was that his clothes were no longer on his body and she was nude on the sofa, like a spectacular goddess right in front of him, her body primed and ready to be worshiped.

And he did.

He worshiped her with his hands, with his eyes, with his lips that eagerly passed over every single inch of her, awed as if he had been allowed access to a shrine.

Dillon couldn't get enough of her.

The more he kissed her, the more he wanted to kiss her. The more his blood heated within his body, demanding that he rush to avail himself of the final fulfillment.

But if this was going to be their one and only time together—and he had made his peace with convincing himself that it would be just this one time—he was determined that it was going to be memorable. Not for him, because it was already that for him, but for her. He never wanted her to look back at this time and feel the sting of regret eating into her soul.

So he made certain that he made love to her gently. He wanted Hailey to remember him as a kind lover. And most of all, he was determined to be a thorough lover.

With that in mind, he brought her up to the point of ecstasy not just once but several times. When her body shivered beneath him, succumbing to a climax, Dillon was quick to start building toward the next one, delivering bone-melting strokes along her body with his lips and his tongue.

With hot excitement rippling through his own body, he methodically moved down along hers, coaxing yet another explosion to reverberate throughout her moist, feverish body.

Struggling mightily to catch her breath, she bracketed his shoulders with her hands. Then she tugged on them. When he looked up at her, she managed to get one word out in a hoarse whisper.

"Together."

He understood.

Seductively sliding his body up along hers, Dillon stopped moving only when he could look into her eyes.

Again he caught her mouth, his lips slanting over hers time and again before he finally moved his knee urgently in between her legs. Silently, he got her to open for him.

Then, weaving a necklace of lingering hot kisses along the top of her breasts and throat, Dillon moved up just a little higher until his eyes were on hers.

And then, with one movement of his hips, he entered her and they became one palpitating unit, driven by one desire: to set the night on fire.

His heart pounding in his chest, Dillon still managed to keep himself in check and move slowly at first.

But as the tempo in his head increased, he began to move faster, and then faster still.

Hailey found that she had somehow managed to feel the same rhythm that was driving him. It propelled her on. She was mimicking each of his movements, recreating them so that the need increased a little more each time she moved her hips against his.

She could hardly contain herself.

They raced one another to the very top of the highest peak before them and then, just for the tiniest of moments, they flew, wrapped up in ecstasy, reveling in the powerful feeling that had seized them, before they slowly began to descend, still joined, still one with the moment and each other.

The euphoria of the afterglow lingered and they held onto one another—and it—for as long as they were able, each loath to surrender to reality and to the world that was waiting to claim them back.

And when it was all over, Dillon lay there on the sofa, feeling her heart beating hard against his.

Part of him was still floating, still wrapped in a delicious, impenetrable mist. But another part of him felt as if perhaps he needed to apologize for letting things go this far when he didn't have the right to allow it to get this out of hand.

Because in doing it, he had made silent promises that he was not at liberty to keep.

He felt Hailey stirring beneath him as reality took on length and breadth. He could have sworn that the room had grown colder.

"I'm sorry," Dillon said, shifting in order to give Hailey as much space as he could on the sofa. It wasn't much.

She took his apology at face value. Dillon was just apologizing for crowding her on the sofa. Granted it wasn't exactly the best place for this to have happened, she silently acknowledged, but even so, it had still been beyond wonderful.

"That's all right," Hailey assured him. "The sofa wasn't built for comfort, not when it comes to this sort of thing, anyway," she allowed with a soft, gentle laugh. "But that's why beds were invented," she told him with a wink.

The next moment, she was sitting up and then wiggling off the sofa to stand before him in what he could only describe as breathtaking magnificence.

Taking Dillon's hand, she drew him off the sofa, as well.

"Why don't we put my theory to the test?" Hailey suggested.

He wasn't following her. "Theory?"

"About beds and sofas. If this was your place, we'd need a compass right about now to get to your bedroom, but my bedroom's just down the hall," she told him. Tugging on his hand, she led the way.

It didn't escape her attention that he paused to grab his slacks—and his cell phone—but she was feeling far too euphoric at the moment to let it bother her.

After all, he seemed to pride himself for being perpetually on call. She accepted it as being part of who he was.

Chapter Fifteen

Feeling blissfully fulfilled, Hailey woke up the next morning with a smile on her face.

Last night had been far and away the most wonderful night of her life. Dillon turned out to be everything she could have possibly asked for in a lover—and more. They wound up making love two more times last night. Each and every time they had, Dillon was even more of a considerate, generous lover than he had been the time before.

The last time they made love, Hailey almost cried. She was that touched by him, that thrilled. Finally too spent to do anything but smile up at Dillon, she fell asleep curled up in his arms.

When she opened her eyes this morning, she was surprised to find that sometime during what was left of the night, Dillon had pulled away from her. As she looked at him now, it was obvious that he had gone to sleep as far over on his side of the queen-sized bed as possible.

It was probably just a sleeping habit of his, she told herself. Some people just needed space in order to fall asleep and they couldn't do it if they felt confined or crowded.

Don't make a big deal out of it. Focus on the fact that Dillon made love with you three times, not that he seems to like to sleep unencumbered.

She was close to convincing herself when her heart nearly stopped as Dillon's eyes suddenly flew open. Her gentle, wonderful lover was looking at her as if she was some sort of invader. Or, at the very least, someone he would have rather not found lying next to him first thing in the morning.

Don't take it personally, Hailey. Maybe your Frog Prince isn't a morning person.

Determined to push past the painfully uneasy feeling that was beginning to form in the pit of her stomach, Hailey forced a smile to her lips as she looked at him.

"So," she asked softly, "how did you sleep?"

"I slept okay." His answer was short, abrupt, his voice distant.

Hailey could have sworn she almost felt the

walls of his fortress resurrecting themselves around Dillon right in front of her eyes. He was regretting what had happened, she thought. She could sense it.

But she *knew* he had enjoyed himself, she silently insisted. Why was he doing this now? Why was he acting as if he didn't care one way or another? Why wouldn't he allow himself to open up to her?

Her heart sank. What did she have to do to get through to him and get him to trust her?

Well, crowding him wasn't going to do it, she thought. With effort, she tried to get herself to back off.

Momentarily at a loss as to how to move forward, Hailey said the first thing that came into her mind. When in doubt, offer food.

"Would you like some breakfast, Dillon?" she asked. "I can—"

"Would you mind if I showered first?" he asked, sitting up in bed and shifting away from her.

She felt as if an arrow had pierced her heart. Did Dillon want to get the scent of her, of their lovemaking, off his body?

Stop it. You're going to make yourself crazy.

Hailey deliberately forced another smile to her lips and said in as cheerful a voice as she could muster, "Sure, go ahead. The bathroom's right over—"

She didn't get a chance to finish. Taking the blanket that was at the foot of her bed, Dillon secured it around his waist. With it draped over his body, he walked into the bathroom.

Maybe he'd feel better once he'd showered, she consoled herself. The man who had made love to her last night couldn't have just vanished without a trace. Not completely. Maybe he just needed a few minutes to himself so he could evaluate what he'd done, what had happened between them.

Maybe—

The sound of the running water in the shower was suddenly interrupted by the insistent beeping of a cell phone. Pulling herself together, Hailey looked around for her phone. Belatedly, she remembered that it was still in her purse. And she'd left her purse on the living room floor.

The sound couldn't have carried this far, she reasoned.

But there it was again, that insistent beeping sound, demanding attention.

Where—?

And then she remembered. Dillon had brought his cell phone, along with his slacks, into her bedroom when they came in here last night.

There it was again. The jarring noise scissored its way under her skin. It didn't sound as if whoever was calling was about to give up.

Given how early it was, she decided that Dillon was probably missing a call from one of his brothers. Knowing how dedicated he was to their projects, Hailey went looking for the cell.

He was probably going to use this call as an excuse to beat a hasty retreat once he came out of her bathroom, but she couldn't very well ignore the call. The more she thought about it, the more she felt that it was probably something important.

Resigned, she began her search, trying to determine where Dillon had dropped his phone.

The annoying beeping sound stopped. The caller apparently had finally given up, she thought. And then she saw it. His phone was lying face down on her floor. Dillon must have accidentally kicked it as he made his way into her shower because the phone was partially under her bed with only an end peeking out.

She picked up the phone, went to place it on the nightstand. But the contact and movement had caused the last series of unviewed texts to pop up on the screen.

The texts were all from the same person. Someone named Julie. The last text was written all in capitals.

WHEN ARE YOU COMING HOME????

Hailey didn't remember sitting down, but she must have. Her knees suddenly gave out and she found herself sinking back onto her bed.

She felt as if she had just been kicked in her stomach.

Julie.

The name seemed to dance in front of her eyes, mocking her.

Julie? Who was Julie?

Was Dillon already involved with someone else? Worse, was he *married*?

Was *that* the reason he had kept her at arm's length—when he remembered his marital status? Because he certainly hadn't acted like he was married last night.

She felt tears gathering in her eyes and she wiped them away. If Dillon was married, then why hadn't he *told* her?

She was a great believer in privacy. Usually. But unable to help herself, she scrolled down through the messages that were available to her, the ones that had been sent and hadn't been looked at yet. She couldn't remember even hearing the phone beeping before now, but then, they had been rather busy last night, oblivious to everything else except each other.

The memory of that didn't console her now. It made her feel as if she had been underhanded. Not as underhanded as Dillon, but hey, they couldn't all be in his league, she thought, a stab of bitterness lancing right into her heart.

Again, she berated herself for reading his private messages like this. But in her defense, she was trying to find something—*anything*—to prove that she was wrong, that this wasn't what it looked like.

But when the same message kept popping up all four times in progressively bigger text, she knew that this *had* to be exactly what it looked like. This Julie woman appeared to have far more of a claim on Dillon than Hailey did.

Hailey knew she had to be right because why else would he have kept this woman a secret from her?

Feeling progressively sicker, she desperately wanted to run away. She wanted to hide from this awful pain that was carving up her insides.

But damn it, this was *her* house, not his. If anyone needed to leave because of this awful discovery, it was Dillon.

Grabbing a robe from her closet, Hailey had just managed to shrug into it to cover herself and tied the sash at her waist when Dillon walked out. Bare-chested and barefoot, he was only wearing his slacks. His hair was wet from the shower.

Without saying a word to him, she got up and shoved his phone into his hand.

Dillon looked down at the screen. Seeing the row of texts, one after the other, he quickly retreated back into the bathroom without saying a word.

Feeling so awful that she found herself fighting

a very strong, very real urge to throw up, Hailey sat back down on her bed, struggling to get a grip on herself.

She wasn't going to cry, she wasn't, she silently ordered herself. Hailey took in a couple of deep breaths, trying very hard not to dissolve in tears.

When Dillon came out again, she was just going to tell him that she wasn't feeling well and would he mind leaving? Permanently?

Hailey fisted her hands beside her. She just couldn't deal with this right now, she couldn't.

But just as she couldn't stop the tears that welled up in her eyes, she couldn't lie or pretend that none of this was happening. She had just made love to a married man—or to a man who might as well be married. He was definitely involved with someone, which to her was the same thing.

The bottom line was she had made love with someone who hadn't been honest with her. And to her, dishonesty was just about the worst.

Hailey jumped when the bathroom door suddenly opened. She swung around just in time to look Dillon straight in the eye.

"Who is Julie and why is she asking you to come home?" Hailey asked him in a shaky voice.

Startled, Dillon looked at her. "You read my texts?" he asked, surprised.

"That's not the important part here," she informed him in a strained, angry voice. "Who is Julie?" she asked again.

"It's not what you think," Dillon began, searching for words that wouldn't escalate what already felt like a totally volatile disaster about to explode.

"I don't *know* what to think," Hailey cried, exasperated. "Because you keep shutting me out. Every time I think we've made a little progress, every time it looks like we've taken one step forward, you do something to push me back not one step but two. I'm through with you keeping things to yourself," she declared, then, out of patience, she demanded, "Is Julie your wife?"

Dillon looked at her, stunned. "No, Julie's not my wife," he answered. "She is—"

He was talking too slow, Hailey thought angrily. She wanted to jump down his throat and physically drag all his words out.

"She's what, Dillon?" Hailey cried, frustrated. "Your girlfriend?"

His blue eyes turning darker, he finally replied, "Julie's my daughter."

Hailey felt as if all the air had just been pumped out of her lungs. For a second, her head reeling, she was totally speechless and could only stare at Dillon, wide-eyed.

"Your daughter," she finally said, repeating the words numbly. The import of what Dillon had just said hit her right between the eyes. "Oh, my Lord, I'm a home-wrecker," she cried.

"No," Dillon firmly insisted. "You're not a home-wrecker, Hailey."

He could see that she wasn't convinced. That was when Dillon did something he never did. He forced himself to open up, at least a little, about his private life.

"There is no home to wreck, Hailey," Dillon told her quietly.

"But your daughter—" she protested.

"Is the product of a teenage romance." He could see that she was waiting for more so he forced himself to keep talking. "When I found out that my girl-friend, Maura, was pregnant, I wanted to step up and do the right thing. I told her that I'd marry her. Hell, I *wanted* to marry her."

"So what happened?" Hailey wanted to know. Heaven knew that if he had offered to marry *her*, to give their child a father as well as his name, *she* certainly wouldn't have hesitated saying yes to him. She would have said it so fast his head would have spun.

She found herself not liking this Maura person

because she could see that the woman had obviously hurt Dillon.

"*She* didn't want to marry me. I thought that maybe she was being stubborn, that she was embarrassed to be in this condition and didn't want me to feel I *had* to marry her.

"But as it turned out, she really wasn't in love with me. She didn't want to get married just because it was the *right* thing to do, or just to give her baby a last name." He smiled ruefully, remembering the scene as if it had been yesterday. "She told me that her baby would have a last name. *Her* last name."

"I don't think I understand," Hailey confessed.

Though it was painful for him, Dillon continued telling her the story. "For whatever reason, Maura decided to keep me from having any contact with Julie. She disappeared right after she had the baby. I tried to keep track of her and the baby because, well, after all, Julie was my responsibility, my *child*.

"I finally managed to track her down a couple of years ago and found that Maura had relocated not all that far away from where I lived. As it turned out, she had gone on to marry someone she did love." He smiled sadly. "As for Julie, she turned out to be a very headstrong, stubborn girl. She got it into her head to look into finding me on her own. The internet can be a very helpful tool if you're as resourceful as Julie is."

There was no missing the pride in Dillon's voice, Hailey thought. He really was a decent human being, she decided, relieved.

"It took some time, but Julie managed to track me down. She's a stubborn girl. I guess she takes after me," he said with a smile. "Once she did, she got in contact with me behind Maura's back. We started exchanging cards and letters. That went on for two years and then she asked if she could see me. By then Callum had gotten involved with building up Rambling Rose and we were all about to relocate. He was counting on me for my help, so I told Julie that we would get together once I got back to Fort Lauderdale. She accepted it at first. Julie's resourceful and bright, but she is still a twelve-year-old girl and they tend to be impatient at that age. I suppose that's the reason she sent all those texts to me. She became impatient."

Hailey ached for the little girl, thinking how she had to feel, finally finding her father and not being able to get together with him. "So what are you going to do?" she wanted to know.

"I haven't figured it out yet," Dillon admitted. "The one thing I do plan to do is see Julie. She deserves a father, her *real* father, and I don't plan on abandoning her for a second time now that we've made contact of a sort. I've already missed too much of her life. I don't intend to miss the rest of it."

"And what about Julie's mother? You said she wouldn't let you see Julie. What if she doesn't change her mind?" Hailey asked. What she didn't add was that Dillon had said Maura had turned him down when he asked to marry her and then had married someone else. That had to have hurt Dillon, she thought. Maura had been his first love. Could he wind up changing his mind about her if she acted as if she regretted her initial decision?

As if reading her mind, Dillon told her, "Anything between Maura and me has long since died. But that doesn't change the fact that I *am* Julie's dad and Julie wants a chance to get to know me. Maura is just going to have to find a way to deal with it," he said with finality. "I guess," Dillon continued after a moment, "getting kicked in the teeth that way at seventeen permanently destroyed any tendency I might have had to view romance with any sort of a positive, rosy attitude."

She knew what he was telling her. That he wasn't able to open himself up and care for her the way she wanted him to because he'd been permanently scarred at a young age. She fought the urge to tell him that *she* wasn't like Maura, but she sensed that he had already opened himself up far more than he had intended to and that she shouldn't push it. So she refrained.

Instead she said, "Not *everyone* is like Maura."

"No," Dillon agreed, "they're not. But putting myself out there and possibly setting myself up for a fall is just too painful. Besides, since Julie is in Fort Lauderdale, my place is there if I ever hope to form any sort of relationship with my daughter."

He took a deep breath and looked directly into Hailey's eyes. "What I'm trying to say is that I'm not free to start anything that would lead to a relationship between us. I can't promise you that I'm going to stick around," he said flatly. Dillon took her hands in his. "As a matter of fact, I can probably promise you the exact opposite." He looked at Hailey seriously. "I'm not about to give up on Julie."

"I wouldn't ask you to," Hailey replied in total sincerity.

Dillon knew she thought she meant that, but things had a habit of changing. There was a time he could have sworn that Maura loved him, but he had turned out to be wrong.

"That's what you say now," Dillon began, "but—"

Hailey placed her finger to his lips, stopping him before he could say anything further. "Why don't we just take this one day at a time and see where it leads?" she suggested.

In his heart, he welcomed that because he really didn't want to just walk away from Hailey. Not while they could still see each other. But he did have his doubts about the arrangement.

"You'd be okay with that?" Dillon asked her in surprise.

"Yes," she answered with a smile. "Look, I know we're in Texas, but I'm not about to throw a lasso over you and hog-tie you so you can't get away. Listen," she continued, "I wouldn't want you if you were uncomfortable being in this relationship just as you wouldn't want me if I was uncomfortable." Then she added what she felt was the clinching argument. "Just as you let Maura go because she said she wasn't comfortable being in a relationship with you."

He looked at her for a long moment. Hailey was making a valid point and it was definitely something for him to think about. But he still knew in the back of his mind that he was going to have trouble putting his fears to rest. Like the very real fear that, if he suddenly decided to stay and opened up his heart to Hailey, something might still happen to make her abruptly change her mind and terminate any sort of relationship that was growing between them.

Once burnt, twice leery…

Still, for now, Dillon felt himself relenting… just a little.

"Like you said, one step at a time," he replied, nodding his head.

Last night had shown her that Dillon knew exactly how to set her world on fire. If he couldn't just leap headlong into a relationship with her without looking back, she was just going to have to find a way to live with that, Hailey told herself.

Live with it and hope for the best. She was going to show Dillon how steadfast she could be and, more importantly, that she was nothing at all like the woman who had crippled his heart.

Chapter Sixteen

Dillon and Hailey continued seeing one another during any free time they could find and stitch together. It was a tall order between his construction projects and her work at the spa. The latter was currently deemed to be another success for Callum and the company, but that didn't mean she had the luxury of dropping the ball either figuratively *or* literally. She worked exceeding hard, which made any free time she spent with Dillon that much more precious and sweet.

However, whenever they did find small islands of time to spend together, Hailey couldn't shake the feeling that they weren't really alone. The specter of Maura and Dillon's failed romance was always there with them in the background, like a nebulous prophesy of doom.

And then, after what had been a promising start, their relationship stalled like a manual transmission stuck in second gear.

Try as she might, Hailey couldn't seem to convince Dillon to loosen up and really take a chance on them.

Added to that was another concurrent problem. Maura continued to throw a wrench into any headway their relationship could have made by refusing to budge on the subject of Julie. The woman was determined that Julie just wouldn't have any sort of a relationship with Dillon.

Ever.

All this made Dillion leery of beginning a new romance. The only time he'd fallen in love, he'd made a mess of things. How could he expect a different result now?

He hadn't expected his twelve-year-old daughter to indirectly provide a solution by finding a way to work around every roadblock Maura put in their path.

For more than two years Maura kept the cards, letters and gifts that he had sent from reaching Julie. For reasons that would forever remain a mystery to him, Maura didn't destroy them. Instead, she locked them up in a box she kept hidden in the back of her bedroom closet.

And then, as fate would have it, when Maura went into the hospital for an appendectomy, Julie accidentally came across a letter he had mailed to her while her babysitter was in the other room. Since it was obviously addressed to her, Julie read it. Surprised, stunned and exceedingly happy that her father cared enough to write to her, he found out that Julie became convinced that there had to be more letters she hadn't seen. A relentless search through her mother's things led her to find the other letters that Maura had hidden.

When he received that first letter from his daughter, he couldn't begin to describe the immense joy he experienced. Although he didn't approve of deception, he felt this was the only way that he and his daughter could get to know one another so he sent the girl money and told her how to set up a postal box in a local office supply store, so that he could send his letters to her there.

The hope was that until Maura could be convinced to allow him to meet their daughter face-to-face, they would continue making contact this way. He knew he could take this to court and fight for visitation rights, but he didn't want an all out war with Maura because he didn't want Julie caught in the middle. It would only hurt her. But neither did he want Julie to feel that he was giving up on her, so he kept writing to the girl.

But he never gave up trying to convince Maura to let him into Julie's life.

Once she was aware of what was going on, Hailey encouraged him to keep working on Maura.

"No luck?" Hailey asked after she watched Dillon terminate yet another phone call to the girl's mother.

Dillon shook his head, frustrated. "She still refuses to let me see Julie, or even talk to her. If she ever realized that Julie and I were communicating, she'd probably disappear with the girl just to spite me. I'd wind up never hearing from Julie again."

Hailey ached for him and the pain she knew he had to be going through.

"Maura can't just take off like that," Hailey said, trying to make him feel better. "You said she was married, right? Her husband has a job, doesn't he?" she asked.

Dillon knew where she was going with this, but he also knew that Hailey wasn't totally aware of the whole situation.

"He does," Dillon answered. "But from what I gather from the things she did tell me, her husband has no spine. That means that he does *every-*

thing Maura wants in order to keep her happy and maintain peace."

The woman sounded like some sort of dragon lady, and in Hailey's opinion, Dillon had definitely dodged a bullet when Maura had turned down his proposal almost thirteen years ago.

Not wanting to sound critical, she kept that to herself. But she did say something that occurred to her just now. "If she keeps refusing to let you even meet Julie and you're worried that they might just vanish if you so much as push Maura to let you see the girl, then why are you still considering moving to Florida?"

He knew she probably thought he was hitting his head against a wall and maybe he was. But he shrugged helplessly, saying, "On the outside chance that I could wear her down eventually."

Because it was her habit, Hailey tried to see the situation in the best possible light. This time, that *best* light was about Dillon's attitude.

"I guess there is a bit of an optimist in you, after all," she said, smiling at him.

"Maybe so, but that optimist is fading pretty fast," he told her.

Even so, Hailey was determined to fan that flame and keep it alive until it could burn on its own. She felt it was also the only chance for them to have any future together.

"If you give up now, you'll never get to see your daughter and that's that," she told him. "But if you keep on trying to get through to Maura, to get her to change her mind, you still have a chance."

Dillon shook his head, amazed. "You really believe that?"

"With my whole heart and soul," she answered with feeling. She put her hand on his shoulder. "You have nothing to lose if you keep trying and everything to lose if you don't."

He laughed, but it wasn't at her. He was reacting to the warmth her words generated. "Do you get these sayings off bumper stickers, or from fortune cookies?"

"From life," she answered, then smiled. "Like I said when I first met you, you could stand to take part in one of my spa sessions."

He slipped his arm around her, pulling her in closer so he could kiss her. Heaven help him, she did make him feel better, even though he didn't quite share her overall outlook, or her peppy sayings. It was the way Hailey said them—and the fact that he needed to have something to hold on to—that gave him a lifeline.

Despite everything he had done to try to discourage Hailey, she continued to maintain her optimism—and to give him hope. He was lucky to have her in his life. "Want to see her picture?" he asked.

"I'd love to."

Dillon took out his wallet and took out a small snapshot. "I made a print of it in case I ever lose my phone."

She loved hearing the pride in his voice. "She's adorable," Hailey told him.

"Yeah," he paused to look at it a moment longer, "I think so, too."

Dillon had just finished going over the final layout for his construction company's next joint project: Provisions, the restaurant that was going to be a joint venture run by his triplet sisters, Ashley, Nicole and Megan, when his cell phone rang. Involved in the review, he didn't hear it at first. When he did, he put down his pencil next to the notes he'd been making.

He had made plans to see Hailey this evening—a rare midweek treat because they were both so busy the last few days—and he thought it was Hailey calling with a possible last-minute change in plans.

"Hi, honey," Dillon said, mechanically swiping open his phone while still looking over the restaurant's layout.

The sharp voice on the other end of the call

took him completely by surprise. Hearing it, Dillon nearly dropped his phone.

"Don't you *honey* me, damn it!" the woman shouted.

"Maura?" It wasn't really a question. Her voice, filled with anger, drilled itself into his head.

Why was she calling him out of the blue like this? And what on earth could he have possibly done to upset her so much?

"Of course it's me!" Maura snapped, her voice shrill. "Don't act like you didn't expect to hear from me."

"I didn't," he told her honestly. "Why are you calling?" he asked, a little frustrated by her tone.

"Like you don't know," she accused.

Dillon sighed. She couldn't have picked a worse time to call. "Maura, I don't have time for games today. I've got a lot on my plate."

"Oh, you do, do you?" she asked in a mocking voice. "Does one of those *things* on your plate include picking up Julie from the airport?" Maura's voice rose as she shouted at him.

"What are you talking about?" he asked when he was able to get a word in edgewise.

"Don't play dumb, Dillon. You know exactly what I'm talking about!" Practically beside herself, Maura was almost screeching at this point.

They were going around in circles, Dillon

thought wearily. It was something he had learned that Maura had quite an aptitude for.

"Why don't you pretend I don't," he told her.

She didn't seem to hear him. "You're responsible for this!" she accused. "Filling Julie's head with a bunch of nonsense, turning her against Bill!" she cried, referring to her husband, Julie's stepfather.

Dillon was struggling to piece things together from the bits of information he was able to glean from her ranting. Why would Maura even think that? "You know I wouldn't do that."

"Right, because you're such an honorable man," the woman on the other end mocked.

Dillon thought that she sounded as if she was growing more and more angry. But beneath the anger, he detected a ripple of fear. Had something happened to Julie?

He needed to cut through all this angry rhetoric so he could find out just why Maura was calling and hurling these accusations at him.

"Maura, you're not making any sense. Now you start telling me what this is all about," he told her.

And then, to Dillon's surprise, the woman on the other end broke down and started to cry. "Julie. It's about Julie," she sobbed.

Fear was suddenly twisting a knife in his gut, carving him up. Maura sounded as if she was falling apart. Maura *never* fell apart. She prided herself on that. Something awful had to have happened to their daughter.

He struggled to remain calm. To *sound* calm. "What about Julie?" he asked, even as his breath was backing up in his throat.

"She's run away from home!"

"Run away?" he repeated. That didn't make any sense to him. Julie was far too stable to do something like that. "Are you sure? Maybe she's just at one of her friends' houses."

"Of course I'm sure!" Maura shouted at him. "Don't you think I've already called all of her friends? She's not there. She's not anywhere," Maura sobbed helplessly. "She's run away, I tell you! To see *you*," she accused.

Maura's mind was conjuring things up now, he thought. He did his best to reason with her and calm her down. "Maura, you're in Florida. I'm halfway across the country in Texas. I really don't think that—"

"She left me a note," Maura cried, cutting in. "She said that since I wouldn't let you come to see her, she was going to go to see you and that I couldn't do anything to stop her!" She was sobbing again. "This is all your fault!" she accused again.

Stunned, Dillon's mind dragged up half a dozen scenarios all involving runaways, none of them good. He needed to find her, he thought, trying not to panic. "Did you call the police?"

"I didn't," she bit off. "I called you. But if you don't bring Julie back the second you find her, I will call them and tell them that you kidnapped my daughter! See if you can talk your way out of that!"

"Maura, calm down!" Dillon said loudly, hoping to get some order into the discussion. "I didn't kidnap Julie. *I don't have her*," he said emphatically. "But I will find her," he promised. Taking a breath, he tried to think. "When was the last time you saw her?"

"This morning—no, last night," she realized. "I had an early meeting with my boss this morning, so I left before she went to school. I didn't see her."

"You left her alone?" he asked incredulously.

"No, of course not. Bill was still home—and don't try to turn things around to blame me! You're the guilty one here!" she cried.

Trying to make Maura see things from his side was frustrating, but she was right—he needed to find Julie before something happened to her. So Dillon continued asking Maura questions, hoping he could get to the bottom of this and figure out if Julie really had run away from home to see him. And somehow, at least for old times sake, he needed to find a way to help Maura calm down.

Chapter Seventeen

He was late, Hailey thought.

She had taken part of the day off because Dillon had told her he wanted to see her. But he was already over an hour late and she was getting antsy. There was no sign of him.

Where was he?

She had reached for her phone several times now, wanting to call him, but she'd refrained each time. She really didn't want Dillon to feel as if she was crowding him. The man didn't need that right now.

She knew that Dillon was worried about his daughter who had been missing since yesterday, and more than anything, she wished she knew what to do in order to help him find her—that is if the girl really had run away the way her mother said she had.

There was the very real possibility that Maura was blowing all this way out of proportion. Secretly Hailey was still holding out hope that the girl had decided to just go to one of her friends' houses to either teach her mother a lesson or just get some time away from her mother who seemed like she could be somewhat overbearing.

Piecing things together from just one side of the conversation as she listened to Dillon attempt to talk to Maura, Julie's mother was apparently bent on making father and daughter pay in their separate ways for daring to forge a relationship behind her back. To Hailey, the woman came off sounding extremely insecure.

Just as Hailey was about to start pacing the floor, she heard the doorbell ring. She instantly snapped to attention and ran out of the kitchen.

Throwing the door open, she cried, "I was beginning to really get worried that you—"

The rest of her sentence died, unspoken, on her lips when she saw who was on the other side.

It wasn't Dillon standing in her doorway, it was a young girl with straight dirty blond hair and bright blue eyes. Caught completely by surprise, Hailey blinked, and then looked at the girl again, this time a little more closely.

Even if she hadn't seen a picture, she would have known her, anyway. "Julie?"

It was more of a greeting than a question. The moment she said the girl's name, she knew she was right. The angry-looking girl on her doorstep looked like a young female version of Dillon.

Julie raised her chin as if she was expecting some sort of challenge from the woman who had opened the door. In a voice that sounded entirely too grown up, the girl asked, "Is Dillon Fortune here? I can't find him."

Hailey couldn't help wondering how Julie had gotten her address—had Dillon given it to her, thinking that another woman might make the girl somehow feel safe if she ever decided to come here?

That had to be it, she decided. Either that or he had mentioned her by name as a friend and the resourceful little girl had looked her up when she didn't find her father at his place. There was time enough to delve into that later. Right now, there were more pressing things to address. Like how she had gotten here.

"No," Hailey answered the girl, "but I'm expecting him any minute now. C'mon in," she invited, opening the door as wide as she could. When Julie made no effort to budge, Hailey added, "Please."

"Okay," Julie finally grudgingly agreed, walking in with some reluctance. "But you *are* expecting him here, right?"

"Actually, he should already be here," Hailey told Dillon's daughter.

She looked over the girl's shoulder, expecting to see whoever had accompanied Julie here from Fort Lauderdale. But there was no one with the girl nor did she look as if she was waiting for someone to catch up to her, like a person who was still parking a car perhaps.

This was really unusual, Hailey thought.

She had to ask. "Did you come all this way by yourself?" Hailey wanted to know, finally closing the door behind her.

Julie straightened her shoulders. "I used my mother's credit card. What of it?" Her tone sounded as if she was ready for a fight.

"Nothing," Hailey told the girl mildly. "You're just a little young to be traveling all that way by yourself," she observed.

Julie's eyes narrowed into small lethal laser beams. Hailey could have sworn the girl's nostrils flared, as well.

"I'm twelve," Julie declared as if that totally negated any question of her being too young to make the trip. "I just said my mother was sending me to stay with my father. Nobody asked any questions," she said proudly.

It wasn't her place to say anything about lying, Hailey thought. She didn't want to antagonize Dillon's daughter. Instead, she asked, "Does your mother know you're here?" she asked, even though she knew the answer to that was a resounding no. She wanted to see what the girl had to say in response.

The answer was typical of a preteen. "She took away my phone, so it's her own fault she can't find me. Besides, my mother doesn't care about anyone but herself," Julie declared dismissively.

Hailey caught herself feeling sorry for both mother and daughter trapped in this dance with no music. "I happen to know that's not true, Julie. Your mother is very worried about you."

Julie sniffed and tossed her head, sending her hair flying over her shoulder. "How would you know? Did she tell you?"

"No, but she told your father," Hailey said. "Your mother called yesterday looking for you and she was frantic."

Restless, Julie began roaming around the living

room and kitchen. Her eyes darted back and forth as she took in every single detail. When it came to Hailey's assessment of her mother's reaction, Julie shrugged dismissively. Instead, she looked at Hailey more closely, as if she was passing judgment on her.

Growing wary, Hailey observed Julie frowning at her. There was an edge in the girl's voice as she asked, "Are you my father's girlfriend?"

She hoped that was what he thought. But she knew better than to reach that conclusion before anything had been said. And she definitely didn't want to risk alienating Julie.

"You're going to have to ask your father that. What I can tell you is that your dad's been beside himself ever since your mother called to tell him that you ran away. He's been calling everyone he knows back in Fort Lauderdale, asking them to try to find you."

Suddenly, the belligerent preteen vanished, replaced by a hopeful little girl who looked at her with wide eyes. "He has?"

Hailey nodded. There wasn't so much as a hint of a smile on her lips. "The last I heard, he was trying to hire a reputable private detective to look for you."

"But I'm here," Julie protested, spreading her hands wide.

Hailey took her cell phone out. "And that's what I'm going to tell him the second I reach your father," she said, beginning to input Dillon's phone number. She paused a second to smile at Julie, relieved that the girl had turned up unharmed. "He's going to really be thrilled to see you."

For a moment, Julie looked undecided and torn, as if she really wanted to believe what Hailey was telling her, but at the same time, she didn't know if she could.

"If that's true, then why didn't he come to see me? I must have asked him to more than a dozen times," Julie told her.

From the tone she used, Hailey could tell that the girl had a giant chip on her shoulder. She knew that if she sounded as if she was lecturing Julie, that would just exacerbate the situation, not alleviate it. She chose her words carefully, watching Julie's face.

"Because your mother told him she didn't want your dad coming to see you. She was afraid that would wind up disrupting your life."

Julie shook her head, looking as if she didn't understand. "But he's my dad," she cried. "He should have come anyway, no matter what my mother said. Didn't he want to see me?"

Hailey looked into the girl's eyes. Empathy ran all through her. Julie was hurting and she did what she could to reassure her.

"You know the answer to that," she told Julie. "More than anything. But sometimes, it's better to go slowly than just barge straight in. Trust me," she assured the girl.

"But—"

After dialing and redialing several times, just to have her calls go to voice mail, Hailey finally heard the phone being picked up on the other end.

Dillon started talking immediately without giving her a chance to say a word.

"Look, Hailey, I know I said I'd be over, but I can't right now. Something's come up and—"

"Dillon," Hailey blurted, cutting him off. "She's here. Julie's here."

"What?" Dillon asked. What was she telling him? It was as if the words weren't registering in his brain. All he knew was that he was waiting for a call he had placed to a detective agency to come through.

"Julie's here," Hailey told him again, not bothering to curb her excitement. After having him go through hell, worried sick about his daughter, she was thrilled to be able to give him some good news. The *best* news, really, she thought.

Numb, Dillon was almost afraid of jumping to a conclusion that might lead to disappointment. "Where's here?" he asked uncertainly.

"My house," Hailey answered. "Julie's here at my house."

Stunned, Dillon could only ask, "When?"

"Just now," she answered happily. "Why don't you—" the call suddenly went dead "—come over?" Hailey concluded, even though she knew Dillon couldn't hear her anymore.

Putting her cell phone away, she looked at Julie.

"He's on his way," she told the girl, then felt that in all likelihood, a warning was in order. "Your dad might be kind of angry and he might yell when he gets here, but you need to keep in mind that he really doesn't mean it. You gave him quite a scare by running off like that. Remember, your dad really loves you."

Julie looked at her uncertainly, clearly torn again. "He said that?"

This wasn't the time to qualify her statement by saying that Dillon hadn't said those exact words, but that was what he meant. If she said that, Julie would discount anything she would have to say after that. No, now was the time for reassurances, Hailey silently told herself.

With that, she told the girl, "Yes. Yes, he did."

For her trouble, she saw an incredibly wide smile bloom on the girl's face.

"Really?" Julie asked again, her eyes shining as she waited to get the same answer.

"Really," Hailey repeated.

Julie paused for a moment, as if she was digesting everything very slowly and with relish. And then she looked at Hailey, curious.

"How did you meet my father?" she wanted to know.

That one was easy to field. "He renovated the spa that I manage."

"When did he—"

Whatever the girl was about to ask was going to have to wait because just then the doorbell rang. Julie's head practically spun as she looked toward her front door.

"That's probably your father now," Hailey told her as she headed for the door.

Julie was right behind her, her eyes never leaving the entrance.

A sudden surge of nerves had her looking toward Hailey for guidance.

"What do I say?" Julie asked, fighting back a wave of panic.

"Hi, Dad would be a good start," Hailey said as she opened the door.

Any other exchanges or warnings were all put on hold because Dillon suddenly hurried inside. The second he saw her, he swept his daughter into his arms, hugging her to him as relief overwhelmed him. It was also the very first time he had ever been able to hug her and he wasn't about to let go, not for a while.

He spun her around and then, finally, before he was completely overcome with emotion, he set her back down again.

"Are you all right?" he asked anxiously.

"I'm okay," Julie cried, her own young voice filled with emotion.

Dillon took a deep breath, attempting to distance himself from all the emotions that were swirling through him right now. "What were you thinking, running away like that?"

"I was thinking that I wanted to see you and Mom wouldn't let me. She wouldn't even let me talk to her about it," Julie cried.

Her eyes were shining with tears and it was obvious that she expected him to understand.

He struggled to be the father she needed and

made another attempt to try to discipline her.
"But—"

This was a very fragile situation, Hailey thought.
One misstep on his part and things could really go
badly for him while he was trying to establish this
shaky relationship. She knew she should keep out
of this, but she couldn't.

"That doesn't matter right now," she told Dillon. "What matters is that she's your daughter and
she's here and you both love each other. You can
work out the rest of that later," Hailey told both father and daughter. "Right now all you really need
to do is get acquainted."

"No," Dillon answered, "We can do that on the
plane when we take Julie back. Right now," he told
his daughter, "I need to call your mother and keep
her from having a nervous breakdown."

Julie looked completely unmoved when he mentioned her mother. She waved her hand dismissively. "She doesn't care."

"Oh, yes, she does," Dillon insisted. "Whatever is going down between your mother and me,
make no mistake about that. She loves you very
much and she deserves to know that nothing happened to you," he told his daughter. He began
to dial Maura's number. "How did you wind up
here, anyway?" he wanted to know. She had obvi-

ously flown here from Florida and airplane tickets weren't exactly going for a song.

"I paid for it," she proudly informed him as he heard the cell phone begin to ring.

"How?" he pressed, still dubious about what she was telling him.

"I've been saving my allowance for something important for a long time now," Julie announced.

This being-a-dad thing was going to take some getting used to, he thought.

Meanwhile, Hailey was smiling at him. "Looks like she takes after you," she said, nodding at Julie. Then, as he looked at her quizzically, she explained, "Patient."

Just then, Dillon held his hand up as the call was being answered.

"Maura?" he asked.

The first words out of the other woman's mouth were, "Did you find her?"

"Yes, Julie's here." He put his arm around Julie's slender shoulders and hugged her to him as he continued to talk to Maura. "She turned up on—my doorstep," he said, changing what he was about to say at the last minute. There was no point adding fuel to the fire and saying that the girl had appeared on Hailey's doorstep, he thought.

"Is she all right?" Maura asked, her voice catching.

He could tell Julie's mother was crying. He didn't ever remember hearing Maura cry. "She's fine, Maura," he assured the woman kindly. "None the worse for her experience."

"Well, I am," Maura snapped, her voice practically choking because of the tears in her throat she was trying to suppress.

Dillon really didn't know what to say to that. Deciding that there was nothing he could say, he just moved on and told her, "We'll be taking the next available flight back to Fort Lauderdale to bring her home."

"We?" Maura questioned.

He knew what she could be like and he wasn't about to get into this with Maura right now.

"I've got to go now, Maura," he told her, promising, "I'll text you the details when I have them."

And with that, Dillon terminated the call before Julie's mother had a chance to tell him what she thought about this whole thing.

Chapter Eighteen

The second that Dillon ended the call to her mother, Julie immediately spoke up. "She's a real pain, isn't she?"

"Don't talk about your mother that way," Dillon told his daughter. A part of him shared some of Julie's frustration, but he wanted to bring about a reconciliation—not escalate the feud that was in progress.

She looked surprised and somewhat betrayed by his admonishment. "Why not?" she cried. "It's true! She won't listen to anyone, not even her husband and he's kind of a nice guy."

"Be that as it may," Dillon told her, "she is still your mother and deserves your respect."

He was really struggling to take the high moral ground, and it was hard. Because all of his arguments with Maura had only managed to get him excluded from Julie's life. It was hardly fair. And yet, he was her father—and he knew this was the right thing to do. For both mother and daughter.

Julie fisted her hands at her waist belligerently. "Why?" she wanted to know. "My mother certainly doesn't give me any respect—or you for that matter," the girl pointed out angrily. She was obviously trying her best to get him to side with her against her mother.

This wasn't going well, Hailey thought. Feeling Dillon could use some help, she decided to step in. Not all that long ago, she could remember feeling exactly the same way that Julie was feeling right now, so she could easily commiserate with the preteen.

"That's one of those things that makes absolutely no sense now, but eventually, it will. I promise," she told Julie. "Trust me on that," Hailey added kindly.

Julie scowled at the two adults who were looking at her. "Well, I think you're wrong," she told them, obviously angry that things weren't turning out the way she had hoped.

"And you are entitled to think that way," Hailey told her, surprising both Julie and Dillon with her answer. "But not long ago I was exactly where you are right now. I was positive that everyone was

against me—but they really weren't. As a matter
of fact, one of those people gave me some very
good advice. They said that sometimes a little bit
of diplomacy goes a long way."

Hailey slipped her arm around the girl's shoulders. Julie stiffened, but Hailey left her arm where
it was and after a moment, the girl began to relent.

"What you have before you is the long-term
plan, not just something for the short haul. You
need to try to get along with your mother and then
maybe, eventually, she'll come around to your way
of thinking. But she definitely won't come around
if you insist on defying her and behaving like you
can't stand her." She looked into the girl's eyes,
searching for a glimmer to indicate that she had
gotten through to Julie. "Do you understand what
I'm saying to you?" Hailey asked her gently.

Julie sighed dramatically. "Yeah. I'm going back
home," she answered, unhappy with this turn of
events, but resigned.

"Yes, you are," Hailey agreed, glancing at Dillon. "And in exchange, your dad's going to try to
convince your mom to allow him to visit you."

"And I won't stop until I convince her," Dillon promised.

Julie looked really skeptical, but Dillon thought
that he could see a trace of hope taking root. "You

think so?" the girl asked, looking from Dillon to Hailey.

"Absolutely," he told Julie. And then he looked around the immediate area. Julie hadn't arrived much before he had, so he reasoned she couldn't have put her suitcase away yet. "Where's your stuff?" he asked her.

Julie shrugged. "I didn't bring anything," she confessed.

Dillon thought he'd misunderstood. "You didn't bring a suitcase with you?"

"No," she answered. "I didn't want to attract any attention."

Amazed, Hailey turned her head away from Dillon and whispered, "You have one very sharp little girl on your hands. Most twelve-year-olds wouldn't have thought things through to this extent."

"I'm going to make reservations for the three of us," he told them, starting to take his credit card out of his wallet.

"The three of us?" Julie asked.

Dillon didn't miss the fact that his daughter sounded decidedly a great deal more hopeful. Even if she hadn't, he had no intentions of losing an ally at this crucial juncture. He knew he was going to need all the help he could get with Julie. Not just to get her home but also to find a way to entrench himself on the girl's good side and stay there.

And then, of course, there was the matter of being able to handle Maura once he got to Fort Lauderdale. This was going to be a challenge all around and he was going to need backup.

"You heard me," Dillon said. "The three of us." And then he finally turned away to make that call to whatever airline had the first available flight from here to Fort Lauderdale.

"Looks like you're going to get to meet my mother," Julie said, looking at Hailey. The girl didn't exactly sound as if she was happy about the prospect of seeing her mother again. "Now you get to see what I've had to put up with all these years," she predicted, followed by another deep sigh.

"Funny thing," Hailey told the girl, "your mother would probably say the same thing if anyone asked her how she felt about living with you."

Julie looked surprised by what Hailey said, then visibly upset. Julie's eyes closed into laser-like slits. "If she feels that way, then why won't she just let me go and live with my dad?"

"Because under all that arguing and rule-setting, your mother really loves you," Hailey told her. Julie's frown only grew deeper. Hailey had to bite her lip not to laugh. "Don't worry, this will all make sense to you in another fifty years. Or so."

"Fifty years?" Julie cried, stunned.

This time Hailey did laugh. "I'm just kidding, honey."

Julie's frown instantly intensified, then after a beat, grew a little less so. Tossing her head, she claimed dismissively, "I knew that."

"Okay, all set," Dillon announced, returning to the room. "We lucked out. A party of four just canceled their reservations. That's one more seat than we need."

"Maybe them canceling is an omen and we shouldn't go," Julie said, speaking up.

"Nice try," Dillon said with a laugh. "Okay, we need to get to the airport right now," he urged, and then he paused as he looked in Hailey's direction. "You want to pack anything?" he asked, giving her the opportunity to get a suitcase.

"Just a smile," she answered, adding, "Something tells me I'm going to need it."

And that's when it hit him. He had just assumed she was coming with him. He hadn't even asked her. "Listen, I just took it for granted that you'd want to come along with Julie and me. But you don't have to if you'd rather not," he told her, trying to find a graceful way of telling Hailey she was under no obligation to come with them.

Hailey looked at him as if he had lost his mind. "You're going to need moral support. There's no way I'm about to let you go alone," she told him.

"Dad's not alone," Julie protested. She squared her shoulders. "He's got me."

"My mistake," Hailey quickly backtracked. "There's no way that I'm letting the two of you go alone. Better?" she asked, looking at Julie.

The girl smiled as she nodded her approval. "Better," she answered.

And then she spared her father a glance as they were about to leave the house. Walking by him, Julie lowered her voice so that only he could hear what she wanted to say to him.

"You know, Dad, I like Hailey. I think she's really nice." she whispered with a wink just as she went out the door.

Dillon stood staring after Julie for a long moment. His daughter's words of approval had left him utterly speechless.

A petite Maura was standing there, waiting for them in her driveway when Dillon, Hailey and Julie pulled up in the car Dillon had rented at the airport. Hailey found herself feeling sorry for the woman.

Maura looked like a very frightened mother who was doing her best not to break down. She still had circles under her eyes from crying and, in general, she looked as if she hadn't slept a wink in the two days since her daughter had run away.

Leaning in toward Julie, Dillon whispered, "Why don't you give her a hug, Julie? She looks like she could really use one. Your mom's been through a lot in the last forty-eight hours."

Glancing at the girl, Dillon thought that Julie looked as if she really wanted to. But at the same time, she looked very reluctant to admit that fact to anyone.

And then she shrugged carelessly. "I guess I can if it means so much to you," Julie said.

"It does," Dillon agreed, playing his part because he sensed that was what Julie wanted to hear.

This time Julie really did appear to have her doubts. "It does?" she asked, looking incredulously at her father.

"Absolutely," Dillon guaranteed, trying to coax her to take the first step. He needed to have Maura in a decent frame of mind if they were going to come to some sort of an agreement about Julie.

"Okay," Julie mumbled. "If it means that much to everybody, I'll give her a hug." She grimaced as she said the words.

The next moment, there was no more time left for any debates or waffling. Maura crossed the distance between herself and her daughter, threw her arms around the girl and hugged Julie close to her as she obviously struggled to keep from dissolving into a puddle of tears.

But after the hugging had passed, Maura looked angrily at her daughter.

"I thought something awful had happened to you, that you were dead, or—" Her voice broke and she was unable to continue for a minute.

"Maura, we brought her back the minute that she turned up. Anyone of us would have been worried sick in your place," Dillon assured Maura. He wanted her to realize that they weren't enemies in this, but on the same side.

Maura looked like she was resisting believing him, but then she must have reconsidered.

"Thank you," she said in a small voice. And then she looked at her daughter. "But you shouldn't have run away like that. Do you know what could have happened to you?" Maura's voice went up as she contemplated the full implications of what she had just asked.

"The important thing is that it didn't," Dillon said, trying to get her to focus on the positive aspect of this reunion.

Maura suddenly became aware that there was someone else at this reunion besides Julie and Dillon. She glared at Hailey, then turned toward Dillon. "I'm sorry, who's this?" Maura asked coldly.

"This is Hailey Miller, Mom," Julie said, doing the introductions before her father could say anything. The girl smiled as she continued. "She's in charge of the wellness spa that Dad built."

"She's also the reason that I was able to get Julie to come back to Fort Lauderdale instead of having her run off again," Dillon told Maura.

Maura's expression was difficult to read as she looked between Julie and Hailey.

"Really? Julie, is this true?" Maura asked her daughter.

"I was pretty angry at you," the girl freely admitted, not attempting to hide the fact. "Some of my friends don't even have dads. I have one and you wouldn't even let me meet him no matter how much I begged you. So I decided to do it on my own," she said, a little defiantly.

"She's your daughter, all right," Dillon said without any intended malice. "Headstrong to a fault."

Maura's eyes narrowed. "Are you trying to insult me?"

"No, in his own way, he's giving you a compliment," Hailey told her, playing peacemaker again.

"It takes a strong, determined woman to raise a child on her own. If you hadn't been as strong as you were, you might not have been able to make it. Or to go on to marry someone you fell in love with," Hailey pointed out.

"Huh," was Maura's only initial comment.

She looked at Hailey for a long moment, silently going over things in her mind. And then she nodded her head, as if agreeing with the conclusion she had come to. Pulling her shoulders back, she said, "Would you like to come inside for some coffee?" she asked. Then, realizing that her question could be construed as only including one of them, Maura clarified, "Both of you."

"Are you sure?" Hailey asked, glancing toward Dillon to see if he was all right with this, as well.

"I wouldn't have asked you if I wasn't," Maura informed her pointedly.

"Well then, I'd love to come in for coffee. Our flight back to Texas isn't for several hours," she told Maura. She looked at Dillon. "How do you feel about coffee?"

"Definitely for it," he answered, following the two women and his daughter into the house. For the time being, peace appeared to have been restored, mostly, he thought, thanks to Hailey.

Chapter Nineteen

Dillon found himself anticipating an explosion, or at the very least, name-calling when the initial dust had settled, but neither scenario materialized. Instead, he and Hailey wound up having an exceedingly civilized visit with Maura, who, it seemed, had actually had time to think the situation over. The woman grudgingly agreed that perhaps allowing Dillon to have regular visits with their daughter was actually for the best.

By the time he and Hailey were at the airport, Dillon finally had to admit that things were beginning to look positively rosy.

"That was really a surprise," Dillon said to Hailey—not for the first time—as they began board-ing their flight. "I honestly didn't think that Maura would ever actually come around." He couldn't believe the amount of relief he was experiencing.

Hailey waited until they had made their way to their seats and sat down before she commented. It didn't seem like the sort of conversation Dillon would appreciate having over the heads of strang-ers.

As she took her seat, she smiled at Dillon. She didn't know how he had managed to get them seats next to one another at the last minute, but he had.

"How could Maura not come around?" she asked him. "She's a mother, first and foremost," Hailey pointed out. "And when Julie ran away, I think it finally hit Maura just how much her daughter was being hurt by this war she was wag-ing against you. If Maura didn't want to risk los-ing Julie again—or permanently—she knew she was going to have to change her tactics. In es-sence, Maura realized that she was going to have to loosen up," Hailey told him.

Dillon nodded. What Hailey was saying made sense. But he knew from experience that sense and Maura didn't always travel in the same circles.

"Still, this could have easily gone another way entirely," Dillon told her.

That sort of mindset could suck him down a dark rabbit hole, Hailey thought. She did what she could to block it.

"Don't think about what *could have* happened, just think about what did—and build on that," Hailey advised with an encouraging smile.

He looked reluctant for a moment—because it left him open to disappointment—but then he gave in.

"You're right," Dillon agreed, his mind already considering possibilities. "When this project is finally finished and behind me, I'm finally going to be able to start spending quality time with Julie."

And less time with me.

Well, what had she expected was going to happen? she asked herself. This was what Dillon had wanted, and in her own way, she had helped to bring about this scenario and make it happen.

While she was really glad for Dillon, Hailey couldn't help feeling sorry for herself.

And that was when it hit her.

She had fallen in love with Dillon.

There was no other reason why she wanted him to be happy in a situation that didn't include her. In order for him to be happy, he needed to spend time with Julie. What it boiled down to, she thought with a sinking heart, was that Dillon was going to be moving back to Fort Lauderdale when his jobs in Rambling Rose were finally wrapped up. Or maybe even before then.

He hadn't said anything about her moving there with him, but even if he had, Hailey thought, it was a hell of a chance for her to take, uprooting her whole life and resettling in Fort Lauderdale on the slim chance that Dillon *might* eventually propose to her.

What if he said he only wanted her to live with him, not marry him? Could she settle for that? Would she be happy with just that?

The empty feeling in the pit of her stomach was her answer.

No, she wouldn't.

Dillon looked at her. "You're being awfully quiet," he commented after ten minutes had passed.

She wasn't about to ruin this for Dillon by doing what she had told him not to do: focusing only on the negative side.

So she said brightly, "I'm just happy for you with how things turned out."

Dillon wasn't really buying that, but for now he nodded. "That's mostly thanks to your doing," he acknowledged. "If you hadn't told me to just hang in there…"

Hailey laughed, shaking her head. "Like someone could have actually bullied you into doing something," she told Dillon, stressing how inconceivable that was given the situation. "Accept the credit where it's due, Dillon. *You* did this. Maura saw how much this meant to you, and, more importantly, how much it meant to Julie. Maura is no dummy. She had to have known that if she stood in your way, she'd be the loser in more ways than one. She would have alienated Julie and, more than likely, by taking a stand against you, she would have lost her daughter."

What Hailey was saying was all true, but there was something in her tone that Dillon found troubling. Something that said while she was happy for him, she wasn't happy in the absolute sense. Something was bothering her.

But he had never been the type to push, to try to burrow deeply beneath the surface. If something was bothering Hailey and she wanted him to know, she would tell him. It was strictly her choice. So he left it—and her—alone.

It wasn't as if he didn't have a lot to occupy his mind. He and his brothers still had the hotel to build, not to mention that the restaurant was in its final stages and some things needed to be reviewed. That would be Ashley, Nicole and Megan's department, he thought. He had taken precious time away from all that to bring his daughter back to Fort Lauderdale. The round trip there and back had eaten up more than a day and he knew he was going to have to explain that. While he was thrilled to have finally met Julie face to face, he couldn't help wondering how his family was going to react about his having kept his daughter a secret from them. He just hoped that they'd understand and ultimately welcome this new member of the family.

"What's wrong?" Hailey asked, looking at the perplexed expression on Dillon's face.

They'd finally landed back in Texas and, since they didn't have the added inconvenience of having to wait for their luggage, they were able to make their way to the parking lot with relative speed. Dillon had driven his own car to the airport and had left it parked there when they began their odyssey back to Fort Lauderdale.

Having gotten into the vehicle, Dillon hadn't started the car. Instead, he had placed a call to Callum to let him know he was back. When his call went to voice mail, he called Steven—with the same results. So he tried calling Stephanie. When *that* call went to voice mail, as well, he began to feel frustrated. It showed all over his face—and that had prompted Hailey's question.

"What's wrong is all the calls I just made aren't going through. Instead they're all going to voice mail," he complained. "Something's up."

He wondered if it had something to do with the restaurant project.

"Are you sure you're getting a busy signal?" Hailey asked. "Maybe there's a tower that's gone down for some reason. Service has really improved in the last year in Rambling Rose, but sometimes…"

"No," he said, holding his phone up just in case she was right. But he could see that he had most of the bars on his cell phone. That wasn't the problem. "I've got four out of five bars, so there's definitely a signal."

"But nobody's answering?" she guessed.

Dillon frowned, putting his cell phone on the console tray.

"No," he confirmed. "Nobody's answering. Something must be up," he repeated, adding, "Something that appears to be involving my whole family."

"Like what?" she asked. So far, she wasn't able to connect the dots and wondered what was running through Dillon's mind.

"Beats me. Look, I can drop you off at your place—" His mind racing, Dillon was already trying to plan for several contingencies.

Hailey's voice wedged its way into his thoughts. "Or you can take me to wherever you're going," she told him. He had already been through a lot these last couple of days and she wanted to be there to support him no matter what came up. "Why don't we go to your ranch and start there?" she suggested. "Someone should probably be there and they might be able to tell you what's going on—*if* there is anything going on," she qualified.

Well, he certainly couldn't argue with that, Dillon thought.

"It's worth a shot," he agreed.

"Any guesses?" Hailey asked as they pulled out of the airport parking lot.

"Not a clue," he said, frustration throbbing in his voice. And then he had a thought. "Unless the city council has decided to pull their support for the new hotel we're building."

That, he thought, was the worst-case scenario. But what other reason was there for this sudden silence on his family's part? He didn't want to entertain any dire thoughts.

"Don't go there yet," Hailey advised. Then, because she had learned what he was like, she decided to qualify her words. "At least not until you have to. Maybe there's another explanation for what's going on."

At least she fervently hoped so.

But neither one of them could even hazard a guess what that could possibly be.

When they got to the ranch, they found Callum there with the twins. But his wife, Becky, didn't seem to be anywhere in sight.

"Why aren't you answering your phone?" were the first words out of Dillon's mouth as he walked into the main section of the mansion.

Completely involved with the twins, Callum looked up, startled. "Sorry, I've been on the phone for a good part of the last couple of hours—at least when the twins let me talk," he amended. Callum looked a little overwhelmed at the moment.

"I left you a couple of voice-mail messages," Dillon told him.

The truth of it was, he had left a couple of messages on both his brothers' phones, as well as on Stephanie's. Since being unable to reach anyone in his family wasn't a usual occurrence, he had gotten really concerned.

Trying to keep one of the girls from leaving her artwork permanently scribbled on the coffee table, thanks to the crayon she had found, Callum was only partially paying attention to his brother.

"Sorry, I didn't see the messages," Callum confessed, confiscating the crayon.

That wasn't like his brother, Dillon thought. Even with his hands full, Callum could always multitask. His initial gut feeling had been right. Something *was* definitely wrong.

"Is there some kind of trouble at work?" he asked Callum.

Callum looked at him blankly. "What?" And then Dillon's question seemed to sink in. "No," he answered. "It's nothing at work."

Hailey interceded, taking Luna, the overactive twin, from him. Callum looked at her gratefully.

"Then what?" Dillon wanted to know. If there wasn't a problem at work, then what *was* going on?

"And where's Becky?" Hailey asked, wiping off traces of jam from the other twin's face. "I'm guessing from that really tired expression on your face, she's not here, is she?"

"Becky's at the hospital," Callum answered. "I'm pinch-hitting for the babysitter who had some kind of last-minute emergency."

There was something in Callum's voice that told Dillon this wasn't just a regular workday for Becky, either. He could swear there was agitation in the air.

Before he could ask again, Callum looked up

and frowned. "Eric brought Linus back to Rambling Rose to see the doctor."

"We already know that part," Dillon said. And then his expression grew more serious. "This isn't just about a cold, is it?" he asked, recalling that he'd heard Linus's dad was worried about the boy.

His brother shook his head. Picking up Sasha, the sticky twin, he began to wash off her face and hands with a wet towel.

"No, I really wish it was, but it's more serious than that. A great deal more serious," Callum emphasized.

Instantly concerned—not just because Linus was the tiny local celebrity, but because she, like everyone else in Rambling Rose, had fallen in love with the boy—Hailey wanted to hear more details.

"Why, what's wrong with him, Callum?"

"According to Becky, a great deal. The upshot of it is that the kid might need a bone marrow transplant," Callum said.

As he spoke, he looked at the twins. Hailey could only imagine how he felt. He'd come to love those little girls in a short amount of time. How would he feel if it were one of the twins who was sick? She knew Callum's empathy as well as his heart went out to Linus's father. And to Linus.

"The poor little guy," Hailey said, thinking of

the hurdles the baby had already gone through: being born prematurely, then abandoned by his mother, who was still missing. It was just pure luck that his father had turned up. When they had broken up, Eric hadn't even known that Laurel was pregnant. He certainly hadn't been prepared to have her take off the way she had. The moment he'd found out what was going on, he had claimed Linus and then taken the boy with him.

And now this.

It just seemed like neither Linus nor his dad could catch a break.

"Well, Linus is rather young," Dillon said, thinking of the surgery. "But his dad's probably a match," he speculated, trying to think positive.

Callum picked up one of the girls and held her in his arms.

"Eric's at the hospital being tested right now," he told them. "If everything's okay, they'll confirm the diagnosis, and then the hospital can begin making preparations to do the surgery as soon as possible."

Hailey nodded. "The sooner the better," she agreed. "You don't want to wait too long. Some other complication might just crop up and then there might be more problems to deal with."

Dillon looked at her, curious. "How do you know so much about the subject?"

"I had a friend once who got very sick. The doctors thought it might be a problem with her bone marrow—but it wasn't." Hailey shrugged, realizing that she had gotten way too serious, reliving one of the attempts that had been made to save Janelle's life.

Clearing her throat, she deliberately forced a smile to her lips. "But that isn't going to happen with Linus. Like you said, his dad's probably a match and they'll do the transplant right away."

As if to bail her out, Callum's cell phone rang. Hailey took the twin he was holding into her own arms, along with the one she was already holding, to allow him to take the call in relative peace. Or that was her reasoning at the time.

Opening his phone, Callum saw that it was his wife calling. "Hi, honey, we were just talking about you." He glanced at his brother. Hailey guessed that Becky had probably just asked him who *we* were.

The next second, she saw that she was right because Callum told his wife, "Dillon and Hailey. They're back and I think—wait, what?"

Callum's entire countenance changed as he listened to his wife's voice on the other end of the call.

Hailey kept her eyes on him, taking everything in as all sorts of half thoughts were forming in her head.

Something more was obviously going on, she thought. Did it have to do with Linus?

Whatever it was, it couldn't be good. The expression on Callum's face was exceedingly serious and almost forbidding.

She and Dillon didn't have long to wait to find out. Ending the call, Callum put his phone back into his pocket as he looked from Dillon to Hailey.

"Well?" Dillon demanded. "What's going on?"

"Eric's not a genetic match to Linus," Callum told them in a quiet voice.

Chapter Twenty

For a moment, the only sounds in the room were the noises made by the twins as they babbled to each other. Dillon and Hailey looked at one another and then at Callum. Neither of them looked as if they could believe what they were hearing.

"What did you just say?" Dillon asked his brother in disbelief.

"Eric's not a match. He can't donate bone marrow to Linus."

"How is that possible?" Dillon wanted to know, confused.

"Well, just because Eric's his father doesn't necessarily mean that his bone marrow would be a match to Linus's. As a matter of fact, there could be a number of reasons why it doesn't match—" Hailey began to explain.

For the second time in less than two minutes, the only sounds that were heard were those being made by the twins as they were jabbering.

Callum shrugged helplessly. "Hey, I'm just repeating what Becky told me." He grabbed Sasha just as the twin was about to pull a throw pillow down from the sofa.

"Are they sure?" Hailey asked him, stunned.

"Oh, they're sure. When he wasn't a match for Linus's bone marrow, Eric insisted on a DNA test. He's on pins and needles until the results come through, but that's not going to be for a while," he told them, setting Sasha down away from anything she could pull on herself. "According to Becky, Eric's reeling. He's terrified for Linus's health." Callum's voice trailed off as he shrugged again.

As shocking as this news was, that wasn't what they should be focusing on right now, Hailey thought.

"Not all parents are immediate genetic matches when it comes to their kids. That's something to be looked into later," she said to the two brothers. "Right now the important thing is to find a bone marrow donor who's a match for Linus." There appeared to be only one solution. She looked from one brother to the other. "We've got to get the word out right away so volunteers can come in and be tested as soon as possible. If Linus is as sick as the doctor says, we can't afford to waste too much time." Her voice rose with each word she uttered.

"I agree," Dillon said, thinking how he would feel if this was Julie who needed to have a bone marrow transplant. A thought occurred to him. "I'll call Steven. Since he's married to the mayor, he can tell her all about this latest development. It's a given that Ellie will want to help," he said. "She can hold a press conference and make an announcement." He looked from his brother to Hailey to see if they agreed with him. "The way I see it, that would be the fastest way to get the word out. We could also send out emails to all the people who were invited to the spa's opening. The more people notified, the better."

Hailey nodded. "And I can have part of the spa close down tomorrow. We can hold the drive there," she told them. "We'll have all the volunteers come to the spa so they can be tested to see if any of them can be a donor. There's got to be a match for little Linus here somewhere," she insisted.

Callum nodded, eager to get started. "I'll call Becky back, let her know that all this is going on. That way she can get a team together to come over to the spa and bring everything they need to conduct the tests." Callum grinned, pleased as he looked at his brother and Hailey. "This is all really coming together fast," he commented as he began to redial his wife.

"I'll call Steven right now so he can get in contact with Ellie to tell her about this," Dillon said, taking out his phone, as well. "He might need time to get through if she's busy or in a meeting."

Hailey nodded. "Once you talk to him, I need to get back to the spa. It might take some time to get ready to handle the influx of volunteers." She tried not to think about how sick the baby was and just focus on the positive side: that they'd find a way to help him. "Since this is for the town's littlest celebrity, I think we should be prepared for a lot of people coming in to be tested."

Both brothers were unable to answer her since they were each on the phone talking to the next link on their particular chain.

Putting the twin she'd been holding into the double-wide playpen beside her sister, Hailey placed her own call. Hers was to Candace, her assistant at the spa, to alert the woman of what was going on. She wanted Candace to be prepared for a large influx of people arriving at the wellness spa, possibly before the hour was up. It all depended on how quickly Ellie could get a press conference together.

The next day, it all went down in what felt like lightning speed. As soon as Steven was told what was going on, he immediately called his wife. Fortunately he got through right away and was able to let her know about Linus and the baby's need for a bone marrow transplant. Ellie quickly called a press conference. Word spread from there like wildfire.

Meanwhile, right after Callum called her, Becky notified Dr. Green, the baby's doctor, about the bone marrow drive being organized at the spa. They lost no time putting together a team to test the volunteers that they anticipated coming in.

As soon as he had called Steven, Dillon drove Hailey directly to the spa. Her assistant was waiting for her and Hailey got right to work.

With the help of several of her people, plus Dillon, Hailey prepared one of the spa's larger rooms to be used for the necessary tests.

For inspiration, Hailey had a photograph of Baby Linus enlarged and taped up on the wall. Hailey felt that ignoring that sweet face was impossible. The more volunteers who came, the better the odds of finding a match.

Hailey moved the massage tables as well as chairs into the spacious room. They would need as many places as possible for volunteers to sit on as they waited for their turn to be swabbed.

Hailey and her people were still in the process of setting everything up when the first volunteers began arriving.

At the head of the line was a soft-spoken burly giant of a man named Riley Evans.

"I heard Mayor Ellie say that the baby was sick and could die if he didn't get something he needed. So I came to see if I could help," Riley told her without any fanfare.

Impressed with how quickly Riley had come down to the spa, Hailey still felt she had to ask the gentle giant, "Do you know what you'll be getting swabbed for today? What you might be donating?"

Riley shook his head. "Doesn't matter," he told her. "If I'm a match, you can have it if it'll help. Way I see it, the little guy's been through a lot and he needs whatever it is a lot more than I do."

Hailey found herself blinking back tears as she led Riley to a massage table.

As the crowd continued to gather and converge in and around the spa, that was the spirit that prevailed through it. Everyone was eager to do their part to try to help save Linus.

It quickly became apparent that almost *every-one* within the small close-knit town was volunteering to have their cheeks swabbed for matching.

The volunteers included Dillon and his two brothers.

"That was very nice of you," Hailey commented as Dillon got up off the table.

He rolled down his sleeve. "Hey, I couldn't very well just stand by while everyone else was being tested. Especially now that I know what it feels like to be a parent, I totally empathize with that situation." He laughed softly to himself. "In a way, since the moment he came into the world, I guess Linus belongs to everyone. Especially since his mother took off and left him." Dillon looked at Hailey to see if she agreed with him.

She thought about the sentiment he had just voiced. "I didn't realize you felt that way," she told him. "I mean, when we were flying to Fort Lauderdale, I thought you made it pretty clear that you considered that home, not Rambling Rose."

He thought back for a moment. "I guess, at the time, I did," he admitted.

At the time.

Did that mean that now he didn't? Before she could stop herself, she asked him.

"And now?"

The moment the words were out of her mouth, Hailey knew she might wind up regretting pushing this. In all honesty, she knew that it was probably better if she just left this alone and let whatever happened progress at its own speed.

But there was another part of her that felt as if she was just deliberately stalling, trying to hold back the inevitable.

That wasn't like her.

She needed to know what was ahead. If she was going to lose Dillon, then she needed to know that, too. She shouldn't be embarrassing herself by desperately trying to hold on when there was no chance for her.

For them.

"And now I can see that no matter what your plans are," Dillon was saying to her, "the universe can be totally unfair. There are no guarantees in life, other than the fact that it's completely uncertain and can all change in the blink of an eye."

Here it came, Hailey thought, trying to mentally brace herself.

But all she could focus on was that her stomach felt as if it were sinking as she waited for Dillon to utter the fatal words that would take him away from her. He was going to tell her that he'd decided not to wait until his part of the project was done. That he intended to go back to Florida as soon as possible.

A wave of heat passed over her as her pulse began to race.

Although it went against what she told herself she should do, Hailey heard herself tell Dillon, "You can't just give up like that, Dillon."

That stopped him cold.

"Give up?" Dillon repeated.

He sounded confused, Hailey thought. As if he didn't know what she was talking about.

Hailey went right on talking as if he hadn't said a word. "You can't," she insisted. "Growing up, I had a friend, Janelle, who was closer to me than my own sister. We did *everything* together and she had such a zest for life! Janelle could always lift me up no matter how bad things seemed. No matter how down I was feeling." She smiled, remembering. "We were going to conquer the world together once we graduated from school."

Dillon couldn't imagine tragedy touching this sunny woman before him. "What happened?" he asked quietly.

Hailey sighed. "The world conquered her. Or at least it tried to," she amended. "Janelle was diagnosed with pancreatic cancer, but she never gave in to it, never let it get her down. She fought it right to the very end. She was my inspiration and she made me promise that no matter what, I would always live life to the fullest. For both of us," she added emotionally. "Because of her, I learned that you have to grab every single thing that life has to offer and make the very most of it because tomorrow, it could all just disappear."

Dillon nodded. "I know."

"You know?" she questioned, confused.

Did that mean he'd decided to stay in Rambling Rose? Or was he saying that was the reason he'd decided to leave?

Her mind was jumping around from one thought to another and her head was beginning to ache. Hailey forced herself to stop, to wait for Dillon to tell her what he intended to do.

"Yes, I do. I get it," he told her. "Life is short, much too short. And I don't want to get caught up in all the tiny details and let that get in the way so that I'm wasting time wading through it. Unscrambling the small stuff and not paying attention to the really important things."

Breathe, Hailey, breathe! Maybe Dillon wasn't saying he was leaving. Maybe he was—

No, no more jumping to conclusions. Let him talk.

"Maybe I'm not saying this right," Dillon continued, a little exasperated. "Actually, I know I'm not—"

This was her chance to stop him, she thought.

Hailey grabbed it. "Maybe you should wait then, until you feel you have the right words. No point in rushing this," she told him.

Especially since you can always say goodbye. At the thought, another strong wave of nausea assaulted her stomach.

This was about finding a bone marrow donor for Linus, not about promoting her romance, she upbraided herself. How could she be so self-centered?

And yet…

Lost in thought and trying very hard to rally, she didn't realize what Dillon was doing until he had dropped down on one knee and taken her hand.

"Hailey," he began.

Stunned, Hailey's mouth dropped open. "What are you doing?" she cried.

"Probably making a huge fool of myself," Dillon guessed. "But I don't seem to have a choice in the matter."

Her breath was backing up in her throat again and her heart was doing an imitation of a jackhammer as she continued to stare at Dillon.

Was he—?

It couldn't be—and yet—

"Dillon?" she questioned uncertainly.

They were attracting attention now, but at this point, she could only see the rugged man before her down on one knee.

"I know that I'm more frog than prince and you do deserve a prince of the highest caliber, but I promise you that if you'll have me, if you say yes, I will love you with all my heart for as long as we both shall live. Longer," he added with feeling. "All I want is the chance to show you.

"But I'll understand if you decide to turn me down, although—"

"Dillon," Hailey cried, desperately trying to get a word in edgewise.

Ready to go on full steam ahead, he stopped abruptly. "What?"

"Stop talking!" she told him.

He thought she was telling him that to save him any further embarrassment.

"So it's no?" he asked, trying to brace himself for defeat.

"No, you big dumb oaf," she laughed. "Stop talking so I can say yes."

"Yes?" He repeated the word as if he didn't understand what she was telling him.

Suppressing a laugh, Hailey spelled it out for him. "Yes, I will marry you."

His eyes widened. "You will?"

"Yes," she cried again, then, for good measure, before he could question her reasoning, she added, "Because I love you."

"You do?" he said it as if he didn't believe that was possible.

"Yes. I've loved you ever since you spilled that jasmine on your shirt and then had a sneezing fit." Her eyes were shining now. "You obviously needed someone in your life. I decided that you needed me," Hailey told him, smiling broadly.

"But—"

She decided that the only way she was going to get Dillon to stop arguing and accept the answer he had made clear he wanted was to take matters into her own hands.

Or, in this case, it wasn't her hands that she used, it was her lips.

She pressed them on his and whatever else Dillon was about to say just faded away.

Happily.

Neither one of them heard the volunteers around them cheering. They were far too busy forming their own little world.

* * * * *

COMING SOON!

We really hope you enjoyed reading this book. If you're looking for more romance, be sure to head to the shops when new books are available on

Thursday 2nd April

To see which titles are coming soon, please visit

millsandboon.co.uk/nextmonth

MILLS & BOON

Coming next month

BABY ON THE TYCOON'S DOORSTEP
Nina Milne

Isobel headed to the kitchenette, scooped powder into another bottle and handed it to Jake, waited whilst he poured the water in from the kettle.

Took it from him and stepped closer to demonstrate. Too close—she was way too close.

Focus. But not on his body, the sculpted forearms, the swell of his upper arms, the strong thighs. Not on his smell, not on the way his hair spiked up— This was a bad idea but for the life of her she couldn't figure a way out of it.

'Put your thumb over the top of the teat, so you're blocking the hole. Then you shake' Like this.' Her voice emerged squeaky…breathless…*ridiculous*.

He'd moved even closer to her now and his eyes held a wicked glint that ripped the breath from her lungs.

'So it's all in the wrist action,' he said dead pan and her gaze flew to meet his, in shock at the double entendre.

'I—'

Then he grinned and wiggled his eyebrows. 'Sorry I couldn't resist. Puerile but—'

'Yes,' she said, trying to keep a straight face. 'Definitely puerile.' But be that is it may she succumbed to a giggle, which morphed into a full-blown laugh. And in seconds he had joined in.

Now their gazes locked and she could feel the shift in the atmosphere, the swirl of desire, the fugue of need. They were even closer now. His scent tantalised; the warm smell of baby milk mixed with a hint of citrus clean sharp shower gel and a whiff of bergamot. Her head whirled and there was an utter inevitability about what happened next. She wasn't sure afterwards who initiated it, who made the fatal decision or whether it was a completely synchronised movement.

But one step took them closer and then she was in his arms and her lips met his and oh god it felt so good. His lips so familiar and yet so new, and her lips tingled as tremors of raw desire shuddered her body. Gentle, hesitant at first as if they both feared rejection and then the kiss deepened, intensified, sent a sear through her veins. His fingers tangled in her hair, she pressed her body against his wanting more, her pulse rate accelerated at his taste, his scent, the way his kiss could drive her to the edge of desperate need for more. Her body alight and craving more of him—of Jake—she wanted his touch, wanted the satisfaction her body knew and remembered.

Continue reading
BABY ON THE TYCOON'S DOORSTEP
Nina Milne

Available next month
www.millsandboon.co.uk

MILLS & BOON

THE HEART OF ROMANCE

A ROMANCE FOR EVERY KIND OF READER

MODERN

Prepare to be swept off your feet by sophisticated, sexy and seductive heroes, in some of the world's most glamourous and romantic locations, where power and passion collide.
8 stories per month.

HISTORICAL

Escape with historical heroes from time gone by. Whether your passion is for wicked Regency Rakes, muscled Vikings or rugged Highlanders, awaken the romance of the past.
6 stories per month.

MEDICAL

Set your pulse racing with dedicated, delectable doctors in the high-pressure world of medicine, where emotions run high and passion, comfort and love are the best medicine.
6 stories per month.

True Love

Celebrate true love with tender stories of heartfelt romance, from the rush of falling in love to the joy a new baby can bring, and a focus on the emotional heart of a relationship.
8 stories per month.

Desire

Indulge in secrets and scandal, intense drama and plenty of sizzling hot action with powerful and passionate heroes who have it all: wealth, status, good looks…everything but the right woman.
6 stories per month.

HEROES

Experience all the excitement of a gripping thriller, with an intense romance at its heart. Resourceful, true-to-life women and strong, fearless men face danger and desire - a killer combination!
8 stories per month.

DARE

Sensual love stories featuring smart, sassy heroines you'd want as a best friend, and compelling intense heroes who are worthy of them.
4 stories per month.

To see which titles are coming soon, please visit

millsandboon.co.uk/nextmonth

MILLS & BOON
MEDICAL
Pulse-Racing Passion

Set your pulse racing with dedicated, delectable doctors in the high-pressure world of medicine, where emotions run high and passion, comfort and love are the best medicine.

JOIN THE
MILLS & BOON
BOOKCLUB

* **FREE** delivery direct to your door

* **EXCLUSIVE** offers every month

* **EXCITING** rewards programme

50% OFF
YOUR FIRST
PARCEL

Join today at
Millsandboon.co.uk/Bookclub